ALL
THAT I
LEAVE
BEHIND

Alison Walsh has worked in publishing and literary journalism for a number of years. She wrote a popular and humorous column on family life for the *Irish Independent* for some years, and this was followed by a memoir on motherhood, *In My Mother's Shoes*, which became a number-one Irish bestseller in 2010. She is a regular contributor to the *Sunday Independent* books pages. Alison lives in Dublin with her husband and three children.

ALL THAT I LEAVE BEHIND

alison
WALSH

HACHETTE
BOOKS
IRELAND

First published in 2015 by Hachette Books Ireland

A CIP catalogue record for this title is available from the British Library

ISBN 978 147 3612822

"Norman Mailer, The Art of Fiction No. 32," interview by Steven Marcus, originally published in The Paris Review, Issue 31, Winter - Spring 1964. Copyright © 1964 The Paris Review, used by permission of The Wylie Agency LLC

Typeset in MrsEaves by redrattledesign.com
Printed and bound by Clays Ltd, St Ives plc

Hachette Books Ireland policy is to use papers that are natural, renewable and recyclable products and made from wood grown in sustainable forests. The logging and manufacturing processes are expected to conform to the environmental regulations of the country of origin.

Hachette Books Ireland
8 Castlecourt Centre
Castleknock
Dublin 15
Ireland

A division of Hachette UK Ltd
Carmelite House
50 Victoria Embankment
London EC4Y 0DZ

www.hachette.ie

To Colm

'It made me decide there's no clear boundary between
experience and imagination'
Norman Mailer, *Paris Review*

Prologue

Michelle

There's no bougainvillea where I come from. There are no snakes or lizards, no sun that sits high in the sky, a hot orange ball; there's none of the dry red earth that coats my toes, that gets into every crevice, the fine lines around my eyes. Sometimes, I've found it in my underwear when I've taken my bra or knickers off to wash. After thirty years in this place, I think it must be inside me, lining my insides, a thin layer around my heart.

Where I come from, the earth is a thick, rich brown, the grass a vivid green and the barley a silver grey, swaying in the fields, and everywhere there is water, rushing over pebbles in a stream, pushing slowly between the reeds in the long bluey-brown of the canal that stretches on into the horizon. There are no mud huts, but two-storey farmhouses which have seen better days or modern bungalows with PVC windows, neat baskets of flowers hanging up outside the porch.

There's a house by the canal that I always wanted, from the moment I saw it, when I first came to Monasterard. I'd point it out to John-Joe when we went on one of our long walks, the way we always did at the beginning, when we had nothing else to distract us, when the life we'd chosen hadn't begun to pull us apart, the dog sniffing around ahead of us, rooting in the grass at the edge of a field for the sniff of a pheasant.

'That's the one I want,' I said to him as we both stood on the bank and peered over the hedge at its collapsing roof, the grey whitewash almost worn away from the pebble-dashed front, a raggy lace curtain hanging in one of the windows.

'You must be cracked.' He laughed, scratching his head, his eyes scanning the rusting tractor sinking down into the mud in the front yard. He had that country suspicion of 'home' as an affectation — of doing places up, extending them, rummaging through bric-a-brac stalls in markets in search of treasure. Homes were where you slept and ate and watched television, as far as John-Joe was concerned. But he indulged my daydream, placing a heavy arm on my shoulder as we both gazed at the house, his handsome face alert, amused. 'Anything for you, my love.' He smiled and, shaking his head, urged the dog on with a whistle.

Anything for me. How funny it seemed later — 'funny odd, not funny ha-ha', as Mary-Pat used to say — that there was a point when John-Joe would have done anything for me, for the girl he loved. Before what happened happened.

How often I think of it these days, that house, that place. When I first came here, months passed when I hardly thought of it at all. I pushed it out of my mind because I had other things to think about, things that made me feel as if my heart was being pulled out through my ribs. But then that was my punishment: to have left them — Mary-Pat, June, Pius and my little Rosie — and yet brought them with me in my heart, where I could never let them go.

Now, after I use the small amount of water that remains at the bottom of the tin bowl to splash that blessed dust off my face, grumbling to myself because I can still feel the dry grit of it on my skin, after I lie down on the hard, narrow bed like an old nun, I can see it in my mind's eye: the way the roof sags, the faded green paint on the front door. Why does the house call me back? Why does it haunt my dreams? I rail against it, knowing all the time why. Because it's everything I once wanted for my husband and family, the life I had planned for myself. The life that I never really had.

And then, because I can do nothing else, I pull the tattered paperback copy of Gone with the Wind *out from under my pillow, the one that I bought in a flea market in Bray because it had a still from the film on it, Vivien Leigh's feline, pixie face staring out at me, unknowable; it fascinates me, that face, the idea that it can be a mask, can betray nothing of what's inside. If only I could have been more like Vivien Leigh. I turn to page 547, to where Scarlett comes back after the battle of Atlanta, and I think about Junie and wonder if she's reading my mother's copy, the huge, heavy hardback that I used to love to read. I wonder if she's found it in the place where I left it for her, and where I left the other things: my plan for the French garden for Pius, because I know how much he loves the garden — he belongs there, just as I do. For Mary-Pat, I left a shell — a perfect whorl of silver and black. We found it on the beach that day we went to Carnsore, that day when my whole life just fell away from me. She made me promise that we'd go back, but we never did. I wonder if she has? For Rosie, I left my ring with the purple stone, the one that John-Joe's friend had made for me, a thick band of silver with a lump of amethyst set into it, rough, but beautiful, a symbol of everything I thought we meant to each other. I hope it brings her better luck than it did me.*

I tucked them into a battered trunk that I'd found in the attic, a huge black thing with big bands of wood set into it that, when I opened it, released a scent of mothballs and foreign travel. The kids used to like rummaging around in the attic, amongst all the debris that John-Joe's brother had left behind: the stuffed trout mounted on a mahogany frame, the box of racing programmes from Cheltenham, the collection of men's hats stored in a battered suitcase, which the girls used to make Pius try on, marching him around the attic, giving each other orders, their footsteps hammering on the ceiling above me as I lay on the bed, my head propped up on a pillow so that I could see the silver ribbon of the canal from my window, could feel that I was part of it, not inside in the prison I'd made for myself. I left them there, because I hoped that, sooner or later, the children would come across them, and because it's the one place where John-Joe never strayed.

I didn't leave a note, because no note would explain to them why I'd left them. No words could ever cover it. Maybe I was fooling myself a little, too, telling myself that, sure, I'd be seeing them again before they'd even have time to miss me. They'd all climb onto the train in Mullingar, piling the old suitcases and bags around them, and when they got off in Heuston Station, they'd stand on the platform for a minute, lost, until they'd catch sight of me, arms open, and they'd run towards me.

How many times have I replayed that scene in my head over the years. Even though, deep down, I probably knew that it would never happen. It just took time for me to understand, and when I did, the pain was so terrible I thought it would kill me. But even though what I did that day cost me everything, I knew that I had no other choice.

I pick up the paperback and open it and that's when the photo falls out. And every time I see it, it's as if it is for the first time. The feeling is physical, like a punch to the stomach, making me wheezy, short of breath. I clutch my hand to my throat and feel the tears hot beneath my eyelids.

They are sitting in line on an old ladder, which Pius has transformed into a boat, paddling with a sweeping brush and a mop at either end. Mary-Pat first, her hair in ringlets, her thighs dimpling under her tartan dress: my happy, plump little girl, with her tea sets and her dolls. Then June, in Mary-Pat's hand-me-down jeans, that watchful look on her face, the one that made me feel that she knew more than she should. Pius is at the end, a half-mad grin on his face, a gap where his two front teeth should be. He'd either done, or was about to do, something naughty. It used to drive John-Joe mad, and the madder he got, the more poor Pius misbehaved. My poor, bold Pius.

Rosie is tucked in front of him, the way she always was, a little doll in a crochet dress, her thumb in her mouth, her hair a vivid flame of red. How I loved my Rosie. It just shows you, family is family, no matter what. I shouldn't have loved her as much as I did. I should have nursed that chip of ice in my heart: the rage against her father should, by rights, have been hers to carry. But instead I loved her more — in truth, more than the others. That's a mother's secret, isn't it? We say we love them all equally, but there's always one, isn't there? To me, it was Rosie, because I needed her. Because she, of all people, could save me from John-Joe and what we were doing to each other.

I run my hand over their faces, their hair, and I kiss them, one by one, kiss them goodnight, as if I'm tucking them up in bed again, that tattered Ladybird copy of Rapunzel in my hand, their noses peeking above the blankets of Mammy and Daddy's bed, where they always had their night-time story. I don't kiss the adults they will have since become, because to me they are forever children. I kiss them and I pray for them in my own way, and then I go to sleep and they are in my dreams.

Part One

Summer 2012

1

*R*osie stood at the door for a few moments, the summer breeze coming in through the open window lifting her hair around her face, tendrils of bright red wafting across her eyes. The breeze was warm and on it she could hear the constant caw-caw of the rooks in the trees near the Protestant church. She'd forgotten how loud they were, the rooks. She used to pass them every day on her way to school, ducking underneath the oak tree and running so that one of them wouldn't crap on her, hands over her ears so that the sudden crack of the bird-scarer wouldn't make her jump out of her skin, terrified that one of the birds would fix her with a beady eye and swoop, like in *The Birds*.

She closed her eyes for a second, clutching her handbag to her, feeling the red leather slick from her sweaty hand. She looked down at her feet and wondered if the espadrilles were a bit disrespectful in a place like this, as if she were dressed for the beach? But then she shook her head. For God's sake, it wasn't Mass, and Daddy wouldn't give a shit about what she wore. He'd consider it highly entertaining that she was fretting about dress codes, she who had hardly worn a stitch of clothing for the first five years of her life. Mary-Pat had had to threaten to take away her collection of stag beetles before she agreed to wear the scratchy jumper and skirt that was her school uniform. 'But I'm a free spirit,' she'd protested, as her sister had shoved her arms into the horrible blue nylon-wool mix. 'Daddy said so.'

'Daddy doesn't have to go to school,' Mary-Pat had barked. 'Daddy doesn't have to do anything he doesn't want to, for that matter. It's easy for some of us to be free spirits. Now, shut up and get dressed, will you, and give me a break?'

A free spirit. That's who I used to be, Rosie thought as she tiptoed into the room, inhaling the smell of disinfectant and something else sickly sweet. Her stomach churned and she remembered that she hadn't eaten since they'd landed six hours ago, a greasy fry under the hot lights of the airport café. She felt her chest tighten again. She reached into her handbag and pulled out her inhaler, taking two deep puffs, clutching it in her hand as she walked over to the bed.

'Daddy?' The man in the bed didn't respond because he was fast asleep, his mouth open, revealing an expanse of pink gum. Oh, she thought, it's not him. It's not Daddy. This man looked like a mummy, shrunken and wizened, his cheeks hollow because they'd taken his teeth out: they were floating in a glass by the side of the bed. Daddy didn't have false teeth, she was sure of it.

'Daddy?' she said again. She went to the end of the bed and saw the medical chart clipped to the frame. She lifted the chart up and examined the name on the top line, a scrawl in blue biro. John-Joe O'Connor. Daddy's date of birth. She swallowed hard then looked at the man in the bed again. His cheeks had collapsed, making his nose even more prominent. She knew that nose, the bump on the bridge of it from when he'd broken it playing football. And she knew the mole on his right cheek. His hair was fully white now, but it still curled around his ears, one of which had a hole in it for a piercing but no silver earring. He wouldn't like that, she thought, being without his lucky earring.

He gave a little snore, a short one, followed by a long silence, and for a second Rosie thought he'd stopped breathing, but then he exhaled loudly. She suppressed the scream which had risen to her throat and instead lifted the inhaler to her mouth and took another long breath in, holding it for a few seconds and then breathing out. She turned around, as if checking to see if there was anyone nearby, and then she tried, 'Daddy, it's me, Rosie.' Silence. 'Ehm, I'm sorry I haven't been to see you in a while. I was away, but you know that, of course.' She blushed as she heard her silly words in the silence. 'Away.' As if that could sum up all those years and all those miles she'd put between herself and this place, her home. If Pius hadn't written to her about Daddy, she knew that she would probably never have returned. It was a mistake — she'd been here five minutes, and she already knew that. But she'd had to come home, because if she never saw Daddy again before - well, she'd never forgive herself.

She pulled up a big red chair and sat right on the edge of it, feeling the plastic stick to the back of her thighs. She pushed her legs underneath, wincing as her calf bashed against the hard commode below the seat. 'How are you, Daddy?' she tried, feeling even more foolish. Then she reached out and took one of his hands in hers and gave it a little squeeze. 'It's good to see you.' She turned his hand over in hers, those long, slender hands with the lovely fingers that he'd used to say were made to play piano at the Wigmore Hall, not dig big bushels of spuds in the arse end of nowhere. When she saw his nails, she swore out loud. 'For God's sake, Daddy.' They were filthy, the cuticles ragged. 'It's a good job you're asleep,' she said, 'that way you can't see the state of your hands.' He'd always been so careful about his appearance. He'd been delighted to discover VO5 hair gel, which he'd nicked from Pius, smoothing down his silvery-black curls in the bathroom mirror, smacking his lips and baring his beautiful white teeth, which no amount of smoking and drinking seemed to have dulled. Then he'd take his brown-leather manicure case out of the drawer in the medicine cabinet and begin his work of filing and shaping. That must be where June got it, that love of making herself look nice. June would have exactly the same expression on her face when she looked into the mirror, one of total absorption, mixed with a fair bit of self-admiration. Rosie wondered what June would look like now. She'd be forty-one and Rosie couldn't imagine her growing older. Maybe she'd have Botox or fillers. June was made for that kind of stuff. The thought made her giggle, before she covered her mouth with her hand.

Still holding Daddy's hand in one of hers, with the other, trembling, Rosie opened the cabinet beside the bed, hoping that she'd spot it now. Sure enough, it was in a blue washbag, sure to have been packed by Mary-Pat, along with a bottle of Blue Stratos, a bar of soap, a toothbrush and a packet of cigarettes, a cheap plastic lighter shoved into a corner of the packet. 'I thought you'd given up the fags,' Rosie said out loud as she opened the manicure set. 'God, I'd kill for a fag, do you know that? But I gave them up, Daddy, would you believe? Yep. Two years and six months ago, but who's counting?' And anyway, she thought now as she looked longingly at the cigarettes, Craig would smell it off her breath. He was like a bloodhound when it came to that kind of thing, could sniff out cigarette smoke and alcohol at a hundred yards. He wouldn't say a word, she knew, but a look would be enough. She'd seen that look once, and she never wanted to see it again.

She extracted a tiny silver nail file from the case and, turning his left hand gently in hers, began to clean under the nails, paring away all the dirt, which she wiped onto a tissue which she'd spread on the bed. She filed away for a bit and then she said, 'Do you remember what you used to say to me at the gate, Daddy?' rubbing a little of the hand cream she'd found at the bottom of his washbag into his hands, smoothing the cream along his fingers, once slender, now distorted by arthritis, which had made his joints swell. '"Don't let the bastards grind you down." Handy.' She smiled as she turned his hand and rubbed cream over the palm, which was cracked. 'You knew what they could be like. Small town,' she continued. 'Small minds.' She could see him then as she stood at the school gate, tipping his invisible hat and announcing, 'Time to head to the office, Doodlebug. See you after school,' and then he'd be gone, a little saunter up over the bridge, Colleen the dog trying to keep up, before the two of them would make a quick right turn, as if Daddy had only just thought of it and not planned it carefully, into Prendergast's. There, Daddy would drink one pint of Guinness and smoke one cigarette and read the *Irish Independent*. He never drank more than one pint in the morning and one in the afternoon: the benders, he kept for Friday and Saturday nights. He regarded it as a sign that he was a man of discipline. Could control himself. Just like any other man, he'd use routine to structure his day, except instead of car and office and home for dinner, his was pub and bookies and only then home to do a few jobs around the house.

Of course, she hadn't seen it then, that this routine wasn't quite like other fathers', wasn't something to be proud of, she supposed. She'd heard it more than once, the slightly-too-loud comment from one of the teachers or one of the girls in the minimarket about 'that fellow, dossing around the town. Sure he's a good for nothing, so he is.' Rosie's cheeks would burn, but with indignation, not shame. How dare they say things like that about her daddy. She knew her daddy. And he was always there for her. Always. How she'd missed him, even though he'd never once written. 'Ah, sure, I'm no good at that kind of thing,' he'd said when she'd pushed him once. 'I'm hopeless with words, you know that, Rosie-boo.' Instead, he'd made a 'trunk call' as he still called it, every second Sunday, never forgetting to reverse the charges, the roar of the punters at Prendergast's in the background, the clink of pint glasses as he brought her up to date with the going at Kempton Park, the favourite for the 3.45 at Leopardstown racecourse – never anything personal, just 'ráiméis', as he called it. He probably felt safe with that, with nonsense, and she did too – the two of them carefully skirting any difficult subjects.

Rosie had made sure to hide the phone bills from Craig, paying them every month from her credit card. He was very careful about expenditure. And then, just after Christmas this year, the calls had stopped, and when she'd rung Pi, he'd told her that Daddy was 'tired', and then he was 'in for a few tests'. Why had she not guessed? Maybe all the wedding stuff had distracted her, made her forget what was really important. 'You're here now,' Pi had said to her earlier, but that didn't make her feel any less guilty.

'I didn't know Prendergast's had closed,' she said now. 'Although I suppose you haven't had cause to go there for a while anyway. Pi tells me that Blazers on the Dublin Road is the place now. Might try it some time.' She grinned. 'Sounds like my kind of place. Not.' She paused. 'Not now that I'm a reformed character anyway. You'll be glad to know that I don't drink any more, can you believe it? I'm very well behaved, Daddy. I know I led you all a merry dance, didn't I? Mary-Pat used to say I had her heart broken. That's why she pushed me onto that bus to Dublin. I suppose I can't really blame her.'

She could see herself still, looking out the window of the bus, in that big hairy coat she'd found at the back of Daddy's wardrobe, the one that smelled godawful but that she wore to annoy Mary-Pat because her sister had taken one look at her the first time she'd appeared in it and had screamed, 'Take that bloody thing off, or I will personally rip it off your back, do you hear me?' It had been an invitation: Rosie had made a point of wearing it to breakfast, dinner and tea, ignoring her sister's look of disgust, because she was so pleased to have rubbed her up the wrong way. That was her mission in life then: to cause Mary-Pat as much hassle as she possibly could, because she knew she could get away with it. Because she thought her sister would love her anyway, no matter what she did. She'd been wrong about that.

Which was why she'd said not one word to her about coming home. The only person she'd told was Pius, because she knew he'd keep his mouth shut. To his credit, he'd said he wouldn't breathe a word, even though he'd written that her two sisters would be 'surprised'. That was one word for it. 'They'll be thrilled to see you,' he'd added at the bottom of the postcard he'd sent her of St Munchin's Cistercian Abbey. He sent a postcard every week, often with nothing more than a scribbled line in his spidery handwriting, or some silly quote from the local newspaper that had caught his eye, but now, he'd written a full paragraph, ending with: 'They miss you, Rosie.' Rosie knew that her brother was just being kind. If they missed her that much, why had neither of them visited, even once? Pi, she could understand, what with his ... illness, but Mary-Pat and June? Apart from the polite letters at Christmas and on her birthday, she'd heard hardly a word from either of them. But then, she hadn't left them on the best of terms, had she?

She could still remember that June had pulled her aside during one of her sister's visits home. Rosie had been wearing the coat for a few weeks, and Mary-Pat had more or less stopped speaking to her. She'd said gently, 'Rosie, love, will you take the coat off? It's upsetting everyone.'

'Why?' Rosie's chin had jutted out stubbornly, her hand on her hips. Truthfully, she was only dying to get rid of the awful coat – it made her itch like mad – but she wasn't about to give in to Mary-Pat.

'It was Mammy's,' June explained patiently. 'It makes people remember her, you see, every time they see you in it. It's ... awkward,' she finished.

Rosie had wanted to pull the coat off then and hurl it as far away from her as she possibly could, but because she was young and stubborn, she continued to wear it, shuffling in and out of the sitting room, making sure that she walked in front of the TV when Mary-Pat was trying to watch *Coronation Street*, making a point of brushing her teeth in the bathroom at night in her T-shirt and shorts and that coat, even though it made her feel sick to wear it. Sick and sorry and embarrassed. But she wouldn't give in, she'd decided, no matter how much it cost.

Rosie blushed as she remembered what she'd been like, the rage that had propelled her forward, out of Monasterard forever, or so she'd thought. 'You needn't fucking bother waiting,' she'd spat at Mary-Pat as she'd pulled her bags out of the Pajero, 'unless you want to make sure I'm going.'

'Sure, there's no need for that, no need at all,' PJ had said, hopping down from the driver's seat and gently taking a bag from her, his big, red face a picture of sorrow. Poor PJ, stuck in the middle of it all, announcing loudly that he was taking the babies for a walk every time herself and Mary-Pat kicked off. John-Patrick and Melissa must be fifteen or sixteen by now.

'It's none of your fucking business,' she'd yelled, yanking the bag out of his hand and turning on her heel. She'd caught a glimpse of Mary-Pat then, sitting bolt upright in the passenger seat, tears streaming down her face. 'What the hell are you crying about?' she'd screamed. 'Haven't you got what you wanted? Haven't you been trying to get rid of me all this time? Well, guess what? It's your lucky day,' and she'd stomped up the steps of the bus, ignoring the muttered tuts of Mrs Delaney. She could just hear her: 'There go the O'Connors again, lowering themselves, but, sure, what else could you expect.'

She'd stomped onto the bus, throwing the money at Paudy, who had driven the 6.15 to Dublin ever since she could remember, barely muttering a 'thanks' and thinking that Mary-Pat would have killed her if she could see her. She'd thrown herself into her seat and glared out the window, her arms folded tightly across her chest. She'd looked at the square, at the monument to the war dead, at the little Celtic well which had had 'Up the 'RA' graffitied on it — by Jim Prendergast, because she'd seen him do it — at the little row of shops: the chipper, at Moran's, with the lovely window displays that spoke to the genteel ladies of the county, at Maggie's general stores, with all the holy statues in the window, and she'd wanted to spit on them, to spit on the whole damn place. And then she saw the Jeep roar off up the road towards the house, a belch of smoke coming from the exhaust, and she'd wanted to hug herself tight and give in to the big, ugly sobs that she knew were waiting. But she didn't. She gritted her teeth and pushed them down, because she wouldn't give into them, she just wouldn't. That would be saying that it was all her fault somehow, when she knew it wasn't.

Of course, she'd had an attack then, a squeezing in her chest, her breathing so tight she thought she'd suffocate. She needed her inhaler, she'd thought, beginning to panic. Where was it? She'd rummaged at the top of the backpack and found it in her washbag, in a special compartment, along with a travel toothbrush and a miniature-size toothpaste and soap. A note had been wrapped around the two inhalers, one brown and one blue, in shaky green biro: 'TAKE TWO PUFFS X 2 TIMES PER DAY, MORE IF NEEDED.' She hadn't packed the washbag, she thought, pulling the inhaler out with shaking hands and sucking on it twice. Mary-Pat must have done it. She'd weakened then, just for a moment, before reminding herself that she hated her sister, really, truly hated her, and that she hoped she'd never see her again as long as she lived.

And then the bus rumbled into life, and the doors of the baggage hold were banged shut, and she found her gaze pulled to the window and down the main street. She kept looking, in case she might see him. He'd come, she was sure of it. It was the

least he could do. And if he came, she'd stay. Even though she
hated the place and everyone in it, hated what had happened
there, she'd stay for him.

She'd kept hoping until the bus pulled away, slowly, past the
Protestant church and over the bridge, the water falling glassy
underneath. And then it was too late.

Rosie closed her eyes, and the dappled sunlight flickered across
her eyelids. She didn't want to think about him now. It was
bad enough that she was stirring up everything else after all this
time, but not him. Not Mark.

'I'm sorry, Daddy,' she said, holding his hand, which was
now slippery with cream. 'I'm sorry for everything.' As she
gripped his fingers, the light caught the single solitaire on the
platinum band on her finger. It was too big, and it slid around,
the diamond jabbing the soft skin on the inside of her fingers,
which were milky-white and covered in freckles. 'I'm getting
married, did I tell you that? Can you believe it?' And then she
continued, as if he'd spoken, 'Oh, I know you think it's all a
load of rubbish, but I suppose I had to grow up some time and
a wedding is as good a way as any, isn't it? I know, it doesn't
sound very romantic, but it's all good, honestly.' As she said
the words, she wondered quite why she felt she needed to tell
Daddy this, why she needed to justify herself. She loved Craig
and he made her happy — it was as simple as that. 'But don't tell
the others, will you? I'll have to break the news to them myself
and I haven't seen any of them yet. I wanted you to be the first
to know.'

She paused for a second, twiddling the ring on her finger
before pulling it off, feeling her finger lighten as she did so.

God, that stone weighed a ton. She'd told Craig that she didn't want a big, silly diamond that made her look like a footballer's wife, but he'd insisted. 'What kind of a guy does that make me, if I can't buy my wife-to-be a proper engagement ring?' And so Rosie had found herself being carried along with the whole exercise, visiting a blingy out-of-town jewellers with Craig and his mum, full of fawning staff, obsequious because they knew serious money was going to be spent.

She'd swallowed her protests because she knew how much it mattered to Craig, and as she oohed and aahed over the outsize stone, she tried not to think of the red piece of string she'd worn on her ring finger for one whole summer, years before. They'd been nine years old and got married in the old gazebo in the garden, with Colleen and Morecambe and Wise, the two goats, in attendance, and she'd thought that it was impossible to be any happier than she was right then, on that hot summer's day. She'd been heartbroken when she'd lost that piece of string – she hadn't even known how; she'd just looked down at her finger one morning and it was gone.

That wasn't why she'd come back, she thought now: to dig it all up, to let it all come spilling out after all these years. Not when she'd worked so hard to forget that angry girl on the bus, to make herself into the kind of woman who'd wear a huge solitaire, who'd come back to Monasterard on the arm of her husband to be, to get married 'in the old country', as Craig called it. His grandparents had come from some little village in Donegal and, to him, her home was a mythical, mystical place where you could have the kind of fairy-tale wedding he wanted. He'd spent months planning it all, looking at photos of country piles, co-opting her oldest friend Daphne into helping out. It was funny how romantic he was about the whole thing, how much of a production he wanted to make of it all — he was out in the car now on his phone, busy hunting down a Norman castle for the wedding photos — when she'd just as soon have gone to the register office downtown in Rivertown and then to Marty's Steakhouse, or the Little Chapel of Elvis in Vegas. She'd tried to put him off, 'forgetting' to send the forms for the posting of the banns home, only to discover that he'd found them under the sofa and sent them off himself. 'Honey, don't you think you're a bit ... forgetful sometimes? Honestly, you'd think you didn't want to get married,' he'd chuckled.

If only he knew. She'd never dared tell him, but she wasn't bothered about marriage. She hadn't exactly had a shining example in her parents, but she also knew that she'd do it to please him. She'd do anything to keep him happy, because he'd saved her and, frankly, it was the least she could do. So what if, some days, she woke up and wondered who on earth she was and how she'd fallen into this life. It was a small price to pay, she reckoned, for a quiet life, a peaceful life.

She leaned over and rested her head on Daddy's chest, feeling the bones of his ribs digging into her cheek. His heartbeat was steady, a solid thump-thump, and it made her feel better somehow that a part of him was still strong, even though he couldn't put his arms around her and give her one of his famous bear hugs that would squeeze the life out of her. She was able to draw strength from him, strength that she knew she'd need when she saw her sisters.

She thought she could stay like that for a long time, just resting with Daddy, the picture of the Sacred Heart looking regretfully down at her, until a noise behind her made her jump.

The nurse was Filipina, dressed in a pink candy-stripe top and black trousers. 'Oh, I'm sorry. I didn't know there was anyone here,' she said.

'It's OK, I was just leaving.' Rosie quickly pulled her bag onto her shoulder and stood up. She had no idea why, but she felt as if she'd been caught doing something she shouldn't. Flustered, she dropped her inhaler on the floor and had to scrabble under the bed to find it.

The nurse held out a hand, as if to steady Rosie. 'There's no need ...' But Rosie leaned over and pecked Daddy on the cheek. 'I'll be back soon, Daddy,' and then she was gone, bolting for the door and then half-running up the corridor and out into the warm air of the summer and the lovely shade of the huge copper beech.

She felt dazed as she walked over to the shiny new hire car parked under a tree, as if the ground was sloping away from her as she walked. She could see Craig inside, programming the sat nav. He'd insisted on doing that, even though she'd told him that she knew perfectly well how to find her way around. 'It's my home,' she'd told him. 'I know where I'm going.'

She took a deep breath and opened the car door, getting in and slumping down onto the passenger seat.

'Everything OK?' Craig's blue eyes caught hers, then slipped away to the screen of the sat nav. When she didn't reply, she could feel him still beside her, waiting. She leaned her head back against the headrest and closed her eyes for a second, seeing herself and Daddy in that room, feeling the warmth of his hand, looking at the rise and fall of his chest. Why had nobody told her, she thought. Why had no one said it was that bad?

And then she felt Craig's hand on hers, the briefest of touches. 'Honey?'

She shook her head and pushed his hand away, her eyes filling with tears.

'You shoulda let me come in with you.' He looked at her, his pale blue eyes flicking over her nervously, before looking away. He didn't like emotion, Craig, because he didn't know how to respond to it. It was too messy for him. Too alarming. He cared, Rosie told herself. He just didn't know how to show it.

'I'm fine. I just needed a moment with him. I'll introduce you the next time when he's better.' If there would be a next time.

'Where to next?' His finger was poised over the sat nav to programme it, and she hesitated for a moment. It's not too late, she thought. I can just call the whole thing off and the only person who will know is Daddy. Daddy and Craig. But then she thought of Daphne, who'd thrown herself into the planning, the organising of food and flowers, the booking of the church, with such enthusiasm, it was as if she were getting married herself. Craig and Daphne had been like two old women, clucking and tutting on Skype over place settings and name cards and favours, insisting on creating a Facebook page, so that the whole town now knew about the wedding, and was inviting itself along to the festivities. Maybe it *was* too late after all.

The more people that knew, the harder it would be.

'Rosie?' He was getting impatient now.

'Sorry. Mary-Pat's,' she said, the words coming out in a big rush.

'Right then, what's her address?' He was all business now, pressing buttons on that bloody machine and looking at her expectantly.

'46 Landscape Villas.' The words came out of her mouth and she knew that things would just happen now, whether she liked it or not. It was too late. He tapped in the code, humming under his breath as he did so. The polite English tones of the sat nav announced that they had to turn right and then right again. As if she didn't know. As if she didn't know this place like the back of her hand, even after ten long years.

'It's kinda cute,' Craig said as they drove towards Main Street. 'All those little houses, and the pub and that old kinda stone bridge. You didn't tell me it was this nice. It's very … picturesque,' he decided, slowing down as they drove past the Angler's Rest, which used to be blue and was now painted a bright pink, with its thatched roof golden in the sunshine.

They drove down Main Street then, which was now festooned with bunting, a big sign announcing that Monasterard was the winner of the Tidy Towns 2011, past Nancy O'Beirne's, which used to be filled with knick-knacks, china country cottages, Belleek teapots, snow globes with 'A Souvenir from the Capital of Ireland's Waterways', a blue-painted strip of river with a tiny boat on it. Mary-Pat had hated Nancy O'Beirne. She'd said Nancy was a witch and Rosie was never to darken the door of her shop. 'She thinks we're knackers,' had been her only explanation, 'but we have more class than that bitch ever will.'

Maggie O'Dwyer's little general stores had gone, where Rosie'd bought her Flying Saucers and Love Hearts when she'd been able to cadge money off Pi, and was now a 99-cent shop, with a bright green plastic sign and a lurid window display. Maggie would have hated that, that her tidy little shop had been replaced by a place that just sold tat. The chipper was still there, although it was called Borza's now, not Aprile's, and the red-and-yellow plastic chicken beside the name had long gone.

As they reached the end of the street, she told herself that she didn't want to see it, the bamboo blinds of the Chinese takeaway, the jade lucky charm in the window. She didn't want to see if it had changed, but then she found the word coming out of her mouth, 'Stop.' Craig slammed on the brakes, so that they both pitched forward, Rosie putting out her hands to stop herself, before falling back on the seat.

'What the heck?' Craig said.

'Sorry, I just thought I saw someone ...' Rosie improvised. Craig gave a small tut and was about to drive off when the door of the restaurant opened, and he walked out, a large black bin-bag in his hand. He was wearing chef's whites and his hair, underneath the small blue hat, was cropped close to his head. He must have heard the car because he looked up, and the bin-bag dropped to the street with a thunk. He peered at the car, with its Dublin reg, and then scratched his head before turning around and going back inside.

She couldn't help it, she felt her chest tighten, and she had to reach into her handbag and rummage around for her inhaler, hands shaking. She pulled it out and took two quick puffs, before shoving it back into her bag.

'Who's that?' Craig's voice broke the silence.

'Oh, no one ... just someone I used to know.'

Craig didn't say anything, putting the car into gear, looking quickly behind him as he pulled out onto the main street. Neither of them said a word as they drove in silence past the Protestant church and the gateway to Monasterard House, where Rosie reached out and switched off the sat nav. 'Sorry, it's driving me crazy. I'll give you directions.'

Craig didn't need to say that he was unhappy. Rosie had learned to read the signs. The set of his jaw, the way his shoulders tensed and his hands gripped the steering wheel. 'Left here.'

'Here?' Craig slowed down and nodded towards the little lane that hardly seemed big enough to fit a car.

Rosie nodded. 'It's a shortcut.' Or at least it used to be, she thought as they eased down the little road, an arc of green stretching above their heads, hawthorn branches brushing off the car. The lane was a long ribbon of road, stretching off towards the bog and the forest, where they'd used to go on picnics on their bikes in the summertime, the two of them stopping every five minutes because he'd cracked some joke that made her laugh so much she had to stop to catch her breath, or she'd spotted a newt or a tiny lizard slinking into the undergrowth.

Stop it, will you, she thought to herself. Don't bring it all up again.

Craig insisted on getting out of the car with her when they pulled up outside Mary-Pat's, a neat terraced house with a riot of knick-knacks in the garden. She'd moved there a year after Rosie had left, leaving Pius to moulder away alone in the old house. 'You'll need back-up.' He smiled and made his hands into the shape of two pistols, aiming them at the house. She had told him as little as she could get away with about her family, but Mary-Pat had figured more than once — she was like that, Mary-Pat. You could hardly ignore her. 'She sounds a real character,' Craig had said, which was one way of putting it.

He was trying to be funny, because he thought it would buoy her up, but Rosie just couldn't smile. 'Hey.' He reached out and gave her hand a squeeze. 'It'll be OK.'

Rosie found herself gripping his hand tightly as she led him up the little crazy-paving front path, picking her way around an ornamental wishing well and a gnome clutching a shamrock. He squeezed back as she went to knock on the door and noticed that it was ajar. Mary-Pat never did lock the front door, she thought as she pushed it gently open. 'Hello?' Silence, apart from a hum of chat from a radio somewhere in the house. She could feel Craig behind her, his keys jingling in his pocket.

The two of them stepped inside the cool hall, which was immaculately clean and smelled of Jeyes Fluid. Rosie stepped forward, then a huge brown-and-white-spotted dog came out of a doorway and stood in front of them.

Rosie froze on the spot, but Craig pushed her gently to one side. 'Honey, it's a dog,' he said reproachfully, 'not a wild animal.' He bent down to the dog. 'Hey, buddy,' Craig exclaimed. 'Aren't you a handsome boy?' The dog turned its head from side to side as Craig spoke, as if trying to catch his words, then licked his hand. 'Yes, you are,' he murmured. 'You sure are a handsome guy.' And then he turned to Rosie, a smile on his face, as if to say, 'See? Nothing to be afraid of.' That's easy for you to say, she thought. You're a vet. If you didn't like animals, there'd be something wrong with you.

The dog turned and walked down the hallway, as if leading the way. Rosie swallowed to try to push the lump in her throat down, before following him.

She could see her sister's shape through the opaque glass of the kitchen door, a blur of blue and white. She was cleaning something under the running tap, the sound of splashing water and squeaking glass mingling with her singing. It was Frank Sinatra, Rosie knew. She'd always loved Frank Sinatra.

She pushed the handle on the door and it swung open, and then the dog nudged past her, its nails clicking off the kitchen tiles as it walked over to Mary-Pat, nudging her with its nose. Mary-Pat looked down at the dog and said, 'Duke, you big eejit. You'd better not be looking for food,' and she fondled his ears, her face splitting into a big beam. She looked the same and yet different, Rosie thought. Her hair was dyed blonde and she could see a line of grey along the roots, and her face, which had always been pink with health, now had a ruddy look to it, a patch of broken veins on her cheeks. Mary-Pat was big on top, her arms and breasts heavy, her legs short and slim.

Rosie cleared her throat then. 'Mary-Pat?'

Her sister turned around, still with a half-smile on her face, and it took a second for the features to change, for her eyes to open wide and for her to give a little scream, as she dropped the glass in her hand. It rolled away over the kitchen titles but didn't break. All Rosie could think to say was, 'You never did lock the front door.'

2

It had been the Yank's idea to have the wedding in the garden at the old house. He'd fallen in love with it as soon as he'd seen it, Rosie said. Fellow must have been blind, Pius thought. But that was the Yanks for you — thought a pile of old bricks and a sagging roof was 'history'. Depends on what kind of history you had in mind.

Mary-Pat said the whole idea made her feel sick to her stomach, and it was typical of Rosie to spring it on them like this, but if Pius was OK with it, she'd have to go along with it. Pius felt as if she'd cast him adrift, left him on his own somehow. And he wasn't really sure that he *was* OK with it — it wasn't the practical side of things, the tidying and painting that would need to be done in three weeks flat, to make it look even halfway decent, and after the weekend he'd spent clearing out the spare bedroom for the two of them. Mary-Pat had sent

John-Patrick up to him in the van with a bucket of cleaning stuff and a Hoover that looked like a spacecraft to do the job. Pius could have taken offence, but he knew his sister had a point. No human could have stayed in the spare room, even if he'd had to shove all those unread newspapers under his own bed. He'd get around to reading them eventually.

No, it wasn't that, it was the fact that the whole thing made him feel uneasy, the way he sometimes did before a thunderstorm, standing at the front door, watching the clouds roll in across the fields. But he'd smiled and said, of course, he thought it was a great idea, just great, and had pretended to be pleased when Rosie threw her arms around him in thanks. He wasn't sure if she was pleased for her husband-to-be or herself — it was hard to tell.

Pius found that if he just concentrated on the present, if he didn't let anything else push its way in, just kept the darkness back at the edge of his mind, he could relax to the point where his unease began to fade into the background, to become just a vague nagging doubt that would surface every so often and which he'd dismiss. 'For God's sake, you're being paranoid,' he'd tell himself whenever he'd wonder about herself and that Yank and how they didn't quite look right for each other, or why there was still that awkwardness between herself and Mary-Pat after all this time. Or if it had really been such a good idea, writing to Rosie about Daddy even though Mary-Pat had told him she'd wring his neck if he breathed a word about it. All that kind of thing distressed him because it made him realise just how bad he was at it. At subtexts.

He could read that she was surprised at the state of him, though, Rosie. There was no subtext there. It was the beard, he supposed, long and grey and bushy, and his hair, like a tangled rosebush on top of his head, the only remnant of his youthful dark colour in his beetle-black brows above a pair of almost-black eyes. Daddy's eyes, so help him. And Daddy's sallow colouring and his high cheekbones. Pius supposed that his clothes could probably have done with some ... updating. He didn't shop much: he didn't like it, only firing up the Volkswagen Beetle to trundle into Mullingar for essential supplies. He couldn't take Dublin at all — he'd get into a panic at all the crowds and forget what he came for. Instead, he allowed Mary-Pat to supply him with PJ's cast-off shirts and jumpers, even though he was three times the size of Pius, and he wore Daddy's old corduroy flares, even though they had great big worn patches on the behind. It didn't bother him, the way he looked, anyway. It wasn't as if he had anyone to impress, after all.

Mary-Pat's son John-Patrick called him 'The Missing Beach Boy'. He'd had to explain to Pius that one of the band had spirited himself away to a remote beach in the middle of nowhere to escape fame and everything that went with it and had emerged ten years later with hair down to his ankles and small animals living in his beard. Pius had found the description oddly hurtful: he lived in the world, didn't he? So what if it was the 'arse end of the universe', as his nephew put it. He was happy with it.

But he'd registered the look on Rosie's face that first time, when she'd stood at the door and looked at him and at the house, crumbling around him, and he'd thought, 'That bad, eh?' And there was something about that look, from someone who hadn't seen him in ten years, that had made him go up to his bedroom — Mammy and Daddy's old bedroom — later that afternoon and stand in front of the mirror and look at himself in a way he hadn't done in a long time. Maybe he did look a bit ... wild, he'd thought, combing his hair with his fingers and tutting in irritation as it stood up even more, tugging the end of PJ's old GAA shirt, bright white with a green St Brigid's cross on it, Cill Dara marked out in dark green letters. He could do with a pair of trousers, he'd supposed, examining the way Daddy's trousers bagged around his knees. He'd stroked his beard again, and the man in the mirror, whom Pius didn't quite recognise, had stroked his beard too. And then it suddenly dawned on him. 'I look shit,' he'd said out loud. 'I really look shit.'

It was funny, thought Pius now, as he bent his head low through the henhouse door, scanning the little space as the hens scattered, squawking and clucking furiously. Maybe it took a visit from someone who hadn't seen you in a while to shift things; pennies could drop and you'd realise something that you'd been hiding from yourself for so long. He pinched his nose at the smell — god, he hated the smell of chicken shit — and looked for Bessie. She hadn't been laying in a while and he wanted to have a closer look at her. She was outraged, of course, puffing up her feathers and giving him what he supposed was an angry look, only relaxing when he lifted her out of the henhouse into the sunshine, stroking her and cooing gently in her henny ear.

He could see Rosie and the Yank marking out spaces for the tables in the garden, the pair of them standing together, hands in their back pockets, examining their handiwork, a look of utter seriousness on both their faces. The way they stood was oddly similar, Pius thought, as he felt Bessie relax in his arms, like they were siblings, not lovers. They seemed to get on well, he had to give them that, and yet there was something ... He was hardly an expert, Pius thought, but there wasn't much electricity — that was it. Surely you needed that in a relationship?

Mammy and Daddy had had electricity, that was for sure, enough to power the national grid, and look where that had got them. The trouble was, theirs was the kind that would give you a nasty shock; it had a too-vivid quality to it, like a flash of blue from faulty wiring. And it was the kind of love that damaged — themselves and others. Maybe Rosie and the Yank had the right idea. Steady as she goes. And she hadn't said she wasn't happy, had she?

He tilted his head back and felt the hot sun on his face. The sky was the palest blue, like a pheasant's egg. The sun felt good after all those months of rain. It warmed his aching bones. The pain had been getting worse lately, a dull ache in his joints that refused to go away. Maybe he should start smoking some of his own weed, he thought. But that was strictly business, a few plants in the old outhouse at the back of the vegetable patch to pay for food and the odd bit of petrol. Wasn't cannabis medicinal anyway? But he was careful not to touch the stuff any more; that's what had got him into trouble before, smoking too much of it. He'd thought it was helping, draping a thick blanket over all the things he didn't want to think about, but, in fact, it had made it all worse. Paranoia: he could write a book about it.

He closed his eyes for a few seconds, and the smell was back in his nostrils, the disinfectant that they spread so liberally around the ward. That bloody smell had clung to his clothes, so pungent that he'd had to get rid of them all once he came out. He'd burned them in a barrel in the back garden. He'd never been able to tolerate it since. Had had to ask Mary-Pat if she minded not using it any more around the house. 'I'm allergic to it,' he'd said, by way of explanation. She hadn't said a word, but the next time he'd dropped in, the kitchen floor had smelled of lemons. She might be a dragon, but she did care, Pius knew that. And he couldn't have managed without her. 'That's what families are for,' she'd told him all those years ago as they'd sat in that miserable waiting room, waiting to see the on-duty guy, squeezing his hand tight. 'That's what they do.'

'Pi, you there?' Rosie's voice came from around the back of the house.

'Here!' He jumped up, Bessie still under his arm, and walked around past the lean-to and Daddy's shed to the back of the house, where the Yank and Rosie were standing, looking at something. Pius couldn't make it out because he was short-sighted but could never find his glasses. 'Wouldn't that be swell for the vows?' the Yank was saying.

'Oh, yeah,' Rosie turned as Pius came towards them. 'It's beautiful,' she said to Craig. 'What do you think, Pi?' and she waved an arm at the old gazebo. Her hair tied up in an old yellow scarf that looked vaguely familiar, her hands in the pockets of her tiny blue jeans, a puzzled look on her face as if she was trying to unravel some mystery — she looked like a little doll, he thought, that if you twisted her limbs too much she'd break. She'd always been tiny, Rosie, but she'd had spirit, a fire inside her. Now, he wasn't so sure. But maybe that's what happened when you grew up. And she'd sure grown up.

She was nodding her head in the direction of the gazebo and it was all Pius could do not to blush a bright, hot red. 'Al fresco,' Katy had called it that time. She'd taken him by the hand and led him towards it, her naked skin almost blue in the moonlight. She'd made him take off all his clothes. He'd asked if he could leave on his underpants, but she'd been adamant. 'No clothes. You need to really feel what it's like, the night air on your skin.' He wasn't bothered about that — after all, he'd spent most of his childhood naked: Mammy had been a big fan of it. But this was hardly the nakedness of a seven-year-old, he'd thought, as he'd felt the cold air on his erect penis, so swollen it was painful to walk. He'd had to half scuttle, like a crab, his cheeks reddening with a mixture of self-consciousness and lust.

'Isn't this amazing?' she'd said, as they'd stood there in the tangle of vines and old buddleia, a canopy of dark green around them. In fact, it hadn't been that amazing, he remembered. The floor was filthy and they hadn't been able to lie down and he'd been in too much of a hurry, coming as soon as he'd slipped inside her. It had all been a bit uncomfortable, but memorable nonetheless. That was Katy — she made you do things you never thought you would. Maybe that's why he hadn't done anything unexpected in about twenty years.

'It's perfect,' the Yank said, pulling Rosie towards him and kissing her tenderly on the cheek, his hand in the back pocket of her jeans. She nodded but didn't reply, and the expression on her face was hard to read. But that was the new Rosie. It was hard to be sure how she felt about anything. In the couple of weeks since she'd been back, he hadn't seen a flicker of the old Rosie. She seemed so ... composed, that was the word.

'I'll give it a lick of paint,' Pius said then. 'White all right? I have some in the shed, I think.'

'Thanks, Pi.' Rosie leaned towards him and planted a kiss on his cheek. He tried to catch her eye but she looked over his shoulder towards the water. 'We'll clear all the ivy off first and sand it down.'

He nodded and turned around, the hen still under his arm, so they couldn't see that he'd nearly cried on them, burst into tears, like a small child, at the way he'd started to remember. God almighty, Rosie, he thought. Why did you ever have to come back?

I need a coffee, he said to himself, and trudged in the kitchen door, wiping his boots on the mat. It was one of those novelty ones that seemed to say 'welcome' until you looked at it from another angle and it read 'piss off'. Mary-Pat had bought it for him for Christmas one year, and she'd thought it was hilarious.

She could be a complete pain in the arse, the same Mary-Pat, Pius thought as he carefully poured water into the coffee maker and twisted the lid, then tapped out the old coffee in the filter and refilled it, pressing it down firmly before slotting it into the machine, the one and only thing of value in this house. He'd ordered it from London, ignoring Mary-Pat's derision when he'd invited her to come up to the house and try it out. 'Oh, la-di-dah,' she'd scoffed. 'Too good for this place now, are you?'

'No,' Pius had said quietly. 'I just like cappuccino.' He'd been gratified to see the look of shame flicker across her face. 'Have a Jammie Dodger,' he'd said, by way of a peace offering. She'd been so surprised to be offered a biscuit that she shut up then for a blessed few minutes.

Poor Mary-Pat. Rosie's homecoming had hit her the hardest. Maybe she still felt a sense of responsibility to her baby sister, not sure what to do now that she didn't have to cook her big dinners and get her out of bed in the mornings. But Rosie was clearly well able to look after herself. Or maybe Mary-Pat was upset that she hadn't been asked to do more with the wedding. Rosie had made it clear that she and the Yank had it all under control. Maybe that's why they all felt a bit unsettled — that they weren't doing the kind of things a family should do for a wedding. They weren't involved.

Pius had gone as far as to say it to PJ when he'd been in to the shop for a bit of groundbait. This year, like every year, he'd promised himself that he'd take up fishing again. He'd spent every single day of his young life on that canal bank, rod in hand, penknife in his back pocket to make a shelter for himself out of the willow branches that hung over the dead pool beyond the bridge. And then, after he'd gone into that place, he'd just stopped. Still, every spring he'd take out his old fishing box from under the dining-room table, and he'd open it, and he'd sit there for a moment, looking at the neat rows of rigs, the line neatly tied around them, and he'd announce to Jessie, because she was the only one who listened and didn't offer an opinion, that he was going fishing again. And she'd wag her tail and look at him expectantly, and he'd close the box and put it away for another year.

Still, it had offered him an excuse to sound PJ out without having to face his sister in the process. It was the coward's way out, he knew, but that way he could persuade himself that he'd done something without actually doing it. His *modus operandi*. Himself and Jessie had called into PJ's Tackle the previous week, Jessie knowing to sit still beside a row of tackle boxes and to keep out of the way, her copper head resting on her two front paws.

'How's herself?' Pius had ventured after a few minutes pretending to peruse the merchandise.

PJ had gone a funny colour, busying himself with lining up packs of mealworm on the counter, before eventually blurting, 'Ah, sure you know yourself. She hasn't been the same since Rosie came back.'

Pius had nodded, picking up a pike lure in his left hand and turning it over. 'I'd say she'd be stressed about it all right.'

'Stressed doesn't cover it. I keep trying to tell her that it's all water under the bridge at this stage and, sure, don't we all change in ten years, but she keeps going on about how she's going to stir it all up again, whatever that means.' He'd scratched his head and looked at Pius hopefully, as if he'd provide PJ with the answers, but Pius had just shrugged. He didn't have any answers.

'Anyway, they're all off to Dublin next week, for the fitting. Mary-Pat's already up to ninety about it. I told her not to bother if it upset her that much, but she nearly ate me.'

'The fitting?' Pius hadn't understood.

'Ah, Pi, the dress fitting, you eejit. That's what all the women do now – they all go into the shop while the bride's having her dress fitted – you know, like on *Bridesmaids*.' Here, he'd rolled his eyes to heaven. 'And they all drink champagne and then complain that they have sore heads for a week after.'

God, no wonder Mary-Pat was keyed up about it. She hadn't managed to be in the same room as Rosie for more than five minutes since she'd come back, so the idea of her spending a whole day with her – how on earth would she cope?

PJ had continued, 'Why don't you come up and watch *Match Fishing* with me while they're all gone? We can have a few beers and put the world to rights.' PJ was always asking Pius up to the house, to watch football on the telly or to listen to a Gaelic match on the radio – and Pius was flattered, because he knew that PJ wanted him to be an ally, a friend, but he just wasn't very good at it. He couldn't really manage the banter and the slagging that you needed to be able to do, the Man-chat, as John-Patrick put it.

'That sounds good,' he'd said noncommittally, ignoring the slight look of disappointment on PJ's face. 'I'll text you.'

'Grand so,' PJ said, for all the world as if his brother-in-law was actually going to come around to watch men on carp lakes hauling them in.

'I'll take this,' Pius had said and put the pike lure on the counter and PJ's face had brightened — 'Pike? Aim high, Pi, that's what I always say.'

Aim high. It had been quite some time since he'd done that.

Pius poured hot milk now onto the coffee in the three white cups. Always cups, never mugs. You couldn't drink cappuccino out of a mug. That waiter in Rimini had told him that, on the one and only holiday Pius had ever taken. Katy had organised it, the way she'd organised everything in his life back then. The waiter had invited him behind the café counter to watch how it was done — the coffee tamped down just so, the black, treacly liquid coming out of the spouts into the white cups, the hissing of the milk frother in the metal jug. 'See?' the waiter had told him. '*Assolutamente perfetto.*' Sometimes, he wished he lived in Italy, imagining himself at some little bar at eight o'clock in the morning, knocking back an espresso on his way to work. He'd talk himself into it on his long walks down the canal to Porterstown, wondering what, exactly, was holding him back. But then he'd reason that, sure, he couldn't speak a word of Italian, and, anyway, it was way too expensive. No, it was better to keep things the way they were. That way, nothing would ever surprise him. He didn't like surprises, Pius. They tended to be nasty ones.

He leaned his head against the cool pane of glass in the kitchen window and let out a low groan.

'Are you all right?'

Pius turned around to see a young woman standing at the door. She was wearing a vivid green dress with a denim jacket slung over it and a pair of battered trainers, but what really struck him was her hair — a long sweep of bright red — not pale red, like Rosie's, or ginger or strawberry blonde, but proper red. Pius's first thought was that she looked like a mermaid. A large mermaid, with rolls of milky flesh around her arms and waist, but a mermaid nonetheless.

He stood bolt upright, heart thumping in his chest. 'You gave me a fright. I was just—'

'Talking to yourself.' The words were spoken matter-of-factly and accompanied by a curious kind of a glare that should have been terrifying but which didn't quite succeed.

He laughed. 'You got me there.'

She didn't reply, just walked over to him and extended a hand and shook his briefly. Her hand was warm and her grip so firm he winced slightly. Her eyes were such a vivid green that Pius was startled by them, before deciding that they couldn't be real. She must wear those tinted contact lenses or something. For some reason, he felt a sudden sense of disappointment.

'Daphne.' Her voice was low and deep, with an almost masculine quality to it.

'Pius. I'm Rosie's brother—'

'I know who you are.'

'Oh. Right.' But who the hell are you? She clearly wasn't going to enlighten him, so Pius cleared his throat. 'Did you need anything ...?'

She'd been looking down at her trainers, but now her head flicked up and there was a faint flush to her cheeks. 'Rosie wanted me to get some sandpaper. For the gazebo thing in the garden.'

'Oh, OK. I have some in the attic …'

'Thanks.'

'Right then.' He was racking his brains now, trying to think of what to say to a woman who clearly didn't do small talk, when Rosie appeared in the doorway. 'Daph, did you get it? Oh, there you are, Pi. We were just looking for some sandpaper.' Then she looked at Pius and then at Daphne, a slight frown on her face. 'Pi. You remember Daphne, don't you? We were at school together. She's my bridesmaid.'

Pius cleared his throat to say hello to the woman, but instead all he said was, 'I'll go and get the sandpaper now.' Like an eejit who couldn't manage a little bit of small talk. But then, he *was* an eejit who couldn't manage a bit of small talk. When was the last time he'd had the chance to practise? There was a flurry of movement then as he bustled up the stairs and the others went out to the garden to busy themselves pulling the ivy off the gazebo and sanding the chipping white paint down.

He found the pole propping the skylight open in the bathroom, gingerly pulling it towards him so that the ancient window wouldn't slam shut and the glass shatter. He hoped the attic door would still open — he hadn't been up there in a long time and he seemed to remember the door was one of Daddy's attempts at DIY, because it never quite fitted into the hole in the ceiling, a draughty gap on one side. He put the hook into the loop in the door and gave a tug and then another and, with a creak, the door pulled open, a great cloud of dust filling the landing. Coughing, Pius pulled the steps down and climbed up.

He rummaged around for the old Bakelite light switch, hoping that it wouldn't electrocute him when he switched it on. To his surprise, it still worked, casting a dim yellow glow over the huddled shapes of a dressmaker's dummy, a music stand and a pile of sheet music. Now, where had he kept that sandpaper, Pius wondered, kicking a deflated football out of his way as he ducked down a little. He was sure he'd stuffed a big pile of it into a box somewhere. And while he was about it, he might as well look for that paint that he'd put away after doing the front gate – he seemed to remember it was a nice pale grey colour. He opened a couple of boxes, to find dusty sheet music in them, and then he spied the black steamer trunk. He'd put a few tins in here, he thought as he tried to prise open the lid, cursing under his breath as he caught his thumb on the rusty catch.

He looked around for something to push the thing open, before pulling a two-euro coin out of his pocket and shoving it under the catch, giving it a twist as he did so. The catch lifted with a sudden snap. He had to tug at it quite hard before the lid lifted with a groan. The smell of must and damp hit his nostrils, and he pinched his nose. He'd always hated that smell, which was ironic considering the state of the house. When the leaves fell in autumn, he'd have to wear a mask over his face to sweep them up, trying not to inhale the smell of decay.

There's no paint here anyway, he thought, pushing aside a set of black tails, obviously part of a morning suit, shiny with age and wear, and a battered-looking top hat. Where had all of this stuff come from, he wondered as he lifted up a fox-fur stole, the head of the fox looking as if something had been chewing on it, its eyes like little black marbles in its head. 'You're disgusting, do you know that?' he addressed the dead fox. 'Mammy would have a heart attack if she could see you. I saw her in action, you know, outside Sunday Mass. Headmaster's wife, as I remember. Poor woman didn't get over being asked if she'd wear her child's skin to Mass. She still looks at me funny. But that was Mammy.'

He threw Mr Fox back into the trunk, feeling suddenly irritable and out of sorts. What the hell was he doing, talking to a dead fox? And where were those tins of paint? He reached up to close the lid of the trunk when something caught his eye, the corner of something hard and shiny. He pushed the dead fox aside and the lacquered top of a box appeared, black, with a pinky-white chrysanthemum painted on the front.

He gave the box a little shake. It felt quite heavy, and whatever was inside it gave a little thud. It, too, had a catch, an ornate one in the shape of a Chinese symbol, and it only took a little push to open it. He placed it on the floor underneath the light to get a closer look, because he couldn't see properly in anything but the brightest light these days, and he scanned the box's contents.

It took a while for him to understand. He could see what each item was, but his brain just didn't register. It should have done, because he knew the writing so well, but he just couldn't understand what it was doing, their names neatly printed on the brown card luggage labels with their string ties and carefully Sellotaped to the objects. Pius picked the book up first, the weight of it too heavy for one hand. The smell of old book hit his nostrils and it was all he could do not to retch as he opened it, the title engraved on the second of the mottled brown pages. *Gone with the Wind*, Margaret Mitchell. The name on the top read 'June Spencer'. Must have been one of Mammy's family. Pius shook his head and closed the book, pulling the luggage label into the light so that he could decipher the name on it. 'June O'Connor'.

He blinked for a few minutes then put the book down. His wrist ached from the weight of it. He looked at the label again, at Mammy's handwriting. His mouth felt dry and he swallowed, pushing the lump in his throat back down a little bit and he could hear the blood pumping in his ears, a steady whump-whump. He only thought for a second about shoving the things back into the box: the desire to hold them, to examine them, to understand them was too strong. His hand shook as he picked up the scroll of rolled-up paper. It had his name on it. Hands shaking, he pulled at the little bit of Sellotape that held the scroll together and rolled it out, squinting in the light. 'A French Potager' read the title at the top, and beneath it, a map of rows of broad beans, cabbages, potatoes, nasturtiums, pansies. A miniature apple tree shaded rows of primula and a raised bed with 'turnips' marked on it.

It was like a voice from the dead. As if she were standing beside him, showing him the map, pointing out the shady spots where the ferns would thrive and the well-drained soil that would be needed for the root veg. If he closed his eyes, he could see her, could hear her voice. 'See here, Pi, wouldn't a climbing rose look just fantastic over the trellis in front of the gazebo, or maybe a vine, what do you think?' Her hands were on her hips, her blonde hair frizzy around her head, tied back with a piece of gardening twine because she didn't care one jot about how she looked. She was smiling at him, the wrinkles fanning out from her grey eyes. 'Well, Pi, what do you think? Will you do it?'

He opened his eyes, blinking in the dim light. He was talking to a ghost. She was gone, had been for nearly thirty years. He'd counted the years like that: the first year after Mammy left, the second, the fifth and so on, until now, more than a quarter of a century, and the pain inside of him was as raw as it had been the day she left. All this time, her message had been lying here, hidden away from him, a message that he'd thought she'd never left him. Never left any of them. Seeing it made her alive for him in a way she hadn't been since she'd walked out the door that summer day.

'Yes, Mammy,' he said into the silence. 'Of course I'll do it.'

He read the other labels, the one with Mary-Pat's name on it stuck on the shell that looked as if it had come from Africa, with its beautiful mother-of-pearl inside, the roar of the sea when he held it up to his ear, the tight wad of Sellotape that held Rosie's name in place around the chunky silver ring. Daddy wore that ring, he thought, but this wasn't his. It was too small. And then he felt bad, because the objects weren't his to see. He'd have to give them to the girls and let them do with them as they saw fit. But then, the thought of what might happen if he did made him panic. He shoved the things back in the box and slammed the lid down, as if by closing them inside they'd just cease to exist. As if he could just erase the last few moments from his mind, could pretend they'd never happened. He put the box back in the steamer trunk and sat down on it, staring into space.

'Pi, you up there?' Rosie's voice floated up to him through the open hatch. 'I thought I'd give you a hand to find the paint.'

He had to clear his throat with a loud coughing noise. 'No need. It's not here.'

'Oh.' There was a long silence and then Rosie's head appeared through the hatch, her tiny face with its scattering of freckles.

A deep line split her forehead as she frowned. 'Is everything all right?'

And even as he said everything was grand, just grand, and that he needed to have a look in the shed, turning off the attic light and practically shoving her down the steps onto the landing, he was thinking, of course it's not fucking all right. Everything's changed, can't you see that? Nothing will ever be the same again. And then the thought came to him: and it's all your fault. Mary-Pat was right. If you hadn't come back, none of this would have happened. And then, he gave out to himself for even having thought such a thing — how was it Rosie's fault exactly?

When she came into the kitchen later and offered to make lunch, he felt so guilty for his disloyal thoughts that he made an extra effort to be nice. Yes, he'd love some carrot and coriander soup, thanks — yes, he knew that it was fantastic to have your own veg and, yes, he really should use them more, instead of that awful packet tomato stuff. And all the time his head was spinning, mind filling with thoughts, one jumbling on top of the other.

He was so preoccupied, he didn't notice the noise of the knife slamming through the onion onto the board, making a loud rapping sound on the wood, but then it grew louder and louder, until she yelled, 'Ow, crap,' and held up her finger, which instantly began to pour blood, a long trail of it dripping onto the board.

Pi was beside her. 'Here, let me,' he said, holding her hand in his and leading her over to the sink, running the cold tap and holding her finger under it, a stream of pink flowing down to the plughole. 'Now,' he said, 'we'll wrap it in a bit of kitchen paper while I hunt down the plasters,' and he pushed a wad around her finger. 'Hold onto that for a second,' and he went into the living room, where he rummaged around under a pile of yellowing newspapers until he found what he was looking for.

'I knew I had some somewhere,' he said, returning to the kitchen clutching the tin of Elastoplast. 'Let's have a look,' he said, and placed one gently around her finger, the thin blob of blood on the cut flattening down under the plaster. 'Pius will make it all better. Just like when you were eight and you fell over the water barrel in the yard and you needed ten stitches.'

'Oh, God, yes.' Rosie smiled at the memory. 'And you distracted me at the hospital by telling me some big long story about a pike eating someone's toes.'

'That wasn't a story,' Pius joked.

'Very funny.' Rosie attempted a smile, but her face had gone a milky shade of white, and her teeth chattered in shock. There was a pause, and then Rosie said, 'Pi, if I tell you something, will you promise not to tell Mary-Pat? Or June?'

Pius sighed and wrapped an arm around her shoulders. 'You can tell your old brother anything, you know that, hmm?'

'I know, Pi. I always could.' She paused. 'I'm not sure I want any of this.'

'What do you mean?'

'Any of *this* —' Rosie gestured to the garden, the house. 'It's all Craig's idea — it's his dream and it's what he wants, but I think it's a mistake.'

'Getting married, is that what you mean?' Pius said, thinking about the Yank and what a long drink of water he was. 'Or coming back?'

'I don't know.' There was a long pause.

'You've been gone a long time, Rosie. It'll take time to settle back in, to get to know everyone again. And Daddy—' Pius tried to reassure her, but she interrupted, 'I got fired, well, made redundant, but it amounts to the same thing.'

'Oh? Oh,' was all Pius could manage. He knew she had some do-gooding job, working with kids – he hadn't been able to see it somehow, but maybe he was thinking of the old Rosie, barely more than a kid herself. This new Rosie, all grown up. Yes, he could see that.

'I worked in a centre with disturbed teenagers – please, no comments about the irony of it,' she added. 'And I got the boot when one of the lads went mad with a snooker cue and smashed the place up.'

'Sounds as if it wasn't your fault, Rosie-boo.'

'It was, because I was really, really crap at it. It turns out that having once been a disturbed teenager is no preparation for dealing with them.' She couldn't help it – she had to laugh.

'Ah, Rosie, I'd say you're being hard on yourself.'

'Not hard enough.' She bit her lip. 'I'm at a bit of a ... juncture, I suppose you could call it. I've always just got along, ever since I left. I managed to find work in Dublin and then I met Craig and went to the States, and it just seemed that life would go along like that for ever, but now ...' Her voice trailed away. 'Have you ever found that, that you've just come to a stop and you've no idea where to go next?'

No, Pius thought to himself, because I've never really got started.

She blushed then. 'Sorry, that wasn't very tactful.'

He shrugged. He supposed she was talking about what had happened to him – but he wasn't going to go there. Not now.

'Are you better now?'

'Ah, sure, I'm all right.' He gave her a little squeeze. 'And you'll be all right, Rosie-boo.'

She shook her head impatiently. 'None of you want me here, do you?'

No, we probably don't, Pi thought to himself, while understanding that this was not the answer his sister was looking for. Because she was right, in a way – about coming home – it had shaken them all.

He had no idea how to reassure her. What to say. And then it came to him. Without another word, he left the room and climbed the stairs to his bedroom, where he'd smuggled the box, holding it behind him as he'd ushered her down the attic stairs to the landing. When he came back into the kitchen, he had a small brown-paper package in his hand. He cleared his throat. 'Ehm, I thought you might like to have this.'

'What is it?' Rosie eyed it warily.

'Open it.'

She took it from him and looked at it, at the crumpled brown paper and the tight wad of Sellotape. 'It has my name on it,' she said.

He nodded.

'Whose handwriting is this?' She looked at the immaculate hand, the 'R' in Rosie an elaborate flourish.

'It's Mammy's.'

Rosie looked up at him and then back at the tiny package, examining it, turning it over in her hand. He'd wrapped it well, burying it hastily under several layers of brown paper, which he'd found under the bed, but he hadn't been able to get the label to stick on properly and it hung off at a funny angle. Eventually, she pulled at a bit of Sellotape, and when it came away, she pulled at another bit, until there was a hole in the paper through which they could see a flash of silver. She pushed back the nest of paper to reveal the silver ring, rough-hewn, with a knobbly purple stone in the middle. When she tilted it towards the light, it took on a muted glow.

Pius nodded then. 'I think he had a friend make them, one for each of them. He still wears his,' Pius added. 'I know, the irony.'

'Why did she leave it for me?'

'I don't know, Rosie-boo. Maybe she wanted you to make the right choice.'

There was a long silence while Rosie slipped the ring on her ring finger, where it wobbled around, far too big for it.

'Do you love him?'

Her head shot up. 'Yes. Yes, I do.'

'Well, then.' And they both looked at the ring. 'Pius's marriage guidance,' he added, 'from the benefit of my vast experience.'

She managed a laugh, and he took his chance then to change the subject. He cleared his throat and asked the question that had been on his mind all afternoon. 'Ehm, your friend Daphne.'

'Yes?' Rosie looked mystified.

'Is she, I mean … is there a Mr Daphne?'

If she was surprised, she hid it well, Pius thought. 'Oh. Yeah, Kevin. He's an idiot.'

'Oh.' He tried to conceal it, but he couldn't help feeling pleased. 'Let's finish chopping that onion, shall we?'

'Right,' Rosie said, punching him playfully on the arm. 'And thanks,' she said, looking thoughtfully at the ring.

July 1969

Michelle

John-Joe has just given me a ring, and I don't quite know what to make of it. I don't even know if I like it, or even if I like him. There's something about him that's so ... powerful, like standing too close to the sun, but do I like him? I haven't decided yet.

It's quite an ugly ring, a battered-looking silver thing with a huge knobbly purple stone in it; I'm holding it between my thumb and forefinger, examining it, while I try to work out quite what to say. It's hard, when you feel that a tidal wave has swept over you, when you feel that someone has come into your life and whipped it up into a whirlwind and the only thing you can do is just give in to it. It's frightening, but then I remind myself that this is what I've always wanted, that sense that life could go anywhere at all, that it wasn't just one dreary day following another, my whole future stretching out in front of me.

How often have I pictured myself in this new life, imagined myself sitting at a long table filled with exotic food that I have to eat with my fingers, drinking wine out of chipped mugs, the sun on my face. I'll be wearing something long and loose, and I will have thrown away the girdle that cuts into my tummy and leaves angry red stripes on my skin. And my hair will be falling around my shoulders, not squashed to my face in those horrible heated rollers. And there'll be a man there too, tall and handsome and brown from the sun – and bare-chested. I have to giggle at that part of the fantasy, because sleeveless jumpers, shirts and ties are also banned in my new world. And shoes! There'll be no more Sunday afternoons in the drawing room, the fire hissing in the grate, listening to the rain beating on the window, the rustle of Pa's newspaper and the tick-tock of the French clock on the mantelpiece as I wait for Mummy to look up and ask, as if she's never asked the question before, 'Sherry, Pa?' And for Pa to reply, 'Is it time, dear?' When I want to scream at the top of my voice, 'Of course it's bloody time. It's been the same every single Sunday that I can remember.' Until just this moment, I thought this other life could never be, that my whole future was mapped out for me, and now I sit here with this man, and for the first time, I dare to think that things just might be different.

He turned up at Miss Marsh's, a single rose in his hands, and demanded that the secretary fetch me out of my typing class. He told her he was my brother and that it was a 'family emergency' and her face was a picture: a mixture of anxiety and distaste as she said the words 'your brother'. I almost said it then, 'But I don't have a brother,' but something made me stay quiet, follow her out of the classroom and down the corridor and into the office, where he was sitting in a chair by the window. For a moment, I had no idea who he was — I'd only met him that one time before, after all, in the gloom of the Students' Club, and even then we'd hardly exchanged a word, just watched the film together in near-silence — but then I remembered the way he'd looked at me when we'd said goodbye, right into my eyes, and he'd kissed me softly on my cheek. And then he'd just vanished — and now, six weeks later, here he was, sitting in the office of the secretarial school, pretending to be my brother.

I hovered by the threshold in my green jumper and my threadbare tweed skirt, my toes pinched in the white stilettos the school insists we wear 'to aid posture'. He'd slicked back those black curls into a side parting, but they still rested on his shirt collar in a way that Mummy would describe as 'scruffy' and he was wearing a suit jacket that looked as if it was three sizes too small for him, and then he caught sight of me and his face split into a huge grin, a lopsided one that showed a set of large white teeth. He looked as if he had a black eye, a purple shadow around his left one, and I took in a deep breath at the sight. Has he been in a fight? I wondered. I couldn't suppress a shiver of excitement at the thought. I'd never met a man before who'd been in an actual fight.

'Well, have you nothing to say to your brother, Miss Spencer?' Mrs McCarthy's voice was sharp in my ear.

'Oh, yes, what is it, William? I have class and you've interrupted my shorthand note-taking.' I tried my best to look annoyed.

He coughed, to clear his throat, his hand over his mouth. 'Yes, well, ehm ... sister, you're wanted at home. Grandad's been taken ill.'

I had to feign alarm then, when all the while I wanted to howl with laughter. 'Sister'? He didn't even know my name! I bundled him out of the office as quickly as I could, thanking Mrs McCarthy profusely for her help, and ran out the door. Only when we had walked around the side of Trinity College, a good five hundred feet from the school, did I dare let out the laughter which had been bubbling up inside.

'What on earth was "sister" all about?'

He grinned that big grin of his again. 'I was improvising. I thought you'd be impressed.'

'I am.'

'Ehm, you see, I don't know your name.'

'It's Michelle,' I said. 'Pleased to meet you again.'

He looked at my outstretched hand and then down at his own, as if he were deciding whether or not it was clean, and then he reached out and took mine, clasping it in his. He didn't shake, just held it there and gave a little squeeze. I could feel my skin tingle. 'John-Joe O'Connor.'

We ran all the way to Macari's café on Talbot Street, the two of us nearly doubled over with laughter as we hopped through the puddles, and then we took a seat by the window, looking down onto the shoppers going in and out of Boyers department store. And now, here we are, sharing a big plate of chips and battered cod, and it feels good, hot and greasy and I lick my fingers, the salt on my tongue. No knives, no forks, no fine dining. Daddy would have a heart attack.

'I suppose you're wondering how I found you again?' He's leaning back on the seat, so far he threatens to topple backwards, rubbing his stomach, before he gives an appreciative belch. I cover my mouth, my eyes wide. In my house, a belch has never once been heard: people retreat into the privacy of the bathroom to do things like that, behind closed doors.

I giggle. 'That's very rude.'

'But you like it.' He smiles broadly. 'You like a man who's honest about these things. Who doesn't pretend to be one thing when he's really another.'

'Hmm ...' I shrug my shoulders, because I have no idea what kind of man I like. The statement seems so odd, when the only men I've ever known are Daddy and a few of the boys at the tennis club. I couldn't imagine Ivan, with his tweed jacket and pullover, his shirt and tie, letting a big burp out like that or talking to me like this man talks to me, directly, as if I'm not 'a lady', just, well, a woman, I suppose. Ivan is far too much of a gentleman — all that opening doors and insisting he drive, even though I know perfectly well how to drive myself. I look at John-Joe and I can tell he's not a gentleman, but there's something about that that I like: it makes me feel that I know him in a way I've never known a man before: as an equal.

'I've been trying to look you up ever since we bumped into each other at the Students' Club,' he's saying. 'I went back a few times, but there was no sign of you. And then I remembered you talking about your "awful secretarial school"' — he does a very funny imitation of me and I find myself giggling again — 'and so I tried all of them until I found you. I had to stand outside for a week or so to see if you walked in the door, but it was worth it.'

I should be scared, I know. That a man — who, incidentally, hadn't seemed terribly bothered about me at our first meeting — should go to such lengths to find me. Me! But then I thought of Jean Seberg and Jean-Paul Belmondo in À Bout de Souffle and how they just found each other, without needing silly things like tennis clubs and respectability. It just seemed so romantic: that he would search the whole of Dublin just for me. And when he lays his brown hand on mine and gives it a little squeeze, my heart gives a little squeeze too.

'How did you know my surname?' The thought suddenly occurs to me.

He leans back in his seat again, a big grin splitting his face. 'You have one of those labels sewn into the back of your coat, like a little schoolgirl. M. Spencer it said. I thought the "M" stood for "Miss".'

I blush a bright red and try to stifle a giggle, thanking God for Mummy's insistence on labelling all my clothes.

He leans forward then, his expression suddenly serious. 'There's a protest on next Saturday. About Vietnam. Fancy coming?'

My stomach flips, a mixture of excitement and nerves. I've never been to a protest before. 'Will it be violent?' I ask.

He looks as if he's trying not to laugh. 'You're very sheltered, aren't you? Of course it won't be violent, unless the guards kick off,' he spits. 'Bastards.' And then he coughs. 'Excuse me. I forget that you're a lady.'

I groan. 'Not all that "lady" nonsense, please. Why can't we just be equals?'

His eyes flash. 'Oh, be careful what you wish for, Michelle. Women's liberation can be a dangerous thing.'

'Oh, really? How, exactly?' I say smartly.

'Well, it's obvious. Men and women aren't made the same. They're different for a reason. Women are born to be mothers – they're soft and gentle and they nurture their young, not like us men – and as for politics or the factory floor, well, it's no place for women. It's too aggressive. Women couldn't survive that.'

'And there was I, thinking that you weren't like other men,' I say tightly, pulling my handbag onto my lap. 'It's because of men like you that we're all at home, chained to the kitchen sink. It's because of men like you that we have no hope or expectation of equality,' I spit. 'Why shouldn't we be doctors or astronauts or soldiers or anything else we want to be?'

'And who'd look after the children then?' he says, his face a mask of disapproval, before he leans back in his chair and roars with laughter.

'You are mocking me,' I say. 'You horrible, horrible man. I'm going. I didn't need to get dragged out of my class for this,' and I pull myself upright, my chair scraping back on the floor so loudly everyone turns around to have a look. I'm about to turn around, when he grabs my hand, tight. 'Sit down,' he says. His expression has darkened and for a moment I feel afraid.

I have to pull myself together. 'No,' I retort. 'Nobody orders me around.'

His face softens. 'Sorry. Sorry, Michelle. Will you please sit down? I promise I won't take the mick any more.'

Reluctantly, I perch on the edge of my chair and he reaches into his jacket pocket, pulling out a battered-looking black velvet box. 'Here,' he says, pushing it across the table to me.

'What is it?' I look at the box as if it is dangerous somehow. He sighs and pulls it back, opening it and taking out two rings, the same rough silver, the same knobbly purple stone in the middle. 'I promised that if I ever found you, I'd give you this,' he said, handing me the smaller of the two. The larger one, he slipped onto the fourth finger of his right hand, admiring it.

I hold mine in front of me, unable to work out what exactly he's asking me. I look at it for the longest time and the place seems to fall quiet around us.

'Well?' he says, taking my hand and stroking my ring finger. 'Will you wear it?'

I know if I get the answer wrong, I'll never see him again, but it's a risk I have to take. I can't let him think he's in charge here. 'I'll think about it,' I say, and I get back up, put the ring into my handbag and close the catch. 'Thanks for dinner.' And I walk out of the restaurant without turning around.

3

The cheap Prosecco was going to June's head, her hand clammy on the glass as the three of them bunched up on the sagging sofa in the bridal shop. Mary-Pat's Melissa was in the middle, chattering away about bodices and dropped waists, while she and Mary-Pat sat either side of her, like anxious terriers waiting for the fox to appear.

'Jesus Christ, it's warm in here,' Mary-Pat was saying, her face red, two circles of sweat under her arms. She was wearing a bright cerise T-shirt and those awful cut-off cargo pants that every middle-aged woman June saw seemed to be wearing. June fingered her cream linen jacket and carrot-leg navy trousers — she couldn't help herself, she felt that she looked good, even at forty-one. But she put a bit of effort into it. She hadn't resorted to anything chemical, not like some of the girls, but she looked after herself: she ate well, avoiding red meat, drank a glass of red wine every night and did Pilates three times a week. It was possibly the most boring way God ever invented of spending forty-five minutes, but it kept all of her bits in the right place, and she supposed that it was worth it. She just couldn't turn into one of those women who'd let herself go, she thought, eyeing her sister's solid shoulders, the flab that hung over the waistband of her trousers. And trainers ... she eyed Mary-Pat's large white pair, complete with those awful neon ankle socks — no one over twenty-five should wear trainers.

'What the hell is she doing in there,' Mary-Pat was saying, 'is she trying on every bloody dress in the shop? I'm baking alive here and I need something to eat.'

'Mum, will you take it easy,' Melissa said, 'anyone would think you didn't want to be here.'

Mary-Pat shot June a look, which June tried hard to ignore, examining the bubbles in her glass before taking another tentative sip. It was cheap and warm, but she'd have settled for anything just to get through this.

'I mean, choosing a wedding dress is the most important decision she'll ever have to make,' Melissa was saying, 'and she'll want to get it just right.' She had a dreamy look in her eye and June felt like hugging the girl — bless her, she was a romantic. If only she knew, June thought, that you had to have so much more after the romance had gone. Something that would bind you both together: friendship, loyalty, common interests, the kind of things that she and Gerry shared.

'For God's sake, Melissa, she's not winning the feckin' Nobel Prize, she's just trying on a wedding dress,' Mary-Pat snapped.

June shot out a warning hand and placed it on Mary-Pat's shoulder. Mary-Pat shrugged it off. 'Mel, why don't you go and see what's happening.' June smiled. 'Maybe Rosie wants a hand.'

The girl was off like a shot, bouncing off in the direction of the curtained area, behind which Rosie clearly *was* trying on every dress in the shop. Lovely Melissa — she was such a sweet-natured girl, in spite of the fake tan and the straightened hair and those spidery fake eyelashes. June thought of her two girls. Georgia would have loved this, if only she didn't have extra violin after school, and so would India, but she'd told June that she was 'up to her eyes' preparing for her maths mocks. June was disappointed — she would have loved to have the girls with her, and it was ages since they'd seen their cousin, but she couldn't argue with hard work. Gerry and she were always going on at them to put the effort in, so she couldn't complain. Mary-Pat thought it was highly entertaining that she had two such studious girls, 'seeing as you never did a stroke of work in your life,' she'd joked. Georgia was a bit of a wild card, though, and June knew she'd have to watch her. She had something of Daddy about her, a twinkle in her eye and a sense of mischief, which June was determined to keep under control. Still, June was proud of them both. Mary-Pat was probably a bit jealous — and boy, could she be hard on Melissa.

'MP, will you go easy on her, she's just having fun,' June said quietly.

Mary-Pat shot her a look. 'Fun.'

'Our baby sister is getting married and she's including us in this ... ritual.' June chose the word for want of a better one. 'Is that so bad? You were complaining last week that she didn't want to include you.'

'I know,' Mary-Pat muttered. 'It's just ...'

'What?' June said gently.

'It's just ... it's been a shock her coming back after all this time, Junie. I just don't know what to think.' Mary-Pat looked anguished and, not for the first time, June felt a flicker of irritation, which she masked. She knew that Mary-Pat was upset, but frankly, she was behaving as if the world were going to end just because her sister had come home after ten years to see them all. Yes, the visit made June feel a tad … uneasy, but she was pleased to see her sister. Delighted, in fact. She really must have Rosie and Craig over for dinner before the wedding, just the two of them, so that she could get to know him a bit better.

'MP, she's not trying to upset you or me or anyone else,' June said, more confidently than she felt. 'She just wants to get married in the town where she grew up, and she wanted to see Daddy before, well—'

At the mention of Daddy's name, Mary-Pat shot forward and grabbed June's arm. 'She wants Daddy to come to the wedding, you know.'

June felt the glass, slippery in her hands. She longed to take another big swig of the nasty wine, to find oblivion in Brides & Co. on South Anne Street. Anything but to have to listen to her sister. 'Oh?' she said carefully. 'Have you told her what he's like?'

Mary-Pat shook her head. 'She's been in a couple of times, but he was knocked out with all the pills and now they have a vomiting bug, so no visitors are allowed, thank God. We have to keep her away from him,' she added by way of explanation.

'We do?' June knew that Daddy wasn't quite right, that he was inclined to say the first thing that came into his head these days, but she couldn't help thinking that Mary-Pat was being a bit cloak and dagger about it all. Rosie would see him sooner or later, before or after the wedding. Maybe she was afraid that Daddy would embarrass them all in public. Well, it wouldn't be the first time, she thought.

She went to reassure Mary-Pat that she and Gerry would

look after Daddy, to make sure she could relax and enjoy the day, because she felt guilty about it. Mary-Pat did all the running after Daddy, bringing him those unhealthy big bars of chocolate and the *Racing Post*, and June knew that it was the least she could do, to offer to mind him for one day ... but one look at her sister made June say, 'You're right. It's not a good idea.' Because she knew that's what Mary-Pat wanted to hear. June always agreed with Mary-Pat, even if her sister was talking nonsense — because it was easier than to face up to her. She'd always let Mary-Pat bully her, and she'd never minded that much, but sometimes she just wished her sister would be a bit ... kinder. A bit less relentless.

There was something June couldn't put her finger on, and she had a sense of the horrible shagpile carpet in the shop shifting beneath her feet. She knew that Daddy was feeling better — he'd practically risen from the dead, sitting up one day last week in St Benildus's after a week in a semi-coma and demanding a fry-up, and that was good, wasn't it? They were all delighted about it, weren't they?

Mary-Pat got up, shuffling forward on the sofa until she could stand up. 'So that's settled then. The bug will do for now, then we'll tell her that he's got the bladder infection back and that he's too ill to come,' and she began to rummage in her handbag for a cigarette. 'What?'

'Nothing.' June knew better than to probe. Mary-Pat must have her reasons, June thought doubtfully, even if she knew that her sister wasn't telling her everything. We all have our reasons. June thought of her little writing box under her bed, with those flimsy blue aerogrammes in it, and for a moment she closed her eyes. No, mustn't think about that.

'I need a fag,' Mary-Pat muttered. 'Where the hell did I put my lighter?'

Alison Walsh

'I'll come with you,' June volunteered, desperate to get out of the stuffy shop. She followed her sister out onto the busy pavement, thronged with people in summer clothes. It was another baking hot day, of the kind they'd grown used to this glorious summer. Mary-Pat found her cigarettes and her lighter and after lighting up and taking a big drag, she leaned against the shop window, her face relaxed for the first time all morning, and she closed her eyes and lifted her face to the sun. For a moment, June wondered if she could cadge a cigarette off Mary-Pat, but she changed her mind. Smoking was so bad for your skin.

The two of them stood there in silence for a few moments, drinking in the hot summer sun, Mary-Pat's cigarette smoke spiralling into the air. 'You all right, June?' Mary-Pat's eyes flicked open.

Mary-Pat's question came so suddenly, June started in fright. 'Why wouldn't I be?' I was under the impression that you were the one who was in a bit of a state, she thought.

'You look a bit … tired, that's all.'

'Oh, God, no.' June shook her head. 'I'm fine.'

'How's Gerry … and the girls?'

'They're fine.'

'Fine.'

'Yes, fine, Mary-Pat.'

'Sure, what would you have to be complaining about anyway?' Mary-Pat threw her cigarette on the ground and put it out with her foot, in its huge white trainer. 'All the servants wiping your bottom for you and making you breakfast in bed.'

'Very funny. Orianna and Luka are hardly servants. Orianna's practically part of the family now anyway.'

'Right. And I bet you have her sitting up to dinner with

you every night. I can just see her, clinking the wine glass with Gerry.' And Mary-Pat cackled at her own joke.

'How's the WeightWatchers?' June knew she was being a bitch, but she couldn't help herself.

'Oh, pile of miserable crap as usual, but, sure, not all of us are blessed with your genes, June.' The way Mary-Pat said it made June blush with shame. She didn't know why she was being so mean. Mary-Pat always teased her about being comfortable, but neither of them really minded. June knew that her sister wasn't bothered about nice things, not really. If she was, she'd hardly be living in Gnome Central, as the girls unkindly called it, that tiny little house, filled with knick-knacks and fishing gear and that dog. June shuddered every time she thought of him, that big horrible brown thing who drooled all over the place. She also knew that things had been tough for Mary-Pat and PJ in the last few years, but her sister had never complained. Once, she'd even broached the subject of giving them a little loan, but Mary-Pat had nearly bitten her head off and June hadn't asked again.

There was another long silence. 'MP?'

'What?'

'Do you ever look around and wonder if it's been worth it?' Lately, June had sometimes wondered just that, even though she'd rather die than admit it to anyone. She'd done everything in her power to avoid it, to stave it off, thinking too much about things. She'd poured herself into the job of homemaker, to use the American term, to make sure that Gerry and the kids never wanted for anything and if June felt guilty about farming out the job to her Filipina housekeeper, she told herself that that's what it took to keep the show on the road. With Gerry hardly ever there, she needed all the help she could get.

And she compensated for her guilt by driving the girls wherever they wanted to go, telling herself that it was because she loved her Land Rover, but really it was because she needed to feel useful. 'It's what I'm there for,' she'd say when India or Georgia would say that they could just get the bus to their piano classes and hockey camps. And even though she saw the looks on their faces, a mixture of irritation and pity, she ignored them. I'm still useful, she thought to herself. I'm still needed. Because she couldn't bear to think what it might be like if she wasn't.

'What do you mean?' Mary-Pat was saying. 'If what's been worth it?'

'Oh, you know, you think you're going along and then ... suddenly everything seems different. I mean, it's the same, but you see it differently.' June was trying to explain how she felt these days, but by the look on Mary-Pat's face, she wasn't making much sense. 'What I mean is—' June was about to continue when Melissa stuck her head around the door of the shop. 'There you are. I might have known, Mum, that you'd be smoking your head off.' She curled her lip. 'Rosie's waiting for you.'

Mary-Pat grimaced. 'Better get it over with then.'

'Behave, MP, will you?'

'I'll try,' Mary-Pat said, pushing the door of the shop open with an exaggerated sigh.

'Ta-dah!' Melissa was standing beside Rosie, a huge grin on her face, and when Mary-Pat and June were silent for a second, she squealed, 'Doesn't she look amazing?'

June was rooted to the spot. Rosie was standing in a shaft of sunlight, which caught her lovely golden-red hair and lit up her pale, freckled skin. And she just looked a vision in antique cream lace, with a dropped waist, that suited her boyish figure, a large damask rose pinned to her hip, her lovely hair piled in a loose bun on her head. She looked like one of those women in the pre-Raphaelite paintings that Mammy loved so much. Oh, she was lovely, just lovely, June thought. How did you grow up so suddenly, Rosie? she thought. How did that happen? And, not for the first time, she felt that guilt that she'd had so little to do with it. That she'd left it all to Mary-Pat.

She could still remember it, the day she'd run away. Not that she'd admitted that to anyone, even to herself. June was nineteen, nearly twenty, and she knew it was her last chance to get out, even though she told herself that she was simply going up to visit Susie at the nurses' home in St Vincent's where she was doing her training, and where she would host illicit parties, her tiny room stuffed full of student nurses and doctors. It was fun, and June wanted that more than anything else. Fun and life and excitement.

It had been part of her Grand Plan. She'd actually called it that, had written it into the pink furry diary she kept under the bed and which June had loved because it had had a little padlock on it. She'd written the heading in block capitals, with a row of bullet points below it. First, she'd learn to talk properly, not like some 'bogger' as they called it in Dublin. Then she'd have lots of acquaintances. Everyone in Dublin had them, to go to the theatre with, to the kind of expensive restaurants June couldn't afford. Nobody in Monasterard had them – they had sisters, brothers, friends, cousins, not acquaintances. It sounded much more sophisticated. And June wanted to be sophisticated more than anything else.

And so she'd told no one, sneaking out the door that Saturday afternoon, everything she'd need stuffed into a little duffle bag that she'd found under Pi's bed. But Rosie had followed her. 'Where are you going, Junie?' She'd bounced up and down on the balls of her feet, her little freckled hands grimy from hours spent on the towpath, messing around the way she loved to do.

'Oh, nowhere special, Rosie-boo, just off to Timbuktu.'

'You are not going to Timbuktu,' Rosie said, her face crumpling and June thought how tactless she'd been. Rosie had a thing about people leaving. It made her anxious and they normally had to explain to her exactly where they were going and for how long. It was funny, really, because she'd had no memory at all of Mammy leaving, not like the rest of them, but somehow she seemed to have absorbed the anxiety about it.

And so, June had lied. 'You're right, I'm not. I'm just going to Dublin to a party. I'll be back in the next day or two.' And Rosie had seemed to accept what she'd said, but it didn't stop her watching June as she walked all the way up the towpath to the village. June could feel Rosie's eyes on her back, and it made her feel awful, because she knew that she was never coming back. Oh, of course, she had — she'd come back the following Tuesday to pick up the rest of her stuff, but she'd never stayed at home again. Not properly. And she'd never thought to wonder how her sisters felt about it. She was gone, leaving Monasterard, and everything else, behind her. And she'd come to Dublin and she'd made a go of things, gathering together a circle of friends-who-weren't-really-friends for cocktails, the theatre, the gallery openings that she attended because one of her boss Paddy's clients owned a place on Fitzwilliam Square. She'd been desperate, she knew, to 'get on'. And because she didn't resemble the back of a bus and had worked hard on her manners, she'd succeeded. Except she knew that she didn't like the word now, 'acquaintances'. It was a lonely kind of a word. And she was a lonely kind of a person.

* * *

Mary-Pat was the first to speak. 'Very nice.' She looked as if she'd eaten something unpleasant, her face screwed up and her mouth twisted. 'Looks expensive anyway.'

There was a silence and Rosie's face fell, her arms dropping to her sides. She looked all of nine again, in spite of her finery. For a moment, none of them said anything. There was a stillness in the room and June willed herself to speak, to open her mouth and say something, anything. She could see that Melissa's fists were balled up, the knuckles white as she bit her lip. Oh, Mary-Pat, June thought, why on earth do you have to be such a bitch? And then she found her voice, rushing forward and pulling Rosie into a tight hug. 'Rosie, you look beautiful, magnificent, utterly fabulous,' and the compliments were so effusive, Rosie burst out laughing, while June pushed her away again to get a really good look at her. 'Look at you. My baby sister's all grown up.' She felt Rosie's bones under her hands, like a little bird's, and then Rosie went a bit grey and her breath began to come in short puffs. 'Do you need your inhaler?'

Rosie nodded, her cheeks flushed, her breath beginning to catch. 'It's all the excitement, I just ...'

'Don't say another word,' June said, motioning for Melissa to fetch Rosie's handbag. 'Just take a couple of puffs and relax.' And she threw Mary-Pat a look over her shoulder. If you had been a bit nicer, the look said, this might not have happened. Wait till I talk to you later. But when she turned around, she noticed that Mary-Pat had tears in her eyes.

By the time June arrived home, she felt so exhausted she could just have gone to sleep in the car. She pulled into the gate and up the driveway, gravel crunching under the wheels of the Land Rover, and when she parked, the dulcet tones of Lyric FM fading, she sat there for a few moments, taking in the silence. She loved this view of the house, the bright yellow front door in the lovely Victorian porch, the two stained glass windows on either side, the bay window above it set into the red-shingled eaves: Georgia's room. The estate agent had called it 'a restoration treasure', which had been shorthand for a complete mess, but June had loved it the first time she'd set eyes on it. It had been owned by a vicar, and the garden was lovely, and even if the rooms had been a little shabby, they'd also been beautiful, with their lovely high ceilings. It was large and gracious and restful – just like the life June had longed to have ever since she was a little girl. And now, she had it.

She sighed and climbed down from the Land Rover, opening the front door, popping her keys and bag on the eighteenth-century oak hall table, and went straight into the kitchen, where she opened the fridge and examined the contents before pulling out a plate of cold chicken, to which she added a large dollop of mayonnaise – the full-fat stuff that she kept hidden at the back of the fridge. There were a couple of cold sausages there, too, so she helped herself to them, starting to eat before she got to the kitchen table, plonking the plate down, fingers already greasy as she shoved the food into her mouth, chewing it quickly and then swallowing before sinking her teeth into the next mouthful. She wolfed it down, that was the expression, like a hungry dog and when she'd finished, licking the grease off her lips, she felt a bit sick. And guilty, and all of the other emotions she felt when she knew she'd failed to control herself. She put the plate into the dishwasher so Gerry wouldn't notice it. He didn't like to see her like this. It upset him.

She jumped when she heard a little cough behind her. 'Oh,

God, India, you gave me such a fright.' She looked guilty. 'I didn't see you there.'

India grunted and continued to stare at her phone and June had to resist the urge to yell at her. She hated that bloody mobile. All India did was take endless selfies on it and text non-stop. June didn't know what on earth she found to say on it — could she not speak to her friends the way June had at the same age?

'I was at Rosie's dress fitting,' June said, trying to make a bit of conversation.

India looked up from the phone and her features softened. 'Did she look amazing?'

'She did. You'll look like that one day.'

India rolled her eyes to heaven. 'Not if I can help it.'

'Oh, why not — isn't it every girl's dream to find Mr Right?' June smiled, taking in her daughter's lovely fair features, her bright blue eyes — when she was a baby, she'd looked like a doll, the kind you'd find in an antique toy shop. Even now, with her skin a bit spotty and her hair greasy, she had a freshness to her, a bloom.

'Yeah, right,' India said, curling her lip in distaste, 'like we have nothing else to be doing, like educating ourselves or getting careers — important stuff.'

'Oh, right.' June felt hurt, catching the unspoken bit — 'not like you', thinking of how carefully she'd looked for Mr Right. How much thought she'd put into it, determined not to settle for the first man who came along. Determined not to find herself with another Daddy.

She was about to say something else, when India got up from her seat. 'Better go and do some study. By the way, there's a gaff on in Alice's on Saturday — can I go?'

Alison Walsh

June winced at the word. 'Gaff'. It sounded so ... unpolished. 'No, I don't think so, India, you have a flute recital the following Wednesday.'

'Please, Mum. If I go, I'll practise all day Sunday.'

June sighed. 'I'll ask Dad – OK?'

'He always says no.' India was beginning to whine.

'Well, no means no then.'

'I'm nearly fifteen, not five,' India blustered.

'I know, India, but we're still your parents and—'

India swore under her breath and stomped out of the kitchen. June closed her eyes for a second. Why did everything have to be so difficult?

'June, is that you?' Gerry's voice wafted down from the landing. He sounded like a small child sometimes, June thought, wondering if he'd heard the clunk of the fridge door closing, the exchange with India. He had the hearing of a greyhound.

'Coming now, love,' June yelled up the stairs.

'*The Apprentice* is on,' he yelled back. He liked to watch it live and got annoyed she didn't watch it with him, and even more annoyed if there were any interruptions. She was fed up telling him that he could pause live TV with the clicker. 'Coming,' she called, putting on her 'face', as she called it, that expression that she'd practised for so long she'd forgotten it wasn't natural. A half-smile, a slight lift of the eyebrow.

He was watching the programme when she padded across to the bed, the TV remote balanced on his tummy, which June noticed was a bit bigger than usual, a round dome under the thickly padded duvet. She'd have to put him on the Atkins again. The two of them: one was as bad as the other with all the monitoring and controlling. It wasn't like that at the beginning. At the beginning, they'd had so much fun. Now, everything was just ... work.

He lifted the duvet and patted the empty spot beside him
without looking up at her. She slid underneath and tucked her
head onto his shoulder, and he rested a hand on her stomach,
under her cream camisole. 'You smell nice.' His voice was a low
rumble in his chest, but his breath smelled of whiskey. Surely
it was a bit early in the week for that — he only ever drank at
weekends.

'It's Jo Malone. You bought it for my birthday.'

'I did? Well, I have very good taste, clearly.' They chuckled,
because they both knew that he'd sent India off to buy it. June
lifted her head to peck his red cheek and fluff his gingery hair,
then they both settled down to watch. He was quieter than usual,
not ranting on about Alan Sugar and how he knew nothing at
all about people. He did this every time they watched and June
knew that this was because, secretly, Gerry had always wanted to
do telly and was annoyed at not having been asked. He'd have
loved to be Alan Sugar, she thought, but she also knew that he'd
come across badly with his ginger hair and that big red face
of his and his old-man sayings. His grumpy catchphrases were
great on his morning radio show: they whipped the nation into
a frenzy of outrage every day between 9 and 12, but on TV — no.
Not that she'd ever tell him. That wasn't her job.

'How was the fitting?'

Alan Sugar was wagging his finger at some cross-looking
blonde girl with a severe hairdo. 'It was fine. Mary-Pat was
rude, of course.'

'She's always rude.'

'I know, but this time, she was extra rude.'

'Is that possible?' Gerry half-smiled. And then there was a
long pause as the girl was told, 'You're fired.' 'Too right,' Gerry
said, nodding in her direction. 'She was a proper madam.'

'She said that the dress was too expensive and that Rosie should wear heels and not "clumpy wedges". And then she had a row with Melissa on the way to the bus – something about her dressing like a slut for the wedding. Oh, Lord, I was never so glad to see the back of the two of them.' Poor Rosie, she thought, trying to banish the thought that if she'd never appeared, if she'd just stayed away, none of this would be happening. It was unfair to blame her, of course, but it was the truth. If she'd never come back, things would have stayed the same. And the same was just fine.

'How's your father?'

'What?' Gerry had never had the slightest interest in Daddy, apart from finding him a figure of mild entertainment. 'He's fine – much better.'

'That's good. It's sad to think that your mind can just take you like that, isn't it, and at that age?'

'Yes, it is,' she thought, suddenly realising that that was exactly what it was. Sad. Then she looked at Gerry, who was now squinting out the window into the garden, his grey eyes watering.

'Do you want your glasses?'

'What? No. I don't need them.'

Yes, you do, June thought. You're blind as a bat. She sighed. 'What's up?'

'What? Oh, you know. Just thinking of your old fellah, wondering if it'll be me next. I never thought I'd get old, do you know that? I never thought it'd happen to me.'

June sat up and put a hand on his shoulder. 'Everyone gets old, Gerry, it's part of life.'

He shrugged. 'Is it? Not in my game. Do you know, I saw an advert for plastic surgery the other week, in the back of one of the Sunday magazines, and I couldn't help it, I just wondered if a little bit of work might do it,' and at this, he mimed a facelift, pulling his eyes back at the corners so that they slanted bizarrely. 'They're all at it nowadays. Look at Simon Cowell.'

'Oh, Gerry, you don't need plastic surgery.' June laughed. 'You are just gorgeous and handsome and perfect, do you hear me?' And she sat up and planted a kiss on his lips. They both knew that she was lying. Gerry wasn't handsome − he looked like a farmer who'd been out in the fields for too long − but she loved him. She'd loved him ever since that first time they'd met in the Shelbourne − she knew that. They used to joke about it because he'd been with his friend Jim, a handsome barrister with nicely silvering hair and a range of pinstriped suits, and yet she'd gone for the short dumpy guy in the crumpled chinos. It was because he was always so sure of himself, so definite, that's what had attracted June, that and his old-world manners. She loved him because he'd always been in charge.

'Maybe I do, Junie. I'm old and past it and ...' He shrugged. 'I just can't help feeling that my best days are behind me. That there are all these nimble youngsters out there, waiting to pass me out while I limp along the road like an old dog. Maybe they'll have to put me out of my misery,' he half-joked.

'Oh, for goodness' sake, Gerry, you're being paranoid,' June said, more impatiently than she'd intended. After the day she'd had, she wanted this conversation to be over. She distracted him then by taking off her camisole and snuggling up to him, asking him if he wanted to take Charlie for a walk. It was their code for sex − silly, but it made them both laugh, and laughing got them in the mood. But he just shook his head. 'Sorry, Junie, Charlie needs a rest.' And then he'd turned on his side and switched off his bedside light, leaving June half-naked and in shock. Gerry had never refused her. Not once in their entire marriage.

4

'Mum, you've got something on your dress.' Melissa's face was screwed up in distaste as she dabbed at the stain on the lapel of Mary-Pat's wedding outfit, a lilac two-piece with a floral trim around her neck that she privately thought made her look about ninety. But PJ said he liked it, and such compliments were so rare these days, Mary-Pat thought it must look all right. 'Honestly, could you not have eaten your breakfast before you got into the thing – you've got muesli halfway down your front.'

'I was distracted, Melissa, in case you hadn't noticed,' Mary-Pat shot back, wishing, as she did so, that she hadn't said anything. 'Let it go, MP,' PJ had said to her earlier. 'Don't pick a fight with her. You'll only make it worse.' He was right, of course, but how could she not? How could she let her daughter out for her sister's wedding dressed like that? 'Trailer trash,'

John-Patrick had called it and he was right. She'd told her not to wear that tiny halter with the stars and stripes motif on it — and she wasn't a small girl. Maybe that was it, Mary-Pat thought, looking at Melissa's ample breasts spilling out of the halter, her thighs huge in a pair of denim cut-offs that showed half her arse. It was because she reminded her of her younger self — all that flesh, those dimpled thighs and fat arms — how she'd hated them. PJ said he loved them, of course, and they'd laughed when she'd accused him of being one of those big-girl fetishists.

But she'd never dressed like trash, that was for sure. She'd never dyed all that flesh that baked red with fake tan, the way Melissa did, so she looked like a Red Indian, those awful false eyelashes that clung like caterpillars to her eyelids. When she looked at her again now, tucking the tissue back in her little bag, swaying in the back seat of the Pajero beside her, Mary-Pat felt like crying. She didn't want Melissa to be the laughing stock of the place, to be humiliated in front of half of Monasterard — at least that's what she told herself, but really it was because she knew it would reflect badly on her. That she'd let her own daughter go out looking like that.

She wished that they hadn't fought, but she knew that she couldn't take it back. It had started when Melissa had been taking Mary-Pat's heated rollers out. She'd been chattering away about the bloody flowers and how they were all organic and natural, and how Rosie'd taken Melissa and that friend of hers, Daphne, to Babington's flower shop in Athy to discuss the order. Babington's, no less, where you couldn't buy a bunch of roses for less than fifty quid. And Rosie had bought Melissa lunch and a new pair of jeans — that fitted her, for a change — and Melissa had come back that evening, cheeks flushed with excitement. When Mary-Pat had asked about what they'd done, though, Melissa had just smiled coyly. 'She made me promise not to tell, Mum — but the wedding will be spectacular. She showed me sample menus and the food is going to be fabulous and the cake ... wait till you see it.'

She could barely contain her excitement and Mary-Pat had felt a wave of jealousy so strong it almost choked her. 'I can't see why she needs to go to Babington's and why she had to order special food when I would have been only too delighted to do the catering. But it probably isn't "sophisticated" enough for our Rosie.' She'd emphasised the word 'sophisticated', making inverted comma gestures with her fingers. But Melissa didn't give her the satisfaction, just shaking her head and rolling her eyes to heaven, a small smile on her lips. Mary-Pat had been left fuming to herself in front of *Coronation Street*.

She had to admit it, she'd thought later. She'd rather die than own up to the feelings, but she was jealous that Melissa found Rosie so fascinating, that they had such an easy way about them, even though they'd known each other all of three weeks. After that bloody fitting, they'd spent all their time giggling and gabbling and going out for coffee. Melissa had let Rosie buy her clothes and yet if Mary-Pat opened her mouth to suggest that they go into Kildare Village to have a look around, Melissa would say that she was 'busy'. But I'm your *mother*, she wanted to yell. You have to like going out with me. That's what mothers and daughters do.

In desperation, she'd confided in June about the clothes Melissa wore. She didn't want to, because June could be such a snob, but she needed some class of advice, even if it was to buy Burberry. 'You can't pay enough for class,' June was fond of saying. Mary-Pat felt like replying, 'Yes, love, but do you know how much it costs?' Bless Junie, but she hadn't a clue what life was really like.

'You should try a different tack with her, MP,' June had suggested. 'Tell her what suits her, not what doesn't. Emphasise the positive, not the negative.' And she'd nodded sagely. You should know, Mary-Pat thought, with your two gorgeous daughters who never put a foot wrong. The only feckin' thing they ever do is tie their cashmere jumpers the wrong way around their shoulders. You haven't been saddled with Daisy Duke and Marilyn Manson.

John-Patrick just looked scary these days. Even his lovely blue eyes were gone — at least most of the time. She'd nearly died when he'd turned around to her in the hall the other day, with coal black eyes glittering. 'Jesus Christ!' She'd barely managed to stifle a scream. 'Your eyes,' she'd finally managed.

'Contact lenses. Sent away for them.' As if it was the most normal thing in the world to look demonically possessed at half-six in the evening.

At least she'd managed to persuade him to wear a suit for the wedding. He'd been reasonably compliant about it too, letting her hire a nice grey one and agreeing to tie his hair back and remove the scary lenses. He looked handsome, with his fine features and strong chin. He was a lovely boy. She suspected the whole Goth thing was to look scary for those little shits in St Munchin's so they wouldn't pick on him, and she supposed she couldn't blame him. She'd have cheerfully broken the legs of that gurrier Johnno Falvey if she thought she could have got away with it. She clenched her fists now as she thought of them. No, she wouldn't think about that right now, she just couldn't, on top of everything else.

She'd thought she was taking a different tack that morning asking Melissa if she'd thought about wearing that lovely cream lace dress June had bought her for her Junior Cert disco. It was some overpriced designer label, but Mary-Pat had to admit her daughter looked lovely in it. 'It really suits you,' she'd said, unable to keep the note of pleading out of her voice.

'I'm happy with the way I look, Mammy,' Melissa had insisted, her mouth set in a thin line.

And that had set her off again, a hair-trigger igniting her rage. She'd whipped her head around to Melissa, eyes watering as one of the rollers got caught in her hair, yelling, 'Do you think I'll be able to enjoy myself with you there looking like a streetwalker? Because that's what you look like, Melissa, make no mistake about it — a tramp.'

Melissa had thrown the hairbrush down then, sent it clattering across the tiles, and she'd fixed her mother with a glare. 'Oh, and you'd know about that, wouldn't you?'

Mary-Pat had remained absolutely still for a moment. 'What do you mean?' she asked finally, without turning around.

'Nothing.' Melissa was sulky now, but her voice was quieter.

'Spit it out, Melissa, why don't you?' It was a command, not a request.

'It was nothing.' Melissa was more defiant now, as she bent over and picked up the hairbrush, breasts nearly falling out of the halter. Mary-Pat had to close her eyes at the sight. Not for the first time, she wished she hadn't told Melissa about John-Patrick, about the way he hadn't exactly been planned, a fact of which John-Patrick himself was unaware. She'd blurted it out once, when she'd come in after WeightWatchers, having had one too many in the Angler's Rest. It was ironic, to get pissed after WeightWatchers, but it was a bit of a laugh after all the tension of the weigh-in and the lecture on portion sizes and fat-free cheese; the lesson, as if they needed to learn it, that life was just a pain in the ass.

She'd been trying to be Melissa's friend when she'd blabbed. It was pathetic — she wasn't her friend: she was her mother — but she'd wanted to bond with her. Melissa had been asking how she'd known that Daddy was the one and she'd said that it was because the minute she'd told him about John-Patrick, he'd asked her to marry him. That yes, that meant that herself and JP hadn't exactly been married when John-Patrick was conceived. And all she'd got for her trouble was Melissa covering her mouth with her hand, a horrified look on her face. 'Overshare, Mum, for goodness' sake.' Jesus, she'd had no idea that young people could be that sanctimonious. Just you wait, she'd thought. Just you wait until you realise that life isn't that easy, Melissa. That it isn't a straightforward choice between right and wrong, good and bad.

'At least I won't look like you, like some ... some dried-up old hag!' had been Melissa's parting shot this morning. Mary-Pat had wanted to hurt her when she'd said that, to damage her, to grab hold of that black hair of hers and pull it out of her head. Her fists were clenched, those two red spots appearing on her cheeks the way they always did when she was agitated.

PJ had intervened then, his mouth set in a thin line. 'Melissa, don't disrespect your mother. Apologise please.'

'Only if she apologises to me.' Melissa stood there, both hands on her hips, just as she had done when she was nine and didn't want to do as she was told. Mary-Pat felt ashamed of herself then. If only you knew how much I love you, she thought. And I'm sorry I can't show you, that I have to spoil it all. Maybe I just don't know any better. Maybe I used up all my mothering before you were born.

But she didn't say sorry. That'd be going too far.

On the way out the front door, PJ had pulled her aside. 'Could you not have apologised first, Mary-Pat? Would it have killed you?' And the look he gave her, of such intense disappointment, had made her hope a hole would open up in the ground and swallow her. Of all people, for PJ to comment. But she just couldn't give in. 'I don't have to apologise to her for wanting to protect her, PJ. I'm her mother, that's my job, in case you hadn't noticed,' she'd said and tried to keep her head high as she walked towards the car.

PJ was sick of it all, she knew that. He'd never said a word, through all the years with Daddy, even when he was living with them and would wander in at all hours of the day and night, insisting on waking the kids so he could tell them one of his Tall Tales, stories of fairies and goblins that they loved. 'But it's four o'clock in the morning,' PJ would explain patiently, appearing in the kitchen while Daddy clattered about, deciding he wanted a big fry. 'Let's leave the stories until they wake up — what do you think?'

And Daddy hadn't even been that nice to him. 'Pee-Jay,' he'd say, with a slight sneer. 'How's the fishing, Pee-Jay?' He'd thought he was better than him, that was it. Thought he was a more exciting kind of a man. Less of a lump. But PJ was a better man than Daddy would ever be. Mary-Pat knew that. But now there was a tiredness to their exchanges, an unfamiliar look in PJ's eyes that took Mary-Pat a while to decipher. Eventually, she'd worked out what it was. Boredom. He was bored with her.

The realisation made her feel lonelier than ever. PJ had always been there for her, putting up with her sharp tongue, pulling her back into line when she went too far, but now he just seemed to drift away, hiding behind the *Daily Star* or announcing that he was going out for a walk at eleven o'clock at night, a man who didn't walk the half-mile to the shops if he could possibly help it. They used to joke that PJ had no legs, because they hardly ever saw him use them.

She couldn't blame him, she supposed. He'd had enough to put up with over the years, but there was something different now. Mary-Pat could sense it. And the real giveaway was that things in bed weren't right. And they always had been. There'd been no complaints in that department. You'd never think it, Mary-Pat supposed, with the two of them. They didn't look like sex machines, but they enjoyed it. It had been such a discovery when they'd started going out together, maybe because Mary-Pat had been asked out so little that she didn't even know about this part of her. This capacity for passion. And then one day, it just happened. Love.

And now, it seemed, that love was over. Somewhere along the line, it had just faded away.

'Where are we going?' Daddy's voice broke into her thoughts, sounding petulant. I shouldn't have brought him, Mary-Pat thought. But she had no choice. Pius had been right, even though she wouldn't admit it in a million years. If he didn't turn up at Rosie's wedding, it would look downright suspicious. She'd have to keep him away, mind. Make sure he stayed in the background, in case he said anything.

One of the nurses at St Benildus's had dressed him in a suit that was two sizes too big for him, but he was neat and tidy, his snowy white hair combed smoothly back off his forehead, his clothes stain free. And yet he looked as if he was ninety, not sixty-seven. A man old before his time, all that swagger gone, that vitality that had been so magnetic and so destructive at the same time. She didn't know whether to be sad or happy about it. He was lost: to them all and to himself.

'We're going to the wedding, Daddy, don't you remember? I told you about it,' Mary-Pat said now, twisting in her seat to look at him.

'The wedding?' He looked blank and his hands made that scrabbling motion on the blanket that was covering his knees, another sign that he was getting agitated. Mary-Pat clenched her fists, a bead of sweat dripping down the back of her neck and repeated, 'Yes, Daddy, the wedding.' Hoping that neither of the kids would intervene, would mention Rosie's name. It might set him off. And God knows what he'd be like when he saw the house. Please God it wouldn't trigger anything.

Something had caught Daddy's eye outside now, the deep green hedgerows, the canal flashing by, a silvery blue, the vivid green and yellow of the lilies that filled it at this time of the year. It felt as if the whole earth had burst into life: the hawthorn in the ditch, the thick blanket of gorse. As they drove over the humpback bridge, the heron slowly lifted himself up from his perch by the water, flapping in a stately manner, his grey-tipped wings spread wide. The blue sky and the small fluffy clouds were reflected in the mirror surface of the canal, its edge alive with dragonflies. It was beautiful, Mary-Pat thought, distracted from Daddy and from everything else, just for a moment.

And then she caught sight of him. His lips were moving and she realised that he was humming that tune under his breath, 'The Rose of Tralee'. 'She was lovely and fair, as the rose of the summer, but 'twas not her beauty alone that won me ...' He'd loved that song, playing it over and over again on an ancient gramophone in the living room, standing on the sofa, one arm pressed to his stomach, the other outstretched, pretending to be Count John McCormack, Daddy's baritone wobbling around the opera singer's fine tenor. He'd always enjoyed the ending particularly: 'But the chill hand of death has now rent us asunder, I'm lonely tonight for the Rose of Tralee.' At the word 'death', he'd throw himself onto his back on the sofa in a parody of dying and send them all into convulsions of laughter. Ah, Daddy, Mary-Pat thought, how we loved you. And then you went and ruined it all.

She looked at him again, humming under his breath, and then he looked at her as if he really saw her, his face lit up with a huge smile. 'Home,' he said suddenly, looking at her. 'Home.'

Mary-Pat reached out and patted him on the hand, a tight knot forming in her stomach. 'That's right, Daddy, home.'

He was mercifully silent then, as they lowered his chair out of the car. He didn't even seem to register where he was. They all stood there for a moment in front of the house and waited, but he'd gone inside himself again, humming a tune under his breath. Mary-Pat realised she'd been holding her breath and expelled it in a rush.

She looked at the place and had to admit Pius had done a great job, him and the Yank. The tatty wooden sign on the front gate that said 'Private' had been removed, and they'd painted the front of the house so that you couldn't see that awful line of plaster, a relic of another one of Daddy's grand schemes, when he'd decided one day that he'd replaster the front of the house and had run out of mortar two-thirds of the way up, never quite getting around to finishing it. The place had looked as if it had a dirty big tide mark on it after that. Now, the three windows above the front door, with its pretty fanlight, and the window on either side were clean, glinting in the sun. The door had been painted a bright red and the brass knocker in the shape of a leaping trout, that had always been a grimy grey, was now a shiny yellow.

And Rosie must have leaned on Pius to tidy the garden up a bit. He'd gone for a cottage-garden look, probably because he had half the stuff growing wild anyway: the beautiful grape-like flowers of the tufted vetch and the lacy fronds of wild carrot. And she hadn't seen granny's bonnet or hollyhocks in years – they looked just right in the border in front of the house. Somehow, he'd managed to coax a lawn out of the mucky soil, a twisting path of bark leading to the gazebo, which was no longer a mouldy green but a gleaming white, draped in white begonias and dusky pink tea roses. Christ, Rosie must have spent a fortune on the place. The Yank must have money, so, because Rosie couldn't have earned much at that social working she did.

'Is that girl wearing any clothes?' John-Patrick's voice broke into her thoughts and they all turned to look at Tracy O'Malley, that knacker, who was striding across the lawn in a dress that looked like a bandage and fuck-me heels. How the hell had she been invited? Oh, well, like mother, like daughter, Mary-Pat thought. She could see her son's gaze following the girl and she jabbed him in the ribs with her elbow – it was bad manners. And then she looked at Melissa, with the caterpillars on her eyes and the boobs announcing to all and sundry that they'd arrived, and she felt like crying all over again.

She managed to lower her bum onto a cast-iron white garden chair, relieved that it hadn't collapsed under her. The two men relaxed in stripy deckchairs, PJ's face turned to the sun, absorbing every single ray of it. She wondered if she should tell him to be careful, that he'd have a face like a tomato later, but decided to keep her mouth shut, to try to relax for a moment, closing her eyes and listening to the hum of chat and expectation, which was broken by a gentle tinkle on the piano, which Pius had lifted all the way out of the living room to sit under the apple trees.

Mary-Pat let the gentle notes soothe her for a bit. She could hear Melissa shifting around on the seat beside her, saying 'hi' to a couple of the girls she knew from the town — perhaps it was best that Mary-Pat couldn't see the looks on their faces. And they were such nice girls — Mary-Pat just couldn't understand why she'd want to stand out from them that much. She willed herself not to think about it, or about Daddy, whom PJ had settled in the shade under a willow tree beside the house. June had said she'd keep an eye on him for once, even if she had managed to make it sound as if it was a huge bloody deal, as if Mary-Pat had asked her to part the Red Sea or something. When Mary-Pat opened her eyes, she could see her sister flapping over the man, talking to him in a too-loud voice, draping his blanket over his knees while he stared into space. That eejit Gerry was hovering nearby, wearing one of those cream Panama hats, like the sort you'd buy in the Sunday newspapers. When he saw Mary-Pat looking, he waved, and she had to wave back.

PJ sat down beside her, squeezing her shoulder as he did so. 'Daddy's fine,' he said.

'I can see that.' She half-smiled, closing her eyes again. 'God help him.'

'Jesus, but Pi's done the place proud.' PJ was trying to talk in a whisper, but the result was a more penetrating than usual rumble. 'He's even draped some sort of a canopy over his cannabis plants, have you noticed?'

Mary-Pat's eyes flicked open and she glared at PJ. 'Shush, PJ, you never know who could be listening.' She'd made her feelings clear to Pi on his little money-earner. Where the hell was he, anyway? She turned her face to the sun, all the while telling herself that she really shouldn't. Her skin would only get even redder. How was it that Junie, who had spent her entire adolescence frying herself in the sun, had perfect porcelain skin, while she looked like an overripe tomato? Junie had inherited Mammy's skin, the lucky bitch, while she'd got the complexion of some bogger throwback from centuries ago.

'Here we go, kick-off,' John-Patrick said beside her, as the tinkling formed itself into the wedding march. Mary-Pat turned her head to see her little sister walking up through the small crowd on the lawn to the gazebo on Pius's arm in that lovely dress. She felt a lump in her throat, which she wilfully swallowed. She was not about to bawl at her sister's wedding. They'd think she'd gone soft. Her sister walked slowly up the path to the gazebo, to gasps of appreciation, and Mary-Pat had to rummage in her handbag, pretending to look for a tissue, so that PJ wouldn't see the tears in her eyes.

He nudged her in the ribs. 'You OK, MP?'

'I'm fine,' she barked back at him. 'I just have something in my eye.'

'Right.' He sounded as if he was trying to smother laughter and she wanted to hit him a belt. She wanted to keep her feelings to herself, not blurt them all over Monasterard. Was there really any harm in it?

The rest of the ceremony passed in a blur of affirmations of love. Father Naul, that new priest, who looked a bit like Sam Shepard, just did a bit of praying and handwaving, because they'd got married in church the day before, with only the Yank's parents, Daphne and Pi in attendance. Mary-Pat told herself that it didn't hurt, that, sure, she wasn't a Catholic anyway, not like her baby sister, for reasons Mary-Pat had firmly blocked from her mind, but it *did* hurt. It made her heart feel heavy in her chest, like a stone.

The priest and the church had been the Yank's idea, as his family were devout Catholics and Rosie had gone along with it because, even though Mary-Pat was sure the girl hadn't been to Mass since the day she'd insisted on making her Holy Communion, it mattered to him. 'It's a compromise, MP, and that's what marriage is all about,' she'd told her.

And what would *you* know? Mary-Pat had wanted to ask, but hadn't. Instead, she'd just nodded her head and bitten her tongue. She'd had to get used to that, with Rosie back. The new and improved Rosie, who didn't seem to need any help with anything. Oh, she'd thrown them a bone with the dress fitting, but apart from that, she had it all 'under control, thanks'. She'd given Mary-Pat an apologetic look then, a 'what can you do', spreading her hands wide, and Mary-Pat hadn't been able to hide the hurt that her sister had excluded her from her biggest day. More than that, she'd have to admit that she was surprised that her sister could manage such a thing. Time was, Rosie couldn't manage to get out of bed and get a breakfast into her without a palaver. Mary-Pat could still see her standing at the door on her way to school, humming a little tune to herself, half a slice of toast in her mouth. Her eyes were ringed with the previous night's mascara and she was looking at her books as if she didn't quite know what they were for. And that coat — that godawful specimen she'd insisted on wearing constantly, just to give me a hard time, Mary-Pat thought. To punish me for having brought her up the only way I knew how.

Of course, Rosie didn't need her any more. She was a grown-up now: she'd been gone for ten years, and during that time something seemed to have happened to her. She looked smooth and sleek, as if she'd grown some kind of shiny outer shell; she wore expensive-looking clothes and her hair tied back in a knot at the nape of her neck, not that fuzzy halo around her head that she used to have. And that bling-ring. Mary-Pat couldn't help wondering where her little sister had gone.

But still, couldn't she let her do this one thing? That was what mothers were supposed to do, wasn't it? And then she'd had to remind herself that she wasn't Rosie's mother. Just her sister, and what's more one who had tried to get rid of her, to shove her away ten years before. And now here they were, a 'normal' family at a lovely summer wedding.

Who would have thought it? We don't look as if we have a hole blasted right through the middle of us, a huge, empty, mother-shaped gap. Maybe that's the way with all families, that they look normal on the outside to make you think that's what a family should be. But who knew what things were really like on the inside?

It was such a bleak thought that Mary-Pat didn't notice that the bride and groom were kissing and hugging and the little gathering was getting to its feet. She felt as if she were in a daze, standing up to join in the applause, the whistles and cheers from the good-looking young friends of her sister's, who seemed so smart and bright, so self-confident. She had no idea Rosie still had so many friends in the village – how had she managed to keep in touch with them all these years, when she'd hardly spoken to her sisters. Her eyes darted to Daddy, who seemed to have fallen asleep under the tree, his mouth open, head tilted back, looking like a small, wizened child. Her heart lifted then with relief. Please let him wake up when it's all over. Please, God.

She started when PJ snaked an arm around her waist and gave

her a gentle squeeze. 'Brings back happy memories,' he said and winked at her, then leaned towards her and brushed her cheek with his lips. She tried to smile back, but all that her mouth did was form itself into a watery grin. She wanted to tell him that she remembered, that it had been the most wonderful day of her whole life, walking along the seafront in Bray, hand in hand, the pair of them tucking into a big bag of salty, vinegary chips, the swell of her stomach just enough to push out the fabric of the pink dress she'd bought with June in Arnotts.

They'd got married in the register office in town, with June and Gerry as witnesses, even though PJ's mother said she'd disown him if he didn't do the decent thing and get married in church. 'She'll get over it,' had been his only comment. He'd known that Mary-Pat couldn't get married in church — sure she hadn't even been christened. And she'd known then, as if she hadn't before, that PJ was the man for her. They'd got the train to Bray, all four of them, herself and PJ trying not to laugh at Gerry's carry-on. He was sulking because they'd chosen chips and the seafront over his preferred choice of lunch at Guilbaud's. They weren't 'lunch at Guilbaud's' kind of people.

PJ and June had gone on the dodgems, but he'd made her sit down on a bench with Gerry and watch, putting a big, meaty hand onto her tummy and rubbing it briefly, flashing her a grin as he did so. They hadn't told anyone else about John-Patrick because they'd wanted to hug the secret to themselves for a bit longer. And so she'd watched June throw her head back and laugh as she crashed into everyone — PJ making a point out of reversing into her more than once — thinking she'd never been as happy. Not even Gerry and his peevish nonsense about the chips being soggy and his suit being ruined by sitting on a damp bench could spoil it.

PJ wanted her to acknowledge him now, she knew that from the anxious look in his eyes, but she just couldn't. The words she wanted to say got stuck in her throat and even though she willed her hand to move, to grab hold of his and squeeze it, it just wouldn't. I love you more than ever, she thought, but somehow I just can't say it.

She followed everyone to the trestle tables that had been laid out against the gable wall of the house and filled with platters of cold meats and salads, all made by someone else, served on artfully mismatched china. It looked like a magazine article for a country wedding, Mary-Pat thought, as she helped herself to a big pile of coleslaw, not the real thing. But it was lovely all the same, just lovely.

'I thought you were looking after Daddy?' Mary-Pat looked over June's shoulder as her sister appeared, all linen and rattly jewellery, her dark curls expensively blow-dried. She looked gorgeous, slim and lovely and about ten years younger than her forty-one years. But there was something about her that just didn't seem right ... Just showed you, you could have everything and still not be happy.

June looked briefly over to the willow tree, before waving her hand. 'Oh, he's fine. He's having a little snooze ... I think,' she said vaguely. 'Oh, pâté! Yum,' and she helped herself to a great big slab of it. Mary-Pat's mouth watered. If she ate pâté, she'd put on a stone before the stuff had hit her stomach. She pushed the coleslaw around on her plate.

'Isn't it just lovely?' June was saying, taking in the crowds and the lovely wedding outfits and the mismatched china. 'So tasteful. Rosie has really done us all proud.'

'Us?'

'Yes, well, you know what I mean. Herself. She's done herself proud,' June added hastily, before looking carefully at Mary-Pat. Mary-Pat knew what that look meant: you weren't very nice at that wedding place, were you? You had your chance and you blew it. She was right, Mary-Pat thought. 'She seems so capable and grown-up, doesn't she? Who'd have thought it,' June said.

Mary-Pat opened her mouth to say something sarcastic, but before she could cut her sister down to size, she felt a little hand on her shoulder. 'How are my two favourite sisters?' Rosie kissed each sister on the cheek. Her lips felt chilly, Mary-Pat thought, like one of those marble statues. 'Thank you both for being here; it means a lot to us, it really does.'

Mary-Pat turned around. 'For Christ's sake, Rosie, we're your—'

'You're welcome, Rosie,' June interrupted. 'Sure, we wouldn't have it any other way, would we, Mary-Pat?'

'No. No, we wouldn't.' Mary-Pat managed to push the words out.

'We're so proud of you, Rosie,' June was saying. 'And look what you've done with the place,' she trilled. 'You'd hardly recognise it, isn't that right, Mary-Pat?'

'That's right.' Mary-Pat knew that she sounded like a robot, but she didn't trust herself to say anything further. How dare Rosie treat them like guests. How dare she.

'Are you sure you've both had enough to eat and drink?' Rosie said, an arm on each of their shoulders. 'The canapés are organic, would you believe. Craig has a thing about it,' and she smiled in that composed way she had now.

'Melissa told me all about it,' Mary-Pat blurted, and of course, at the expression on Rosie's face, she knew that it hadn't come out right. It had sounded sarcastic and hurtful. But it was far from the kind of 'organic' they'd been reared on and she wondered if Rosie remembered crying for three days when they'd had to wring Denise the hen's neck and put her in a pot. But she felt June's hand on her arm then, a steady, firm pressure, and she forced herself to say, 'It's lovely, very tasty.' And, yes, they had everything they needed, thanks, and, yes, they'd help themselves to more, then they both watched their sister dance off into the crowd, where she was pulled into an embrace by a young man with a flaming red beard, a stranger to them both.

June snaked an arm around Mary-Pat's shoulder. 'That's your work, Mary-Pat.' June squeezed her shoulder gently. 'She's a credit to you, even if she doesn't know it.'

'Oh, I'm not so sure, Junie,' Mary-Pat said and she just couldn't help the note of bitterness that crept into her voice. 'I can't help thinking that our Rosie's put a lot of thought into herself all the same.'

June looked puzzled and Mary-Pat thanked God that her sister could be a bit slow on the uptake and wouldn't grasp what she'd been trying to say, that her sister wasn't the same Rosie that had stomped onto that bus ten years before, and that it wasn't the normal change that growing up brought — it was something that made Mary-Pat feel uneasy, something not quite real. But she didn't want to be bitter and nasty on her sister's wedding day. She really didn't, and so she patted June on the hand. 'Thanks.'

'If only Mammy could see her now.' June sighed. 'She'd know just what a good job you've done, MP.'

Mary-Pat felt that there was something just beyond her reach, something she didn't quite get, and she looked at June, who was biting her lip. She was about to ask her, but then June said, 'C'mon, let's go and get drunk and make holy shows of ourselves.'

Mary-Pat nodded vaguely, scanning the crowd. 'In a minute. I need to find Pi. You go on and pour me a drink ... a large one,' she called out to her sister's retreating back.

He was in the kitchen, filling the old tin bath with the contents of a plastic bag of ice. His back was turned to her, but she could see that he'd scrubbed up well. That awful bush of hair had been tamed into something halfway presentable and he was wearing a smart-looking shirt and slacks that she'd never seen before and that looked as if they'd cost actual money. 'Pi?'

He turned around, a look of shock on his face. 'You gave me a fright, MP.'

'If I didn't know you better, I'd say you've been avoiding me this last week.' She knew that she was bullying him a bit, using 'that tone' of voice, arms folded across her chest, but she couldn't help it.

She was almost glad when he blushed and put the bag of ice down in the sink. 'Ah, no, it's just that I had a big long list of things to do for the wedding, and the garden needed a bit of tidying, you know.' He shrugged. 'And then Rosie dragged me into Mullingar to some men's shop. It wasn't my kind of place – full of half-naked men waving aftershave in the air – but I did it to please her.'

Mary-Pat felt it again, the jealousy pushing up inside her, making her throat constrict. For fuck's sake. She'd just swanned back here after ten years and taken over. Where was Rosie when he'd needed to go into that awful place, when he'd had to put his head in her lap and bawl his eyes out like a baby while they were waiting to see the shrink? Where was she when he couldn't dress himself without bursting into tears, or eat without herself or one of the kids sitting with him to make sure he took even just a few mouthfuls? She wasn't there, not for that whole long year when he'd hardly been able to set foot outside the house, when PJ had had to take him and Jessie for 'little walks' down by the canal, him shuffling along like an old man. She hadn't been there when it really mattered, and now she was taking him to boutiques and doing him up like he was some kind of a doll.

Mary-Pat folded her arms across her chest, feeling a trickle of sweat slide down into the neck of her dress. She wanted to yank the awful thing off and throw it into the garden. 'Haven't I been on at you for years to tidy yourself up? Much good it did me.'

'I know. I suppose I just needed a bit of a push, by someone … you know, someone outside the family, I mean, someone who hadn't seen me for a while, that's it.' He stood there at the sink, his arms folded across his chest, and she was suddenly struck by how like Daddy he looked, with those lovely fine features, those flashing dark eyes. The bloody Judas.

And then he said, 'I have something for you. Wait a minute till I get it.'

He left her standing in the kitchen, the sounds of the wedding filtering in through the door. It was nearly dusk now and the room was filled with a rosy pink glow, the same kitchen in which she'd spent her whole young life, cooking dinners and drying clothes on the range, trying to bite back her impatience as Rosie tapped her pencil off her copybook, tilting her chair backwards so that, any minute, she'd fall and hit her head. Sometimes, Mary-Pat would throw the wooden spoon down with a clatter and go over and yank the back of the chair so hard it would squeak in protest, righting Rosie with a thump. 'Get on with your bloody homework, will you?' And then she'd slap back to the range and bash pots and pans about for another half an hour, before yelling at them all to come down for their tea.

She'd been so angry, she thought now, her skin prickling with heat and guilt. Such an angry young woman. She still was.

'I've found it,' Pius was muttering as he came back into the room, his head bent. He didn't look at her but instead thrust a small package into her hand.

'What is it?'

'Don't open it now.' His hand on hers was firm. 'Leave it till later.'

'For feck's sake, Pi, you're scaring me. What's in here — a bomb or something?' She went to open the little parcel, picking at the Sellotape which stuck the brown paper together. The thing felt as light as air, as if there was nothing at all inside the package. She looked up at him and the expression on his face was one she'd never seen before. He looked anguished.

'Mary-Pat.' His tone was so firm that she looked up from her task. 'Don't. OK? Put it in your bag and leave it and we'll go and get drunk and we'll talk about it in the morning. I have a lethal punch which I spent three days making and which would knock an elephant stone cold.'

'Thank God, I thought you'd never ask,' she said, shoving the package into her shoulder bag, tucking it underneath her fags. 'I'll race you.'

They were heading towards the makeshift bar beside the henhouse when they heard the commotion, the raised voices, the loud shriek. Mary-Pat turned her head to see Rosie running down the garden, her hands pressed to her face, a look of horror on those tiny, pretty little features. She was barefoot and the daisies in her hair had formed into tight clumps, the red hair knotted around them, her mouth a big round 'o' of alarm.

'Rosie!' Mary-Pat called out to her as she ran past, extending a hand as if to catch her, but Rosie just shook her head and disappeared around the side of the house. What on earth ...? Mary-Pat looked at the knot of people gathered at the pergola, the voices male this time, one of them clearly the Yank's, that nasal twang that she couldn't stand. 'Couldn't you leave her alone, old man? Couldn't you let her be?'

Oh, shite, Mary-Pat thought, her step quickening as she hurried towards the pergola. I thought June was taking care of him. I thought he was out of the way.

She arrived in time to see Daddy, half-out of his chair, looking mystified. 'But I only said—' he was saying.

'I know what you said, you old bastard.' The Yank was leaning towards him now, his face a livid red, both fists clenched. His tie, unknotted, hung around his neck and his cream suit had grass stains on it. For a second, Mary-Pat was sure he was going to hit Daddy, and even while she put out a hand to stop him, the thought entered her head: Go on. Do it. Hit him.

The thought made her stop dead for a second, but then she pulled herself together and bustled in to the little group, clutching the handles of Daddy's chair. 'What's the matter, Craig?' Her voice was flat.

'That bastard.' Craig was gulping, trying to get enough breath into his lungs. 'Could you not have kept him away from her?'

And then Daddy tried to stand up, that awful blanket falling from his knees. 'But I only told her — it was for her own good. She had to know,' he was saying, his voice shaky, the look on his face confused, as if he couldn't understand for the life of him what had gone wrong.

Mary-Pat's stomach lurched. 'Told her what, Daddy?' As she

asked, she lifted a hand to silence the Yank, who'd been about to interject, his eyes bulging with rage.

'That she isn't mine.'

There was a deafening silence for a few minutes, during which Mary-Pat could hear the blood swishing around in her ears. She opened her mouth to say something, but no words would come out. For fuck's sake, she thought. Could you not have kept your mouth shut after all this time?

And then Daddy added helpfully, 'You see, I had to send her away then, that little knacker, I had to. I couldn't have that. That child is not mine. No, no.' He was shaking his head now, and then he looked at Mary-Pat. 'Don't you see?'

'Daddy, you're talking nonsense. You know who Rosie is: she's your daughter. Your flesh and blood.' And she tightened her grip on the handles of the chair, as if to drive it forward, away from here.

But then Daddy turned and grabbed her by the wrist, his black eyes locking on hers. The look on his face was so intense, it frightened her. She wanted to pull away, to run, to bolt for the safety of the car and home. She licked a bead of sweat from her upper lip.

'She tried to pin it on me, you know, she tried to tell me that it was all my fault. Filthy bitch ...' And he shook his head. 'Do you understand, Mary-Pat? I just couldn't let it go on.' And now his eyes filled with tears. 'That woman tried to trick me, to make me believe that Rosie was mine, but it was all lies. You know, Mary-Pat, you know the truth.' He spat the last word out, covering Mary-Pat's face in a thin mist of his spit, and she had to fight the urge to vomit as she wiped it off with the back of her hand. She looked down at her arm, which bore the mark of his fingers. Her breath was ragged now, coming in short gasps, and she clutched her throat. She pushed him firmly, with all her strength, back into the chair, pressing his shoulders down as hard as she could until he landed on the seat with a thump. 'Daddy,' and her voice sounded like a cracking whip. 'You're not yourself. It's time to go home now for a little rest. Let's go.' And she yanked the chair back into reverse, cursing as it caught in the gravel and tugging it harder. She didn't dare look up to see the expressions on their faces. The dirty O'Connors, doing it again, lowering themselves.

'Here, let me.' Pius's voice was firm in her ear as he took the handles from her, gently hauling the chair out of the gravel and across the grass, ignoring Daddy's bleated, 'But I was only saying ...' He simply pretended Daddy wasn't there, throwing over his shoulder, 'PJ, I'll stick him into the back of the Pajero for you.'

'Thanks.' PJ's hand on her arm was warm. 'C'mon, love, it's time to go.'

Where did you come from? she thought, as she said, 'I can't fucking get into a car with *him*,' turning to PJ then, ignoring the snot streaming from her nose. 'Did you not hear him?'

'I heard. And he doesn't know his mind,' PJ said gently.

'I told you this would happen if she came back — I knew it would happen sooner or later. I couldn't keep it in for ever.' The words were out of her mouth before she had time to edit them, and Mary-Pat clamped a hand over her mouth, to prevent anything else escaping. 'I mean, I—'

But PJ didn't seem to have noticed, thank God. His voice was low now, a soothing rumble. 'Shush, shush, let's go, MP, let's go.' He put an arm gently around her shoulder and tugged, and she found herself following him in the direction of the car, where she could see Pius wheeling Daddy up the ramp into the back, Duke trotting close behind.

'Sorry, Craig, so sorry.' Mary-Pat turned and extended a hand to him, which he threw off, a look of disgust on his face. 'Your family,' he hissed. 'You're all insane, do you hear me?' and he mimed a 'gone in the head' expression with his hand.

'Now, Craig, there's no call for that.' PJ was gentle, but firm. 'He's an old man who has Alzheimer's; he doesn't know what he's saying.' This was addressed to Craig's back, as, muttering, he'd turned away and was striding across the grass to the house.

'You take him back to the car,' Mary-Pat said to PJ. 'I'll go and see how Rosie is.' And she made to follow Craig back to the house, until he turned on his heel and yelled, 'You stay away from her. Do you hear? Stay away from my *wife*.' He was jabbing his finger at her now and his face was red with rage.

'C'mon, love.' PJ grabbed hold of her sleeve and tugged gently, and when she turned around, he was giving her that look, the one she knew meant that he was taking charge.

'But she needs me ...' Mary-Pat began, but PJ was shaking his head. 'No, let herself and Craig sort it out tonight. You can ring her in the morning.'

She allowed herself to be guided into the car, PJ clambering in beside her. 'I'll drop you all home and then I'll leave Daddy in, all right?'

Mary-Pat nodded, not trusting herself to speak, her fists clenched tight on her knees. I want to kill him, she thought. I just want to finish him off. She shook her head, unable to believe that she could think such a thing about her own father. And yet, the words must be true, because they'd come from somewhere deep inside, from a place where you couldn't lie.

The silence lasted all the way home, Mary-Pat not even turning to say goodnight to Daddy, just letting PJ carry him off into the night, going inside and letting Melissa make her a cup of tea and smoking three fags in a row. The light in the kitchen was too bright and so she turned it off and sat there in the dark, watching the moon rise, telling herself that she hadn't really meant it, that dark thought that had pushed its way into her head on the way home from the wedding, and that just because Daddy had said what he'd said, it didn't mean that anyone had to believe him.

She was so lost in thought that she didn't hear PJ come back, keys jangling as he stood in the kitchen door. 'Why are you sitting in the dark?'

At the sound of his voice, Mary-Pat jumped up and gave a little scream. 'God almighty. You might have let me know you were there.'

'Sorry.' He looked sheepish, shifting slightly from foot to foot. He had a yellow can of air freshener in his hand, which he put gently down on the counter beside him.

'Yes, well. Where have you been? It's half-one in the morning.' She looked up at the kitchen clock.

'Ehm ... well, I put Daddy to bed at St Benildus's. The nurse said she'd give him something to help him sleep. And then I, ahm, I had to get something in the minimarket.'

'What?'

'Sorry?' He looked startled.

'What did you get at the shop?'

'Oh. Ehm, we needed some air freshener.' He nodded at the yellow can. 'The car stinks. Must be the heat.'

'Oh.' Mary-Pat couldn't understand why he needed to go to the minimarket in the middle of the night, even if it was open

24 hours. Could he not wait until the morning? But she was too tired to ask.

'PJ, would you help me up to bed?' she said quietly.

'Sure, love,' and then he was beside her, her big rock of a man, his arms around her. He gave her a brief, tight squeeze and then led her gently up the stairs to bed.

Only when they had closed the bedroom door behind them did PJ speak. 'Love, you've had a shock, that's all. You're not to listen to him. He's talking rubbish. It's the disease. I'm just sorry that Rosie had to hear that. Even if it *is* a load of bollocks, she'll still be wondering ...' he said, his voice tailing off when Mary-Pat didn't move to contradict him. She felt a wave of intense exhaustion so strong it felt impossible to resist. She looked around at the bed and wondered if she could lie her cheek against the bedspread, just for a minute, and close her eyes and just drift away.

'It *is* a load of bollocks, isn't it?' PJ caught her eye, and she knew that if she didn't look completely blank, he'd rumble her — he always knew when she wasn't being truthful.

She nodded again. 'Utter and total bollocks. I'll go and see Rosie in the morning and put her mind at rest.'

'Good idea.' The hand, when placed on her shoulder, was warm and heavy and full of quiet hope. When she made no move towards him, the hand was removed, and she heard him sigh gently, and she felt a wave of sorrow wash over her. But she couldn't yield to him, she just couldn't. If she did that, she'd end up blabbing, she knew she would. She had to be vigilant, for Rosie's sake.

5

*R*osie had to use Pius's bike in the end because she couldn't run fast enough in bare feet. She'd tried, but the stones on the towpath had hobbled her, digging into the soft flesh on the underside of her foot, making her scream in pain.

She crept around the side of the house to where Pius kept an old racing bike, a tall narrow-framed Raleigh with the handlebars that curved under, like rams' horns, bound with dirty white gaffer tape. Tucking her dress up into her knickers, she swung a leg over the crossbar, putting out a hand to steady herself on the gable wall. She'd have to be careful – she hadn't ridden a bike in years.

She pushed on the pedals, gaining a little speed before removing her hand from the wall, gripping the handlebars as the bike moved forward with a wobble. Oh, Christ, she thought,

I'm going to come a cropper, but she kept pedalling until she was down the garden path and veering out onto the bank, where she managed to steer the bike towards town.

The moon was up now, a huge silvery ball which hung over the row of gloomy leylandii that marked the boundary to Sean O'Reilly's chicken farm, the fishy smell of feed and chicken poo now floating over the hedge to her.

Her hair flapped around her face as she picked up speed, but she didn't dare tidy it behind her ears with a hand in case she lost her balance. She just needed to keep going, not to stop until she got there. If she stopped, then she'd think and if she thought, then she would just turn around and go back home again. Home to her husband, curled up on the bed, his back towards her.

At first, he'd refused to utter one word to her. She'd tried: after everyone had gone home, murmuring and whispering and laying regretful hands on her shoulder. She'd trudged up the stairs to their bedroom to find him sitting on the bed, his back to her. He'd taken off the cream linen wedding suit jacket and his shirt was rumpled, a grass stain just above the left elbow. He was completely still. She knew that stillness. She'd witnessed it many times before. It didn't bode well. When she'd put a hand on his shoulder, he'd whirled around, his face twisted into a snarl. 'Don't say a fucking word,' he'd hissed. 'Do not speak to me, do you hear?'

Rosie had shrunk back against the door. 'But, Craig, I didn't know this would happen.' As she tried to explain, the thought flitted across her mind: nobody said anything to *you*: they – he – said it to me. My father told me that I wasn't his. That my mother was a knacker. Daddy said it to me. His favourite.

'What did I say? Do. Not. Open. Your. Mouth.' His face

was a livid red and spit flecked the corners of his mouth so that he looked as if he was having a seizure. He yanked the bow tie off and threw it on the ground. 'Jesus Christ.' He ran a hand through his thick, dark hair, those pale Midwestern eyes blazing. 'Why didn't you warn me about them? To pull that shit on us, on our wedding day.' He shook his head, bewildered. 'I mighta known. Since you came back to this dump, you—'

'I what?' She tried to overlook the word 'dump', even though she wanted to say that she'd told him so: that there were no castles or fairies in Monasterard.

He tutted and swore under his breath. Craig never swore. 'You've become someone else. Someone I don't really know.'

She didn't even try to answer. There was no point — and besides, he was probably right. Instead, she'd said, 'I need to go out for a second,' and turned and closed the bedroom door behind her. She'd slipped quietly down the stairs, stopping only to pull her platform wedges off her feet. Mary-Pat was right about them — they were totally, stupidly impractical and they'd cost a fortune. She'd quietly placed them next to Pius's wellies and opened the door as silently as she could. And now, she was cycling under the huge copper beech, the darkness under the branches, with their thick covering of purple leaves, swallowing her. For a second, she panicked, unable to see the path in front of her, but then she steadied herself, looking to one side to where she knew she would see the remains of the bright blue rope hanging from the lowest branch. Pius had put it up for her one day, when she was ten, after she'd spent an entire afternoon whining at him about how bored she was.

She'd spent the rest of the summer on that swing, back and forth, back and forth, watching the others as their lives played out before her, from her safe vantage point. Pius's regular departures in Daddy's old Volkswagen, the distinctive rattle of the engine as it drove along the gravel road by the canal, on his way to meet the girlfriend he had at the time. Katy, the one who was always laughing and didn't mind playing Monopoly with her even though Rosie had to win all the time. Then there were Mary-Pat's trips to the clothesline and back, to the hen-run and back, to the vegetable patch and back, the clatter of the screen door as it bashed against the wall, the huff and puff as she bustled across the garden, the brisk tutting to herself, the tight snap of the clothes as she took them off the line and folded them. When Mary-Pat came out, Rosie would stop swinging, afraid she'd draw attention to herself and be asked to help.

June never appeared at all. She was always in her room, the record player on, singing 'Waterloo' at the top of her voice. Rosie had been able to hear her at the other side of the canal, warbling away, out of tune. If Rosie managed to sneak into her sisters' bedroom, she'd find June lying on the bed, a homemade facemask on, two teabags on her eyes, a discarded copy of *Jackie* on the bed beside her. If she was lucky, June would have nodded off and wouldn't hear her as she lifted the magazine from the bed and sneaked it off, to take it back to her lair and peruse the mystifying articles about meeting boys with funny names at the school disco and things like periods and spots and a world she didn't know existed. Not here, anyway. She was sure people didn't have periods and spots in Monasterard.

Of course, there was another reason for the swinging. Before that, she'd stood at the stile, watching. Once Pius had built the swing, she could scramble up onto the chunk of wood and see the path across the field all the way to the town. She could watch to see if anyone came down the track, the head visible first, then the shoulders and finally the whole shape: of Sean O'Reilly, the farmer, or Daddy, or June if she'd gone to the chipper. No one else. Never anyone else.

But she never gave up looking, she thought now. She never gave up. How foolish it seemed, that childlike belief that if you wanted something badly enough, it would happen. That the birthday wish made before you blew out the candles would actually come true. That one day, she'd look up from her swing and see her mother's blonde head, then her shoulders, then her whole self, arms outstretched, inviting Rosie to run towards her, enfolding her in a tight hug, the way she'd seen other mothers do.

She was at the edge of the cornfield at the back of the town now. Her foot slipped on the pedal and she stubbed her toe off the hard earth, sending a jolt of pain up her leg. She had to stop then, tilting sideways so that she could place a foot on the ground, then sliding off the bike, which she had to heave over the narrow stile into the cornfield, grunting as she pulled the back wheel off the ground, then trying to hold on as she slid the bike back down the steps and onto the ground.

She was standing at the top of the stile, looking down at the bike when it hit her. He'd loved her the best — she knew that. He'd told her often enough.

So, how can it be true, she thought as she looked down at her feet, blue in the moonlight, at her wonky knees, at the way her hips jutted out in the dress, at her tiny, flat chest. How can it be true when I'm still the same me?

Rosie blinked and nearly lost her balance. She put out a hand to steady herself, then slid down the steps of the stile onto the ground, landing with a thump. She suddenly felt tired, sitting there at the edge of the field, the stalks of the golden corn now a silvery blue in the moonlight, swaying above her head. I'll just stay here, she thought, feeling the ground warm through the fabric of her wedding dress. If I stay here, nothing else will happen.

But then she remembered her purpose and managed to pull herself up after a while, to walk the bike over to the road, where she clambered up on it and wobbled off again towards Main Street, passing a huddle of people outside the chipper. The cream lace of the wedding dress was now smeared with dark soil, a large rip at the hem from where she'd stood on it, trying to get back up on the bicycle. Half of it was still tucked up into her knickers, which, when she looked down, she saw resembled a Victorian lady's bloomers. Her feet were filthy and her toe, where she'd bumped it, was now bleeding. She kept going, past the neat Protestant church with the lovely manicured lawn, the clean tombstones in the graveyard at the side, so organised, somehow, so tidy. She'd spent more or less her entire adolescence in the place, long summer evenings, puffing away on a joint that she'd nicked from Pius, letting the smoke drift into the damp night air, and then the brown plastic bottles of cider, guzzling the stuff, enjoying the fuzzy feeling that would sweep over her, the numbness on her tongue that would make her slur her words. And all because she'd wanted to fit in with the girls in the Protestant graveyard. She'd wanted their approval so badly, those bitchy girls without a brain cell between them – badly enough to flunk her final year of school and end up in a secretarial school at the bottom of South Great George's Street in Dublin, bashing out the letters AFCD over and over again on a huge manual typewriter, thinking that she'd never been so bored in her entire life. Badly enough to trash the one person in her life of any value. The one person who really mattered.

Rosie could still remember the first day she'd seen him. 'Vuong's here to give a hand with the housework,' Daddy had said when the two of them had just appeared at the gate, looking like birds of paradise in the grey, watery mist. 'It's getting too much for Mary-Pat.' And even aged nine, Rosie had wondered where Daddy was going to get the money to pay this tiny lady, in her black trousers and pink jacket that had funny ties across the front and a little collar, and her son, in his yellow shorts and a T-shirt with a faded Coca-Cola logo on it. She had never seen anyone like them before, with that colour hair, so black it had a blue sheen to it, and their faces a deep nut brown. The boy looked at her with black eyes that folded at the outer edges, that looked like splashes of ink on his face. The boy's mother had nudged him with her elbow and said something in a nasal, sing-song tone and he'd nodded and then looked at Rosie expectantly.

'Do you want to see Morecambe and Wise?' she'd asked him, thinking that he'd probably like to see the goats.

He'd followed her out into the garden then and they'd done a tour of the place in complete silence. Rosie had pointed out the things she'd thought he'd like: the henhouse and Colleen, the sheepdog, and the goats nibbling the grass behind the vegetable patch, which contained only a few scraggy onions and a few potatoes. The boy had looked at it all but had said nothing, not one word, and she'd wondered if he had something wrong with him, if he was a deaf-mute or something like that. One of the saints she'd studied in school was deaf-mute.

'He doesn't speak English,' Daddy had told her later after tea. 'He comes from a place that's thousands of miles away, love, where they speak another language altogether. Like Chinese.' And he'd ruffled her hair and she'd wondered what kind of a language Chinese was.

'They're like those refugees,' Mary-Pat had thrown over her shoulder. 'Boat people.'

At the mention of the word 'boat people', Pius had looked up from his work of tying a fly in the hope of catching a rare sea trout on the river, and Rosie remembered that he'd said he'd take her after tea. She'd caught two perch the last time. 'For God's sake, MP, they're not boat people – they've just come in search of a better life. The boat people were refugees from the war. And the poxy government only took in a hundred and fifty of them. Left the rest of them to float around the South China Sea until they drowned or starved, whichever came sooner, and all that after being napalmed by the Yanks in the first place.'

'Pi, take it easy.' Daddy had looked up from the *Evening Press* then and had shot his son a look over his reading glasses, with the big lump of Sellotape on the bridge because he'd fallen over one night and broken them. 'The child doesn't need that level of detail.' Rosie had been surprised then, that Daddy would talk to Pius like that, because he normally didn't say much to him at all.

'Oh, and you'd know about detail, wouldn't you,' Pius had muttered then, putting the fly down and taking a long pull on his cigarette, shooting Daddy a glare. 'A grand man for detail, aren't you, Daddy? Well, you know what, I think you've forgotten a couple of things over the years.'

Daddy had looked up from the paper, but his eyes hadn't met Pius's. Then he'd just shrugged and continued to read the paper and Pius had taken another furious pull on his cigarette, exhaling with a frustrated hiss.

She still wasn't sure what a refugee was, but anyway, he couldn't speak English so when his mother came, on Tuesday and Thursday mornings, they had to climb trees instead or build shelters on the towpath out of branches, Rosie miming instructions and the little boy, who she had learned was called Mark, dutifully obeying.

And then one day, a few months after he'd arrived, he'd dragged a heavy bag onto the old sofa in the attic, the one that was filled with dusty horsehair, and had pulled out a big, black leather-bound book. Rosie had been fascinated because it had looked like a book of spells, but when she'd looked over his shoulder, she'd seen row after row of black, spidery letters. She couldn't work out what they were — maybe it was a secret code — but then he'd pointed to them and then to himself and said in English, 'My language.'

Rosie hadn't been able to understand why his language looked like hers, but didn't spell anything, and why the letters had little hats on them, but then he'd pointed to one word and spoken in that musical, twanging way, and she'd tried to copy him, and he'd laughed so hard he hadn't been able to speak for a whole five minutes. Laughing until the tears streamed down his cheeks. She didn't care. That's where they'd become real friends, when she'd started to speak his language, enjoying the nasal sounds the words made, and he'd started to speak hers, pointing to Morecambe and Wise and saying 'goat', only it had come out 'goash', because of her accent and it had been her turn to laugh at him.

She pulled up to The Great Wall with a squeak of brakes, only just putting out a foot to stop herself crashing to the ground. The place was quiet, Rosie thought as she opened the door of the restaurant, a wall of steam hitting her as she did so. A knot of local boys were hanging around the high counter, the way they always had done, hair stiff with gel above their ruddy faces, the air filled with the smell of cheap aftershave. They all hunched over, hands in their pockets, muttering to each other, a sudden burst of laughter indicating that someone had cracked a joke. The kind of boys she'd used to hang out with when she was a teenager. The kind of boys who'd still be here in twenty years' time, grown men.

Behind the lads, she could just see the top of his head, a thatch of inky black, bent low over the wok. She fought the urge to run. She could hear the pans hissing and spitting fat on the gas, the deep-fat fryer sizzling in the corner. He was probably making short work of a few bean sprouts, throwing them into a pan along with a chunk of ginger and garlic paste, then tossing in a big handful of prawns, swishing them around the pan, then a sprinkling of spring onions, sliced long and thin, the way Vuong liked them. His mother had been very precise about that. She liked things to be just right. In that sense, he took after her.

He looked up then, to ask one of the lads if he wanted extra chilli, and then he saw her. His eyes opened wide in surprise and a smile touched the corner of his lips. He's pleased to see me, Rosie thought for a second, before the smile was replaced by a hard stare from those black eyes, the lids folded down at the sides, the smooth wide face unchanged apart from a frown line that ran from his forehead to the bridge of his nose. He still had the cleft in his chin. She used to tease him about it, running her finger along the fissure. 'Do you know what they say? "Cleft in the chin, devil within."'

'Oh, I'm not the devil,' he'd used to laugh. 'We both know who the devil is,' and he'd reach out and grab her then, tickling her until she had to scream at him to stop, then kissing her the way he knew she liked, long and hard and slow, so that when he'd finished, she'd feel she needed to come up for air.

The boys left, clutching brown paper bags, all guffaws of laughter and slaps on the back, one of them giving her a curious look as he headed out the door.

'I'm sorry,' she said into the silence that followed. She wasn't sure what for, just at that moment, but she knew that she had so much to be sorry about, it seemed appropriate. It might cover all of the bases.

Mark didn't respond, instead lifting the hatch and shuffling around the few tables in front of the counter, tidying up the discarded chopsticks and any leftover cans. She didn't remember there being tables, just two plastic benches either side of the high counter. He had a tea towel thrown over his shoulder and his white T-shirt was pristine. She wondered what his chest was like under the T-shirt, if it was still as smooth and flat, the shoulders a little too broad for his narrow waist and small hips, before she told herself to stop it. What his chest looked like was no longer any of her business.

Now, he wiped and tidied for a while, piling up sideplates and chopsticks and putting them onto the counter, then wiping down the tables with a damp cloth. He said nothing and neither did she. She just waited. After a while, he looked up at her, taking in her torn dress, her bare feet, the tangle of daisies and knotted hair on her shoulders. 'Sorry about what?'

She shrugged and cleared her throat. 'About turning up like this. I should have come to see you earlier.' Ask me why I'm here, she thought. Ask.

'I heard about the wedding. That there was trouble.'

'Jesus Christ, already?'

He shrugged. 'News travels fast. There were a few of them in here ... after.'

She bit her lip. 'I suppose you consider it well deserved. Justice being meted out at last.' She couldn't help the bitter tone in her voice.

He shook his head and looked down at his food-spattered clogs. 'No, that's not true.'

'Oh, no? I'm not so sure. You've been waiting for a long time for this, Mark.'

He gave a tut of impatience, flicking the tea towel up over his shoulder. 'Don't blame me for whatever happened, Rosie. Don't take it out on me.'

'It was Daddy ...'

He stopped dead, dirty wine glass in his hands, before putting it down carefully on the table. He didn't look at her when she added, 'He said something at the wedding. He said—'

He put up his hands in a 'stop' motion. 'No, Rosie. No Daddy. Please.'

'Look, I need to tell you.'

He shook his head, his face impassive. 'I can't help you.'

'How do you know? I haven't told you yet.'

He sighed. 'Look, nothing your father says would surprise me, Rosie.'

'What do you mean?'

'Oh, please. The whole of this place knows what kind of a man he is.' He spat the word 'man' out.

First Daddy and now Mark. She didn't know what she'd been expecting, but not *this*. 'I made a mistake coming here. I'm sorry I bothered you.'

She turned to leave, but she didn't hear him come up behind her, reaching out and grabbing the upper bit of her arm. The grip was so sudden it made her take in a sharp breath. 'Don't touch me,' she hissed.

He looked nearly as shocked as her. 'I'm sorry, I just wanted to stop you. I didn't mean—'

'Oh, fuck off.' The anger took her now, great fat tears rolling down her face. 'Where were you when I needed you? Oh, I know, holding the high moral ground, I'd quite forgotten. Well, do you know what, I hope you're fucking well happy now.' And with that, she swivelled on her heel and made to grab the handle of the door, to pull it open.

She felt his hand on her shoulder then, gently now, the other one cupping her elbow. 'C'mon, Rosie. I'll make some tea. We can talk then. It's OK, Rosie.' His voice was a low, soft whisper and she allowed herself to be turned gently around; she let him wipe her face with his tea towel. He was so close that she could smell him, the clean scent of soap, the sharp tang of ginger, the medicinal smell of the cleaner he used to wipe down the surfaces. She closed her eyes for a second and when she opened them, his face was just inches from hers. His expression was soft now and his hands were on her shoulders, warm and heavy, and she nearly gave in to it then, the feeling that she wanted to lean against him, to press her head into his shoulder, to feel the warmth of it, the solidity.

But she wouldn't give in to it. She wouldn't. She pulled back abruptly. 'You feel sorry for me,' she said, her voice a near-whisper.

He was rubbing his hand up and down her arm now, and she could feel the callouses on his fingers. 'No, Rosie, that's not true.'

She shook her head. 'You do. And do you know what?'

'What?' His expression was hopeful now.

'You can take your pity and shove it up your ass.' And then she turned and wiped the dust off the hem of her dress, where it had been trailing on the floor. 'I'm going home now. I should never have come.' And she opened the door and slammed it shut behind her, so hard that the bell jangled against the glass, grabbing the bike and hobbling up Main Street, cursing and muttering under her breath.

How quickly it had happened, that turning into her old self again, she thought. Maybe that's what happens when you go home – the clock is rewound and, next thing, you find you're the person you were all those years before. Maybe it had been wasted, all that work on herself – it had all come to nothing. And then she felt it, that familiar tightening, that sense that her chest was being pressed in a vice. She didn't have her inhaler and just the thought of it made her panic more, her breath coming in short gasps. A sweat broke out on her forehead and she had to bend forward as a wave of nausea overcame her. But she wouldn't go back to The Great Wall, she just wouldn't – she wouldn't give him the satisfaction, even if it killed her. And so she limped home, wheezing, a short, tight cough tearing at her throat, and as she ransacked the bathroom for any sign of her inhaler, her face grey in the bathroom mirror, she thought, I should never have come back. Never.

October 1970

Michelle

I'm wobbling around on John-Joe's knee, the two of us crammed into the back of the smelly old Volkswagen Beetle that Bob is driving at speed down the narrow country roads. John-Joe's got his hand up my long suede skirt, his chilly fingers pushing under the elastic of my knickers and I have to slap it away. 'For God's sake, John-Joe,' I say, irritated.

'What's the matter?' he murmurs, nuzzling his head into my breasts, hidden under a voluminous cape, a black-and-white Navajo Indian affair which looks and smells like a dog blanket but which I wear because Bob makes them by hand and it would seem rude not to. 'We are married after all,' he says slyly.

I have to laugh at that and return his kiss, feeling the sandpaper stubble on his chin, because, in the end, our 'wedding' was a simple affair, attended by no one but ourselves. I finally accepted the ring he'd offered me on that winter's afternoon, and I was his. And now, we are married, not in a church but in the only way that matters.

The air in the car is stale, and the plasticky smell of the seats, mixed with Bob's sweat and the smell of Melody's patchouli, is making me feel ill. They're friends of John-Joe's and they're part of one of these new communes in Tipperary, where they live off the land. Bob's nice — he doesn't say much, but I know he's a good man by the way his eyes crinkle at the corners and by the way he always includes me in the conversation. 'What do you think, Michelle?' It feels new, and nice, someone asking me what I think about things. John-Joe, for all his pretence, doesn't much care — he's too busy talking — and so I have to push my way into the conversation with him, to insist that he hear me. I need him to understand that he can't push me around.

Melody is a complete twit — all she does is giggle or say the first thing that comes into her head — even if she is very pretty, with her huge brown eyes and that lovely dark hair of hers. How I wish mine wasn't such a dry frizz! I put a hand through it now and it's like sandpaper, all coarse and wiry; it's the water here — it's so hard and I've given up on heating it every time I want to wash my hair, because it takes so long to warm on the old range, so I sluice it in cold water, and *voilà*, a horrible Brillo Pad on my head.

I have a terrible cramp in my leg, but I can't budge because there's a big placard wedged in the seat beside me ... 'No to Nixon, No to Vietnam'. 'Make Peace, Not War', 'US Foreign Policy Kills!' We spent all night painting them in thick, black emulsion on the white board Bob brought down, then pinning them onto wooden batons — it took all night because we drank so much of the German wine Bob and Melody brought along with them.

I drank plenty and now my head aches, a low throb just above my eyes, but I'm glad I didn't touch the hash Bob produced, a sly grin on his face. 'Amazing what you can get in Morocco these days.' He smiled. 'It'll blow your mind. Try it.' Amazing indeed. If only we could afford to go to Morocco: for Bob, the kind of life we're leading, close to the land, asking nothing of anyone but ourselves, is just a hobby, something to do to annoy his rich parents, but for John-Joe and me, well, we have to live it, even if sometimes it's almost unbearably hard.

When we first moved to the cottage, John-Joe had great plans to fix the place up, but it's hard when the chill seeps into your bones and when the ancient electricity meter has switched off again because you can't find one of those new 50p pieces to shove into the slot. We didn't have too many of them, 50p pieces. I only had a few pounds which I'd managed to scrape together by emptying my post office account, and the little wad of cash John-Joe brought with him, the proceeds of a summer's labouring on a building site in Chapelizod, is getting smaller by the day. And it's hard to grow your own food in winter, even if I spent most of the autumn clearing the front garden. It's better now, though. I have a couple of rows of potatoes and a row of dark cabbages, as well as lettuces and peas. This summer, I even managed to grow tomatoes in the shelter of the gable wall. They're a bit green and pebbly, but not bad for a beginner. When I look at my little garden, I feel a dart of confidence in myself; that I can do this, I can live the life I want. It's hard, but it is possible.

And besides, it's easy to moan and see the dark side of things here. The truth is, John-Joe and I are happy, strange as that might seem, in our little hovel, just the two of us. Sometimes, we feel as if we are the only two people left on earth, waking up every morning in the big double bed, our breath streaming out into the icy air of the bedroom, daring each other to be the first to get out of bed to go downstairs and get the range going. Whoever draws the short straw has to bring the other a cup of tea in bed, to which we'd both then retreat for the rest of the morning, holding each other to keep warm, laughing and making love, then talking about our hopes and dreams. 'I can just see it,' John-Joe will say, 'we'll tidy this place up and grow all our own food to sell in the village and then, with the money, we can invest in a bit of livestock. Nothing too elaborate, just a few hens and a couple of goats. Once we have eggs and goat's milk and veg, sure we're laughing. We'll hardly need to buy anything.'

I'll nod eagerly back. 'And then we could fix the fruit trees out the back and grow our own plums and pears and make jam and bottle the rest to see us through the winter.' Of course, the reality is much, much harder than that, but there are small victories that make it all seem worthwhile. And even if, sometimes, John-Joe seems to prefer spending the morning in bed to working outside, I don't mind. I like being outside and I like having the time to myself, working alone, watching the silvery light through the bare branches of the trees, the scrawny little robin that comes to watch me work. That is the only good thing about the cottage: the soil is good, thick and rich, but not too clay-ey; Mummy would declare it just perfect for her roses.

It's not easy to be true to yourself, to live by your own lights. It requires so much more of you than just to trudge along the same way as everyone else. It's exhausting. Sometimes I find myself wondering if it wouldn't have been easier to have just gone along with Mummy's wishes and married Ivan with his awful sleeveless pullovers and resigned myself to a life of deathly boredom. An easy life, a life of comfort and polite wealth. But then I remind myself that it's a life that would suck the soul out of me.

'Happy?' he says now.

I bite my lip, nodding.

'It'll be OK,' he insists. 'We'll be OK.' And he nuzzles against me then, his hot tongue darting into my ear, making me squeal.

'Oh, you're disgusting!'

'But you like it,' he says slyly, and I have to agree that I do. Not the tongue — that is disgusting — but having John-Joe by my side. I feel braver like that, as if I can withstand anything. And if I feel homesick sometimes, I remind myself why I'm doing this, so that John-Joe and I can be together. And it makes it all seem worthwhile, even if the cost is losing Mummy and Pa for ever. Losing home and the boiled egg on the table every morning, the milky coffee. The sound of O'Brien pushing the roller over the lawn; the noise of the fat wood pigeons on the tree outside my window; lovely JB and throwing the ball for him on our walks by the river. Sometimes when I get melancholy like this, I wonder if Mummy was right. That maybe I'm more conventional than I think. 'It's a simple choice,' Pa said to me on the day I left. 'Him or us.' A choice which I know he thought I'd make in his favour. But he was wrong, and even though my throat constricts with the pain of it, I know that I made the right decision. It was wrong of Pa to make me choose.

Maeve was the only one who asked me how I really felt. We were standing on the steps of the church in Bird Avenue, a big Catholic barn of a place, and she was getting married to lovely

Alan, in a gorgeous broderie anglaise dress which she and her mum had toiled over for months, and she just glowed. 'I'm so happy, Michelle. I didn't know it was possible to be this happy.' And then she frowned. 'Are *you* happy, Michelle?'

I squeezed her tight. 'Of course I am, you silly girl.'

'It's just ...' she bit her lip nervously, 'with all the trouble with John-Joe and your parents ...'

'Shush,' I said. 'This is your day, not mine, and we are not going to breathe a word about Mummy and Pa. They will come around. They'll understand how much I love him, I know they will, and then, well, they'll be happy for me.' My bottom lip trembled as I said the words. 'Because I'm happy, Maeve, truly I am. I've found my other half in John-Joe.'

Maeve couldn't help it, the doubtful look that crept into her eyes, and I felt the hurt spring up inside me. 'You don't believe me either. You're like them. You just think it's an infatuation; that any day I'll change my mind and announce that I'm marrying Ivan, with his horrible sweaters and that musty smell ... ugh.' I shivered, and we couldn't help it: the two of us exploded into giggles.

'Oh, Michelle, how I'll miss you.'

'For God's sake, Maeve, I'm only going to Kildare.' I laughed, but the look in her eyes told me the truth. That I might as well be going to Timbuktu.

But I don't care. I don't. I have the man I love and that's all I need. It's just the two of us now. The two of us, and the new life we've made together.

'Guys, this looks like the place,' Bob says quietly, and he slows the engine, pulling the car into a gateway by the side of a tiny country lane. When we climb out of the car, the air is damp, a cold wind blowing a mist into our faces, laced with the smell of manure that always seems to hang in the air here. There isn't another soul to be seen and it's hard to believe that in just one hour the car of the President of the United States of America will pass through Timahoe village, his ancestral home.

'Where the hell is everyone?' Bob is saying, looking around him. 'They said they'd all be here,' and then he smiles as a man steps out of what looks like a hole in the hedge, followed by another and then another and then a woman, and then four women, and soon there are about fifty of us huddled together against the rain, which has begun to fall more heavily now. There are handshakes and stamping feet and cigarettes are offered and smoked before one slight, dark-haired man claps his hands and says, 'Right, lads. The place is full of guards and the secret service, so we only take the designated routes to the site, understood?' There is a murmur of agreement and I can't help wondering about the military language. He didn't learn that in the army, that much is obvious. With his stripy jumper and straggly brown hair, the man looks an unlikely soldier. 'We know what the plan is.' He pulls a map out of his pocket and unfolds it onto the bonnet of the Beetle, a patter of drops falling on it as he indicates the points at which we are to stand. 'Here, here and here. Now, remember, don't interfere with the convoy or we'll get ourselves arrested, just maximum visibility and lots of noise, OK? And look out for any cameras, make sure you keep right in front of them. If they get the shots, we'll make the front pages tomorrow. Right?'

More murmurs and nods. I squeeze John-Joe's hand and we look at each other, sharing the excitement. The blood begins to pound in my ears as I take my placard from Bob. Just as quickly as it appeared, the crowd melts away, crossing the fields to the village, and Bob motions us to slip quietly up the lane to the crossroads, where a statue of the Virgin Mary has been adorned with the Stars and Stripes, a huge banner draped over her head. 'Timahoe welcomes Richard Milhous Nixon'. Red, white and blue bunting is strung from the lampposts, and small children are waving little American flags on white sticks. We stuff the placards into the hedge and try to see over the heads of the crowds who've gathered by the roadside, six deep. As we wait, there's a low murmur of conversation and lots of stamping of feet to keep the cold out. A little old lady is standing beside me wearing one of those fold-up plastic rainhoods and a brightly coloured rain jacket. On her feet, she wears sturdy black lace-up shoes. 'The Lord hasn't seen fit to bless us with the weather, but, sure, we have to make the most of it, don't we?' She smiles. 'To think, the President of the United States is coming to our little town. Even if he is a Quaker, but, sure, God loves all his people, so he does.'

I nod, 'That's right,' suddenly feeling guilty that, in just a few minutes, we are going to spoil her day, but then, I reason, it's the only thing to do. That man can't be allowed to go on destroying all those young lives in Vietnam. It could have been Bob, I think, if he hadn't managed to get out. He's what they call a draft-dodger. It sounds kind of cowardly, but I think he's brave to stand by what he believes: that the war is wrong, and has cost so many lives, and for what? American imperialism.

'Do you not have a nice umbrella or something,' the woman is saying, 'that lovely blonde hair of yours will be wet through. Here, I think I have another one of these,' and she rummages in her big black bag, producing a little fold of plastic with a flourish. 'Here we are, pet,' she says, pulling it open, 'put that on now, and you won't catch your death.'

'Oh, it's all right, thank you,' I say, but then I see the look in her eye and I take it. 'Thank you very much.' And I put on the plastic hood with the pink flowers on my head, while John-Joe snorts with laughter beside me. I give him a sharp dig with my elbow and he leans towards me and whispers in my ear, 'Oh, what I'd like to do to you with that lovely rainhood on.'

I blush. 'Stop it,' and I smack his hand, which has wandered around my waist, away. And then the quiet murmurs in the crowd build to an excited roar. The little old lady clasps her hands. 'Here he is, thank the good Lord,' and John-Joe pulls me back through the crowd to the hedge, where we take the placards out and wait until the roar becomes louder. 'Wait till I see where things are at,' John-Joe says and goes to the edge of the crowd, craning his neck, looking down to the end of the road and then back at me, motioning at me to come forward. 'Right, the car's about two hundred yards away, so when it gets to the statue, we begin, OK?'

'OK,' I agree. And he peers up above the heads of the crowd, my lovely handsome man, and we wait and then we hear the low rumble of the convoy. If I stand on my tiptoes, I can just make out the top of a huge black car, the American flag fluttering in the damp breeze. 'Right, in ten, lift the placard and begin, right?' John-Joe is shouting now over the roar of the crowds, and I don't know whether it's the noise or the excitement but I feel a sudden jolt of energy and it doesn't feel like me, but I'm surging forward, pushing my way through the crowd, oblivious to the tuts and murmurs and the 'careful, loves'. I can feel John-Joe's hand on the edge of my sleeve, but I just shake it off and then I'm at the front of the crowd, the grey, slick road in front of me. I'm facing the Virgin Mary and for a second I think, 'Sorry, Mary,' and then I look to my right. He won't be in the first car, I reason. I pull the placard behind me, apologising as it catches someone's leg, and tuck it in beside my feet so that the slogan doesn't show. By now, the first car is level with me and the granite face of a secret service man is looking out the window, and he seems to be staring right through me. Just for a second, I falter, then there's a small gap before the second car approaches, and I don't know if that's the car with the president in it, but I know what I have to do, and so I find one foot pushing out onto the road and then another and then I'm standing there, feeling the damp wind around me, and I don't know why nobody stops me and I don't care, I just lift my placard high above my head and I yell, 'Nixon out of Vietnam, stop the killing now!' I must look such a sight, with my plastic rainhood and my Navajo cape, but I don't care. I don't care when a man the size of a house comes lumbering towards me, his arms open as if to embrace me, but I know it's no embrace and so I turn and I hurl myself back into the crowd, and I feel his hand take hold of the back of my coat and pull it, hard, and I just keep pushing forward and then I can see John-Joe's hand and I reach out and I grab it and he pulls me to the back of the crowd.

'Jesus Christ, Michelle, are you out of your mind?' he says, but his eyes are flashing and I know he's as excited as me. I feel that I really, really want to laugh, but I'm too scared and so I just let him pull me down the narrow country lane again, the wind slapping against my face, my breath ragged in my throat. 'Bob and Melody,' I manage.

'They're coming,' he says, and then he turns around and I see the look of panic on his face.

'What is it?'

He shakes his head. 'Just run, will you. Run!' And so I run, my feet pounding against the mud and the stones of the lane, and I keep running until I see the black shape of the Beetle at the bottom of the lane and then John-Joe is pulling open the doors and starting up the engine with a roar. I barely have time to get in, half-hanging out of the front door, when he reverses the car, then pulls it forward, and for a second I think we're going to fall into the ditch. The huge man is running towards us now, the thud of his feet heavy on the road, and then we roar off up the lane, the car belching a big cloud of smoke behind us.

I can't help it, I have to let it out then, a big whoop, and John-Joe yells, 'Woo-hoo,' and slaps the wheel of the car so that the horn beeps and then we are both laughing so hard we can hardly breathe. I look in the wing mirror and see the man, bent over, his breath steaming out into the damp air. Fuck you, I think, and then I hold my hand over my mouth as if I've said the words out loud. If only Mummy could see me now.

'We've forgotten Bob and Melody,' I say then, my hand on John-Joe's arm.

'They'll be all right,' he says. 'One of the others will take them.' And then he leans across to me, one eye on the road, and runs his free hand through my hair and pulls me towards him, planting a sloppy kiss on the side of my mouth. 'My God, Michelle, you are fuckin' amazing.' He laughs and shakes his head. 'What the hell kind of woman have I married?' and he roars with laughter. And I feel so proud and happy and alive. As if everything we've gone through since we came here has melted into the distance. This is what I'm here for, I think proudly, as we whizz along the country roads. This is what I was born to do.

And then later, when we've prodded the damp turf in the range to some kind of warmth and spread the little bit of bread we have left with a smear of butter and a dab of jam, washing it down with a pot of hot tea, he pulls me on top of him, on the only chair we own, an old red armchair with a wonky arm that leaks stuffing, and he begins to take off my Navajo cape, which I wear all the time to keep out the cold, and then my green woollen jumper and then my vest, and then I'm half-naked on top of him, and his lips are on mine, and he whispers, 'Let's make a baby.'

I sit up on his knee then, my hair around my face, and I look into those black eyes, searching them for any sign that he's joking. That it's just one of his pranks and that he'll turn around any minute and say, 'Got you there!' And a little voice in my head says, 'I don't know, it's too soon. My life is just beginning. Didn't you see what we did out there, what we achieved?' But I don't know how to say this to him without hurting him, and so I say nothing.

'If it's a boy, we'll call him Richard.' He grins, and then we both collapse into giggles and then we're kissing and pulling off our remaining clothes and, because at that moment I want so badly to give him what he wants, I find myself saying, 'Yes.'

Part Two

Autumn

6

June found that she was getting pretty good at lying these days. Mammy had raised them not to, had drummed it into them: as far as Mammy was concerned, the truth was the only thing that mattered. But even though June might not be as bright as Mary-Pat or Pius or Rosie, she knew that Mammy had been wrong about truth. Sometimes it was better avoided. That way, you didn't ruin people's lives with it.

And so she'd kept it all to herself for the next few weeks after Daddy had ruined everything with his nonsense. She'd watched her little sister struggle with it — she must have been feeling so *confused* — but all she'd done was visit once or twice, bombing down the motorway and back in an afternoon, to nod and to pretend to listen, to agree that he'd just lost his mind and that was all there was to it, all the time feeling that she shouldn't really be there. That she didn't deserve it, the right to comfort her sister.

That was why she'd had to pretend when Pi had given her Mammy's book, her copy of *Gone with the Wind*. He hadn't known what to say, poor lamb, that look on his face as he'd handed it to her, and she couldn't tell him that it didn't mean that much to her. It was nice to have it, to feel the weight of it in her hand again and to remember all the times she'd lain on her bed at home and lost herself in the sheer romance of it, but it didn't feel to her like it must feel to the others, she thought. It didn't feel like Mammy was back with her, because she'd had her all along. And so, every time she got back from Monasterard, she'd go up to her bedroom the way she always did, to get ready for Gerry, to make a bit of an effort, and she'd pull the writing box out from under her side of the bed, and she'd unfold the aerogrammes and read them, her eyes scanning the flimsy paper for clues.

She was a great secret-keeper. She knew that. That was why the letters had been sent to her. Because she wouldn't tell a soul and besides, she told herself, it wouldn't change things. It wouldn't change what Daddy had said, would it?

When Maeve had first rung, all those years ago, June had been living in Dublin, working in that funny little office on Fenian Street. She'd loved it: keeping her little flat just the way she wanted it, going out with the girls from the office to race meetings and to the Shelbourne Hotel and the lovely bar, where, after a few near misses, she'd bumped into Gerry. It was as if she were a new woman, had been given new life. She'd made something of herself, just as she'd planned, and now her whole life lay in front of her, full of promise.

It had been a glorious, sunny morning, the trees a bright,

zingy green, the city alive with colour and life. She'd been just about to leave her flat on Haddington Road for work and had hesitated about answering the phone, figuring she'd be late, and then decided to pick up in case it was Mary-Pat. Mary-Pat was always ringing her at funny times, even though she'd tried to explain to her a thousand times that she worked all day; suppressing the flicker of guilt that Mary-Pat was still at home, cleaning up after Daddy, while she'd managed to escape. 'What's happening in the big smoke?' Mary-Pat would ask, that eager tone in her voice, as if she were living her life through June.

At first, she'd politely listened to the woman at the other end. It had taken a while for the penny to drop, to realise what it was the woman was saying. She was 'an old friend of your mother's'. Could they meet for a coffee some place convenient for June? Maeve – the woman had cleared her throat and said, 'Maeve with an "e"' – had something that she thought June might like to have. Something of Mammy's.

June's first instinct had been to say 'no', that she didn't want anything of Mammy's. That, quite frankly, she'd rather die. 'Do you have any idea,' she wanted to ask Maeve, 'what I've been through for the last ten years? Do you have any idea at all what you're asking?' She opened her mouth to say as much, but then stopped herself. Because, of course, she did want something of Mammy's. Any tiny crumb, she'd reach out and grab it, because she wanted to know, to understand, to find an answer, no matter how much she tried to persuade herself otherwise. She needed to understand what she'd done to make Mammy leave like that. She needed to *know*.

And so, she found herself agreeing to meet Maeve at the Mont Clare hotel. 'It's a nice hotel, dear, quiet and out of the way. We won't be disturbed.'

The morning had dragged by. June had felt she was wading through treacle, dragging her feet up and down the office, trying to pretend that she was filing so that Paddy, her boss, wouldn't notice how distracted she was. At the dot of one, she'd grabbed her handbag and stuck her head around the office door. 'Just popping out, Paddy,' and she'd run before he could ask anything further.

She'd bustled around the corner of the maternity hospital, a little cluster of women on the steps, resting their huge bumps on their knees as they took in the sun. She passed them every day on her way to and from the office, and every time she did, she'd wondered if one day she might like to be there, on the steps, in a snuggly dressing gown, a baby in her belly. Once, it had seemed a faraway dream, but with Gerry on the scene, the idea had slowly been taking shape in her head. But now, it just seemed sinister, fraught with danger. She knew what mothers really did. She knew.

She'd passed Merrion Square, then shivered as she'd stepped out of the bright sunlight into the gloom of the hotel lounge. She'd hardly been able to make out anyone in the near-darkness of the hotel, but her stomach had heaved at the smell of the lunchtime bacon and cabbage. She should have brought her glasses, she'd thought. She was normally too vain to wear them, but she could have done with them as she'd squinted into the cavern of the lounge.

In the end, Maeve hadn't been that hard to find, a dark twist of hair piled on her head, a nut-brown face with two eyes like currants pushed into dough above a button nose. She looked like one of those friendly dolls made of fabric, with buttons for eyes. She'd been sitting alone with a bowl of soup and a copy of *The Irish Times* in front of her. 'I feel a little like a spy,' she'd chuckled, standing up to meet June.

June couldn't bring herself to smile back. She managed to shake Maeve's hand briefly then perched on the edge of the worn velvet banquette. No, thank you, she said, she wouldn't have coffee or soup. She'd cleared her throat then, saying, 'Maeve, I don't mean to be rude but I've only got half an hour lunch break ...'

'Of course.' Maeve had sat upright then, all business. 'I'm sure you're wondering why I suggested we meet.'

'You know something about Mammy,' June had said baldly. 'What do you know?' The question didn't come out the way she'd meant it, and Maeve shrank back slightly.

'Sorry,' June had muttered. 'It's just, it's hard after all this time.'

'I know,' Maeve had said. And when she didn't add anything, June had blurted, 'Where is she, Maeve?'

Maeve had shaken her head then, just slightly. 'I'm afraid I can't say. And not because I'm hiding anything,' she added hastily. 'I don't honestly know, June. But I can tell you she's safe.'

June had had to bite her tongue then, clenching her fists tight, trying to suppress the urge to stand up and yell, '*Safe*? Do you think I care whether or not she's safe? After what she did?' In that second, New June just melted away and in her place there was a desperate young girl, and June hated herself for it. For her weakness. 'I know that she is — was — alive. She left word with Granny Kate in Donegal. I just want to understand, Maeve, that's what it is.' The statement was more like a whimper, and June had felt her eyes fill with tears. She took a hankie from her bag, dabbing at her eyes with it. 'Sorry.'

Maeve had nodded silently and reached into her own

handbag. June had flinched, as if the woman were reaching for a gun, but instead she'd pulled out a white envelope with June's name on it. 'Your Mammy wanted you to have this,' she'd said. 'Don't read it now,' she'd added hastily, placing a hand on June's. 'When you have some time. I think you'll probably have some questions and I hope I'll be able to answer some of them anyway. Give me a call then?' And she'd got up, squeezing June's shoulder. 'And now, if you'll excuse me, the number 45 bus is a rare bird and there's one due any minute.'

And then she'd left, and June had sat there, looking at the fat white envelope, holding it in her shaking hands. And then she'd walked out of the hotel and into the glare of summer and had walked home to Haddington Road, ringing Paddy and telling him she wouldn't be back after lunch, because she had a really bad headache. And she'd sat on the bed and composed herself, sitting up straight, hands folded in her lap. The envelope she'd placed in front of her on the bed and she'd stared at it until the writing on the front became a blur.

As she sat there, she could hear the sounds of the traffic outside, a child laughing, a siren far away near the canal, and it seemed strange to her that life could just be going on outside the window, that people could be going about their daily business, just like that, when her life had stopped. And the gap between her two lives, the one she could have had and the one she now faced, opened up in front of her. When she reached out a hand and grabbed the envelope, tearing it open so quickly that great, jagged lumps appeared at the top, it was as if she were standing outside of herself, looking at the girl with the two spots of pink on her cheeks, at the way she pulled out the wad of flimsy paper, held it in her hands, lips moving as she read the words, the way they always did when she read. Mary-Pat said it gave her the creeps, like she was some old nun saying her prayers, but it helped her to get the words into her head. It helped her to understand them better.

'*My dear June, I don't know where to begin. How to tell you about the past ten years and what they've been like for me.*' She'd had to stop then, to look out the window and twist a lock of her hair into a tight, hard knot. What about what they were like for *me*, Mammy? What about that? When she'd looked back down, the letters had swum in front of her eyes. '*I just need to tell you that I never intended to leave you. Not for ever. I thought that you'd come with me, you see, and we'd all be together, but then ... it didn't work out like that. I had no choice, Junie. You have to believe me.*' June had shaken her head then, unsure. There was no such thing as 'no choice', not really. Even she knew that.

'*It's very hot where I am. Hot and dry and there's no rain for months at a time. The sun burns down day after day. You'd think it was Hell, if you didn't know better, and sometimes I think it is. But it's what I deserve, I suppose. It's my punishment for running away. My penance. And I try to serve it as best I can. I'm helping mothers and little girls and it's good work, June. Meaningful work. I feel that what I do makes a difference to another person ...*'

June had put the letter down then. She was trying to understand it, but she just couldn't, even though she was reading the words out loud. She knew what the words meant, but it was hard to see why Mammy couldn't do that kind of work at home, with them. Why she had to leave them all to go and help other people. Surely that wasn't enough reason to leave your children?

'*Please try not to blame me. One day, when you're older, you'll understand what can happen when love spoils, when it goes off, like sour milk.*' The viciousness of it had always made June feel a bit sick — the idea of love 'going off' — like Daddy was a pint of milk with the top left off. Oh, he was no angel, Daddy, but he had *stayed*. '*I miss you all so much, it feels as if my heart has been squeezed in a vice with the pain of it, but then I hope that, some day, you can forgive me.*'

Whenever June got to that bit, she always shook her head. No, Mammy, she thought. I can't forgive you. '*You were always such a tough little girl, Junie. Much more so than Pius. You were twins, but it was as if you were two halves of the same person, the ying and yang*' — God, Mammy was still into that nonsense — '*I imagine he took it hard, and Mary-Pat, too, even though she'd never admit it. She'd bury it deep inside and let it eat away at her*' — Mammy had been right about that — '*but you, June, I think you'll triumph. I never really knew what was going on inside your head, Junie, but I did know that you had some inner strength that would help you to pull through.*' That bit was the most upsetting for June: the idea that she somehow didn't feel it as much as the others.

'*Do you think that you might write to me, Junie, and tell me about your lives, about what's going on for you all? That way, I can feel I'm part of it, that even though I'm far away I'm still, somehow, in your lives. Does that make sense?*' The first time she'd read this, June had sucked in a huge breath, holding it inside her chest. It took her a while to realise that she wasn't breathing and she let it out then in a big rush. She knew, of course, that she'd say yes, that she'd agree to whatever her mother asked her to do. And that, by saying yes, her life would be stolen away from her, the life that she could have had.

And sure enough, that new hope she'd had for herself just went up in smoke with the burden of it, the weight of responsibility for keeping the secret. She'd kept up appearances, but it had cast a shadow over her whole life: Gerry, the births of the two girls, his success at Talk FM, the good times they'd had together, all of it. Oh, how she'd longed to break free of it; so many times she contemplated finishing it all, but she never could. What kind of a daughter would do that? Would spurn her own mother? And so, once a month for the next twenty years, she'd pull her writing box out from under the bed and take out the lovely cream notepaper that Gerry had ordered for her from Smythson, and she'd sit down to compose her letter, nonsense about holidays in Portugal and Spain, about Mary-Pat and the kids, about PJ's business and silly local gossip, carefully crafted lies to spare everyone's feelings, hating herself as she put the words onto the paper. And she'd hand it to Maeve and a week or two later a letter would be sent back. And over these twenty years, not a word of the truth would be spoken by either of them.

It was a lifeline, the connection between them, June knew that. She knew that she was keeping something alive by writing to Mammy like this and by reading the letters that would be sent back via Maeve. But if it was, why did it make her feel so bad?

It had been coming for a long time, June thought that morning as she drove past Avoca Handweavers, thinking about the lunches she and the girls had enjoyed there, sharing those enormous plates of quiche – which June had avoided – and salad, a half-glass of Chardonnay so that she wouldn't get pulled over on the way home. June hadn't even realised it until she'd opened her mouth last night to tell Gerry that she was going to see Rosie today. 'You'll be gone in the morning,' she'd said, tapping on his study door. 'I'll be back for dinner.'

He hadn't even turned around, just looked up from his computer, throwing half a glance over his shoulder and waving an arm. 'Have fun.'

I'm hardly going to 'have fun', June thought, as she passed the garage on the way into Monasterard, the lovely manor house that she'd dreamed of living in, the bridge over the river, then left towards the canal. I'm going to see how my sister's doing and I'm going to try not to torture myself with guilt, if you call that 'having fun'.

It was a blustery day, gusts of wind blowing a warm drizzle over the water, and June pulled the Land Rover up in the parking space just before the humpback bridge and watched the September rain fall. A mother duck and her nearly grown ducklings were marching up the towpath, she leading the way and they shuffling along behind, feathers ruffling in the wind. She seemed to know exactly where she was going, June thought, as they waddled along. She was in charge of her own destiny, Mother Duck. June thought for a few moments, then turned the key in the ignition again and drove slowly over the bridge.

Mary-Pat's house was to the right, the little cul-de-sac behind the church, but June turned left instead. She drove down past the school before turning left again, bumping over the rutted narrow road that led to the garage. It had a sign with a Michelin Man on it hanging from the wall. June stopped the car and sat there for a few seconds before climbing down and walking out of the bright sunlight into the dim shade of the workshop, the smell of rubber and petrol filling her nostrils.

She stood by the door for a minute, taking in the grey-painted walls with the rows of tyres lined neatly along them, 'Goodyear' written above them, the tools arranged in order of size along magnetic strips above a large workbench, on which two order books were placed below a small filing cabinet, and a manual on Nissan Micras. He always had been neat, Dave. 'A tidy workshop means a tidy mind,' he was fond of saying. It was one of his more interesting quotes, but as she stood there, trying to adjust to the gloom after the brightness outside, June tried not to think about Dave's limited command of the language, or his smoking habit, or the way he used to smell of diesel. Or to think about why she was there for the first time in twenty-five years. Why she'd come.

A radio was humming in the background, a murmur of chat and then a rising tone of indignation as the presenter held forth on the Troika. June realised that it was Gerry. She looked down at her watch – 11.30, he was nearly finished his show. She should have taken it as a sign, but instead she just ploughed on.

'Is Dave here?' she asked the pair of feet sticking out from under a Ford Focus.

The feet slid out from under the car and a freckled face streaked with oil beamed up at her. 'Well, well, if it isn't June O'Connor, the Belle of Monasterard. After all these years.'

June stood there for a moment, looking down at Dave O'Leary, before clearing her throat. 'It's June Dunleavy now.' As she spoke, she blushed, not sure why she was insisting on using her married name. After all, she was hardly going to be in a position to be protecting her status, was she? Not when she was about to do what she was about to do.

He scratched his head. 'Oh, yeah, you married that fellow on Talk FM. He's quite the man, isn't he?' and he nodded in the direction of the radio, giving her that sly grin again, the one she remembered from twenty-five years ago. He hadn't changed, really. His hair was still black and those eyes still bright blue, and his face still had a youthfulness to it that Gerry's had lost – too many steak dinners in Shanahan's on the Green had seen to that.

'To what do I owe the pleasure?' Dave said, rolling up the sleeves of his overalls to reveal tanned brown arms, the ropes of veins twisting upwards to where she could see pale skin. A workman's tan. June swallowed, eyes darting around the room. It's not too late, she thought. You can still leave.

'Oh, it's my car,' June improvised. 'It's been making a funny rattling noise.' And as June said the words, she realised how implausible they must sound. After all, how many garages were there in her neighbourhood? And anyway, the dealership on the Navan Road was the place to go, everyone knew that. 'I want someone I know to take a look at it.'

Dave looked at her steadily for a few moments. 'C'mon in for a cup of coffee,' he said. 'We'll take a look at her after. Unless you're in a hurry.'

'No hurry,' June replied, following him into his office, closing the door carefully behind her.

September 1972

Michelle

I've taken to pushing the massive pram down the towpath, watching it rock and sway as I drive it over the bumps and tufts of grass, my little girl gurgling with laughter. We've called her Mary-Pat, after John-Joe's sister, a name which seems to me to be very old-fashioned, like a nun's, but I gave in to him only if I could name the next baby. I've already decided that if it's a girl I'll call her June, after Mummy. Mind you, I'm so big at this stage that I wonder if I'm going to have two! I'm six months along now, but I feel so heavy, and the pain in my back and hips is so bad that, sometimes, I worry that I've made a mistake and got my dates wrong.

I didn't intend to have another baby so quickly after Mary-

Pat, but nature had other ideas. Of course I know about birth control, but there certainly isn't much of it around here, and Dr Meade only gives the pill to married women – and he'd ask for my marriage cert, I know he would. My only hope would be to get on a train to Belfast and come back waving condoms, like those brave women I see on the front page of *The Irish Times*, triumphantly getting off the train, armed with enough contraception for half the country. I look at them and I think, God, I wish it was me. They are marching forward and doing brave and remarkable things, and I'm trudging up and down the canal with one baby and another on the way. You'd never think I'd read Betty Friedan – not that Betty Friedan's ideas would hold much sway in Monasterard. Father Fathom would, no doubt, denounce her from the pulpit, had he even heard of her – but I can't help wondering how easily I forgot what the book taught me, that there was another way of life open to me, one of freedom, of self-realisation. I swore to myself that I wouldn't become like Mummy, content with keeping house and gardening and knowing her place. I'd forge my own path, my own destiny. And yet, children have a way of making your world shrink, making your options just seem that much smaller, so that, at the end of the day, just going into the village for a walk can seem like an achievement. So much for Betty Friedan!

I wonder if she had a husband who pestered her, wore her down with charm and persistence, even during those tricky times of the month: it seems he can't get enough of me. It's exciting, I know, and it seems worth it at the time, until I miss a period and my heart sinks to my boots. I suppose I could say no, if I really felt that strongly about it. But I don't. Because I like it, and because I like the way, when we're together in bed, John-Joe belongs wholly to me. To me and to no one else. I wonder if that's why I give in to him so much, because I don't want him to look elsewhere. And I have a feeling, an intuition, that he would. Oh, he hasn't so much as given another woman a look, but I've seen the way some of the women around here look at *him*, particularly that cheeky Fidelma at the post office — she practically waves her bosom in his face, which he thinks is hilarious. I don't find it quite so funny, particularly when I look like a hippo nowadays.

But my baby is my reward. My reward and my consolation. I love babies. It's a contradiction, I suppose, but I love Mary-Pat's milky, rusky smell and silky hair, the little murmurs and gurgles. When I look at Mary-Pat, I know that she's completely mine.

It's a beautiful summer's day and I sit down to rest on the canal bank, exhausted from the walk. I put the brake on the huge pram and lift Mary-Pat out, my arms aching, and put her down on the grass. I sit there beside her for a while, feeling the sun on my face, and I thank God it's summer and that I have a beautiful baby with me to enjoy it.

Bridie nearly ate me, of course, when I told her I was pregnant again. 'What in the Lord's name can you be thinking?' she scolded, as she sat opposite me, looking around her with a sniff, her watery blue eyes taking in every inch of the peeling wallpaper, the grubby linoleum, which no amount of scrubbing would rid of its scuff marks and blotches of old food. Bridie is a big woman, with a broad bosom and greying hair which she ties into a funny kind of sausage roll at the back. She has a face scrubbed raw by the wind and rain and a long nose from which often hangs a drip, which every so often she blows away loudly into a huge white hankie, while John-Joe and I try not to laugh.

'You need rest and good food and the Lord will take care of the rest,' she said the first time she asked me to lie on the bed while she examined my bump, her huge hands pushing and prodding. 'And you tell that husband of yours that this room is to be clean and tidy the next time I come.' She looked around our bedroom, with the mould clinging to the walls and the condensation on the windowpane, sceptically. 'I'll send my fellow down with something for the damp.'

'Yes, Bridie,' we both chorused then, like guilty children.

She nodded brusquely. 'Yes, well,' and she patted my shoulder absently. 'A child like you giving birth to a child. You need every bit of help you can get.'

'I'm twenty-one,' I protested.

'What did I say?' She folded her arms across her bosom, a satisfied look on her face. 'A child.'

Without Bridie, I really don't know how I'd manage. She gave me this huge pram, appearing at the door one day with it, an ugly grey thing that bounced and sprang on huge silver wheels. That pram has been my lifesaver, my key to the outside world, to the canal bank and then to Monasterard, across the wheatfield and up the little road, past a lovely Protestant church with a tiny, neat little graveyard, the gravestones like teeth, planted in the ground, then onto a long, straight street – accurately called 'Main Street' and, by rights, the only proper street in the village. It's only about a hundred yards long, but it has six pubs in it – I counted them – as well as a funny little draper's painted maroon with the word 'Moran's' picked out in white. The pram takes me on then to Maggie O'Dwyer's grocery, with its single basket of fruit in the window and the flies stuck to the fly paper that makes my stomach heave. Inside, it's a little dark cavern, with shelves up to the ceiling, packed with what look like very ancient boxes of Lux soap flakes and Brillo pads and big tubs of Bisto gravy mix, for some reason. Maybe everyone in

Monasterard is hooked on Bisto. The thought always makes me laugh and distracts me from the sight of Betty's husband, Pat, in his string vest, hovering behind the counter, an unsettling leer on his face.

'Well, if it isn't herself. How's the good life, eh?' and then he laughs, until his smoker's cough gets the better of him and he has to hack into his handkerchief. He's revolting and it's all I can do not to vomit all over him as I ask for a few slices of ham, carefully counting out the money into his greasy hand, then running out of the shop to Mary-Pat in her pram, as fast as I can. And then we're off again, pushing gently up Main Street, past Joyce's pub and general goods store, wondering if I dare ask Jim Joyce for credit again, figuring that it's been a while since I went in last to ask if he had any offcuts of wood. John-Joe has an idea that he wants to make a crib for the new baby.

I managed to get some nice bits of birch from Jim a couple of months ago. I didn't like having to ask, but he'd been so nice about it, wrinkling his freckled face under his sandy hair and pushing the pencil he'd used to measure the wood behind his ear. 'Sure you can give me a few of those potatoes when you're next in. I love a home-grown spud, so I do.' I change my mind, deciding I'd better dig a bag of potatoes before I cross the threshold. It's funny, the way things work here in the country. In town, you just go into shops and pay for stuff, and if you haven't got any money, God help you. They put that sign behind the cash register: 'Please do not ask for credit, as a refusal often offends.' Here, people are too kind to turn you away and too clever to offer charity; instead they pretend that a girl like me has something valuable to offer them. John-Joe says it's because they're like every other Irish person, afraid to speak their mind, to call a spade a spade. 'They all dance around things,' he says, 'pretending that they're not the way they really are.' But I like that about people here. Their kindness.

Today I'm going to see a farmer who has hens to sell. Bridie told me about him, Sean O'Reilly. I imagine him to be another old man, as I place Mary-Pat back into the pram, in spite of her protests, and push on, until I see the big red corrugated iron shed of his farm, from which seems to be coming an alarming sound of squawking and clucking. At the neatly painted white gate, I call, 'Hello?' and after a few moments there's a shout from the shed and a man appears and strides across the yard. He's huge, like a barn himself, with bright blue eyes, red cheeks and a thatch of black hair standing upright on top of his head. He's wearing a pair of battered corduroy trousers and a blue shirt which is open to his chest and through which I catch a glimpse of black chest hair. For some strange reason, I find myself blushing.

'Sorry, I didn't hear you above the din,' he says, reaching out a large red hand and shaking mine so vigorously I think it will fall off. He eyes the pram then, and my bump, and I think I must look such a fright.

He scratches his head before saying, 'Come in and have a cup of tea before we look at them, will you?' He's being kind of course and I accept gratefully, glad to rest my swollen ankles in a comfy armchair by the huge, shiny range in his kitchen, which is also spotless. I sit Mary-Pat on my knee, where she babbles and plays with her feet before bursting into a peal of laughter when a black-and-white collie slinks into the room and comes up to her, giving her an experimental lick on her toes.

'Get out of it,' Sean orders, and the dog darts away, tail between its legs. 'It doesn't do to get too close to animals,' he says, as he takes the hissing kettle off the range. 'They need to be themselves, without having to please humans.'

'That's very philosophical.' I smile, accepting the steaming cup of tea he offers me and taking a grateful sip.

'Ah, well, we have to respect each other as species.' He smiles back, taking a seat in the opposite chair before getting out of it again and coming towards me, arms outstretched. For a second, I think he's going to embrace me, and I shrink back in the chair, but instead he says, 'Here, let me take this little miss while you have your cup of tea.' I'm about to object, but before I can, he's lifted her high into the air, swinging her up almost to the rafters, while she gives another gurgle of laughter.

'You're very good with her.'

'That's because I'm the eldest of nine. I had plenty of practice.' And then he sits down, bouncing Mary-Pat gently on his knee. And for a second it flashes into my head. What if I were married to him and not to John-Joe? What if this lovely kitchen, with its dresser packed with delf and the shining flagstones, was mine, and this handsome man was sitting opposite me every night? Almost as soon as I have the thought, I push it out of my head. It must be the pregnancy, I think to myself: it's making me think all kinds of thoughts. I love John-Joe: I love his laughter and his singing and the way he lights up the room; I love the way that he thinks every day should be lived to the full, should be an adventure. And there was bound to be a Mrs Sean O'Reilly anyway, a grand country girl with big hips and a way with livestock. The thought makes me giggle and he looks at me for a second before asking, 'So how's John Dermot's place shaping up? Bridie tells me you've worked wonders with it. Mind you, it needed it.' He grins sheepishly. 'John Dermot was a singular man, that's for sure.'

'Well, the garden's coming on,' I say. 'I've planted quite a lot for the summer and I haven't had too many disasters, bar a

patch of leeks that ended up tasting like soap! But the house ...'
I give a little shiver.

'I'd say there's not a lot you could do with it all right.' He
nods. And Mary-Pat nods too, then, her little head bobbing
up and down as she imitates him. His face lights up. 'My word,
who's a clever girl?' he says, and he gives her a little tickle under
the arm, and she responds with a squeal. 'Sure, maybe Mammy
would leave you behind, would she?' he coos gently. 'Would she?'

'She would not.' I laugh. 'Sure, I couldn't leave her for five
minutes, never mind with a stranger – oh, sorry,' I say, covering
my mouth. 'I didn't mean ...'

He smiles briefly, the lines at the corners of his eyes crinkling.
'I know you didn't,' he says, bouncing Mary-Pat gently on his
knee. 'It's a mother's instinct, isn't it? Not to want to let her
child out of her sight. It's nature's way to bond us to them, so
we can't wander away from the nest and leave them motherless.'

'I suppose it is,' I say weakly. I feel a little uncomfortable at
this Biblical turn of events. It seems to me that Sean O'Reilly has
a very definite way of looking at the world, where things are either
right or wrong, not a mixture of both. I wonder what he makes of
me, the hippy in John Dermot's place, with my daft ideas?

'I suppose I'd better be getting back. My husband will be
wondering where I am by now.'

'Oh, of course.' He looks embarrassed for a moment, before
getting up, Mary-Pat tucked under his arm. 'Will you listen to
me, ráiméis-ing on, old bore that I am.'

'You're not.' I giggle.

'What? Old or a bore?' He grins, as I try to get up from the
chair and find myself pinned there by my bump. 'Here, let me
help,' and he pulls me gently to a standing position, his arm
solid under mine. 'You have a lot on your plate,' he says gently.

'I do, but my husband does his share,' I say stoutly. 'He's great with the baby and he helps me in the garden ...' I feel the need to defend him, because I know that there's 'chat', as Bridie puts it, about the amount of time John-Joe spends in Prendergast's.

'Well, then you're a lucky woman,' he replies. And then, as if the subject is closed, 'Let's lead the way to the hens, little lady, shall we?' And off he marches to the squawking barn, opening the large wooden door, whereupon a tiny little black hen darts out underneath his legs. Deftly, he leans down, Mary-Pat still in his arms, and plucks the hen up with one hand. 'Making a bid for freedom, eh, Bessie?' and the little hen turns her head to the side, as if she's listening. Then Mary-Pat reaches out a little hand and pats her gently on the head. 'Oh, she's been chosen, so,' he says. 'And now, let's see what other little ladies we can find inside, shall we?' and he goes into the barn, talking softly to Mary-Pat as she gurgles and coos. And I have that sudden thought again, that picture of myself here, in another place, in another life. I have to shake my head to dislodge it from my brain.

Only when we've selected our little menagerie, and he's pushing them gently into the crate I've brought, balancing on the wheels of the pram, does he say, 'Well, I suppose the cottage will be getting a bit small for you, once the baby comes along.'

'I suppose it will,' I agree, fighting a sense of weariness at the thought of four of us crammed into that tiny place.

'Why don't we take a look at my brother's place?'

I shake my head for a second. 'Why?'

He's taken aback. 'Well, because ... it's habitable anyway and it's got a nice patch of land, and I've been looking for a tenant for a while, truth to tell.' He runs a hand through his black thatch, which now stands upright on his head. He looks a bit lost and I feel sad that I've offended him in this way, when he's clearly doing me a favour. I'm sure he probably doesn't need a tenant for his brother's house.

'I'd love to see it, Sean. Thanks,' I say and he beams and says, 'We'll lead the way again, little lady, shall we?' He hasn't relinquished Mary-Pat and she's growing sleepy in his arms, her tiny thumb in her mouth, eyelids drooping. 'Here, let me take her,' I say and put her gently in the pram. She hardly protests before turning onto her side, the way she always does when she's going to sleep. Sean looks disappointed and sticks his head under the hood of the pram. 'Night, night, sleep tight,' he says and when he stands up again he blushes, as if it's not right for a man to fuss over a baby like that. But I think it's very endearing. He'll make a good father, I'm sure.

We chat about growing vegetables and what works best in the soil here, and about the finer points of hens, about which I confess I know nothing. 'You just have to handle them gently,' he says, 'and talk to them a bit, they like that.'

'I'll remember that.' I smile, as we walk up towards a rusting gate, over which a thick green arch of privet grows. The house is a plain two-storey farmhouse painted pale yellow, and it's regular in build, like the kind of shapes I used to draw as a child: a neat rectangle with a row of smaller rectangles inside for the windows and a larger one for the door, which is a faded, peeling red. It looks a little tired, as if someone hasn't loved it for a long time, and the garden is a neat lawn of green, devoid of any embellishment. 'I just keep it tidy for him. It needs a lick of paint, mind you, and the guttering needs to be fixed.'

'It's perfect,' I say. And I want to run all the way home to tell John-Joe, to look at his face when I tell him that I've found it now. My home. Our home.

7

Pius was in the cabbage-and-wax-smelling hallway of the parish house. He must be one of the few in Monasterard who'd never been in it. The thought made him smile for a second. He wondered what Mammy and Daddy would have made of it.

He and Rosie were ushered into Father Naul's office by Bridie O'Reilly, now bent almost double over a walking stick, a thick cardigan buttoned tightly over a blue floral dress, even though the heat in the house was sweltering. They must have the heating on, even in summer. Bridie must be in her nineties, Pius thought, following her through the door into a surprisingly modern room with a cream carpet and a new leather sofa and very little in the way of religious iconography. She'd always made a big deal about being the priest's housekeeper, bustling around the main street, a self-important look on her face, announcing to all and sundry that she was 'doing messages for Father Fathom'. Pius wondered what she made of Father Naul.

As if answering his question, she muttered, 'Ye'll have tea,' shooting the priest a disapproving look. Clearly, she wasn't his number-one fan.

'Indeed we will, Bridie, and thanks,' Father Naul replied, jollying her along. The old bat.

She turned to go out the door, but then stopped and, as if she'd remembered something, turned back again and shot Pius a look. 'Whose are you?'

'Whose what?'

'Who's kin?'

Jesus, you have a way of asking, Pius thought as he cleared his throat. 'John-Joe O'Connor, and my mother was—'

'I knew your mother,' Bridie interrupted, beaming. 'A fine woman she was. We were great friends, so we were.' She shook her head, and muttered, 'That fellow ...'

There was a long silence. That fellow indeed, Pi thought.

'And you're the baby, I suppose,' she said, darting a look at Rosie. It was funny, Pius thought, for a second the old lady looked as if she were afraid.

'Yes, that's right,' Rosie began, before Father Naul interrupted. 'That tea would be just lovely, Bridie, and biscuits if Father Fathom hasn't eaten them all.'

'Tea and biscuits,' she repeated, as if he'd asked for champagne and caviar, and then she was gone, the door banging behind her.

'You'll have to excuse Bridie. She has her ways,' Father Naul explained. 'Anyhow, I hear you're a great man for the fishing, Pius. I like to fish for trout myself, although of course it isn't the place for it. So I've been trying to perfect my roach-catching techniques to compensate.' He smiled, and the lines which were etched into his skin suddenly smoothed out, his steel-grey hair waving around his tanned face. He really did look like Sam Shepard. Pius could see why all the ladies at the wedding had been flirting with him.

'You need to know the canal better for roach,' Pius found himself saying. 'All the best spots are the ones only the locals know about.'

'Well, maybe you could show me a few of them some time.' Father Naul beamed.

Pius nodded and said of course he would, wondering what Daddy would have made of it, going out on a little jaunt with the parish priest. 'Religion is the opium of the masses' had been one of his favourite sayings, and every time he'd said it, it had been in the same self-congratulatory way, as if he'd been the very first person to think of it, not Karl Marx or whoever it was. Daddy, the little shit.

Father Naul was perching now on the edge of his desk, sleeves rolled up to reveal hairy, muscular forearms. He clearly wasn't a man for sitting behind a desk. Of course not, Pius thought. Sam Shepard didn't either. He was always on the back of a horse, and Pius could see Father Naul on one too, a battered cowboy hat on his head. He looked out of place in this sterile lunchbox of an office.

'So, Rosie, I've dug out the parish records that you asked for – 1981, I think, is that right?' and he leaned over and picked up a large red volume from his desk, opening it and scanning the contents, a frown of concentration on his face. 'Now, I just need to find the entry ... ah, here it is,' and he turned the book around to show them both, his index finger on the second column down, which had been filled in with an immaculate hand.

'See? Rose Michelle, daughter of Michelle Spencer and John-Joe O'Connor. And there's Pius, the godfather.'

Rosie looked at him with a puzzled expression on her face and then back at the register and finally back at him again.

Pius managed a smile. 'Believe it or not. Not sure how well I executed my pastoral duties at eight years of age. Or later, for that matter.' Especially as he could hardly be a spiritual guardian, what with him not being a Catholic. He never had understood why Rosie was the only one of them to be baptised — it was hardly as if Mammy and Daddy had found religion, now, was it?

'Oh, Pi.' She reached over and squeezed his hand, giving him a watery smile. She looked down at her shoes then and there was a little sniff.

Oh, Lord. 'C'mon, it's OK, Doodlebug. It'll be OK,' Pius said, and he looked meaningfully at Father Naul. 'It's all been a bit emotional …'

Father Naul nodded but said nothing further and Pius admired him for it, that, in spite of having officiated at a wedding which was now the talk of Monasterard, he was able to keep his mouth shut when needed. That he didn't feel the need to witter on about it being the Lord's will and all that nonsense, when the Lord had shag all to do with it.

She seemed to rally then, lifting her head and asking Father Naul, 'Who's the godmother?'

'Well, let's have a look … someone called Jasmine … I think,' he said. 'Hang on, I need my reading glasses.' And he rummaged around in his shirt pocket, producing a pair of battered-looking spectacles, which he perched on the end of his nose, looking down through them at the book. 'No … Frances. Frances O'Brien. Mean anything?'

Rosie shook her head. 'Never heard of her. Pi, you must remember,' and she looked at him hopefully.

God, Pius thought. Frances O'Brien. He hadn't thought about her in years. Who'd have thought that the woman who was now the life and soul of the parish council would have been an old hippy once — she'd been friends with Mammy and Daddy at that stage. He'd had a bit of a crush on her, if he remembered right. He used to like her because she smoked weed and didn't wear a bra. He'd spend hours watching her breasts move under whatever tiny top she was wearing, mesmerised by them, by the way they were soft and the nipples hard at the same time. It had kept him amused for that whole summer. But she smelled, too. He hadn't been so keen on that. And when she'd moved in with them that time — he'd been even less keen because he'd had to give her his bedroom and sleep on the sofa for two months. He'd had to box up his collection of stag beetles too, because she'd found them 'creepy'. He'd been delighted when he'd woken up one morning to find that she'd vanished.

'She was someone Mammy and Daddy knew at the time. She's still around, I think. Lives up the way.' He didn't see the need to explain any of the details. It didn't merit digging up after all this time.

'Oh.'

'Well, there you are, Rosie, mystery solved.' Father Naul smiled, a flash of white, even teeth. 'Does this put your mind at rest?'

Rosie nodded, thoughtful, before agreeing. 'Yes, thanks, Father Naul. I really appreciate your help.' But she seemed dazed, Pius thought, dazed and confused.

'C'mon, Doodlebug, let's go home.' Pius took control, shaking Father Naul firmly by the hand, promising to drop by to take him fishing some night and leading Rosie out of the parish centre and into his car, not saying anything until they reached the house, when he turned to say the words that he'd been composing in his mind all the way back from Monasterard. But she was fast asleep, slumped against the window of the car, her head propped up against her elbow.

He hesitated for a bit before deciding that he couldn't leave her in the car, and so he got out as quietly as he could and went around to the passenger side, opening the door gently so she didn't fall out and lifting her as carefully as he could. She weighed nothing in his arms, a little bird, and she didn't even wake, head nodding back on his elbow as he carried her through the front door and into the living room, where he nudged aside Sunday's paper with his foot and placed her gently down on the sofa. That should have been your husband, he thought, as he dragged Jessie's blanket out from under her feet. That should have been him, carrying you across the threshold. He felt a huge sadness for her then, sleeping on his sofa like a young child, sadness and irritation that she was like a boil on his skin that he just wanted to lance, to cut it away from his flesh, so that he was clean again. Clean and free.

He made himself lunch — packet tomato soup and a hunk of stale bread because Rosie wasn't around to lecture him about it — and sat at the kitchen table to read the newspaper. He looked forward to having a few moments' peace, but the second he sat down, he felt his eyelids begin to droop, resting his head on the table. When he woke up, sweaty and disorientated, a feeling of panic rose in his chest as the doorbell buzzed, a long, insistent ring.

He opened the door and stood stock still for a moment.

The Mermaid was standing there, holding the hand of a little boy in a pair of faded blue shorts, a red T-shirt with 'Ban the Bomb' on it and a pair of bright green Crocs. Her red hair was crammed into a horrible woolly hat with a Euro 2012 logo on it and she was wearing mismatched tracksuit bottoms and a top.

'Hi,' he managed.

She ignored the greeting. 'Is Rosie in?' And she looked behind him, as if Rosie might be lurking in the hall somewhere.

'Ehm, yeah, in the living room,' he said, standing back to let her in. 'Hi,' he said to the little boy.

'Oh, this is Dara,' the Mermaid said. 'How is she... after the visit to the priest?'

'Oh, you know ...' Pius said.

'No.' She shook her head.

'She's ... still a bit upset.' Jesus Christ. Her husband had left her, and she'd discovered that her father possibly wasn't her father. Upset just didn't cover it. Mind you, he could never admit it, the dart of happiness when the Yank's rental car had disappeared off up the towpath, two weeks after the wedding. Apparently, he was going back to the States to 'clear his head'. Leaving his wife to deal with the fallout. Some guy, he was. Pius hadn't asked Rosie what her plans were: he kept telling himself that it was because he didn't want to interfere, but really, it was because he didn't want to know — it was all far too messy for him.

'Right. I'll go up and see her then. Will you keep an eye on Dara?' She clumped off into the living room in her battered trainers.

Pius looked down at the child, wondering what on earth she meant by 'keep an eye'. Could he just go and have a cup of coffee and let the child out into the garden, or should he go with him? What did you do with a boy his age anyway?

He sighed and looked down at Dara uncertainly, about to suggest a walk, when Dara rescued him. 'My mum says you have hens.'

'I do.'

'Can I see them?'

Pius cleared his throat then and nodded in the direction of the garden. 'The hens are outside.'

'OK', the little boy said, and then he slipped his small hand into Pius's, looking up at him expectantly, as if to say, 'Lead the way.' The boy's hand felt odd in Pius's much larger one, so small and soft. It felt good, Pius realised. 'Right,' he said, more confidently, 'let's grab a bucket and we'll give them their breakfast. They'll be starving.' It was a lie – he didn't normally feed them after midday and they'd be half-asleep, but hens never say no, he thought.

Pius gave him Mabel to hold, a fine black speckled hen with a nice personality, who sat in Dara's arms and clucked appreciatively while Dara stroked her. 'She's very nice,' he said.

'She is. She's a gentle lady. Now Gwyneth over there, she's another kettle of fish altogether.'

Dara wrinkled his brow and looked over to where Pius was pointing at a small, brown hen who was scuttling around on the grass, an anxious look on her face. 'I saw her scare the fox once,' Pius said. 'Gave him the fright of his life, so she did.'

'How did she do that?' Dara looked up at him, eyes round.

'Well, it was early one morning, just before dawn. Norman wakes them every morning,' he nodded in the direction of the cockerel, 'but this morning there was a commotion in the henhouse, lots of fluttering and clucking and I knew something was wrong. So I tiptoed down the stairs,' Pius began, and then paused for dramatic effect.

'And then what happened?'

'Well, I've never seen anything like it. I saw him out the kitchen window, slinking around to the front of the henhouse, head bent low, and suddenly the door just burst open and she came at him, clucking and squawking and, I don't know what it was, but he turned tail and bolted over the field there towards the canal.' He didn't add that he'd also been standing by the gable wall, pointing an air rifle at the mangy beast. It sounded better that Gwyneth be the hero of the day — and she was a feisty girl, that was for sure.

'She looks very brave,' Dara said.

'She is. And because of her, I've never had a problem with a fox since. She's like Cerberus at the gates of Hades.' As he said it, he chastised himself. The child wouldn't have a clue about Greek mythology — they were all into computers and stuff nowadays.

But Dara nodded. 'Hmm, I know, Daddy told me that story. His name is Kevin and he lives in New York. He's coming to visit me soon because I'm seven. Do you think he can come and see your hens, Pius?'

I'd rather die, Pius thought, before managing a smile and a change of subject. 'Maybe we should call her Cerberus, what do you think?'

Dara shook his head and burst out laughing, and the sound was so sudden Pius started in fright. 'Oh, no, Pius, she's a girl, silly. Cerberus is a boy.'

'Of course. I'm such an eejit.' Pius smiled. 'Now, let's go and pick a few peas for tea. If you and your mum are staying, I'll have to do better than packet soup, which is what I normally have.'

'I like packet soup. Do you have Quick Soup? I like the tomato one, even though Mum says it's junk.'

'A man after my own heart,' Pius said, thinking as they walked back towards the house about how it must feel to be a child, finding things out for the first time. When everything was new and surprising and changed the way you thought about things for ever. And how you could look up to adults, the way this little fellow was looking up to him. It came as a shock to him, that someone would actually look up to him in this way. Him. A drug dealer. And it came as even more of a surprise when he remembered that he had looked up to Daddy in the same way once.

He remembered that Daddy had taken himself and Mary-Pat out into the back field when they were both children. He'd lifted them both onto the fence and said, 'Look up, and tell me, what do you see?'

They'd both been transfixed for a bit, looking up at the stars in the inky black sky. It was full of them, and a wisp of what looked like candyfloss that Daddy said was the Milky Way. He'd been talking about the planets. 'We can see Venus,' he'd said, pointing to the Evening Star, 'but why can't we see Mars or Mercury?'

'Because the sky's too small?' Pius had said. He'd thought that the sky was like a canvas, stretched over the earth, with not enough room to fit all the planets. Those that couldn't fit in would simply fall off the edge.

Daddy had laughed then, throwing his head back and roaring, the earring in his left ear flashing in the moonlight. The earring he wore because he was a gypsy, or so he told them, a Traveller whose family had wandered the roads of Donegal.

Then he'd reached out his hand and ruffled Pius's hair. 'The sky goes on forever, Pius, on and on into infinity. We're just hanging here, spinning around in space on our tiny planet.'

Pius hadn't been able to get his head around how the sky didn't end somewhere — didn't everything end somewhere? Wasn't there an end of the road, where things kind of piled up in a great big heap? It was bewildering and exciting at the same time. And the person who had told him about it all was Daddy, a Godlike figure who seemed to possess knowledge about just about everything. Maybe Dara thought about his father in the same way. And maybe that, too, would change, Pius thought, as Dara skipped ahead of him up the front path. And maybe that was why he'd never become a dad, because he didn't want to risk it, falling from grace. He didn't want his son to feel about him the way he felt about Daddy.

Pi still remembered the time Eoin Prendergast had called the house at three in the afternoon and asked Pius if he could come and collect Daddy. 'He's taken a little turn,' had been the man's explanation. Only thirteen, Pius knew the lingo: 'A little turn' could mean anything from a sugar low to a cardiac arrest, so he'd jumped into the car, which he barely knew how to drive, and roared off up the towpath, hoping to God Garda Kelly wasn't around to catch him — he was a stickler for illegal driving, probably because half the county had no licence.

When he'd pulled up at the door, bumping the car against the pavement before remembering to brake, Eoin Prendergast had been waiting, a cigarette clamped between his lips. He looked like his pub, Eoin, sagging and grey and dishevelled, a brown cardigan buttoned up over his substantial belly, his face unshaven. He had hair coming out of his nose and ears. Pius had thought he might vomit at the sight of it.

'He's in the kitchen,' and he'd nodded to the little laneway at the side of the pub. Pius had hurried into it and through the half-open door into the kitchen. He'd never been in the kitchen of Prendergast's. He'd had no idea they had one, considering the only food they served was ham sandwiches on white bread. Daddy had been lying on one of the big steel tables under the glare of a flickering striplight, entirely still, and for a second, Pius had thought he was dead. He'd been rooted to the spot, thoughts careering through his head — how would he organise the funeral, or should he bring him to hospital first. How would he break it to Mammy and would she be sad or pleased? Did that mean he was the head of the family now — did it all fall on his shoulders and how would he be able to manage ... and the final thought, that he almost didn't let himself think, thank God. Thank God it's all over.

'He was in mid-pint when he just keeled over,' Eoin had explained, breaking into his thoughts. 'You'd better take a closer look at him.' And he'd nodded in Daddy's direction.

Pius had crept over to take a look, his heart thumping in his chest — at which point his daddy gave a little snort, like a pig, and had opened his eyes. 'What the —? Where am I? Am I dead?'

Pius had let out a little scream, and the two of them had stared at each other for a few seconds, his father's face a mixture of alarm and rage. 'No, you're not, Daddy,' Pius had eventually managed.

'Just resting so,' Daddy had said, lying back down on the table, his eyes closing again.

It had taken four of them to manhandle him into the back of the Beetle, an audience gathering on the other side of the street. Pius felt the hot flush of embarrassment, and he'd wanted to just disappear into any available black hole.

'Are you driving that thing?' Eoin Prendergast had had the grace to assume a concerned expression on his face, but not the wit to get an adult to drive them both home. Instead, Pius had wobbled off up Main Street and over the humpback bridge, whereupon Daddy had slid sideways towards him and he'd had to push him back against the window, almost losing control of the car in the process. It would have been comical were it not so awful, Pius would later think. When Pius had got home, shoulders stiff with the tension of driving, Mammy had been standing on the doorstep, arms folded. She hadn't said a single word as he'd got out of the car, legs like jelly.

'He's in the car.' He'd nodded towards the Beetle, as if it were the most natural thing in the world for his father to need to be taxied home because he was in a coma at four in the afternoon.

'Make sure you throw a blanket over him,' had been her only words, and then she'd turned and gone inside, leaving Pius standing there, unsure what to do, Daddy snoring away in the car.

He used to call me a 'Mammy's boy', Pius remembered, because I liked to spend time with Mammy in the garden, because I liked to talk to her about propagation and the best ways of keeping weeds down. That was why Daddy didn't like me. Pius thought Daddy loved him, but knew for sure he didn't like him, because he'd sided with Mammy.

He tried to shake off that feeling while he made risotto for his guests for supper, hardly able to believe, as he stood there for a full half an hour stirring, that he was capable of such a thing. He'd found some arborio rice in the cupboard, which he supposed Rosie had bought, and had followed the instructions on the packet. He didn't have wine so used a glass of beer instead, but it didn't taste that bad. Rosie had even managed to praise him. 'Very nice, Pi. I didn't know you were such a good cook.'

'Thanks,' he said, chuffed.

Rosie seemed to be a bit brighter this evening. Maybe it was the visit from Daphne. She was sipping from a glass of the white elderflower cordial that the Mermaid had brought, even managing to smile at Pius's ridiculous attempts to make conversation. 'Honestly, Pi, who would have thought that once upon a time you couldn't stop talking? You were like a machine gun, spitting out words so fast no one could keep up. And remember, you just couldn't keep still.'

'Daddy used to make me sit on my hands at the dinner table and count to a hundred before he'd let me start my dinner, because I'd wolf it down so fast,' Pius said.

'What happened to you?' Daphne asked.

Pius leaned back in his chair, surprised. 'What do you mean, what happened to me?'

'Well, you're not like that now, are you?'

'No.' Jesus, you have a way of asking a question, he thought to himself.

'Why?'

Pius thought for a long time before answering. 'Because … I was unhappy. It made me ill in the end.'

He thought of the hospital corridor in St Loman's, a sudden flash of distemper yellow, a smell of Jeyes Fluid in his nostrils. It had been six months after Katy left when it had all stopped for him. He'd been worse than ever those previous few months, drinking till he couldn't stand up any more in the pub then pouring himself into Daddy's old Beetle and roaring up the road, weaving all the way home along the towpath. And then he'd take all his clothes off and jump into the water, at three o'clock in the morning, before deciding that what he really needed to do was paint the living room, while listening to Daddy's old Count John McCormack records, with the water of the canal still dripping off him and not a stitch of clothing on him.

Then he'd woken up one morning and found that he couldn't keep his thoughts in a straight line. That they'd all got jumbled up in his head. One thought didn't follow another any more and no matter how he tried, they just wouldn't join up. He'd sat bolt upright in bed, panicky, almost hysterical, trying to pull the thoughts together and lay them out in a line, like a row of dominoes, but they just kept jumbling up. His hands had shaken as he'd pulled on his jeans, an old sweatshirt. He'd said the words out loud to himself, as proof that he was still functioning: 'jeans', 'sweatshirt', naming each item as he put it on. 'Car,' he'd said to himself then. 'Drive.'

But he hadn't driven to Mary-Pat's — he hadn't trusted himself — he'd cycled instead. He'd raced along the towpath in the lashing rain, the pedals slippery under his feet. He'd arrived, soaking wet, just standing there on Mary-Pat's doorstep. He couldn't open his mouth to Melissa, who'd opened the door. In the end, he'd managed, 'Help.'

Melissa had taken one look at him and yelled, 'Mum,' then bolted into the kitchen.

Mary-Pat had come out then, in her pink dressing gown. 'Pius? What is it? What's the matter?'

He hadn't been able to answer. His lips had moved, but the words wouldn't come out. He'd tried, 'Thoughts,' and then pointed to his head.

'Your thoughts, I know,' his sister had said soothingly and pulled him towards her, cradling his head as she hugged him tight. 'You poor cratur. Poor Pius.'

And he'd sobbed then, great gulping wails that didn't even seem to come from inside him. He'd been like an animal, moaning and wailing. 'I'm finished, Mary-Pat, finished,' he'd yelled, as she patted him and tutted.

'Indeed and you are not. Now, let's go inside out of the rain.'

He'd had to lay his head on her kitchen table then, the oilcloth cool under his cheeks, which seemed to be burning. He'd closed his eyes for a while, letting the murmurs between Mary-Pat and PJ roll over him. And when Mary-Pat had sat down beside him, the smoke from her cigarette reaching his nostrils, she'd said, 'Pi? I think you need a rest. Would you go into St Loman's for a few days?'

He hadn't even lifted his head from the table, just nodded and said, 'Yes.' And when he'd come out again, six weeks later, he'd been quiet and had remained so ever since.

'Ill? What kind of ill?' Daphne was leaning towards him now, the red of her hair glowing in the sunlight from the kitchen window.

Pius shrugged. 'Hospital ill.'

She nodded. 'And you recovered.' A statement, not a question.

'You know, I don't think I did. Not really,' Pius said, getting up and gathering up the plates. 'I just … returned, I suppose.' As if he'd come back from some conflict, battered and bruised. From a war zone of his own making. And then, signalling that the conversation was over, he said, 'Dara, let's go and pick some veg for you and Mum to take home,' and he extended his hand, enjoying the feeling when Dara slipped his hand into Pius's. He squeezed it gently.

It wasn't quite dusk and they were still in the vegetable patch when Daphne called from the house, her voice echoing down the garden. 'Time to go home, Dara,' Pius said, standing up and clutching the small of his back as he did so. Jesus, that hurt.

She was waiting for them both, leaning against the back doorframe, scratching her head through the hat, and he wondered if she knew just how horrible it was, and just how beautiful she looked in spite of it, with that pale skin and her eyes, which seemed to capture the light. 'Rosie's gone for a walk with Jessie,' she offered. 'I left her to it.'

'Oh, right.' There was a long pause, during which Dara ran around the side of the house in search of the hens again.

'It's not true you know,' Pius said. She looked puzzled for a moment and he realised he'd need to elaborate. 'What Daddy said. The trouble is, Rosie seems to believe it. She's been like a dog with a bone. I can't persuade her to leave it alone.'

'Well, she needs to find the truth, and when she does, she'll stop,' Daphne said, as if it was the most reasonable thing in the world.

Jesus, Pius thought, glaring at Daphne.

'Look, it's family stuff, Daphne, and you're best off out of it.'

She just shrugged, her lovely red curls catching the light.

'Family stuff,' she said blankly. 'Maybe you're just blaming her for everything that's happened in your family. It's not her fault, you know.'

You'd be right, he thought, not that he'd give her the satisfaction. 'Thanks for the psychoanalysis,' he said shortly. 'Will you see yourself out?'

'Fine.' She glared at him. 'Whatever.' She shouted into the garden. 'Dara, time to go.'

They both stood there in complete silence, Pius thinking that if he ever had to see the woman again, it'd be too soon. But then she started cramming her gorgeous hair into that hideous hat and it made him want her all over again.

8

*M*ary-Pat peered in through the window past the Lotto stickers and the small ads written out on little cards, advertising cattle feed and baby-minding and Spanish lessons. She'd begun to come up every day and just sit there, in the Pajero, waiting for a glimpse of that puff of blonde hair, watching to see how the woman talked to the customers, if she was like that with all of them or only with PJ. Joking and laughing, a flash of teeth ringed with bright red lipstick, that peroxide blonde quiff bobbing up and down as she bent over the till or reached over to the cigarette machine to extract a packet of cigarettes for a customer.

Mary-Pat made sure that PJ didn't see her, parking across the road from the shop so that he'd have had to look behind him to spot her, which he never did. Too intent on looking ahead, she thought, to what might be about to happen. Even so, when he appeared, as he did every day at a quarter to one, pulling up in front of the door in the little van and getting out, his big chunky frame far too big for the van, she'd duck down behind the wheel in case he might catch a glimpse of her. Because if he did and asked her what, exactly, she thought she was doing, she'd have struggled to find an answer. 'I'm checking to see if you're having an affair with that young one at the counter.' No, it sounded too final, too bleak for her even to contemplate. It was bad enough thinking that he was making a point of going there every single day, before he came home for his lunch. That he'd arrive home to her barely fifteen minutes later, barrelling in the door in his Kildare jersey, a big smile on his red face, 'Howya, love, what's for lunch?' And she'd want to punch him or to pick the plate of quiche and salad up and throw it in his face, with a yelled, 'Here's your effin' lunch. Why don't you shove it where the sun don't shine?' Oh, how she longed to do it: her fingers would itch as she handed him the plate, but because she was so used to keeping bad feelings at bay, she would no more have thrown a quiche at him than flown to the moon. It wasn't her style. Instead, they'd both sit there, the drone of the one o'clock news in the background, and make polite conversation, the sound of forks and knives on plates punctuating the background chatter about burning the bondholders.

And the worst thing was, he was happier now than she'd seen him in a long time. She supposed she had Marilyn Monroe at the minimarket to thank for that. Until just three weeks before, PJ would have slunk into the kitchen, a wary look on his face, a muttered 'Thanks, love' as she'd hand him his ham salad or hard-boiled eggs, shooting her anxious glances as he forked the food into his mouth, but saying nothing for fear of upsetting her. Ever since the wedding, the poor fellah had been able to do or say nothing right. Now, though, he was positively chatty, regaling her with stories of crazy Hughie O'Leary and his order for half a ton of maggots, because he thought they'd make great fertiliser for his vegetable patch. 'Can you imagine, MP, them all crawling over his tomato plants?' PJ had nearly choked on his lunch, he'd been laughing so much, and it had been all Mary-Pat could do to raise a half-smile, to look as if she were enjoying the story when all she really wanted to do was to go upstairs and lock herself into her room and never come out. Oh, she'd been such a fool. A silly fool. She thought of the night he'd come back with the damned air freshener, and she felt it again, that hot blush of shame and rage.

She'd tried to talk to him once. She'd told him that she'd gone to see the doctor, deliberately waiting until he was watching *Grand Designs* before spitting it out, and being grateful that he only half-noticed. 'Grand, love, that's good,' he said, his eyes fixed on a converted barn in Buckinghamshire. 'Did she give you anything for the anxiety?'

'She did – half a kilo of cocaine,' she'd said, to see if he was really listening.

'Oh, good, great,' he'd said, continuing to look at the screen, patting her absently on the knee. 'I'm sure it'll have you feeling better in no time.'

She'd had to laugh then, a short bark of laughter, at which he'd turned and looked at her curiously. 'What's so funny?'

'Oh, nothing, love. I'll stick the kettle on,' she'd said and got up and left the room before he'd notice the look on her face. Fuck him, she'd thought as she filled the kettle and banged it down on the counter. Fuck him. I don't need him. I can manage just fine on my own. Sure, isn't that what I've been doing for the last while anyway?

ALL THAT I LEAVE BEHIND

How had it come to this, Mary-Pat wondered. How had they both gone from not being able to get enough of each other to ships passing in the night?

She could still remember the day he'd called up for her. It was burned on her mind. She was twenty-six and she'd thought her chance had passed for another life, that she'd be stuck here for ever. She'd been standing over Rosie, trying to coax some sums out of her, trying to resist the urge to clatter her around the head, when the doorbell had rung. She couldn't imagine who would be calling to the house — no one ever called, apart from the postman — so she hadn't even opened the door. She'd just yelled through the closed door, 'Who is it?'

A throat had been cleared outside and a voice had said, 'PJ.'

There had been a long pause while Mary-Pat had racked her brains, trying to remember who PJ could be, and then the voice had said, 'From the tackle shop? You came over last week with an order for Pius.'

Christ almighty. Mary-Pat had done a little spin in the hallway, like a dog trying to settle in its bed, going round in a circle until she'd managed to calm herself, pulling off her apron and patting down her hair. She'd opened the door and he was standing there, in jeans and an open-necked shirt, the top of his chest burnt bright red from the sun. He'd clearly showered recently, because a smell of shower gel wafted across to her and his red-gold hair was still damp. He was holding a box in his hand.

'I've some groundbait for Pius,' he'd said. 'He ordered it a while back, so I thought I'd drop it down. Special delivery.' He'd smiled.

Mary-Pat had swallowed and had opened her mouth before realising that she didn't know what to say. It was an unfamiliar feeling, because she wasn't often lost for words, but something about this man made her tongue-tied. And when he'd asked her out, she hadn't known what to say. No one had ever asked her out before. He'd blurted, 'I wondered if you'd fancy the session going on in O'Dwyers?'

'Oh, no,' Mary-Pat had found herself replying, 'I don't drink at all. I've never been in one of the pubs down the town.' It had been one of Mammy's things. That they weren't like the rest of them in this place, falling out of the pubs at all hours. By 'the rest of them' they knew she'd meant Daddy. Mary-Pat had stuck to it, even though, with Mammy not there, she could have done whatever she liked.

He'd blushed a bright crimson, sticking his hands in his pockets and examining his feet in their blue Gola trainers. And then he'd mumbled, 'I actually meant the trad session. There's one on a Sunday afternoon. You don't have to drink. You can just have tea or coffee.'

'Oh. Are you asking *me*?' Mary-Pat had pointed to herself, as if there was someone else in the vicinity that he might be asking, someone lurking in the bushes. When he'd blushed and looked down at his feet, she'd felt sorry for having made him work for it. Are you cracked, Mary-Pat, she told herself. For God's sake, say yes. 'Because if you are, that'd be grand.'

He'd looked up then and a grin had split his freckled face. 'It would? That's great. I'll be down so on Sunday. Around two.'

She'd shrugged then, as if she wasn't that bothered, and had turned on her heel. 'See you then,' she'd said, in what she'd hoped was a casual voice, a voice that disguised her excitement, her disbelief that there was someone out there who wanted *her*.

And that was it. He was the man for her. The first time they'd done it had been in his place, on the sofa, just a week after that first date, bouncing up and down on the thing until she thought the springs would break. They hadn't even bothered climbing the stairs to bed, just shedding their clothes and climbing onto the sofa. She'd never enjoyed herself so much. God, she'd thought after, collapsing into his arms, both of them succumbing to fits of the giggles, what the hell had she been missing? Why hadn't she known about this before?

'Mary-Pat, you're a fantastic girl,' PJ had said, burying his head in her breasts and making loud farting noises. 'All that lovely soft flesh. I think I'm getting a hard-on again,' he'd moaned.

She'd burst out laughing.

Later, when she'd discovered that she was pregnant with John-Patrick, she supposed they shouldn't have, really. Didn't that make her a bit cheap? But they couldn't keep their hands off each other, and anyway, PJ had every intention of making an honest woman of her. He was the one for her, and she'd known it the minute he'd turned up at her door, box of groundbait in hand.

And better than everything else, they made each other laugh. Great belly laughs as they watched re-runs of *Fawlty Towers* or comedy videos that his friend had got for him, bootlegs but the quality wasn't bad. They'd watch them and fall around with laughter and then, if the fancy took them, just make love on the sofa, lying there after, telling each other stories.

It was that she missed the most, she realised now, the cuddles and the close times. And the woman she used to be.

She hadn't breathed a word about PJ's fancy woman to anyone, for shame. Not even to her therapist. She couldn't even believe it, that she had such a thing, even as she'd thought the words: 'my therapist'. It sounded like something Junie would say, something else she was prepared to waste her money on when she wasn't having colonic irrigations and that kind of shite, pun not intended. His name was Graham and he was from England — at least, judging by his accent; he wasn't from Naas, that was for sure. He was a slight man, whose outfits seemed to be composed of various shades of the colour beige.

He'd never mentioned where he was from, as it happened. Never said anything, in fact, or at least very little. It had taken her a while to get used to it, the way he'd just sit there, waiting, when she arrived.

He'd only asked her one really difficult question, at the very first session: 'Why are you here, Mary-Pat?' It was an obvious one, of course, but she'd been flummoxed. Why exactly am I here? she'd thought, as she'd examined the pile on his expensive-looking beige carpet. 'Well, I've been having these panic attacks, at least that's what the doctor calls them, you know, Jennifer on the Dublin Road ...' she'd begun, trying not to think of the huge wall of grey water that rose up in front of her, the feeling that she had that she was drowning, every time it happened. And it happened a lot these days. Eventually, three weeks after the wedding, she'd been able to bear it no longer and had trudged up to see Jennifer, mainly because she was new to the place, unlike Dr Meade, who knew every last thing about her. 'And she thought it might be the stress, you know, what with Daddy — my father — in a home and the kids growing up and all that ...'

As she said the words, Mary-Pat knew that they were true, strictly speaking, but she also knew that they weren't the whole truth. How to explain to Graham that feeling she'd had, ever since the wedding, that her whole life had been turned upside down, that everything she'd believed about herself no longer made sense, after Daddy had said what he'd said. I'm the carer, the one who looks after everyone, she'd thought. I didn't want the job, but I got it and I did it well, and I thought it counted for something. Only now did she understand that it had all been a waste. Caring for someone who didn't deserve it, making that daily pilgrimage to St Benildus's, *Racing Post* in hand, like an eejit. She'd gone in to see Daddy for a couple of weeks after the wedding, telling herself that he still needed her, that if she didn't go, he'd miss her. But that wasn't true. She hadn't been to see Daddy in an age now, but she couldn't go there, she just couldn't. She needed time, time to work things out, and she knew that he'd only muddle up her feelings by making her love and hate him at the same time.

To think, she'd put ... that man before her own sister, had banished her from her life, for what? So that she could keep a lie intact?

Graham was like a bloodhound, she had to give him that. He'd sniffed out the lie, interrupting her, politely but firmly. 'Yes, but why are you here?' He hadn't been impatient or annoyed, just smiled encouragingly when Mary-Pat had stopped in her tracks and looked at him blankly. Shite. The game's up, she'd thought.

'I'm not sure what you mean ...' she'd ventured. He hadn't offered any explanation, just a shrug of the shoulders. They'd spent the next half an hour in complete silence, while Mary-Pat covertly examined the nice pictures on his wall and admired the tasteful wallpaper with its subtle print, the exotic statues lined up on his bottom bookshelf.

It'd be nice to have a lifestyle like Graham's, she'd thought, as she'd settled herself into the expensive-looking leather sofa, where everything looked as if it had cost real money, not a cheap imitation of it. She wouldn't want to be like Junie, mind, that was taking it too far, but just quiet taste that looked as if it had cost just enough, with a few touches of the foreign to make it look as if she'd travelled. She'd wondered where he'd got the pretty carved masks on the wall from, with their round, painted eyes and funny smiles: the home store in Kildare Village might have some. Of course, she'd only be pretending that she'd travelled — herself and PJ having ventured as far as Lanzarote the sum total of once when PJ had been flush and they fancied something different to their usual week by the sea in Wexford —

'Mary-Pat, time's up.' Graham's voice had been gentle, but she'd still jumped in fright.

'What? But I've only just arrived,' she'd begun.

'Actually, we've been here fifty minutes.'

'We have? But we haven't discussed anything, like my panic attacks or my family or what have you.'

Graham had nodded. 'Well, we have next week. Maybe you can think about the question I asked you in the meantime?' And he'd got up then and Mary-Pat realised that she would have to, too.

But the funny thing was, Mary-Pat thought about that question for the rest of the week, when she was making the dinner or walking the dog or pretending to listen to that eejit Imelda at the minimarket, going on about the weather and everyone who might be sick or dying in Monasterard.

She even thought about it when she went for a power walk with the girls — her first in ages — and only half-listened to the gossip and chatter as they strode along, out past the creamery and left at Sean O'Reilly's, her eyes flicking over the outline of Pius's roof as they crossed the bridge over the canal and then turned left, following a narrow path at the bottom of Sean's field of corn, now ripe and golden after the hot summer.

The stalks were a dull, sludgy brown, the same colour as the earth to which they would return, and the cobs a rich, buttery yellow. Mary-Pat could taste the sweet kernels in her mouth as she walked past, imagined eating them with a nice slab of melted butter, never mind that they stuck in your teeth. The other two, Mary-Lou and Mary-Pat's oldest friend, Bridget, were chattering away about Christmas, of all things, and Mary-Pat tuned out for a few seconds, enjoying the smell of the rich brown earth and the damp grass. Autumn had always been her favourite season.

'Did you hear about Frances O'Brien? She's running for the town council. She came around the other week, canvassing,' Mary-Lou said. 'She's a fierce holy-Joe, so she is — or should that be "Josephine".' She chuckled.

At the sound of Frances O'Brien's name, Mary-Pat suddenly tuned back in again. Rosie had been all gung-ho about seeing the woman after she'd dragged Pi to the parish house. Even the thought of it made Mary-Pat's heart nearly stop in her chest. She wasn't sure how she could prevent it, how she could spare poor Rosie the pointless visit, because Mary-Pat knew it would be pointless. Frances O'Brien wasn't about to tell her anything, not any time soon.

At the mention of the name, Bridget shot Mary-Pat a look and said vaguely, 'Is that so? Well, it'll be nice to have a woman's touch on the council. I've had enough of that fat Pat Mooney with his sweating and his greasy handshake. Gives me the creeps, that fellow does.'

Thank you, Bridget, Mary-Pat thought, as her friend tried to move the subject away from Frances O'Brien.

'Oh, he's some class of mover and shaker, the same Pat Mooney,' Mary-Lou agreed, taking the bait. 'God knows what he gets up to half of the time, and that's not even the politics — did you hear, he was supposed to have bribed John-Paul O'Sullivan to get the Lidl built on the Dublin Road. "Bringing Jobs to Monasterard" — bringing brown envelopes, more like.'

'Oh, be careful, Mary-Lou.' Mary-Pat laughed. 'He might sue you for defamation of character if he hears you, and you know he has eyes and ears everywhere.'

Mary-Lou was off now, cheeks reddening with indignation. She was a bit excitable, was Mary-Lou. 'If I thought I could knock the so-and-so off his perch, I'd even vote for that woman, in spite of all her holy-moly. She asked me if I believed in the power of prayer — can't see what that has to do with voting, but sure it could be worse. Anything's better than Fat Pat. Do you know, there's a rumour going around that he's visiting that young one at the minimarket every night. Can you imagine? He leaves the wife at home and drives up Main Street, bold as brass, and then pulls in to the shop in broad daylight. Doesn't seem to care who sees him.'

Mary-Pat's ears were aflame, her throat tightening as she dropped ever so slightly behind Mary-Lou so that she wouldn't have to walk beside her. She didn't want her to see the expression on her face. She wasn't stupid, Mary-Lou, she'd know something was up. And then the story would be all over town.

'Who is she anyway? Haven't seen her around here before. Is she a blow-in or what?' Bridget asked, oblivious.

'Foreign,' Mary-Lou said, nodding her head as if that explained everything. 'I tell you, ever since she got the job, the lads have been flocking to that minimarket like bees to honey. Men: sure they're pathetic, they're so obvious.' And then she turned. 'Mary-Pat, are you not able to keep up?'

Mary-Pat saw her chance and pretended to huff and puff a bit, putting her hands on her hips and stopping for a few seconds, as if to draw breath. 'You know, girls, I think I'll call it a day. I'm knackered. I'll cut back along the canal and go into Pi for a bit. I'll be better able for it next time,' and she turned with what she hoped was a cheery wave and bolted for the safety of home. Christ, it was worse than she thought. Her husband was just a fool, a complete and utter fool. And she was a worse one to let him away with it. She'd have to do something about it, she thought, something that would make him sit up and take notice.

In the meantime, though, there was that question. The answer had only occurred to her when she was back in Graham's sitting room the next day, looking out the window at the trees, their leaves now russet and yellow. They'd been sitting there in silence for a full twenty minutes, Graham perched on a cream armchair, like a bird, eyes bright, Mary-Pat half-disappearing into his squashy sofa, when she said, 'I've thought about your question.'

He didn't say anything, just gave her that watery smile, and when the urge to beat him over the head with one of those masks had passed, she said, 'Do you know, my husband is seeing another woman?'

He raised an eyebrow and leaned forward slightly in the chair. He cleared his throat and said, 'I see.'

'Yes, this blonde young … young woman at the minimarket.' It sounded so silly when she said it out loud, as if she were hanging around at the till in a pair of denim cut-offs, the way they did in the movies, offering people fill-ups in a sultry southern accent, instead of behind the counter wearing a green check pinny and doling out breakfast rolls. But Mary-Pat knew that appearances could be deceptive – she'd seen it often enough with Daddy.

Graham said nothing, merely nodded, and Mary-Pat took this as a signal to continue. 'He goes in to see her every day at lunchtime ...'

'How do you know?'

'Because,' Mary-Pat cleared her throat as the hot flush of shame crept up her neck, 'because I follow him.'

Graham's face betrayed no evidence of judgement as he asked, 'And what do you do then?'

'I wait outside in the car and I watch through the window.'

His features softened and Mary-Pat thought she saw an expression that looked suspiciously like pity on his face. 'You don't have to feel sorry for me,' she said.

'Is that what you think?'

'What?'

'That I feel sorry for you.'

'You have a look on your face.'

'What kind of look?'

'A look like —' and Mary-Pat did as polite an imitation as she could manage of his sympathetic gaze, which, by the look on his face, he seemed to find terribly amusing, the flicker of a grin twitching at the corners of his mouth.

'Do I look that bad?' He half-smiled.

'You're all right,' Mary-Pat said gruffly, looking down at her shoes. She had never been as mortified in her whole life. She was used to speaking her mind and not giving two shits about it, but this was different. She didn't want to upset the man, to cause offence. He seemed so fragile, as if the smallest thing would make him disappear in a puff of beige smoke.

'It must be a very busy place, the minimarket,' Graham said neutrally.

'Oh, God, yes, sure the whole town goes in there, the Centra at the other end is too expensive altogether.'

'Aha.' And then, as if he'd only just thought of it, 'So would there not be other people going in and out, as well as your husband?'

'Well, yes, I suppose ...'

'Particularly at lunchtime?'

'Are you saying that I'm imagining it?' The cheek of it, Mary-Pat thought as she attempted to pull herself upright on the sofa.

He smiled, and his brown eyes were soft. 'No, Mary-Pat. I'm not.'

'Because I'm not, you know,' Mary-Pat huffed, crossing her arms as best she could, given that she was half-buried in a cream sofa. 'I know what I saw.'

'I just think that you should talk to him.'

Mary-Pat shook her head, tears blurring her vision as she reached in her handbag for a tissue, to find that a box was gently pushed under her nose. 'Thanks.' She blew her nose, honking into the tissue, trying to collect herself. 'Look, I want to talk to him: it's just that I have no idea where to begin. It's not just him going to the minimarket, it's just ... she makes him laugh. I can see it through the window. She says something and he throws his head back and roars – I can hear him from the Jeep. And it really upsets me, because he used to laugh like that with me. He used to find me funny.' And sexy and gorgeous, all of that, she thought, not knowing if Graham was quite ready for her sex life just yet. There were some things you couldn't discuss with a strange man, she thought. 'It kills me, knowing that I'm not enough for him.'

Graham leaned forward onto his knees, the fawn of his jumper crinkling as he did so. There was another long silence, after which he said, 'Have you ever felt you weren't enough for someone before?'

Mary-Pat shook her head, puzzled. 'What do you mean?'

'I mean, is this the first time you've felt like this, that you're not enough?'

Mary-Pat opened her mouth but no words came out, and so she shut it and then opened it again, like a goldfish. She shifted slightly on the sofa and looked at her feet in their white bulky trainers, at her legs in their navy tracksuit bottoms, so solid, so strong, as if they anchored her to the ground.

'No,' she finally said, her voice no more than a whisper.

There was a long silence, and when she looked up, Graham was looking at her expectantly. She sighed and reached down into her handbag and pulled it out, the shell. It filled her hand, its matt black surface marked with bumps and craters. She turned it over and looked in to the lovely mother-of-pearl centre. It felt warm in her hand, solid. 'My mammy gave me this,' she said, and when Graham didn't reply, she added, 'I never knew about it until a few weeks ago. All these years, I thought she'd left without a single word. I could never make sense of it, you know, the way she left like that. But she didn't. She left me a message.'

'What kind of a message, Mary-Pat?'

'I don't know,' Mary-Pat said. 'I suppose I'll have to find out.' And with that, she felt the tears come, a tidal wave of them, which she didn't have the will to stop. So she just let them come, flowing down her face and onto her hands, splashing onto the surface of the shell, then sliding off. She didn't even bother reaching for a tissue or wiping them away, she just waited, wondering as she did if they would ever stop, or if she would simply cry for ever.

June 1974

Michelle

The funny thing is that it was only when we moved to the house, the place I'd imagined so often in my dreams, that things began to go wrong. That the unhappiness began to take a grip on John-Joe. The unhappiness and the fear. I suppose it's hard not to succumb to it when you suddenly realise that you're not living in a dream any more. When the reality is ten draughty rooms that need heating, three tiny children that need feeding and a vegetable patch that stubbornly refuses to yield more than a few rotten potatoes. How ironic that it was the soil in the old hovel that produced the best crops; this stuff is awful: big hard lumps of clay that stay waterlogged and are impossible to dig. John-Joe says that it's because we're closer to the canal so the soil is damp, and I've managed to settle it now, but it's taken me almost two years of hard work, adding compost and not over-digging. I have a fine crop of leeks and cabbages laid down now and even garlic, and I've sewn some hardy lettuces, including lamb's lettuce, under a big sheet of polythene.

I'm not a fool and I know that we can't live on lettuce over the winter, so I've got a little job at Sean O'Reilly's; he says it's because he could really do with a hand, 'and you have a gift for the land', but I think he's just being kind. He can see how difficult things are, how hard it is to keep afloat; honestly, sometimes when I wake up on a dark winter morning, my breath misting into the bedroom, I wonder if I really want to face the day at all. Sometimes the weight of it just pins me to the bed, the sense that if some little thing fails, we'll starve, but then I reason with myself that at least I'm living the life I've chosen. I'm totally free, and if this is the price of freedom, well, I'll just have to pay it.

After I've done my morning jobs, I leave the babies with John-Joe, kissing him on the top of his head as they clamber over him while he sits in front of the range, feet up, cigarette in hand, and I try to suppress the flicker of resentment that he can sit here, relaxed as you like, while there are logs to be chopped for the fire and potato drills to be dug. But he's a good father, I know that. He loves the babies and he just seems to know how to talk to them, how to get down on the floor on all fours and let them climb all over him, while I feel myself quickly grow bored of it; he doesn't mind spending hours in the one spot on the canal with them in their tiny little wellies as they dig around in the mud and pick up snails and worms between finger and thumb. Only Pius seems to try him. He doesn't like his son's restless nature, the way he learned to pull himself up and over the bars of his cot as soon as he learned to stand up. 'That child was sent to try me,' he'd often say. Ironic, I thought, seeing as he resembles you to a tee.

I put on my wellies and I walk the thirty yards or so and push the gate into Sean's yard and, as I do so, I feel my heart lift. A whole afternoon to talk about plants and hens and seedlings; to pick up a fluffy hen and to feel her little body in my hands, as her head gently turns to one side and she fixes me with a beady eye; to help Sean fill the rows of feeding troughs and to check their claws for any sign of disease. And then, when the work is done, to follow him into the kitchen and munch on the batch of scones I left in the range to stay warm, and to drink tea and to talk about world events, the end of the war in Vietnam, the boat people and how terrible their suffering is. Sean is full of curiosity about the life we're leading; he asks me the kinds of questions I should probably have asked myself. Like how we plan eventually to do without money at all. He scratches his head. 'Do the ESB accept eggs in payment of bills?'

'No.' I laugh. 'John-Joe's working on a generator at the moment that runs on diesel oil, which is much cheaper than electricity.' At least, he says he is. He pulls out the big rolls of wallpaper which he found behind the wardrobe in the bedroom, on the back of which he's drawn elaborate plans which look rather like Leonardo's drawings for some of his gadgets. I pray that he knows what he's doing. And I pray that he finishes the job this time.

'I'm thinking of getting some livestock,' I say then.

He thinks for a bit. 'Well, a cow would be a bit of a challenge just yet, with the milking and all; and you'd be needing the vet every so often — the badgers are a divil for passing on TB, and there's brucellosis and ringworm — but you'd get all the milk and cheese you need.'

'I was thinking of a couple of goats, actually,' I say. 'They produce milk too and they're easier to mind.'

'As long as you don't mind them eating all the crops you've lovingly tended.' He smiles. 'And the stink of them; and then there's the slaughter, I suppose ...'

'The slaughter?' I turn to him and I see that he's grinning at me. 'You're teasing me.'

'Well, I am and I amn't,' he says. 'If you get any kind of livestock, you have to be prepared for that possibility. I used to keep a few pigs myself, and it nearly killed me to slaughter them because they're intelligent creatures. I could see it in their eyes, the day I was going to do it. They just knew.' He sighed. 'But that's the way of the land and you have to accept that.'

'I didn't think you'd be soft-hearted about it, Sean. I thought you farmers were all far too practical for that.' I smile.

'Well, maybe I'm more soft-hearted than you think.' And he smiles and his eyes crinkle up at the sides and I get the sense that he likes me, maybe more than he should. And I know I should feel guiltier about it than I do. I should probably make more of my status, drop John-Joe's name into the conversation more, but I tell myself that I'm making money to support my family, accepting the few eggs that Sean hands me or the sack of spuds that he says is just going to waste, and giving him an extra big smile and seeing his eyes melt. He's a friend, and friends are hard to come by in this life.

'You'll make some woman a fine husband,' I say now, watching his face flush a livid red. He doesn't answer me, just fills another cup of tea from the pot on the range, and I know that I've offended him in some way, making light of his feelings. I'm about to apologise, when he says, 'I'll find out about the goats, if you like. Some mad eejit or other will have a pair, I'm sure.' And before I can answer, he's gone out the door to the henhouse. When I leave, he's still there, the door closed. I don't open it to shout goodbye, the way I normally do.

When I come home, the kids are sitting up having their tea, little hands grasping carrots and slices of apple, the bread I made that morning. John-Joe is sitting at the table, and opposite is a woman I've never seen before, a girl. She's pretty, with long brown hair and a dusting of freckles on her nose. She's also young, sixteen if she's a day. I have no idea what she's doing in my kitchen. There's no reason for her to be here.

'Hi,' I say.

She blushes and mutters something into the cup of tea sitting in front of her.

'This is Aileen, Paddy Mitchell's girl. She came down to see about giving us a hand with the kids,' John-Joe says. 'Is that right, Aileen?' and he winks and she blushes again, but I catch the look he gives her then, a sly flash of the eye that makes my stomach flip. Oh, I think. There's something about that look that I don't like. All I know, and I can't even voice it in words, is that it isn't the kind of look a man of John-Joe's age should be giving a girl of hers. I feel queasy, and I need this girl to leave.

'Well, that's a great idea,' I manage, 'but we'd probably need to have a think about it to see if we can afford it. I'll discuss it with my husband, and then we'll be in touch, Eileen, is that OK?' The mispronunciation of her name is deliberate, and as I say it, 'Eileen', she winces. She opens her mouth and I know she's going to correct me and I cut her off. 'We need to put the babies to bed now, so let me show you out,' I say brightly, lifting the thin coat she's draped over the chair, a child's coat, in my hand and leading her out to the hall. The girl clearly has no choice but to follow me, but not before saying something under her breath to John-Joe. I don't hear his reply.

I watch her walk down the path to the gate, her shoulders hunched, her hair flying behind her in the wind. And when I'm sure she's gone, I shut the front door with a bang and stride back into the kitchen. The two cups of tea are still on the table, barely cold, and when I see them, I can't help it, the words just come rushing out of my mouth. 'Why was that girl here, in my house?'

He blusters at first. 'What the fuck are you on about?'

I nod at the teacup.

'For God's sake,' he protests. 'I was trying to help you. I can see how much the kids take out of you and I thought we could do with a hand, that's all.' But he doesn't quite catch my eye, turning instead to rummage in his jacket pocket for his cigarettes.

'She's too young for you,' I say quietly, turning to put the kettle on the hot plate of the range.

He tuts, puffing smoke out through his teeth. 'You know, that's rich, coming from you,' he says. 'With your boyfriend across the way.' I turn around because his voice is suddenly loud and Mary-Pat looks up from her tea, eyes round. She looks as if she's going to cry.

I feel the rage grip me then, a sudden wave of it. 'I'm earning money to put food on the table,' I hiss. I go to my purse and empty it out onto the table with a clatter of coins. 'Which is more than I can say for you.'

His eyes flash and he grabs hold of the edge of my jumper, pushing his face into mine. 'Is that right now? The boyfriend pays well, does he?' And he grabs me and starts pushing his hand under my coat. 'Get off me,' I shout and push him onto the floor. I don't push him hard, just a little shove, but he's doubled over and he's not making a sound, until I hear a sob. And then the babies are crying, all three of them, a frightened wail that makes my hair stand on end. Mary-Pat has climbed off her chair and goes to stand behind her daddy's knees, her tiny head sticking out, thumb in her mouth. 'Get up, Daddy, it's all right. We'll put a plaster on the boo-boo,' she's saying, nudging him gently with her hand. 'Get up, Daddy.' Why doesn't she stand behind me, I wonder.

He lies there for a while, crying softly, and I turn my back, clutching the rail along the edge of the range for support.

When he speaks, his voice is quiet. 'For God's sake, Michelle, do you know what you're doing to me? I can't stand this. I need you. I don't care about her or your fancy man ...'

'Well, that's good to know.'

'Ah, for Christ's sake, will you just come here to me?' And he comes up to me and wraps his arms around me, and I can feel him against me. And then he starts to kiss me behind the ear, the way he knows I like, and he murmurs, 'Wouldn't do this with that O'Reilly fellow, would you? Smell of chicken shit would put you off. I don't smell of chicken shit, now, do I?'

I'm forced to laugh, and he tickles me then. 'Well, do I?'

'No.' I giggle. 'No, you don't.' He always could wrap me around his little finger.

In the end, we leave June in the playpen in the living room, and we give Mary-Pat some crayons and a big roll of wallpaper and we ask her to draw us something special. We tell Pi it's bed time, because that's the only time he will actually let us put him to bed, and maybe he wonders why Mammy's in too much of a rush to wash his little face and hands and read him a story, instead popping him into bed and closing the door tightly, turning the knob that little bit extra so that the snib jams in the lock, the way it does, because the door's broken. I try to tell myself that I'm not locking my child into his room so that I can make love to my husband and I try to ignore his thumping on the door, his plaintive, 'Mammeee – need a wee,' as we crash into each other on the landing and do it right there, him pulling up my skirt and pushing my knickers down and me pulling at the belt of his trousers and grabbing hold of the zip on his fly and pulling so hard that he gives a yelp, 'Jesus Christ woman, hold on, you'll have my balls off,' and as he pushes me up against the wall and lifts me so that he can slide inside me, and I give a little scream and then we're both laughing and panting and sighing and licking and it feels like never before. But when I feel him coming to the end, I whisper, 'Wait.'

He groans and stops for a second, his breath rasping in my ear. 'What is it? What's wrong?'

'It's just … no more babies, John-Joe, please. I can't.'

He looks as if he will die of disappointment, so I say, 'I have an idea,' and I slide off him. 'Come on.'

'What the –?' His face is a mask of disappointment, his breath coming in rasps, his trousers around his ankles. I go into my bedroom to the little drawer beside the bed, to where I put the brown envelope that Bridie gave me and for which, until now, I've had no need, and I take one of the foil-wrapped condoms out and I call out, 'John-Joe, in here.'

There's a rustle and a crash, followed by a shouted 'fuck' from the landing and then he shuffles in the door, his trousers around his ankles, penis still erect. 'What is it, Michelle? I'm in agony here.' He looks comical, but when he sees the condoms, his whole face lights up. 'You beauty! Where the hell did you get those?'

'I have a source,' I say coyly, 'now hurry up.' And he jumps on top of me so enthusiastically I think the bed will give way underneath us. And I try not to think of Bridie, or that girl with her lovely hair, or how he must laugh with her the way he doesn't with me any more, or about Sean and the way he looks at me sometimes.

We lie on the bed after, catching our breath, a tangle of sheets, clothes and limbs, and I lean on his chest, listening to his heart, feeling it beating steadily underneath his ribs.

'You know, I don't love anyone but you,' he says. He's not looking at me but staring up at the ceiling. 'You know that, Michelle. From the day I first met you, you were the only one for me. You have to believe me.'

I don't say anything for a few moments, because I'm thinking. I'm not really sure I do believe him, because I've seen it. Not just silly Fidelma in the post office, or this young girl, but the way women are with him, fluttering around him. He seems to bring that out in them, the butterfly. How strange, I think, that he never brought that out in me. Instead, he's made me hard, impatient, as if he's a boy and not a grown man and I'm his mother, not his wife, or his lover, or his companion. His bloody mother.

I try a different tack. 'Look, I know you're scared,' I say. 'I'm scared too, sometimes, that we won't make it here. But it'll be OK, I know it will. We just need to remember what we're trying to do here. What we're trying to achieve.'

I know I've made a mistake when he groans. 'Achieve. For fuck's sake. You make it all sound like some kind of cow-shit enterprise, like we're some bacon factory in Ballina or something.' He sits up then and begins to pull his trousers and underpants on, grunting with the effort. Then he curses and lies back down beside me and gives a heavy sigh. 'Look, I am scared. Scared that we'll starve in this place, that we won't survive another winter, and it's all so bloody hard.' He thumps the bed. 'Why the hell does it have to be so hard?'

I sit bolt upright then. 'John-Joe,' I say quietly, 'I know it's hard, but we both went into this together, you know that. And I can't do it without you. Please don't give up on me.'

He just shrugs then, his eyes full of misery. 'I'm trying to be someone I'm not, Michelle. I don't belong here, in this life.' And then he turns on his side and I wonder how, one minute, we are making love as if our lives depended on it, and now this. This sense that there's something between us: something we can't name, that's pushing us apart.

Later, I have to change Pi's pyjamas where he's wet them and quietly wipe away his tears, while I give him a little bath, filling the basin and letting him sit in it. His sobs have subsided into hiccups and when I give him a squeezy bottle and a sponge, he's content to fill it and empty it over and over again, humming to himself. And I thank God that he's too young to have understood what his parents were doing. I allow myself a minute of self-loathing, that I put John-Joe before my son, but I had to. I needed to. Without John-Joe I'm not fully myself. And I want him back. I want him to be mine and mine only.

9

John-Patrick had said he'd drive her and wait around outside for a bit. 'Shag-all else to do,' he'd said, but Rosie knew he was trying to help. He was supposed to be helping PJ in the shop at the weekends, but 'All those kids wreck my head,' he said, about the nine-year-olds on bikes who'd pitch up in search of free bait. He preferred to be outdoors, helping Pius in the garden.

They were on their way to see Frances O'Brien, even though Rosie had no idea if she'd know anything. 'It's total crap, the whole thing,' Pius had said to her. 'But if it'll put your mind at rest, go ahead.' But keep me out of it, had been the unspoken words. Fair enough, Rosie had thought. Put your head in the sand as usual.

'John-Patrick,' she said now. 'Ehm, would you do me a favour?'

'Sure,' he said doubtfully.

'Would you mind not telling Mary-Pat about this … this visit? It'd only upset her. I mean, she'd only worry about it and she has enough on her plate.' Not to mention the fact that she has barely spoken to me in the six weeks since the wedding. She has barely passed the house and if Pi wants to see her he has to call up. She's avoiding me. I know she is.

He didn't say anything, just nodded, eyes fixed on the road, but his cheeks flushed a bit. He was a good kid, John-Patrick. Mary-Pat was worried about him because he preferred manga and Japanese cartoons to Gaelic football, and had thus marked himself out as an oddball in Monasterard. Rosie thought he had guts to stand out in this place.

John-Patrick pressed hard on the brake and screeched into the verge with a spray of gravel. He drove like a Formula 1 racing driver, all handbrakes and roaring engines — it took a bit of getting used to.

'I think this is the place,' he said.

Rosie sat there for a few moments, looking out the window at the pristine little bungalow. It looked as if it had recently been scrubbed with a toothbrush, the render a blinding white, the slate roof an immaculate shiny black, a neat pebble path leading up to the front door, with its stained glass window that gleamed as if it had been blasted with Windolene. Pi had said she was 'an old hippy'. Could a hippy really live here?

She tried to compose herself. 'I have no idea why, but I feel nervous.'

John-Patrick nodded, clearly out of his depth with this information. Eventually, he cleared his throat. 'I suppose it's better to know, like. Better than not to know … ah, shit.' He shook his head and banged the steering wheel.

Rosie stretched across and squeezed his arm. 'I know exactly what you mean. Thanks. Look, would you mind if I walked back? It might clear my head.'

She could see his solicitous expression clear, to be replaced by one of relief that he'd be spared any emotional fallout from the visit, and she almost smiled. Men. They were all the same.

'Grand so.' He nodded, trying to look regretful, and as she got out on wobbly legs and nervously opened the little wrought-iron gate to Frances O'Brien's cottage, he screeched off back up the road, more gravel spraying behind him.

Rosie was distracted for a moment by the doorbell. When she pressed, it played the 'Star Spangled Banner', a tinny whine, and when she looked in through the porch window, she could see a sticker with the American flag on it and the slogan '*Is Féidir Linn!*' – Yes, We Can. The hall door opened and a trim middle-aged woman in a red business suit with big gold buttons was squinting at her from behind the porch door. Rosie gave a little wave. The woman didn't wave back, and her face was expressionless as she opened the door just enough to stick her head out. 'Ms O'Brien? I'm sorry to bother you, I'm Rosie O'Connor.'

'I know who you are.' The woman opened the door a fraction more, but not to invite Rosie in. Instead, she stood there, arms folded across her chest, as if she were barring Rosie from entering. She looked like an angry Sarah Palin, a helmet of red-gold hair sprayed onto her head, a pair of reading glasses around her neck on a long gold chain. The idea that this woman could once have been a hippy seemed utterly ridiculous.

Rosie pinned a smile onto her face. 'You do? That's great. You see, I've come to ask you a few questions if I could. It's about—'

'I don't know anything.' The line was delivered with such force, like bullets from a machine gun, that Rosie hesitated for a second, wondering if Pius had been confused and there was some other Frances O'Brien and she'd got the wrong one. 'I'm sorry, I thought ... Do you remember my parents, John-Joe and Michelle?'

Suddenly Frances was all movement, bustling forward towards Rosie, her arms outstretched as if she wanted to push her away. Instinctively, Rosie took a step back onto the garden path. Frances rushed past her to the front gate, opening it and then closing it, as if to check if anyone was outside lurking on the canal bank. Then she turned to Rosie. 'Who sent you?'

Rosie didn't understand the question for a second. 'No one,' she answered. 'I came myself. You were at my christening.'

The woman was hovering by the gate, her hand on the metal handle, and Rosie noticed that her hand was shaking, trembling. And then she shook her head. 'No.'

'Oh. It's just ... I saw your name, on the parish records. Father Naul showed them to me. And you're on my baptismal cert – your name is beside my name and my parents' names in the register. It said you were my godmother.'

The woman turned to her now and pinned a smile on her face, revealing a set of shiny white dentures, like tombstones in her mouth. It made Rosie feel uneasy. She suddenly wanted to push past the woman out onto the canal, but the woman was blocking her way. 'Rosie,' she began. 'Is that your name?'

Rosie nodded. I just told you what my name is, she thought.

'Look, pet, I'm sorry, it's just ... I think you've made a mistake. I don't know anybody by that name. Those names.'

'Oh.' Rosie knew that she sounded like a child, but she couldn't help it. This wasn't how it was supposed to be. How it was supposed to turn out. 'My father's ill, you see, and, well—'

'I'm sorry to hear that. But I can't help you. I don't know who they are. And now, if you'll excuse me, I have a cumann meeting. The *bainisteoir* will kill me if I'm late.' Frances O'Brien pushed out the gate and trotted onto the towpath, where she eased herself into an immaculately clean red Nissan Micra with a clutch of holy medals swinging from the rear-view mirror, then drove off.

Rosie stood by the gate of the bungalow for a few moments. She felt as if she'd been buffeted by something, by some huge wave, and had been left on the shore, a mouth full of sea water, that feeling of nausea at the back of her throat. She'd had it all written in her head, the script, the two of them sitting side by side on an immaculate sofa, reminiscing, munching biscuits and drinking tea. She would tell Rosie all about her parents, what they'd been like. Maybe she'd tell her what Mammy was like, so that Rosie could get to know her. Could hang onto more than just sensations, smells, feelings. Things she couldn't get a grip on, no matter how hard she tried.

Maybe Frances hadn't liked them. Maybe that was it — she wouldn't be alone there, at least with Daddy anyway. He hadn't bothered much about whether people liked him or not. 'I couldn't give a flying fuck,' he'd said once, when Mary-Pat had asked him not to hang around Prendergast's after closing time, shouting at anyone who happened to be passing. 'I had to hear about your carry-on in the minimarket,' she'd scolded him. 'Do you not know you're making a holy show of us?'

'Caring what people think about you is the road to ruination, Mary-Pat. It's what's made this country an effin' Valley of the Squinting Windows, do you get me?' he'd said, waving his cigarette while his daughter rolled her eyes to heaven, rambling on about how the only judgement he'd accept would be God's in heaven.

'You're an atheist,' Mary-Pat had barked. 'Now, eat your dinner.'

She walked back, trying to compose some kind of an explanation to Pius while she had the time. The towpath was straight here, a long line of grassy track stretching away into the horizon. Rosie trudged along, head down, watching her feet, in their muddy trainers, slice through the thick grass, the purple knobs of the clover flowers disappearing under her feet. She could hear the warble of the moorhen as she shuffled in the rushes, the little 'peep' of anxiety as she became aware that someone was approaching. Rosie had always loved this season – the stillness of the water, the murky sheen over the September trees, but now she found it hard to enjoy it, because her mind was filled with random thoughts, with Frances O'Brien, with Craig, with Pi and Daphne and Mary-Pat and Daddy up in St Benildus's, unaware, as usual, of the havoc he'd wreaked – they were all jumbled in her head, talking to her, and she wanted to yell at them all to shut up.

Craig had gone home, two weeks after the wedding. 'It's best, in the circumstances, to let you sort everything out,' he'd said. He hadn't even looked at her as he'd folded the expensive waterproofs he'd insisted on buying 'for the terrain', even though she'd tried to explain that there wasn't much terrain in Monasterard. He hadn't needed them even once.

You have no idea what a relief that is, she'd thought, sitting there on the bed, the suitcase open beside her. She'd felt light-headed about it, almost gleeful. It wasn't that she didn't love him, it was the relief that she didn't have to keep it up for much longer, the pretence. She felt she had to protest, though, putting a hand on his, which he'd hastily removed. 'I haven't changed. It's just Daddy ...'

He'd shaken his head and only then had he looked at her, his blue eyes sorrowful. 'You're not the woman I thought you were, Rosie. That's what it is,' and then he'd nodded, as if he'd finally understood something he'd been wrestling with for a while.

You're probably right, Rosie had thought. I could keep it up in the States. I could be anyone you wanted me to be, that nice sensible girl with the neat hair and the job helping others and not one, but two, pairs of walking shoes. We matched, and I was careful to keep it that way, to make sure I didn't express too many opinions but just echoed yours instead, intercepting things that might annoy you, tuning in to your responses to make sure I didn't overdo it. It was exhausting, she now realised. And now that I'm back here, well, I just can't.

'I'm sorry, Craig,' she'd said then. 'I really am. I'm just very tired.'

He'd looked at her, and she understood that he meant it when he'd reached out and took her hand in his, wiggling her wedding ring gently on her finger, as if he were deciding whether or not to take it off. 'I think we both need a bit of time,' he'd said helpfully.

She was so preoccupied that she didn't hear or see him until he was practically on top of her, a sudden rustle of branches and a thud, followed by a 'Christ'. And he was standing in front of her, panting with exertion, hands on his hips.

'I nearly tripped over you there.' Mark didn't look at her as he spoke, instead looking just beyond her, at the horizon.

'Jesus, you gave me a fright.' Rosie clutched her throat. 'You might have said something.'

'You were busy ranting and raving to yourself.'

'I was?' She looked at him and saw the ghost of a smile on his face. She used to talk to herself all the time, gesticulating and muttering, until she'd trained herself out of it because Craig said it made her look unhinged. 'I was thinking about something,' was the best she could offer by way of explanation.

'I gathered,' he said, and they both looked out over the canal for a while, the choppy silver water, the reeds bent double in the wind. 'What are you doing all the way down here?'

Rosie thought of Frances O'Brien. Of her helmet of hair, her big teeth. She'd been terrifying, that's what it was. That was the word. 'Oh, just going for a walk.'

'Right.' He looked doubtful. His breathing was slower now, but his T-shirt was stained with sweat and drops of it clung to his hair.

Rosie felt her heart beating rapidly in her chest as the thoughts flitted around in her head. There was so much she wanted to say to him. She wanted to tell him about her life without him, about how it had been, what that other place had been like, how she'd fucked it all up, what it was like being back here ... about Frances O'Brien ... She wanted to tell him everything, the way she'd used to when they were twelve years old, but the words just wouldn't come.

'We used to go swimming here. Do you remember?' He turned to look at the grey water, now covered with a mass of green lily pads, turning slightly now that it was autumn. Soon, there would be nothing but silvery water and the fish would retreat to the shelter of the reeds, to slink around the muddy edges of the bank until the weather grew warmer.

'God, yes,' she said. 'Once I thought the pike had got me.'

He grinned briefly. 'You were pathetic. Fancy being scared of a tiny little old pike.'

'Ha ha. It was huge. And deadly. I thought it'd take my leg off.'

He snorted with laughter, and then there was another silence as they both looked at the water for a while longer, and Rosie played that film in her head of the last time they'd gone swimming together, when she'd been wearing June's bikini because she wanted him to think differently about her, wanted him to see that she wasn't his childhood friend any more. Her breasts were ridiculously small in it, as if she were a girl trying to pretend she was a woman. She *was* a girl trying to pretend she was a woman, she thought now, reddening at the memory. She remembered the way his eyes had flicked over her, just for a second, but she'd seen him look.

'Why don't we jump in?'

'What?'

'Why don't we jump in and have a swim, like old times?'

'Oh, very funny,' Rosie began, looking down at her worn jeans, wondering if they would withstand immersion in water, and then up at him. The look on his face was mischievous, a sly grin revealing a flash of white teeth, his eyes crinkling with amusement. She remembered that look: she'd missed it, she thought. That lightness, that way of seeing joy in ordinary things, of taking pleasure in jokes and silliness and fun.

'You're serious.'

'Course.' And then he took off his shoes and socks, rolling them into a ball and stuffing them neatly into his trainers, then his jeans, which he folded neatly on top of the trainers. He was wearing swimming togs, baggy shorts with pictures of palm trees on them, which looked completely out of keeping with the grey dampness around them.

'You've cheated,' Rosie said, pointing to them. 'That's not fair.'

He shrugged again, as if to say, 'What can you do?' and then pulled his T-shirt over his head. Rosie looked down at the ground. She hadn't seen any bit of him in a very long time, and she didn't want to stare, but eventually she turned her head to catch a glimpse of that golden skin, the heavy set of his shoulders, the broad chest that had not a single hair on it. She felt her stomach flip. Oh, Christ, she thought. I'm not twelve, I'm a grown woman. He caught her eye and she swallowed nervously.

'I go for a swim every day after my run,' he said, by way of explanation. He was standing two feet away from her, almost naked, and all she could do was stare down at the ground.

'Are you going to swim with all of your clothes on?' He nodded at her jeans and sensible rain jacket.

She thought of the horrible grey underwear she'd dug out from the bottom of her suitcase this morning, as she didn't have anything clean. She couldn't possibly show him that. Then she had an idea. 'Turn around,' she said.

'What?'

'Turn around. I'm getting undressed.'

'Oh, right.' His voice wobbled with laughter and she wanted to punch him, but he did what he was told, and before she could talk herself out of it, she quickly pulled off her clothes, taking care to leave her T-shirt on to cover the awful underwear. She tiptoed through the grass at the edge of the water and eased herself in, gasping as the water reached her navel. 'It's cold,' she said, and turned her head to see him standing above her on the bank, looking down at her, an expression on his face that she couldn't quite read. She lowered her body into the water, feeling its silty coolness surround her, and paddled over to the other side, trying not to think of what might be lurking in the water.

She perched on a little shelf of shingle on the other side of the water. 'Your turn.'

He was standing with the water up to his chest now, teeth chattering. With a yelp, he dived in, submerging himself completely. She waited for him to come up again, but all that she saw was a ripple in the brown water where he'd dived in. She waited. Maybe he'd hit his head on something, she thought, wondering whether to jump in and drag him up from the bottom. But it was only a few feet deep. She looked anxiously left and right and didn't see the pair of hands that shot out and grabbed her hips, pulling her down under the water.

She screamed and then laughed as they resurfaced, an arc of water splashing over his head. 'You bastard!' She giggled. 'I thought you were drowning.'

'Not drowning, just waving.' He smiled and leaned back in the water, lifting his feet up so that he was floating. The sun had come out now and the water had turned from a steely grey to a bright blue, the lily pads a vivid green and the rushes a browny-silver. Rosie tilted her face up to the sun, letting the water buoy her up as she lay back and floated, looking up at the blue sky, hearing nothing but her breathing, in and out, and the burble of the water underneath her. She closed her eyes and opened them again, blinking drops of water from her eyelashes, feeling the ripples at her feet. I love this place, she suddenly thought. How could I have forgotten? All those years in that other place, that grey, dusty town with no flowers or trees, just acres of brown fields, low buildings. It had felt dry, dead, but this place ... Under every bit of grass and reed, there was something growing, or burrowing, or nosing into the brown earth. It felt so intensely alive, and so did she. In spite of everything, she'd somehow come to life again.

She didn't see him, but felt him instead as he bumped against her. She got such a fright, she swallowed a mouthful of water and had to stand up, coughing and spluttering.

'Sorry.' He was still lying on his back, looking directly up into the sky, eyes half-closed against the sun. Rosie had the sudden desire to float over to him, to lie on top of him in the water, to cover his body with hers, but as soon as she'd felt it, she'd pushed the thought away. No, Rosie, control yourself, she thought, you'll only ruin things the way you always do. She splashed her face with water, then wiped the droplets off. 'I'm getting out,' she said, tiptoeing gingerly through the water, feeling the silt squeeze between her toes.

He was still lying on his back, not looking at her, but when she passed, he grabbed her hand and squeezed it tight. She stood there for a second, unsure what to do. If she let go of his hand and climbed out of the water, maybe she'd never get another chance. But if she stayed ...

She held onto his hand while he leaned on her other arm to stand upright in the water, facing her. 'I'm cold,' she said.

'I know.' He pulled her towards him then, enveloping her, wrapping his arms so tightly around her that she had to turn her head against his chest to be able to breathe. His skin was wet and cold, a rash of goosepimples against her cheek, and when she leaned against him, she could hear his heart beating, a steady thump-thump. She took in a deep breath and let it out again. I can breathe again, she thought. I can breathe.

'Mark —' she began, but he interrupted her.

'No. Don't say anything,'

For once, she did as she was told and just let him kiss her, silently, her eyelids, her nose, her lips, her chin, the base of her throat, while she clung to him, her hands gripping the waistband of his trunks. She tilted her head back as he kissed her collarbone and she looked up at the sky, feeling the warmth of the sun on her face, and then she stroked his wet hair and his sticky-out ears and, lifting his face to hers, his nose and then planted a gentle peck on his lips, which were now blue with the cold.

When she kissed him on the mouth, she could feel something in him then, an energy, like a wave, coming towards her. His eyes opened for a second and he returned her kiss, forcing her mouth open with his, his tongue darting into her mouth, finding hers, but as soon as she felt it, it was gone. No, she thought. Don't stop, please. But he was pulling away from her, and the shock made her wake up and realise that the sun had gone in and everything looked cold and grey again.

'Rosie?'

'Uhmm?'

'I could stay here all day, but I'm freezing. C'mon,' he said gently, 'let's dry off and warm up a bit.'

Rosie nodded and allowed him to lead her out of the water, his hand still in hers, pulling her gently through the rushes at the edge and up the gentle slope of the bank. Her T-shirt clung to her now, and the outline of her awful bra and her nipples could be clearly seen through the wet fabric. Blushing, she reached for the safety of her raincoat, and then felt the warmth of his towel around her shoulders. 'To cover your modesty.' He smiled. 'Not that I'm complaining.'

Rosie blushed, pulling the towel down over her shoulders. 'Thanks,' she managed, and then ducked behind a bush to take off her wet clothes, rubbing her body — which had now turned a greenish colour with the cold — with the towel, then gingerly pulling her waterproof jacket on and zipping it up tightly, stuffing her wet clothes in her pocket.

He was sitting on the bank when she got back but said nothing, just patted the ground beside him, and she sat down, shuffling her bottom until she was touching his.

'We need a brandy to warm ourselves up,' he said. 'I sometimes bring a hip flask with me, when it's really cold — strictly for medicinal purposes, you understand.' He rested his arms on his knees and his elbow touched her bare leg.

'Actually, I don't drink spirits,' she said, then added, 'What?' when she caught the look of incredulity on his face. 'I hardly drink at all these days,' she said. 'I know, hard to believe, isn't it, that I have a modicum of self-control.'

He didn't rise to the bait, just said quietly, 'When did you stop?'

'Oh, ages ago. As soon as I got to Dublin, really. I knew that I had to or else I'd ruin my life completely.' She didn't think it tactful to mention that it was when she'd met Craig. He'd been in Ireland doing a diploma in dairy herd health, and she'd been working in the bowels of an office on Leeson Street, filing tax forms, when one of her typing friends had made her go to a student night. He was the squarest man she'd ever met, but she'd seen that as a bonus — he was perfect because he wasn't Mark. It wasn't fair, she knew that, but she'd been determined. He'd made it clear that he didn't like her 'partying', and it was the look of alarm on his face, distaste, that had made her stop. Because she needed Craig, needed what he had to offer.

Mark looked at his feet fixedly and Rosie noticed that there was a faint flush to his cheeks.

'You were young and you had nobody to look out for you,' he muttered, as if he only half believed what he was saying.

'I had you.'

The pain flashed across his face. Don't be sad, Rosie thought. Please don't be sad. She reached out and rubbed a hand across his hair, feeling the bristles sharp against her palm. 'Mark, I'm sorry. I know I promised ... But look, there wasn't a day when I didn't think about you, about us, but I thought you'd finished with me, given up on me. In case you'd forgotten, you made it pretty clear that you didn't want me around any more.'

'I know,' he said bleakly. 'It was my fault. I judged you. I thought you weren't good enough.'

'I wasn't.' Rosie closed her eyes for a moment, and she could see herself that summer, all those years ago, her hair streaming behind her as she cycled down the towpath to the old Norman tower. She'd been in such a rage, she remembered, pushing the pedals around as fast as she could, even though the exertion made her breath come in short, jagged puffs and she remembered that she hadn't brought her inhaler. She had to slow down then. The last thing she needed was an asthma attack.

She'd arranged to meet Declan there, even though she didn't even like him, even though the leer on his spotty face when she saw him at school made her feel queasy, and when he put his hands on her, she wanted instinctively to slap them away. She was only doing it to spite Mark, because the week before, she'd asked him, and he'd said he wouldn't. He'd been horrified when she'd asked, his black eyes widening in surprise, then a look of distaste creeping over his face. 'I can't do that, Rosie. Your first time should be special, with someone you love. You shouldn't want to throw it away like that.'

'But you love me, I know you do,' she'd said then and had been gratified to see the faint flush on his cheeks as he looked at his feet. And I love you, she thought. 'So what's the problem?'

He'd looked around then, furtively, as if to see who might be watching. 'Have you lost all reason, Rosie? I am not going to ... do that, because you are my friend and I have too much respect for you.'

'Oh, fuck off,' she'd spat. 'You do not. You don't respect me at all. You think I'm dirty, I know you do. It's because you're looking down your nose at me, that's why. Well, you know what, I'll save you the bother.' And she'd stomped off then and climbed up on her bike and sped off home, throwing herself on the bed and staring into space, teeth grinding with frustration and rage.

And then she'd gone to the postbox in the village and she'd called Declan. Declan had been only too willing, and it had been horrible, of course, painful and undignified and traumatic. She'd had to stifle a scream as he shoved himself inside of her, his face scrunched up in a grimace, and then rammed himself in further, his breath coming in short puffs as he ground in to her. There was a sharp stone under her left buttock which kept digging into her and her bra, where he'd roughly shoved it up over her breasts, was strangling her. 'Oh, Rosie, Rosie, Rosie,' he'd chanted. Please shut up, she'd thought. Please don't call my name.

After, he'd been triumphant, his eyes glittering, rolling off her with a whoop. 'Jesus Christ,' he'd panted, laughing. 'Fuckin' A, that was, pure fuckin' A.'

'I need a wee,' she'd said, wiping the grass off her bottom and wincing in pain as she pulled her knickers up. She couldn't button her jeans because the crotch cut into her, and so she had to half-waddle over to her bike, which she proceeded to push slowly up the towpath. She'd been able to hear him shout then. 'Rosie, where are you going? Come back.' But she knew he wouldn't get up and follow her. He wasn't that kind of man. He was the kind of man who took what he was being offered without a second thought, who grabbed it and manhandled it and soiled it. Rosie sobbed all the way home, great big sobs that shook her whole body, snot pouring from her nose, which she had to wipe with the back of her hand because she had no tissue. Mary-Pat would kill me, she'd thought. She says that every decent woman should have tissues; you never know when you might need them. But then, she wasn't a decent woman, was she?

'I had a miscarriage, did you know that?' Rosie said.

Mark's eyes widened, and then he looked down at his feet. He shook his head and didn't say a word, just picked up a twig that was lying on the bank and began to dig away with it, hacking at the grass.

That September, Mary-Pat had brought her to the clinic in Mullingar, a discreet place tucked away on a backstreet, with a small brass plaque with a polite 'Women's Clinic' engraved on it. She was sixteen years old. Mary-Pat had barely said a word to Rosie from the time she'd come down to breakfast that morning, face chalk white. She'd put her hand there, low down, beneath her stomach, where the pain gripped her, feeling as if it were pulling everything inside her into it, like a black hole. She'd barely got the words out, 'Mary-Pat, I think ...' and then she'd looked down to see the blood streaking down her legs. She'd given a little moan then and had fallen onto her knees, a wave of pain pushing her down towards the floor. 'What is it, Mary-Pat, what's wrong with me?'

Mary-Pat had said not one word, but instead she'd been a blur of motion, wrapping her in the old Foxford blanket, then stomping up the stairs to her bedroom. There was a clattering and a creaking as the wardrobe door was opened and then closed again, and then her footsteps echoed along the landing to the bathroom, where the medicine cabinet was opened. Then there was silence, followed by the slam of the cabinet door, and then Mary-Pat's heavy footsteps on the stairs. When she came into the kitchen, her face was red with exertion and she was carrying a greying black duffle bag. She hardly glanced at Rosie, but instead filled a glass of water and then handed it to her with two paracetamol.

Rosie's face was now shiny with sweat and the pain in her abdomen had spread to the top of her legs, which were now numb. 'It's bad, Mary-Pat,' she moaned. 'Am I going to die?'

In reply, Mary-Pat gave her hand a brief squeeze. 'You are not, do you understand me? We just need to get you to the doctor. Now, can you put on a pair of tracksuit bottoms?' and she pushed Rosie's feet gently into a baggy pair of grey jogging pants, pulling them gently up towards her thighs, so that Rosie could shuffle her bottom into them.

'Can you stand up?' Mary-Pat had said gently. 'We need to get you into the car before Daddy and Pi get back.'

Rosie had looked at her sister, but her expression was neutral, businesslike, as she'd helped Rosie into her favourite pink sweatshirt, and Rosie was glad of it. If Mary-Pat wasn't panicking, maybe she'd be OK. Mary-Pat had picked her up under the arms and manhandled her through the open door, down the path, opening the passenger door of the car, grunting with the effort, then pushing Rosie's legs into the footwell and slamming the door. She'd run around then to the driver's side and got in. 'Right, let's go.'

Rosie had leaned her head against the window, even though it rattled so much she thought her teeth would fall out of her head.

The doctor had been kind, gentle when she said she needed to 'take a little look'. 'It might hurt a bit, so just try to relax,' she'd said. Rosie had to grip Mary-Pat's hand, squeezing it so firmly, her sister had given a low moan. 'Easy, Rosie.'

'Sorry,' Rosie had said. 'It hurts, Mary-Pat.' She was a child again, complaining when Mary-Pat brought her to the dentist. And then the doctor had said that the neck of the cervix was open and they'd need to do a D&C. 'They just need to make sure there's nothing left, so that you don't get an infection,' Mary-Pat had said quietly.

'Nothing left.' She hadn't seen it as a baby then. She'd just seen it as something terrible that had happened to her body, that was being expelled, like an alien. 'I don't *know* what's happened to me,' she'd gulped, sobbing. 'I don't know.'

'Rosie, you do know, and it's not nice, but you need to accept it.' Mary-Pat had been firm. 'There's no other way.' And something about the words, about the closed expression on Mary-Pat's face, made Rosie shut up. She knew what her sister was saying. 'Grow up. Accept what you've done.'

'I'm sorry,' she'd said quietly.

Mary-Pat hadn't replied, but instead had put the blanket around Rosie's shoulders and led her to the car, opening the passenger door and easing her into the seat. And Mary-Pat had been silent all the way home, but the pile of fag ends in the ashtray told a different story.

* * *

'Yes, I did,' Rosie told Mark now, as if he'd asked her to tell him everything, instead of sitting there, digging a hole in the bank, completely silent. 'And then Mary-Pat said she couldn't put up with it any longer, so she said I had to leave.' She was being mean now, rubbing it in, but she was angry with him, so angry. Can you not think of a single thing to say, she thought. Not one word?

She remembered what she'd told Mary-Pat that morning. 'I know you think I'm a slapper, but I only did it once.'

Mary-Pat had replied, 'Let's get this straight. I don't disapprove, love. I don't have any moral objection, in case you think I do. It's just that I'm afraid — that's what it is. I'm afraid because nothing I say or do matters any more. I can't control you and I'm frightened of what might happen next.'

Rosie turned to Mark now. 'I was scared, really scared, because I had nowhere to go, not really. I begged her, but she said it was too late.'

She was trying to provoke him, to get a reaction. He cleared his throat, finally finding his voice. 'Where did you go?'

'Does it matter?' she snapped. She didn't want to tell him about that night, the last one she'd spent at home, even though she'd never forgotten it. She'd fallen into a deep sleep on her bed, and she awoke to find Mary-Pat standing beside her, looking down. She'd jumped in fright, wiping a sliver of drool from the corner of her mouth. 'What time is it? How long have I been asleep?' She'd half-sat on the bed, looking out the window to the soft early-autumn light.

'It's eight o'clock. Your friend is outside.'

For a second, Rosie had thought she'd meant Declan and she'd panicked, but then Mary-Pat had said, 'It's Mark.'

Rosie had been silent for a few seconds before answering, 'Tell him to go away. I don't want to see him.'

And, until just a few weeks ago, she hadn't.

He turned to her now, his eyes soft. 'No, of course, it doesn't bloody matter. I'm sorry you had to go through that. Sorrier than I can say. I was your friend and I let you down. I should have been there for you and I wasn't. If I'd known—'

'You'd have done what exactly?' She wasn't going to make it better for him now, even if it was true.

'I'd have done *something*,' he protested, but they both knew it wasn't true. What could he have done? 'Rosie, I ...' He gave a long sigh, and began to say something, but then changed his mind. 'What'll you do now?'

'No idea,' Rosie said shortly.

'You're not happy, I can see that. And I don't blame you, after everything that's happened ...'

'I could be happy. You could make me happy,' she said in a small voice.

He stuck his hands in his pockets now and looked down at the towpath, running a foot back and forth across the grass. 'I couldn't, Rosie. I can't take it all away, everything that's happened. I love you, but that's not enough. It wasn't enough then, and it won't be enough now. Because no matter what I do or say, you won't accept yourself and like yourself, and it'd be like loving someone who isn't the real Rosie, if you see what I mean.'

She wiped the tear that was dripping off the end of her nose. He was right. She wasn't happy and it wasn't the wedding, or even Daddy, it was something else, something right inside her that didn't work. That was empty. 'I know,' she agreed sadly.

'Sorry,' he muttered.

'Don't be.' Rosie sniffed. 'Because you're right.' She stood up, straightened herself, pulling the hem of the coat down. 'I'll see you around, OK?'

His face twisted into a grimace. 'Ah, Rosie, don't be like that.'

'I'm not being like anything.' She sighed. 'I've just had enough, OK?'

'OK.' He looked stricken, the almond shape of his eyelids visible as he looked down at the ground, before picking up a stone in the grass and tossing it into the canal, where it landed with a gentle 'plop' and a ripple spread outwards, right to the edge of the irises that lined the canal bank.

'So, I'll see you,' she said and walked away, and even though as soon as she'd got twenty yards from him she'd burst into tears, great streams of them running down her nose, gulping down the lump in her throat, she didn't turn around. Not once. She just kept walking.

October 1978

Michelle

'Mammy, do you think we'll know when the world's going to end?' Pius is sitting at the kitchen table, tapping a pencil repeatedly off the surface, and I wish he'd just stop. Then Mary-Pat reaches out and knocks it out of his hand. 'Ow!' he protests and pushes her copybook off the table, a cheeky grin on his face. She leans over as if to pick it off the floor, sticking out a foot while she's at it and flipping the stool from under him so that he lands on the floor with a thump.

His face creases into a grimace and then the tears come. 'She ... hurt ... meee,' he wails, as I go to him and pick him up, setting the stool back on its feet and whispering and murmuring soothing words, while shooting Mary-Pat a dagger look. She looks triumphant, returning to her task of writing out a poem about Hallowe'en in her lovely handwriting.

I feel my fists clench, and I have to push the anger down inside myself. It's always there these days, that anger, hovering just below the surface, ready to break out at the smallest excuse. I have to take a deep breath now, to hold it in, and I say quietly, 'Mary-Pat, we've spoken about gentleness, haven't we?' as I settle him back on the stool, feeling his thin body vibrate with rage. Her smug smile tells me that she didn't exactly take our conversation to heart, and once again, I wonder about the savagery siblings feel towards each other. I never really understood it, being an only child and the centre of my parents' universe. I never had to fight for love; it was given to me for nothing. All I had to do was just stand there and receive it, to bask in the glow of my parents' attention, but my children circle each other like wary animals, waiting for their chance to grab their moment, to triumph over their siblings and get a little sliver of Mammy, a crumb of a kiss or a story told only for them. They're prepared to fight each other for this, to injure each other; it's so raw, so basic, this need and this struggle that sometimes I find it just so overwhelming; I wonder if I can satisfy this need, if I'm enough.

'I don't think we would know,' I say, once order has been restored and the three heads are bent over the copybooks. 'It'd probably happen too quickly for us to realise.'

'But Brother Marcus says that there will be a big plague and pestilence and people pretending to be God only they're not, "And ye shall hear of wars and rumours of wars: see that ye be not troubled: for all these things must come to pass, but the end is not yet,"' he intones in an imitation of a deep baritone.

'And because there are lots of wars now, doesn't that mean the end is close?'

What on earth are they filling the children's heads with in that school? I knew that they should never have gone there, but John-Joe insisted, even though he hates that kind of thing, the religion that so dominated his early life. I don't know, but it seems to me that being a Catholic isn't just about going to Mass and praying; it's about culture, about sharing, about sin, about feeling guilty about everything all the time. I can't honestly understand why he'd want to subject the kids to that, but he says they need structure, that Frau Hunkel's little Steiner school at the end of the towpath will just fill their heads with 'Teutonic rubbish', which alternately makes me laugh and want to kill him. Whatever happened to wanting them to take a different path? It seems being a father has turned him into an arch conservative. At least in some ways. He is such a contradiction, John-Joe, and sometimes I think he just takes a position to be contrary. We aren't legally married, the children aren't baptised, so let's beg and plead to allow them to go to a Catholic school instead of the obvious choice. Oh, it's maddening.

But I'm trying to be conciliatory at the moment. We've reached a truce after months of arguments, of skirmishes over the breakfast table, in bed, in the bathroom, in the garden; mostly about food and bills and the goats. Those bloody goats. Morecambe and Wise. To think I once wanted goats when, now, they just seem to me to be a symbol of everything that's gone wrong for us.

He came home with them late one night, crashing and banging about, cursing and muttering under his breath. I woke with a start, pushing June off me, as she'd sneaked into my bed, and sitting up. I remembered a moonlit night almost ten years before, when he'd stood below my window and quoted Shakespeare. Now, all I could hear was a stream of expletives. 'Where the hell did I put my effin' keys?' Under the stone beside the front door, I thought silently to myself, gritting my teeth. Look under the bloody stone. But it's too late: 'Michelle,' he yells. 'Michelle, are you awake? I can't find my keys.'

For goodness' sake, I think, pulling myself out of bed and going to the window. I open it and Romeo is standing below me, swaying. He has a bit of frayed blue rope in either hand at each end of which, I realise, is a goat. When he sees me, he throws his head back and beams. 'My love. Look what I brought home for you.' He tugs the rope to which the two animals are tethered and they bleat forlornly.

I slam the window shut without a word and stand there in the bedroom. Did I just dream that, I wondered, or was John-Joe standing there, drunk as a lord, clutching two goats? I peer out the window, and he's still standing there, head down now, like a naughty schoolboy. I pull on an old jumper of his and I shuffle down the stairs, wondering as I do what would have happened all those years ago if I hadn't answered his call when he'd stood beneath my bedroom window. If I'd just stayed in my bed? Would he just have slunk off into the night, allowing me to marry a man in a sleeveless jumper and live happily ever after? I debate, just for a second, not answering him now, not opening the door to him in the hope that he might just disappear into the darkness, with his two goats trotting along beside him. And for that second, I think I hate him. I truly, truly hate him. The feeling is so strong that my heart speeds up, my breath coming in short puffs. I have to lean on the kitchen door for a moment until I feel it subside.

I open the door and he's standing there, his breath streaming into the night air. 'I told you I'd find us a pair of goats and, lo, it came to pass,' he says triumphantly. 'Michelle, meet Eric and Ernie, or Morecambe and Wise.'

'Where did you get them, John-Joe?' My tone is flat and I'm aware that I sound like his mother, but I can't help it. As time has gone on here, I've become the mother and he the naughty, wayward child who won't do what Mammy tells him. This isn't a partnership — it's something useless and decaying and ugly and we both hate it, but neither of us seems to be able to escape it.

'I thought you'd be pleased,' he says dully.

'Where did you get them?' I repeat.

He lifts his head up now and I see a flash of defiance in his eyes, a flicker of mischief. The old John-Joe returns just for a moment, the John-Joe I remember, and I want to pull him to me and kiss him, hard. He puts his hand to his chest and sucks in a deep breath. 'I won them, fair and square.'

'You won a pair of goats.'

'I did. There was a quiz in Prendergast's and they were second prize.' He beams. 'Who'd have thought it? Just when we were looking for a pair, the Lord provides. It's a miracle,' he says with a wink.

I'm about to say something, when I hear the bedroom window open above me and a little head sticks out. It's Pi and he turns and whispers, 'I knew it, MP, there's a pair of sheep in the garden, look!' Mary-Pat's head appears now, a tumble of curls. 'For God's sake, Pi, they're goats, you big eejit.'

With the audience, I can't say anything to him. I can't hiss at him, 'How the bloody hell do you expect us to look after a pair of goats, when we can hardly look after ourselves? What'll we feed them on, John-Joe, thin air?' Instead, I just stand there, and so does he.

'I've fucked up again, haven't I?' he says eventually. 'I don't get it, Michelle. You spend two years going on about shaggin' goats, about the cheese and the milk and shite, about how the kids will end up with effin' rickets if they don't get enough calcium, and I bring you two goats and you're not happy. You're never happy, no matter what I do. I can't do anything to please you.' He sounds like a sulky child.

I curl my bare toes and clench my fists. 'Most people don't go to the pub and come back with a pair of goats, John-Joe. Where will we put them? How will we feed them?'

'I'll put them in Colleen's old kennel and sure they'll eat any old crap, you know that, scraps and the like.'

Now I'm properly angry. 'Scraps of what, John-Joe? Leftovers, is that what you mean? Sure, we'd have to have food to have leftovers, wouldn't we? And to have food, we'd have to actually do some work instead of sneaking off to the pub, and then God knows where.' I hiss the words, because I don't want the kids to overhear and be upset, and yet I wonder who on earth I'm fooling. We both know what I mean by 'God knows where'. We mean to a cottage half a mile down the canal or to a council house up the town, and they're only the two I know about.

Bridie told me about the girl in the council house, even though I didn't want to know. I just didn't want to hear it. I wanted to hold my hands over my ears and shout 'la-la-la' at the top of my voice. But she made me listen. 'Michelle, you need to wake up and face reality. He can't go around like that. He can't do that to you and the children.' Her mouth was pursed in a thin line. 'I mean, the girl is still in a school uniform, heaven help us.'

'Oh, God,' I managed, trying to avoid the feeling of nausea which hit my throat at the thought of it.

'I'll get Maurice to talk to him,' she said, crossing her arms, her eyes glittering at the mention of her husband, a big, softly spoken bear of a man with a certain stillness to him that makes others wary. 'He can't be making a fool of you around the town. It's a disgrace, Michelle.' And I hear the unspoken accusation: why can't you keep your husband in check? Why can't you keep him under control? Because it's what women do: they keep their husbands' base instincts in check; they apply a tight pull of the reins if they threaten to misbehave. I never believed that, that men were some kind of animal that had to be kept on a leash. Maybe that's my mistake. That I let him be free.

At the accusation, he steps backwards, and his silver earring flashes in his ear. He purses his lips and clicks his teeth. '"God knows where", eh? Well, anywhere would be better than here, with you, listening to you go on and on at me. Nagging, carping. "Why haven't we got firewood, John-Joe? Why haven't you dug the potato troughs? Why don't you get up off your lazy arse and get a job? Why aren't you good enough for me, John-Joe?"' He mimes my voice, a sour expression on his face. 'Well, you know what, love, at least I'm good enough for someone else.'

'I'm going to bed. I have an early start. I'm going to Wexford in the morning, in case you've forgotten. And you said you'd come.'

He looks blank for a moment, and then his lip curls into a sneer. 'Oh, of course, the nuclear demonstration, as if the world can't do without heroic Michelle making her stand. The moral majority herself. Oh, such principles!'

'The last time I looked, you used to have principles, John-Joe.'

'That was before I realised they made shag-all difference.' He lights a cigarette now and blows the smoke out in a cloud above our heads. He flashes the kids a grin and a little wave, as if we're just having a nice little chat and not spitting insults at each other.

I don't say anything for a long while, before I blurt, 'Well, it's a bit more productive than shagging half of Kildare.'

There's a sudden, deathly silence, during which I can hear his breathing, a little snort in and out of his nose. He's really drunk, and one of the goats shifts a bit and gives a little forlorn bleat. Poor goats, I think, ending up here. And then he's beside me, so close that he has to tilt my head to one side, as he grabs my hair and twists it into a tight knot.

'You're hurting me,' I wail.

'Shagging half of Kildare, is that it, pet? Well, you'd probably know more about that than me, now, wouldn't you? With your boyfriend across the way there. Does he have a nice big bed or a little hard single one for a bachelor? Is it a bit of a tight squeeze, eh? Or maybe he's into sheep shagging or the like?'

I have to twist my head to face him, my scalp now burning from where he's pulling at my hair. I murmur, 'Oh, I don't think so, John-Joe. This seems to be all your idea, this free love. What's the matter? Are you jealous?'

'Piss off,' he hisses, and I can tell that I've got him and I feel a dart of triumph.

'Jesus Christ,' I hiss. 'A fifteen-year-old? And it's illegal, in case you didn't know.'

His face goes as white as a sheet and he stumbles backwards, knocking into one of the goats, who gives a forlorn bleat. And I feel like bleating forlornly as well. His hands are down by his sides now and he looks defeated.

10

June told herself that it was as if she were possessed, as if someone else, not June, was sitting up into the Land Rover, Pilates gear and gym bag on the seat beside her, and driving down to Monasterard. She always stopped at the bridge, though, and looked out for Mother Duck. If she saw her, she'd drive on. And she always went to see Mary-Pat anyway, so that, in some small part of her brain, she could tell herself that that was precisely why she'd come, and not to spend half an hour in the dingy office of a mechanic's garage. Half an hour. They didn't exactly chat, herself and Dave.

That first time, they hadn't discussed the car. There hadn't been time. Dave's hands, large and hairy, had been on her bottom and then on the tops of her thighs, just under the seam of her knickers. 'Is this what you want, June?' He'd leaned over her, his breath hot in her ear. She'd tried to ignore the smell of Nescafé and cigarettes on it, tried to concentrate as he'd fumbled at the top of her blouse with his left hand, his right staying put as they'd bent over his desk, a grubby receipt book, stained with oily fingers, and a half-open packet of Marlboro Lights the only two things left on it. She'd thought suddenly of the stains his hands would make on her silk top — would she ever get oil out of it? She'd have to Google it, she thought as she allowed him to push her skirt up and pull her knickers down.

'Why did you come here?' Dave had asked her after, as they'd draped themselves over his desk, a pile of invoices pushed to the floor along with June's handbag and shoes. Neither of them had fully undressed, and Dave's overalls had hung around his knees. He'd passed the cigarette he'd lit over to her and she'd taken a big pull on it, the way she used to when they were teenagers, but she was out of practice and had ended up coughing and spluttering, Dave banging her back.

'God, I don't know.' June had pulled herself up to a sitting position, pulling her blouse closed over her bra, tugging at a loose strand of hair. Dave wouldn't be offended by the truth — he'd always been like that: thick-skinned, oblivious to insult, unlike Gerry, who'd take offence at the slightest comment. But the truth was, she *did* know. Mary-Pat had said it once: it was because Mammy had left that she was so 'buttoned up. You think you have something to hide.'

'Will I see you again?' Dave's voice had been hoarse and when she'd turned around, her clothes neatly rearranged, her handbag on her arm, he was still lying on his desk, cigarette in hand, a big grin on his face as if all his Christmases had come together. Oh, what have I done? June had thought. What on earth have I done?

ALL THAT I LEAVE BEHIND

'Get dressed,' she'd said, before turning on her heel and walking back out to the car.

Now she was in Mary-Pat's kitchen, pale autumn sunlight streaming in through the windows — what was visible of the windows anyway, with the row of knick-knacks along the windowsill, the walls full of china plates and photos of the kids, and that awful dog, who was currently lurking in the bathroom on his 'special' mat. A dog, in a bathroom. Mary-Pat said it was his favourite place, but it made June shudder. She insisted on using the upstairs bathroom, even though it was coming down with potpourri. But now, she felt grateful for the clutter. It made her feel safe, as if she were in a little cave. And she needed to feel safe these days, when everything seemed fraught with danger.

What I was afraid of all along — it's finally happened, she thought. She'd been running away from it for her whole life, and it had caught up with her anyway, Dave or no Dave.

It was that feeling that had always been with her, that she was the only person in the whole world and that, one day, she'd end up alone. She knew it didn't make sense logically — she was a twin, for a start, and didn't they say that twins always had each other? But she'd never been that close to Pi. She'd always felt that there was something between them, a distance, as if they didn't really understand each other. Didn't speak each other's language. Maybe she was jealous because he'd been Mammy's favourite. Maybe that was it. Mary-Pat had always been beside Mammy when they were children, helping her with the washing-up or with straining that foul-smelling goat's milk through a muslin cloth to make yoghurt. She was Mammy's helper and, God knows, Mammy, and then Daddy, had needed her. And Pi made Mammy laugh; June could still remember the two of them, heads tilted slightly towards each other, snorting with laughter at some shared joke. When she'd ask them what the joke was, they'd just shake their heads. 'It'd take too long to explain,' Pi would say, but June knew what he really meant: 'You're too thick anyway.' She seemed always to have been standing on the edge of things, looking in.

Everyone in the family knew what to do, who to be, except her. She didn't know who she was.

'Where is that brother of ours?' Mary-Pat broke into her thoughts. 'I have to go up to PJ's in an hour to take over. He's off to Dublin to some fishing expo.' Mary-Pat had made a huge pot of tea and was slicing big slabs of fruit brack, which she liberally slathered with butter. June felt her stomach heave. There was no way she could touch that stuff, even though normally she looked forward to it. There was no fruit brack at home, or any other treats for that matter, unless you counted a fridge full of kale, which was Georgia's latest wheeze, the sight of which June found terribly depressing.

'Is Rosie coming?' June asked quietly.

Mary-Pat stopped pouring tea into their mugs and put the pot down on the table. She shrugged.

'You didn't ask her.'

Mary-Pat looked guilty. 'I'm used to it just being the three of us.'

That's not very nice, June thought, but she couldn't help but feel relieved.

'I don't know what she's going to do about that fellow,' and she nodded her head in the direction of the window, as if he was lurking in the back garden and not six thousand miles away. 'I asked her if she was thinking of going back, but she looked at me as if I had six heads.'

'Has she said anything more about Daddy?'

'She has not. And we've let the subject drop.' Mary-Pat shot June a warning look over the top of her 'I Love Mum' mug. Have we? June thought. How exactly could we have done that? But she knew better than to quiz her sister.

'You're looking very fresh these days, Junie,' Mary-Pat was saying, lighting up a cigarette and blowing a big cloud of smoke out into the kitchen.

'For goodness' sake, MP, everyone goes outside to smoke nowadays.' June tutted as she got up to open the window.

'My home is my castle,' Mary-Pat said nonchalantly, taking a big drag. 'Tell me something, is Gerry on the Viagra? You look as if you're getting plenty.'

'Mary-Pat!' June felt her stomach flip. She'd seen that 'look' before, but on other women's faces. Doreen Carmody had it when she was having sex with that dentist, and Susie had it too, with that personal trainer in the gym. June had been horrified when Susie had told her, eyes bright, face flushed with guilt and excitement. June knew what she was doing was wrong. So wrong, and if Gerry found out ... And yet, she felt it, even as she thought about him, about what they did in the 'office' behind the garage, a surge of electricity, a jolt of energy that ran through her. It must be written all over her face.

June blushed bright red at the thought of it. What would her sister think if she knew that June had been pressed against the wall of Dave's office, her skirt up around her waist, breasts hanging out of that expensive bra she'd bought herself for her fortieth birthday. The thought of it made her squirm in her seat.

'Are you all right, June? You look a bit flushed.'

'I just need to use the bathroom for a second,' June said,

getting up and quickly running to the toilet, nearly tripping over the dog in her haste to get to the bowl, which she gripped in both hands as she heaved up the contents of her stomach, what little there was of them. She flushed and rinsed out her mouth, patting it dry with a towel. And she looked at herself in the mirror, two spots of red on her cheeks. 'You are committing adultery,' she mouthed, to see what the words would look like spoken from her own lips. They didn't look good.

As she turned, the dog was sitting in front of her, an anxious look on his face. He came towards June and she shrank back against the sink, but he nudged her hand gently with his head and then he licked it solemnly, before looking at her as if to say, 'Any better?'

'Thanks, Duke,' she said quietly. 'Good boy.'

He wagged his tail in return.

'Must be a tummy bug,' she said to Mary-Pat when she came back to the kitchen, walking over to the sink and helping herself to a glass of water, gulping the contents down, not turning around to face her sister. She looked out the window to Mary-Pat's back garden, at the ornamental pond stuffed with koi, surrounded by gnomes with fishing rods and a large plastic heron.

'Did I tell you, Rosie went to see Frances O'Brien?' Mary-Pat said. June didn't reply because her limbs were trembling and her mouth felt dry. She sat back down at the table and reached out and helped herself to a bit of tea brack, biting into it, feeling the spicy fruit and the thick butter coat her tongue. She swallowed and felt instantly better, the sugar giving her a little boost.

'She did? What on earth would that woman have to say to her?' That woman, who had spent a summer in their home. Who had offered to French plait June's hair and smooth electric-blue eye shadow over June's lids. 'We're best buddies,' Frances

O'Brien had said to June once, and she'd been thrilled that this woman, who just seemed to pulsate with life, would be her friend. Would spend time with her, the one no one wanted to spend time with because she was too 'thick', too slow to keep up with them all. But Frances O'Brien didn't think so: she thought June was 'an amazing little girl'. And June had treasured that — even when she'd woken up one morning to find Frances's place at the breakfast table empty. When she'd asked where Frances was, Mary-Pat had given her a look of such venom she'd felt like hiding under the table. Frances had vanished as suddenly as she'd arrived, and even though she now lived less than a mile away from here, it might as well have been Timbuktu.

'Lord knows. She was on Rosie's baptismal cert and she thought she might know something. Wish to Christ she'd let it go.' And Mary-Pat gave June that look again, the warning one, although June couldn't quite work out what her sister wanted to warn her about.

She didn't know what to say, so she decided to change the subject. 'I'd better go. Gerry's off early today and we've booked La Firenze.'

At this, Mary-Pat looked visibly brighter. 'Oh, very posh,' she said, in a mock south-Dublin accent. 'Well, what is it Gerry always says? "Have fun,"' and she did an imitation of Gerry that was pitch perfect.

'Piss off,' June said. 'Tell Pi I said hello. I'll be down to you next week.'

'What's with the weekly visits, Junie? Next thing, you'll be moving back.'

'Oh, there's no fear of that,' June said, picking up her handbag and holding it in the crook of her arm. 'No fear of that at all.'

She had the front door open when Mary-Pat asked her, 'June, are you sure you're all right?' She turned to look at her sister. She had never been able to lie to Mary-Pat. One look and she'd be blurting out the truth in no time. But she wasn't about to do that now. If she told the truth, God knows what might happen.

I need to go and see Maeve, she thought, when she got back in the car. She wasn't sure why she'd left it so long, but now it seemed urgent, something she absolutely had to do. Maybe she was looking for salvation, she thought grimly as she looked at her watch, calculating how long it would take to drive around the M50 and south to Bray, then back home again. Gerry would kill her if she was late. He'd already given out about restaurants having two sittings and how dare they throw you out after an hour when you'd paid good money for your dinner. She didn't want to upset him — there was a board meeting in a few days at work and they always stressed him out. It was funny, she thought as she drove along, how that part of her brain could still work, could still mind him and look after him and care about him, while the other part ... She blinked furiously. At least she could do one good thing today. Just one thing.

The road around the city was empty at this time of day, but June wouldn't have noticed if it was jammed with traffic: she just kept driving, the white lines of the road markings disappearing under the car as she drove and drove. When she looked around to see where she was, she was almost surprised to see that she was coming up to the roundabout for Loughlinstown hospital, ten miles out of town, the icing-sugar dome of the Sugar Loaf mountain in front of her. It was as if the car had driven itself south towards Wicklow. It was funny how that happened, June thought as she drove, how your body still knew how to do the things your mind had forgotten about.

As she bumped off the motorway and down the narrow roads to Bray, June clutched the steering wheel and gritted her teeth, manoeuvring the Land Rover into a tight spot between a white van and an ancient Citroën. The act of completing the task made her feel stupidly pleased with herself. She wasn't much good at reverse parking. When she got out, her knees were wobbly, her hands shaking as she fiddled with the car keys. She looked at the house, a granite Edwardian block with a white-painted balustrade over the porch and a shrivelled palm tree beside the red front door. 'Elsinore' was painted in the fanlight above the porch. It looked grand, shabby and genteel all at the same time, with the two white-painted lions that flanked the front doorstep, a riot of geraniums in pots lined up on either side of the tiled entrance.

The bell played a little tune when June pressed it. It sounded incongruous in the surroundings, a tinny 'When Irish Eyes Are Smiling', and when it finished there was silence. June was wondering if she'd have to press the bell and hear the awful song again, when there was a shuffling noise inside. 'Just coming,' a reedy voice called from the other side of the door.

Maeve opened it, her black hair, now streaked with grey, pulled back into a bun, her currant-black eyes squinting in the sun. June knew that Maeve was older than Mammy, but wondered if this is what her mother would now look like: her face a criss-cross of wrinkles, dotted with liver spots. Her hands twisted with arthritis. 'I'm sorry, Maeve,' she began, 'I should have called first, I—'

'June!' Maeve's face crinkled up in a smile and her eyes all but disappeared. 'Musha, for God's sake, why? 'Tisn't often we get visitors these days, I can tell you. C'mon in.'

June couldn't work out who she meant by 'we' — Maeve's husband, Alan, had died years ago — but at the sight of Maeve's face, she wanted to cry with relief, to grab hold of the woman and hang on to her, sobbing, like a little girl. She remembered her manners then and instead cleared her throat to keep the tears down. 'If you're sure?'

But Maeve was already gone, shuffling gently down the hall on her walker and into the living room, clearly expecting June to follow her. She was talking as she went, a stream of chat that June couldn't hear and so she just 'aha'-ed and 'yes'-ed at what she thought were appropriate moments. God it was depressing, she thought, as she watched Maeve shuffle through the gloom. The half-drawn curtains only let in a small trickle of light, through which danced dust motes and which dimly illuminated the piles of old newspapers scattered on almost every surface.

'Excuse the mess,' Maeve was saying as she lowered herself into an armchair. 'The cleaning girl only comes once a fortnight now — I hardly think there's much need with only myself ... Oh, I forgot to offer you a cup of tea — where on earth are my manners.' She chuckled and made to get up out of the chair.

June made a motion with her hand, urging Maeve to stay put. 'It's fine, thanks, Maeve. I can't stay long.'

'Oh?' Maeve looked disappointed now, her liver-spotted hand clutching the handle of her walker, her face a mass of wrinkles as she peered at June, like a little walnut. June had to damp down a shiver of revulsion. To think, one day she'd look like that.

'No. I have to ... well, I've come about Mammy, Maeve.'

Maeve didn't stop smiling, but waited, still, like a bird.

'It's just ... I think I might need to show someone else the letters.' As she said it, June suddenly wondered why she was asking Maeve's permission. She could have shown them to half the world and Maeve would be none the wiser. But she hadn't, because the weight of it had felt so enormous, a secret that only she and Maeve shared. Maybe that's why she was here now, she thought, because she didn't want to keep that secret any more — because she wanted to break it, to be free of it once and for all.

Maeve shook her head. 'Oh, no, June. She was very clear about that. Just you. She thought she could rely on you to keep your counsel, so to speak.'

June twisted her scarf in her hands. It was an expensive scarf, black with a white skull motif on it. McQueen, so India said. She'd helped her pick it out in Brown Thomas, forking out a couple of hundred euro for it. 'It'll make you look younger, Mum,' she'd said, to June's amusement. As if a *scarf* could make you look younger. Now, she looked at it for a second, wondering why on earth she was wearing it — it seemed so silly, somehow, so … superfluous, that was the word.

She looked up and realised that Maeve was waiting for her to say something in response. 'Maeve, I've never breathed a word to anyone. Not even Mary-Pat.'

'Oh, I know you haven't, pet, I know. That was precisely why Michelle trusted you. It shows she was right,' and Maeve beamed, her little curranty eyes squished up in her face.

June could feel herself growing impatient. Get on with it, June. 'It's just, well, something's happened. With Rosie.'

'Ah.' Maeve looked out the window, her hands clasped in her lap, as if trying to find something in the windblown seafront outside.

'Yes. Daddy said something to her. On her wedding day, in fact,' June said, rolling her eyes to heaven. Maeve knew Daddy. She knew what he was like. She'd understand.

'Is that so?' Maeve was such an expert at non-committal politeness.

'Yes, Maeve, he did.' June tugged at the end of her silly scarf. 'He, ehm ...' June looked down at her hands, with their immaculate nails covered with just a sheen of clear nail polish, at her wedding band, her diamond eternity ring and the large emerald engagement ring that had belonged to Gerry's mother. 'He denied she was his.'

There was no response and when June looked up Maeve was still and entirely silent, her features giving nothing away. Eventually, she said, 'Not very tactful.'

'No.' June had to smile at the understatement. 'No, it wasn't. But what I need to know is, is it true?'

There was a sigh from Maeve. A small, soft one. 'Well, your daddy was – is – an interesting man, June. Complicated, that's for sure. And your parents' relationship was complex – not that they didn't love each other. They did, but, well—'

'I know about Daddy, Maeve.'

'Of course.' Maeve pulled herself slowly into a standing position, a look of pain flickering across her face as she did so. Leaning on her walker, she shuffled slowly over to where June was sitting on the overstuffed sofa and eased herself down beside her, reaching a withered hand out and patting her gently on the knee. 'I know what you think, pet, but it's easy to judge, when there were two of them in the marriage. It was difficult to live the life they'd chosen. There were a lot of hardships.'

At the mention of the word 'hardships', June swallowed down the anger which was threatening to bubble up again. You think I don't know about the bloody hardships, she thought; you think I don't *know*?

'You know, your mother wasn't an easy woman either, June,'

Maeve said quietly. 'She had high standards, for herself and for others, and they could be hard to live up to sometimes. I think John-Joe struggled with that a bit and it brought out the naughty boy in him.' She smiled. 'Try not to be too hard on your father, June: he wasn't entirely to blame.'

'Do you mean for her leaving?' June said, her senses on alert.

'Not exactly,' Maeve said. 'Your mother was a passionate person, June. She was such a trailblazer. Oh, I still remember her in secretarial college, telling Mrs Joyce that it was time she wised up and joined the twentieth century, and asking her if she'd ever heard of Women's Lib.' Maeve chuckled. 'And she refused to learn shorthand because she said it made no sense and, anyway, she wasn't going to be a secretary. She was going to forge her own path. She wanted to change the world. And when she met your father, she thought he was a kindred spirit. But, sure, he wasn't really able for her, the same John-Joe. He couldn't keep up with her.'

The stuffy room seemed to settle around June, dust motes circling in the late-summer light. There didn't seem to be enough air, and when she breathed in, it tasted of old books and mouldy newspapers. 'Did she have an affair, Maeve? Is that what you're saying?' June said.

Maeve didn't answer straight away, and in the silence, for some reason, June thought of Sean O'Reilly and how good he'd been to her, to them all. Even as a child, she'd known how much he'd liked Mammy, by the slight flush on his neck every time he caught sight of her, by the way his eyes followed her across the yard — not in a creepy way, but like a lovelorn boy, but there was no way ... He was a good man, Sean. She'd spent half her childhood in his kitchen, nursing the sick hens he kept in a little crate by the range or playing with Bessie's pups. Once, they'd had to warm one of them up, when the little creature had strayed out of the barn and had ended up soaking wet and cold. They'd placed the little black-and-white bundle carefully into the warming drawer of the range, Sean's huge, spade-like hands scooping the pup up and onto the cast-iron grate at the bottom. 'Will she get cooked?' June had asked, worried.

He hadn't laughed at her, just shaken his head seriously. 'There's only just enough heat here to warm her through. She'll be fine, but you'll have to keep a close eye on her. Do you think you can do that?'

June's chest had puffed up with importance. 'Yes, Sean.' She'd nodded. And she'd spent the rest of the afternoon by the range, watching the little body as it slowly uncurled, the pale blue eyes opening, a little mewl escaping its lips.

Maeve was talking now, looking down at her hands. 'Well …' she added. 'Not as far as I know. Your mother didn't tell me everything, you know. We weren't that close,' she said.

Well, that was a lie, so what else was Maeve lying about. June remembered the smile of satisfaction, the look of self-importance in Maeve's eyes every time she'd hand over a letter. I'm the secret-keeper, it said. Without me, where would you be? And June remembered then why she found it so hard to trust her, because she thought she could control her, doling out access to Mammy like it was a bag of sweets. Well, not any more.

'Tell me the truth,' she ordered, shocked as the words came out of her mouth like bullets. She wasn't normally like that, so aggressive. Maeve recoiled, a frightened look on her face.

'That *is* the truth,' Maeve whispered. 'As far as I know, June. Your mother was at a low ebb. Your father's drinking was getting out of control and the smallholding wasn't working out and,

well, there were your father's ... indiscretions; but an affair ...
I don't know ...'

For God's sake. June didn't know which of them was worse.
Mind you, not that she was anyone to talk. She gripped the
handles of her handbag so tightly her knuckles were white. She
could feel the two bright spots of red on her cheeks. 'Maeve, if
you know something, can you just tell me? Rosie deserves it.
She deserves to know who she is. Please.' She almost choked on
the word 'please'.

Maeve nodded without speaking. There was a long silence,
while the house around them shifted and groaned, like a creaky
ship, and June felt that herself and Maeve were floating along
on it, the two of them the only people alive.

'I can still see your mother standing on the doorstep, you
know, with Rosie beside her. It was an awful day, just awful.
Grey and dreary and the rain hadn't let up all morning,' Maeve
began. 'Oh, she was in such a state, your poor mother. I was
worried about her, I really was. She'd been under so much
strain for the previous few months,' and here Maeve blinked and
looked down at her hands before taking a deep breath. 'I think
all the years of hardship had just worn her down. All those years
of trying to live a life that just put so many demands on her,
and, well, she just stood there, soaking wet, little Rosie standing
there beside her in a little coat and knitted bonnet, and all she
said was "help". I can still remember it as if it were yesterday,'
Maeve said softly. 'Just that word, "help" – it has such a finality
to it. I could see that she was finished, just hollowed out.' She
sighed. 'And so, that's what I did. I rang the mailboat company
and I booked a ticket and then Alan took her to Dun Laoghaire
...' Maeve stopped. 'So help me, June, I still think I did the
right thing.'

'But *why*, Maeve?' June didn't know what question she was really asking. Why did she have an affair, if she did, why did she leave, why did she marry Daddy? All of that. There were so many whys.

'You know, it takes a lot for a mother to leave her children, June. And to be honest, I probably didn't understand myself. Alan and me weren't blessed with children ...' Here, she paused for a second, clearing her throat. She put a hand to the small gold crucifix that hung around her neck, her bottom lip trembling. For a second, June felt sorry for her. She said nothing, just looked at Maeve expectantly. 'I couldn't see how ...' Maeve hesitated. 'Well, I think she counted the cost of that every single day.'

I've had enough, June thought. I don't want to think about how Mammy felt, I really don't. She stood up from the sofa so quickly she felt giddy for a second and had to steady herself as she pulled the strap of her handbag over her shoulder. She looked down at Maeve, at the little collection of bones in the too-big cardigan, the shapeless skirt, and she almost felt sorry for her. 'Thanks for seeing me, Maeve,' she said blankly. 'Don't get up. I'll see myself out,' and she turned towards the door, trying not to bolt.

'But that's not everything ...' Maeve protested.

'I've heard enough,' was June's only reply. She tried not to run to the front door, tap-tapping down the hall with its parquet flooring and carefully opening the door, a gust of wind pushing into her, sending her hair flying around her head. She almost didn't hear Maeve's reedy voice following her. 'Talk to Mary-Pat. She knows.'

* * *

I hate her, I hate her, I hate her, the mantra kept spinning in June's head as she drove towards the seafront, a line of silver-grey on the horizon, then turned left again in the direction of Dublin. The mantra stayed in her head all the way home, and it took her a while to understand who she was ranting about. It wasn't Maeve at all. It was Mammy. All these years. All that time spent protecting her memory and keeping that bloody secret — for what? Who on earth gained from it — not Rosie, not Mary-Pat and certainly not her. Look at what she'd done, trying to wreck her own life. June thumped the steering wheel, screaming at Lyric FM, which was warbling away in the background. As if classical music could give her a bit of class.

By the time she got home, she'd burnt herself out. She pulled up the gravel drive and switched the car off, wearily getting out and clambering down, opening the front door and stepping inside, the cool air of the hall enveloping her. She could barely put one foot in front of the other and had no idea how she'd get through the evening. Maybe she could cancel — say she had a migraine, but no, she couldn't do that to him, she thought. She looked around the hall, taking in the silence in the house. Gerry mustn't be back yet. God, she hoped the board meeting hadn't gone on for too long or he'd be in a terrible mood. At least, she'd have time to shower and change, to wash the smell off her now. She threw her handbag on the table and went to climb the stairs, and then she let out a little scream. Gerry was sitting on the top step in the semi-darkness, a glass of whiskey in his hand.

'Where have you been?'

August 1979

Michelle

The sun is beating down through the open windows of the car and I can feel the seats sticky underneath me. I'm in the front seat and Bob's driving, and Mary-Pat and June are in the back, bickering over who gets to sit closest to the tinny stereo that's blasting out the charts into the car. I've let John-Joe go with Melody and Pi in the other car. Serves him right, she can bore him to death. She'd probably be just about the only woman in the world he wouldn't make a pass at. And besides, I can't bear to look at him. Every time I do, I see him, his hands on that girl.

I close my eyes for a few seconds and just feel the sun on my face, the heat of it, warming me to my bones. And it feels good, the warm breeze in my hair; I feel myself relax, my shoulders drop, my muscles soften. Mary-Pat and June are singing along to 'My Sharona', the two of them miming, then yelling out the chorus, 'Muh-muh, muh, My Sharona.' And I can hear them both laugh, and Bob cracks a joke and they giggle and Mary-Pat says that he's quite funny for an old man. She's such a funny girl, Mary-Pat, so forthright, so cheeky — she can make anyone laugh, and yet she's more sensible than any of us. It was she who walked the goats over to Sean this morning and asked him if he'd mind them for the couple of days.

If anyone ever asked me what the final straw was, I'd have to say, 'the goats'. It seems laughable, the notion that once I thought they were our salvation; that if only we could get hold of a pair of goats, all our problems would be solved — the goats would be a symbol of our lifestyle, of our choices, and all that lovely, creamy milk and cheese an emblem of our success in the life we'd chosen, a sign of richness, of completeness. What a joke.

I lean back against the headrest and I find myself nodding off, and as I do, I can feel it wash over me, the exhaustion, the feeling that I could sleep forever. Just then, as if she read my mind, June begins to tap me, her fingers sharp in the flesh of my upper arm, little jabs. My eyes shoot open and, before I can stop myself, I'm reaching around into the back seat and slapping her hard on the top of her legs, one, two, three times. I can see my hand moving, the marks of my fingers bright red on her little brown legs. Her mouth opens in shock, a little 'o', and then she's wailing, a long, almost silent howl, and Bob is saying, 'Michelle, take it easy, they were only messing.' And I turn around and face forwards again and look out the windscreen at the green trees flashing by, hear the tiny snatches of birdsong, the hum of a tractor in the distance, and my hand is shaking. Did I just do that? I wonder. Did I just hit my child? And it's all I can do to stop myself opening the door of the car and throwing myself into the ditch.

* * *

The campsite at Carnsore is a riot of orange canvas and cars, all jumbled up behind the sand dunes, the large white catering tents in the distance, and already I can hear the music floating across the hot, dry grass. People are sprawled out on the dunes, sunbathing and smoking, their placards on the grass beside them: 'No to Nuclear', 'Nuclear Power, Nein Danke'. We clamber out of the car and I try not to look at June, and we gaze around us at the sea of tents. 'That man's not wearing any clothes, Mammy,' Mary-Pat pipes up, as a naked man dives into the sea with a whoop.

'I can see that,' I say. 'Let's see if we can find Dad, will we?'

The two girls are subdued as we walk towards the stalls at the corner of the site, a long row of white canvas. In one, a German couple is cooking sausages and the aroma, along with the rich stew of frying onion, makes my stomach rumble. I desperately want to eat one, but I know that we'll have to make do with the rations we brought: a few eggs from the hens, a big bag of potatoes and, the *pièce de résistance*, a big slab of ham donated by Bridie. What would I do without Bridie? Just the thought of the food makes my mouth water.

The girls know better than to ask for something I can't afford, but I say it anyway. 'We'll get our eggs and ham as soon as we find Daddy and set up the stove.' But they're distracted by the sight of a naked man in what looks like a large cage, a beard down to his ankles, the bones in his shoulders sticking out, his cheeks hollow. A hand-painted sign stuck to the front of the cage says 'Blanket Protest'.

The girls start to giggle and I find myself joining in, the three of us with our hands over our mouths. 'Why is he protesting about a blanket, Mammy?' Mary-Pat asks.

'I think it's to do with the Troubles,' I say vaguely. 'The

prisoners are protesting about their rights. At least I think they are.' The Troubles seem a million miles away right now.

'Oh, yes, Sister Fidelma makes us pray for all the poor people in the North,' June says, talking for the first time since we'd arrived. When I look at her, she doesn't meet my eye but looks down at the ground instead, the toe of her sandal scuffing along the sandy ground.

'Well, that's a lovely thing,' I say. 'I'm sure they can hear your prayers.'

She gives me the look then that I deserve.

'C'mon, let's go down to the water,' I say, and the two girls scream in delight. They haven't been to the sea, not really, and the size of it, the flat blueness, intrigues them. They are used to the warm brownness of the canal and Mary-Pat shrieks as she dips a toe in the water. 'It's freezing. Mammy, can we swim?'

I nod and they strip to their little red knickers and hop up and down in the tiny waves, letting out little screams of delight. And I remember that Mummy used to take me to Sandycove every day during the summer and I'd watch her swim out to the buoy about a hundred yards away, a firm, ladylike breaststroke, her head high above the water in her frilly rubber swimming hat. She'd get out of the water then in her black swimsuit, her thighs heavy and mottled, her toes turning in with bunions and she'd sit down beside me and reach a damp hand into her purse and pull out two sixpence pieces. 'Off you go,' she'd command and I'd run up to the ice-cream van, returning with two 99s to see her in her tent, a big circle of blue towelling with an elasticated top, under which I could see her arms move, her knees lifting to pull off her togs and pull on her roll-on. She'd send me for ice-creams so that she could preserve her privacy, her dignity, and as I watched the girls, I wondered what dignity

I had to preserve. What sense of myself I still had left, what kind of a mother I could be to my children.

And then I see it, the shell. It's hard to miss because it's about four times the size of the other shells on the beach. This one is big and black and has a bumpy matt surface, a bit like the surface of the moon, and when I hold it in my hand, it feels warm. I hold it up to my ear and I hear the hiss of the sea, and then I think of my childhood swims with Mummy and it's all I can do not to let out a bellow of pain, right here on the beach.

When Mary-Pat comes up to me, shivering, water dripping off her hair, I give it to her and tell her to hold it up to her ear, and when she does, her mouth opens in wonder. 'Every time you listen to it, think of me, will you?' I say.

She doesn't reply because she has no idea what I mean, and so I just shake my head and tell her not to take any notice of my nonsense. 'Let's go and find Daddy, shall we, and we'll have our tea,' I say, rubbing the girls dry with the small hand towel I've brought, then watching them run off together up the dunes. They'd be all right, I think, if I wasn't there. They have each other. It's Pius I'd worry about. He'd miss me more than any of them.

I can't believe I'm even imagining this, I think, as I tilt my face up to the hot sun, that it's even entered my mind. But more and more these days, I find myself wondering what it would feel like not to live this life any more. Not to have to face another day of disappointment, of looking at John-Joe over the kitchen table and thinking about just how much I've come to hate him. You've let me down, I think. You've let us all down. You're not the man I thought you were. Maybe you never were.

I pull myself up to a standing position, and my bones ache; they feel stiff and tired, as if the years of damp and cold have lodged in them permanently. I trudge off up the dunes to find the girls, wandering through the sea of orange until I see the yellow tent that Bob brought with him. It's not hard to pick out because it's decorated with huge Tibetan prayer flags that he brought back from his 'pilgrimage' to that country. That and a tendency to preach about spirituality and being at one with the universe.

I walk towards the tent and see that Bob and John-Joe are bent over the guy ropes, pinning them into the dry ground. Beside them, drinking from a bottle of beer, is a nut-brown girl with auburn hair and a ready smile. 'I'm Frances,' she says, reaching out her hand. 'Your hair's really beautiful.' And something about that compliment makes me realise. And then John-Joe stands up and lights a cigarette, and I catch his eye and he looks away. And I think of Mummy again in her towelling tent and I understand that I have nothing left. Nothing.

'Christy Moore's on next,' Frances is saying. 'You coming, Michelle?'

'In a bit – I need to make the kids their tea,' I say, and that phrase should give me my dignity, but instead it makes me feel like a nobody.

'Of course you do,' she says. 'You're a mother,' in a tone of awe.

'Yes, that's right,' I say, as if I need to remind myself. At least the girl has the grace to blush, because there's nothing as unassailable as a mother, nothing so sacred, is there? I thought it would protect me, like an amulet of sorts, keeping John-Joe beside me and other things away, but now I see that it has no value at all in this new world that I, for one, insisted upon. And I feel a fool. There would be no such thing as a title in my world, or a boundary, or a notion of status; it would all, somehow, blur into a happy nothingness, where respect and status were irrelevant, would come from hard work and self-satisfaction. Now, I realise that I've given away the only thing of worth I have.

I muster up as much defiance as I can manage and I look that nut-brown girl in the eye and I say, 'A mother'.

I plead a headache so that I can leave later, even though Christy Moore is still warbling away on the stage. I've been standing behind the nut-brown girl, inhaling her scent of patchouli and sweat. I can see her shoulders tense, her head held rigid, the beer bottle she's been clutching in her hand waving around and I think, good, I'm glad you feel tense. When I declare that I have a headache, I can see her shoulders relax and it's all I can do not to rip every hair out of her head. Instead, I say that I'm taking the girls back to my tent, that they're exhausted after the trip down and the heat. 'Of course they are!' nut-brown girl declares and tries to pull Mary-Pat to her in a hug. Mary-Pat goes rigid in her arms, like a board, and I want to pull her towards me and kiss the top of her plump little head and thank her, but then June lets herself be hugged, putting her skinny little arms around the woman's neck, just for a second, and I see it, that they've met this woman before, and I wonder how often and where.

They're subdued, the two of them, as if exhausted by what's going on around them, absorbing all the unspoken tensions between their parents without even knowing it. They lean into each other as we walk back across the crowded dunes, stepping over bodies or around people sitting cross-legged on the grass, a cloud of dope smoke rising up in the sky, which is the palest pinky-blue, the grass crackling beneath our feet. Mary-Pat tucks an arm into June's and the two of them bump along, June's head touching Mary-Pat's shoulder, bouncing off it, the wisps of her brown hair flying around her head, and Mary-Pat lets her lean in, accepts the weight of her, supports it. They have each other, my two little girls, together with that silent language they both speak, pushes and shoves and hugs, and I think how lucky they both are. And I wonder, just for a moment, if I wasn't behind them, what might that be like. Would they even notice or would they just keep on walking, moving forward together? The thought is so frightening, so distressing, that I have to run to catch up with them both, an arm around each shoulder, breaking their perfect circle by sticking my head in between theirs and planting a kiss on each cheek, which they suffer with a silent smile.

When we get back to the tent, Pius is sitting outside with Bob, the two of them cooking marshmallows over the fire Bob has made, the light flickering orange in Pius's monkey features, his currant-black eyes, his eyebrows sharp black lines above them; he's jabbering away to Bob about some theory he has – Pius always has a theory, whether it's about fishing or the stars or the lifecycle of the newt. 'I have a theory, Mammy ...' he'll say. My clever, restless little boy.

Bob normally just does small talk, harmless chat, the odd dry one-liner, because he's a shy man, particularly with women. Melody is the only woman he trusts, and I wonder what that must be like, even if she is a complete twit. She's his twit. But now, he pats a place beside him on the grass. 'Sit. Have a marshmallow.'

I can hear the girls squealing in the tent, something about a spider, and I sit down, feeling, as I do, the fight suddenly go out of me; my bones are melting into the ground, sinking down into the earth. I fight the urge to lean against Bob, but in the end, I give in and allow the top of my arm to rest against his. And then he puts an arm around me and squeezes my shoulder and kisses the top of my head. And I feel like a child being comforted by a parent, and it feels good. So good.

'I'm sorry, Shell. It's not right ...'

I shake my head. 'I can't help thinking that somehow I asked for it. I brought it upon myself.'

His voice is a low rumble in my ear. 'You did nothing wrong, love. Nothing.'

The hot tears come then, filling my eyes and spilling down my cheeks, and I shake my head vigorously, wiping them away with the back of my sleeve. 'Oh, I did, Bob. If only I'd known. I forced him into being a person he isn't, and I suppose I have no one to blame but myself for the way things have turned out. He told me, you know, that he didn't want this life, but I ignored him. I just ploughed on, hoping he'd just go along with me, and I suppose this is his way of showing me, isn't it? He's been trying to show me how he really feels, because when he told me, I didn't listen.'

Bob sighs. 'He's an adult, Shell, he can act of his own free will. Nobody forced him to live this way. He chose it. The place in Kildare, don't you remember? It was his dream. Turns out, he just liked the idea of it, not the reality. Who'd have thought it, that you'd be the one with the grit?' And he gives a little laugh. 'When I first met you, I thought, this girl will never make it. She'll be gone the first time the pipes freeze or the range packs up. But you didn't. You stuck it out. You stuck by your principles.'

I give a short laugh. 'Principles don't pay the bills, Bob. And I'm tired of it, to be honest. Tired of doing it all alone. I don't really think I can go on much longer.' And as I say the words, I realise that they're true. That I have nothing left to give.

II

*M*ary-Pat closed her eyes as she held a matching pair of red satin briefs and a slinky top, wondering if she could squeeze into them, then opened them again, almost surprised to find herself in the middle of a lingerie shop at Kildare Village. It was all too much: too overwhelming, to be knee-deep in thongs and cut-price designer clothes, confronted with the way she'd been feeling all these years. She just didn't know how to process it all. Graham had said to be kind to herself, but she didn't know how when she'd done so much wrong.

'You made the best of an impossible situation,' had been Graham's parting words, but she couldn't accept that. She just couldn't.

She could hear Melissa's voice from the other corner of the shop, laughing and chatting – she must be on her mobile.

Mary-Pat had sent her off to the shoe place because she didn't want her to see her mother shopping for fancy underwear.

'Mum, are you in there somewhere?' Melissa's voice drifted towards her over the racks of lace and satin.

Oh, Christ. Mary-Pat threw the red slinky thing back on the rail and grabbed a pair of not-too-hideous-looking blue lacy undies that came with a matching corset that looked about her size and made for the till, her eyes scanning the rows of clothing to make sure that Melissa wasn't about to appear.

'Very nice.' The girl at the till smiled at her as she folded them carefully into pink tissue paper. 'Must be a special occasion.'

'You could say that,' Mary-Pat agreed, looking at the girl for the first time. She was Eastern European, judging by her accent, a lovely slim girl with sallow skin and lustrous dark hair and the kind of fabulous figure they all had, all long legs and tiny waists – none of the blubber of the Irish. Mary-Pat blushed then: she'd bet this girl would look fantastic in a lacy bra and knickers, not like an elephant.

'It's our anniversary,' she blurted.

'Oh, congratulations. He will be pleased with his present.' The girl laughed.

Oh, Christ, Mary-Pat thought. Why had she said that? It wasn't even their anniversary, but she could hardly tell the girl the truth, that she was trying to seduce her own husband in the hope that it might put him off the competition. That she hoped a nice bit of underwear might tempt him to forsake the pleasures of a gingham pinny and a puff of blonde hair. It sounded pathetic, when you put it like that, but Mary-Pat couldn't think of anything better. She needed to make a statement to PJ, to show him what he'd be missing if he thought a bit of Polish totty would do him.

ALL THAT I LEAVE BEHIND

At least Graham would be pleased with her, she thought, taking the bag off the girl with a muttered 'thanks'. Pleased that she was taking a positive approach to things and not resorting to anger or recrimination. 'Confrontation is your *raison d'être*, Mary-Pat. Have you considered another approach?' he'd asked her once. Stifling the urge to tell him to feck off and thereby proving his theory right, she'd said that, funnily enough, she had. She was going to have a nice dinner with her husband and discuss their relationship in a calm and rational manner. Not that she'd told Graham what she'd be wearing.

She hadn't told Graham, either, that she'd paid the opposition a visit. She knew he wouldn't like that. He'd think badly of her. That she was the kind of woman who would pour paint on her rival's car or would chop up her husband's suits in a jealous rage, but she wasn't. She knew that she could be a bit ... direct sometimes, but she wasn't prone to losing it like that. It wasn't her style. She just wanted to look the woman in the eye to see what she was dealing with.

She'd waited until the lull after lunch, when the sales reps had bought their greasy rolls full of fried food and bombed off up to Dublin, when the locals would be at home after lunch or at work and, more importantly, when she'd known PJ would be at the shop, and before she could think twice about it, she'd pulled up in front of the minimarket and hopped out, taking in a deep breath before pushing open the door and going inside.

She'd lurked down the back for a few minutes, trying to catch a glimpse of her over the tops of the plastic bottles of oil and antifreeze, the deodorising trees that you could hang from your rear-view mirror. She had been able to hear her, a gentle murmur of English with a foreign intonation, a tinkle of laughter which had made Mary-Pat want to scream. Maybe that's why PJ liked her, because she laughed like that, like a young woman, a carefree youngster with her whole life before her and boobs that didn't hang around her ankles.

Mary-Pat had grabbed one of the little trees and made for the counter, her feet carrying her forward even while her mind was darting around frantically, asking herself what, exactly, she thought she was doing. She hadn't looked up as she'd handed the tree over and rummaged in her purse for a few euro.

'Lovely day, isn't it?' The woman's voice had been warm and lively and, as the question had been directed at her, Mary-Pat had known she'd have to look up to answer her. She'd found herself looking into a pair of vivid green eyes, outlined with a big sweep of dark eye-liner, and that hair, piled into one of those topknots that were all the rage.

'It is.' Mary-Pat had found herself agreeing, handing over a few coins. She'd hesitated, wondering what else she would have to say to this woman. Stop bothering my husband? Leave him to come back to his wife and children? 'Ehm, can I have twenty Benson and Hedges as well?'

'Sure,' the girl had said brightly and turned to the cigarette dispenser, giving Mary-Pat a glimpse of a slender waist, a curvy bottom. Oh, Christ, no wonder he fancied her.

'Eight-twenty please,' she'd trilled. Handing over the change, the girl had said, 'Have a good day!'

'You too,' Mary-Pat had muttered, grabbing the cigarettes and trying to bolt out of the shop.

'Excuse me?'

Mary-Pat had been at the door and had contemplated pretending she hadn't heard, but she'd looked up and the girl had been waving the bloody cardboard tree at her. 'I think you forgot this.'

Mary-Pat had had to walk back up to the counter, her head bowed. 'Thanks.' She hadn't even been able to look the woman in the eye, let alone speak to her. It had just been too much. Just too hurtful. It was all she could do to dash back to the safety of the Pajero and sit there and sob.

It was funny, Mary-Pat thought, scanning the racks of clothes and bags, trying to catch a glimpse of her daughter's dark head, how history could repeat itself. She'd never have thought that PJ had it in him, that weakness, just like Daddy had. Maybe all men had it, even Graham, with his beige sleeveless jumpers. Some part of her knew that it wasn't fair to lump PJ in with Daddy, but she couldn't help it. She wanted to kill him. Now she knew how her mother must have felt, all those times. How betrayed, how lonely. And none of them had done a thing about it. They'd just left her to it, to her shame and humiliation.

The pattern was always the same. Daddy would be morose for a while, puffing away on his cigarettes and looking out the window, tapping a foot agitatedly on the kitchen floor, before announcing that he was 'going out for a little drive'. June would look up from whatever she was doing and catch Mary-Pat's eye and then they'd both continue, as if the unspoken thought had never existed in either's mind. Daddy would come back from his 'little drives' whistling and humming to himself and be full of the joys, bursting into one of his songs as he opened the fridge and then closed it again, there naturally being nothing inside. He'd turn to them then and boom, 'Well, ladies, how's about we treat ourselves to a trip to the chipper? I fancy a single of cod and chips.' And he'd pat his stomach expansively. To Mary-

Pat's shame, they always said yes, acquiesced to being bought for the price of a bag of hot, greasy chips.

Frances O'Brien had been different, though. She wasn't one of the usual, the local slappers with high heels and short skirts that just wanted a bit of excitement, who thought that Daddy, with his silver earring and flashing dark eyes, was a loveable gypsy rogue. For a start, she was the first one that Daddy had brought through the front door. Mary-Pat should have known, from that one act, that it was the beginning of the end.

She smelled like ripe cheese, Mary-Pat had thought, as she'd stood beside Daddy in a ragged T-shirt with 'I love NY' on it in faded lettering. Her nipples could clearly be seen through the material, and she was tanned a rich, dark brown, like the mahogany sideboard in the living room. Mary-Pat had had to give Pius a good dig with her elbow to get him to stop staring at her breasts, although she could hardly blame him — they were fairly noticeable, along with her dirty feet in a pair of flip-flops and her grimy fingernails. Only her hair seemed clean, a lustrous auburn that spiralled around her face in thick waves, her hair and her teeth, which were white and strong. She should have been revolting, but instead she radiated sex, Mary-Pat had thought. As a nine-year-old, she couldn't name it, but she could see it. Sex and health and joy. Next to her, Mammy's pale beauty seemed insubstantial, ghostly, as if you could blow it away with one puff of breath.

'This is Frances. She's come to have a look at the goats,' Daddy announced. He was almost shy with her, reverential as she stood there, leaning against the doorframe, head tilted towards his, a bright smile on her face.

'Hi everyone,' Frances had said, giving a little wave and a

flash of those teeth, a little wiggle of her hips which set her breasts jiggling again.

'Hi,' they murmured, and while they all returned to whatever they'd been doing beforehand, it was clear that something had changed. From the moment she'd set foot in the house, there was a different vibration, one that Mary-Pat couldn't quite put her finger on. It filled the house with a treacly, oily atmosphere and they all seemed to wade around in it, pulling themselves through it, herself and Pius and June and Mammy and Daddy.

When had she understood how serious it all was? That Frances wasn't just another one of Daddy's flings? Mary-Pat remembered now, it was the day they'd gone to the festival at Carnsore and herself and June had jumped into the sea in just their knickers. Neither of them had ever been in the sea before, not even once. The stones had been hot under their feet, she remembered that, burning the soles of them as they'd hopped down to the water. It had looked so blue and inviting and she'd wanted to jump right in, but the moment the waves lapped over her toes, she'd gasped in shock, looking at June, the pair of them collapsing in giggles. 'On the count of three,' June had said, holding her nose, her teeth chattering with the cold. And the two of them had plunged in then up to their shoulders, the icy water sluicing over them. Mary-Pat could still recall it, the cold, and the two of them squealing, splashing each other, great arcs of water catching the sunlight. They hadn't wanted to get out, but Mammy had called them then and they'd hopped out to her, teeth chattering, the sun warming their shoulders, and they'd allowed her to towel them dry and hand them half a banana each.

'Mammy, did you see me swim?' Mary-Pat had been so excited about it, she remembered, thinking she was like Mark

Spitz in the Olympics and that, next thing, she'd be winning gold medals for Ireland.

'I saw you both.' Mammy had smiled, squinting up at them against the glare of the hot sun. 'You were like mermaids, the two of you.' And when June had scuttled off up the beach, chasing after a puppy she'd seen, Mammy had said, 'Look what I found for you.' And she'd handed her a large black shell, about the size of an orange. 'Hold it up to your ear and, tell me, what do you hear?'

Mary-Pat had looked at the shell for a long time, her fingers running over the bumps on its matt black surface, poking into the mother-of-pearl inside. It was beautiful, and it didn't look like any of the other shells on the beach, the tiny little yellow ones or the flat razor clams. She held it to her ear and she heard it then, the soft hiss of the sea. 'It's magic,' she'd exclaimed.

Mammy had laughed, a soft laugh, and had pulled Mary-Pat to her, giving her a squeeze. 'You keep that shell, Mary-Pat, and every time you listen to it, think of me.'

'I will, Mammy,' Mary-Pat had promised, 'but I won't need to if you're here, will I?' And Mammy had shaken her head then, looking over her shoulder as if she'd seen something in the distance, and when she'd turned back to Mary-Pat, her eyes had been wet.

'Some day you might, pet, so look after it, won't you?' Mary-Pat had been about to say that she would, when she heard a little giggle. The two of them had looked up to see Daddy and Frances O'Brien standing at the top of the dunes above them. Mary-Pat had seen Frances lean towards Daddy and whisper something in his ear. He'd smiled at her, a shy, private smile and then the two of them had laughed and clambered down to Mary-Pat and Mammy. Daddy had a cigarette in his hand and he'd kissed

Mammy on the top of her head, which she tilted to one side so that the kiss landed on her ear. 'Stop,' she'd muttered.

'Jesus Christ, Michelle,' he'd said, his face colouring. Mary-Pat was used to their rows, so it wasn't the exchange that bothered her: it was that there was something wrong with the way they were positioned, Daddy and the woman standing beside each other, looming over Mammy, while she'd squinted up at them. Then Daddy had said, 'C'mon, Mary-Pat, I'll race you down to the water,' and she'd forgotten all about Mammy, rushing back into the icy waves again. If only she'd known what Mammy had been trying to say to her, if only she'd known she would have done something, but what could she have done? She was only a child, but even so, the guilt had never left her. The guilt and the blame.

After that summer – the summer of Frances O'Brien – when she practically took up residence with them and then suddenly vanished, Mary-Pat didn't see the woman for another six months. Then one evening, Mammy had sent her down to the minimarket for a pint of milk. 'Tell Dympna I'll settle up with her next week,' she'd said when Mary-Pat had been leaving, shutting the door and running off down the towpath, glad of fifteen minutes to herself. Glad to get away from the door-slamming and the whispers, the way Mammy would leave the room when Daddy came into it, his hands in his pockets, looking like a naughty child.

She'd made sure to take her time in the minimarket, browsing the aisles, taking in the packets of biscuits and the big boxes of cereal, her mouth watering, plucking up the courage to ask for credit – again. And then she'd seen her, Frances O'Brien, except that she hadn't recognised her at first. Her hair was lank and greasy and hung around her face, which was pale and drawn. Gone was the flimsy T-shirt and instead she was bundled up in a heavy fisherman's jumper, her dirty feet now hidden in a pair of trainers. And she was unmistakeably pregnant, her belly a round bulge underneath her jumper. She hadn't put on weight, Mary-Pat knew that, because everywhere else was skinny, her wrists, which were poking out of her jumper, were twig-thin and her legs a mottled blue beneath her gypsy skirt.

She didn't know how she knew that this had to do with Daddy, but Mary-Pat knew. As an animal instinctively knows when it's spring, she sensed it, knew it inside, in her heart, if not yet in her mind.

The woman must have sensed that Mary-Pat was watching, because she'd turned around and, before Mary-Pat could duck out of the way, she'd been caught. 'Mary-Pat?' Her voice was a tiny squeak now as she shuffled down the aisle towards her.

'I was just getting some milk,' Mary-Pat had murmured, hardly daring to look at the woman. 'How's your mammy?' The question was such an odd one, Mary-Pat shook her head for a second and then found her voice. 'She's grand, thanks for asking.' And then she'd added, 'Daddy, too. He's grand as well.'

The woman had flinched as if she'd been hit. 'Good, that's good. Well, tell them both I was asking for them, would you?'

'I will. Ehm, I have to go now.'

Frances O'Brien had nodded and Mary-Pat was sure she'd seen tears in the woman's eyes. Mortified, she'd shuffled awkwardly from foot to foot, eyeing the rows of milk cartons behind Frances O'Brien's head. And then she'd stuck her hand out and placed it on the woman's arm. 'Hope you feel better soon.' And then she'd almost bolted out the door of the shop, grabbing a carton of milk and waving it at the girl behind the counter, ignoring the filthy look she was given in return.

The phrase had come back to her again and again that summer. 'Hope you feel better soon.' As if the woman had simply had a bit of a head cold when, later, Mary-Pat would come to understand. The woman had been ruined. There was no other word for it.

That was the last she'd seen of Frances O'Brien for a long, long time: the back of a woolly jumper shuffling up the aisle of the minimarket, head bent low in shame.

The rumours started to spread that winter. About what had happened to 'that young one' Frances O'Brien. That she'd gone to the nuns, or to England 'to have it seen to', conversations that ended the minute Mary-Pat opened the door of the post office or the bookies to place a bet for Daddy.

How could she have forgotten, Mary-Pat wondered now. When Pi had given the shell to her, it hadn't meant a thing. She must have blanked the memory of that day on the beach. In the chaos that followed Mammy leaving, a shell was probably the last thing on her mind, or perhaps she couldn't bear to listen to it and so she'd put it away. It's funny, she thought, as she stood beside a rack of leopard-print thongs, how we can so easily forget. She reached into her bag and pulled it out, the shell, and held it up to her ear, listening to the hollow hiss of the sea. 'Every time you listen to it, think of me.' I will, Mammy, she said now. I will.

'Mum, I've been looking for you everywhere!' Melissa hobbled up to her in a pair of fuck-me heels, black, with great big spikes on the back. 'What do you think?'

Mary-Pat swallowed and shoved the shell back into her handbag. I think that old habits die hard, Melissa, that's what I think. But she was quite pleased with herself when she managed, 'They're lovely. Very fashionable.' Graham would be proud of her, that, for once, she hadn't picked a fight. Hadn't judged.

Melissa giggled. 'Oh, Mum, you are *so* funny. I look like a complete tramp. I was just trying them on for the laugh. I have a pair of Converse here in my size that I'm going to get.' And she shook her head, as if her mother were the greatest eejit in the world.

'Oh, right,' Mary-Pat said weakly.

'Vanessa has a pair in maroon, so I thought navy would be good,' Melissa was saying. Mary-Pat had only been half-listening, but at the name, her ears pricked up. Vanessa was the new girl in school – she'd moved down here with her family from Dublin, and they all thought she was the height of glamour. Melissa had taken to quoting bits of wisdom from her, beginning every sentence with 'Vanessa says ...' and it had irritated Mary-Pat, but still, it seemed to have jolted Melissa out of her *Dukes of Hazzard* phase, so she should be grateful to the girl.

'Why don't you ask her over to tea some day?' she said now. 'She could give us the benefit of her Dublin sophistication.' As soon as she'd said it, she knew that it sounded more sarcastic than she'd intended.

'For God's sake, Mum.' Melissa looked hurt.

'I'm sorry,' Mary-Pat said quickly. 'I didn't mean it to sound like that.' Clearly, I haven't changed that much, she thought morosely to herself. 'Invite her over. I'd love to meet her.'

Melissa gave her the sceptical look she deserved. 'Look, you can't say anything if I invite her over. None of your usual.'

'My usual?'

'Yes, your usual sarcasm, Mammy.' Melissa looked at her pointedly.

Mary-Pat tutted. 'Look, I won't show you up, if that's what you mean.'

Melissa brightened. 'Well, OK then. Thanks, Mum, I will.' She nodded at the little paper bag that her mother was clutching. 'Must be a very small dressing gown.'

'What? Oh, they didn't have any in my size, so I got a few napkins instead,' Mary-Pat said, knowing that that would put Melissa off. She'd never want to look at napkins. 'C'mon, let's have a coffee.' And she linked her arm through Melissa's and made for the café. 'We'll pretend to share a cake but eat two of them instead.'

Melissa gave her arm a squeeze. 'Thanks for taking me, Mum. It was fun.'

Mary-Pat looked at her daughter in surprise. 'Good, pet. That's good.' And, even through the numbness, she was glad of that. She could see that it was a good thing – herself and Melissa together and actually enjoying themselves. She spent the rest of the afternoon trying to have fun with her daughter, trying just to focus on that and nothing else. Living in the moment, Graham called it. It sure beat living in the past.

She didn't hear her phone buzzing in her handbag, so she didn't get the text until she got home, stashing her purchase in the back of the wardrobe where PJ never looked.

'We need to have family conf. Tuesday eve suit all? June x.'

12

*P*ius drove as slowly as he could through the November gloom to Mary-Pat's. He knew it was a bit daft because he could only delay things — he'd have to arrive sooner or later. He couldn't actually refuse to go either. He'd never refused his sisters anything and he had no intention of doing so now. Life was awkward enough without having them on his back, he thought.

At least now he had the plan, and it gave him something, a focus and a connection to Mammy. Every time he weeded or hoed or picked out loose stones to get the soil ready for carrots, he felt that he was closer to her, could hear her voice in the tiny pencil notes on the back of the plan. 'I think we'll have snapdragons here, what do you think, Pi?' she'd say as she'd draw in the tall spears of the plants, with their gorgeous pink and red rosettes. 'And here, a few wallflowers and maybe some cosmos, oh, and some stock. We want lots of scent in the garden, plenty for the nose as well as the eye. Now, don't plant the carrots too close together, or you'll have crooked roots.' I know that, Mammy, he'd smile as he put a good covering of mulch over the green shoots so that the leaves wouldn't go bitter. And even though he wasn't sure she was right about planting three leek seedlings in the one hole, he thought he'd give it a go. If Mammy had been able to grow them this way, it must work. And as his potager took shape, the interlinked circular beds planted exactly as Mammy had instructed, he began to feel as if a puff of new life had been breathed into him. That in some way he was taking shape too.

That's what had given him the confidence to ask Daphne to that reading at the literary festival in Monasterard House, and what's more, not to be daunted when she said no. To understand that she was right. 'Look, don't take this the wrong way, you're nice,' she'd said. 'It's just … I want a man who's active, you know what I mean?' Pius hadn't known what she'd meant, at least, not initially. 'I want a man who's going places. Who has plans for life. I can't afford timewasters because of Dara. I don't want to make the same mistake again.'

She was right. That's what he'd been doing his entire life. Wasting time. Sitting in his living room, knee-deep in old newspapers, or making bloody coffee, or wandering around the little grow-house he'd rigged up in Daddy's old shed, stripped down to his underpants because of the heat, the lamps dyeing him a nice shade of blue. When you looked at it that way, it didn't add up to much of a CV. So instead of sulking, he'd taken a deep breath. 'Daphne, I know you think I'm not exactly a catch, but I'll prove you wrong. I have plans, believe it or not,' he'd said, thinking of his garden, 'and when I put them in place, I'll ask you again and hope you'll say yes. Will you give me that chance?'

She'd looked at him for a long time, then nodded. 'OK.'

'Good. Great,' he'd said. 'That's just ... great.' And then, because he couldn't think of another word to say, he'd bolted back into the safety of the kitchen, leaving her and Dara to see themselves out. He hadn't been feeling that brave.

His phone buzzed again and he tutted in irritation as he pressed the button, while trying to keep an eye on the road, and looked at the text. 'We're all waiting. Get a bloody move on.' Mary-Pat — she'd kill him if he was late.

When he turned into Mary-Pat's cul-de-sac, he had to manoeuvre around June's huge Jeep, parking the Beetle as close as he could to her back bumper, hemming her in, because he knew it would annoy her later on. Serve her right if she was going to drive one of those eco-disaster tanks.

He stepped over the huddle of garden gnomes beside the gate and walked up to the front door and was about to knock, but the door opened to his touch. Pius didn't know why, but his heart sank. Either Mary-Pat had been burgled or they were all waiting for him, and he didn't know which was worse.

When he stuck his head around the kitchen door, three heads turned to look at him. Mary-Pat, arms folded grimly in her electric blue fleece, June, a vision in cream silk and Rosie, in a pair of jeans and a Boston College sweatshirt, her hair piled on top of her head in a topknot. Christ, who died? A picture of Daddy in his wheelchair flashed into his mind, and before he could dismiss it, he felt it, that surge of relief. A feeling of lightness that both embarrassed and excited him at the same time. But no, it couldn't be Daddy. They'd have told him straight out.

'Sit down, Pi,' Mary-Pat ordered and shoved a mug across to him, filling it with a stream of dark brown tea. Pius felt his stomach flip. Strong tea always made him feel faintly sick.

'Thanks,' he muttered, pulling off his jacket and folding it over the top of the chair. 'Sorry I'm late.'

June sighed. 'Well, you're here now, so we can get started.'

Get started with what? Pius looked at Mary-Pat and then at June, faces set, mouths in a straight line, and then at Rosie, who was examining the bottom of her teacup, red head bent over it, worrying away at the enamel with a fingernail. It was always like this, the two of them, Mary-Pat and June, ambushing with their plans and orders. He felt a flicker of resentment and reached out and patted Rosie on the shoulder. We're in it together, the gesture said. Two of us against two of them.

June cleared her throat and, as he looked at her, Pius realised that she looked awful — big, dark shadows under her eyes, mouth pulled down. 'I have some news that I want to share with you all.' He looked at Mary-Pat in surprise, because she was normally in charge of these things. June's hands were shaking as she reached for the envelope which had been sitting in front of her, a pale blue flimsy thing with a foreign-looking stamp on it. She opened it and said, 'This is very difficult,' and then her eyes filled with tears. 'Sorry.'

Mary-Pat reached a hand out and squeezed June's. 'It's all right, love. Whatever you have to say, just say it.' June nodded and sniffed and accepted the tissue offered to her by her older sister. She tried to compose herself, fanning herself with her hand and taking in a deep breath, before exhaling again. 'OK, it's OK,' she said to no one in particular. Then she straightened her shoulders and shuffled in her chair until she'd regained her composure. 'Sorry, everyone, it's all been a bit overwhelming.'

What was overwhelming? Pius had that all-too-familiar feeling of having come in halfway through a conversation and having to work out what subject was being discussed. He shot Mary-Pat a look but was surprised to see that she didn't have her usual know-all expression on her face. Instead, she looked worried, and Pius felt a jolt of panic. If Mary-Pat didn't know anything, it must be bad.

'It's, well, it's about what Daddy said at Rosie's wedding ...' June blushed a deep red, glancing briefly at Rosie, who gave no indication that she was actually listening. 'Mammy had an old friend, Maeve. She lives in Bray and they went to college together. I ... ehm, thought she might know something about what Daddy said, so I asked her. And, well, it's difficult because it involves something I haven't told you all.'

At this, Mary-Pat removed her hand from June's and sat back in her chair, before rummaging around in her handbag, producing a cigarette which she lit, inhaling deeply and blowing smoke up to the ceiling. The smell filled the air, as usual – they were all used to it at this stage – but Rosie looked up and said, 'Mary-Pat, could you just put it out? It's making me feel really sick.'

'Oh. All right.' Mary-Pat took one last drag then ground the cigarette out on a saucer, which already had a little pile of butts on it.

'Rosie, do you want to go outside for a bit?' Pius said, eyeing the kitchen door, an escape for both of them.

She shook her head. 'It's OK.'

Mary-Pat tutted impatiently. 'Go on, June.'

For a moment, June's face crumpled and Pius felt sure she was about to cry again and he wished she'd stop and just spit it out. 'I'm sorry, Rosie, I really am. I didn't know, I really didn't.'

Rosie was sitting up now, her tiny face like granite, jaw set, eyes pale. Pius noticed that she'd let go of the mug and instead she'd gripped the edge of the tablecloth which she'd twisted into a tight knot.

June dropped her head and looked at the letter again. 'Years after Mammy … went away, Maeve called me. I had no idea who she was and when she told me she was a friend of Mammy's, I honestly didn't want to know. I was living in Dublin and it was ten years then, and I'd forgotten …' Her voice wobbled again. 'Anyway, she asked if I'd meet her and I did and she gave me a letter. A letter from Mammy.' June's voice was barely a whisper, but it sounded like an explosion in Pius's ears, as if she'd lobbed a grenade right there into the kitchen. She ploughed on. 'I didn't read it for ages. I tried to forget about it, to get on with the life I'd been leading, but I couldn't. I just couldn't seem to get it started again, knowing what I did. It just seemed so pointless, just a big lie. So I read the letter.'

When no one responded, June continued. 'I just needed to know … she seemed to vanish in a puff of smoke. I mean, we knew that she'd gone to England somewhere, because Daddy found out, but nothing after. And then I got this letter and it was as if she was there with me again, do you know? In the room, telling me one of her stories. She asked how you all were and what you were doing and she told me she'd gone far away to a place where people needed her more than we did.' At this, her voice broke.

Pius didn't move to help her, to offer her a tissue or to put a consoling arm around her shoulder, because he felt so angry. He felt that he was looking at a woman he didn't recognise, who would keep something to herself that could have helped them all. All the years of wondering why she'd left. Wondering where out there in the world she might be, wandering. Wondering if she was happier now without them all and trying to build a life without her. And June knew. She knew and yet she kept it to herself. How selfish, because she wanted to be the important one, the one with the secret. She was sick, Pius thought, just sick.

Mary-Pat spoke the words that were on his mind. 'Why the hell did you never tell us? Why did you let us go on wondering, when all along you knew?' She shook her head. 'I mean, what's wrong with you?'

'Mammy made me promise not to tell. She said that if I let you all know, she'd stop writing, because she couldn't be responsible for the way you'd all feel when you found out.'

The three of them all looked at her in baffled silence, a silence which June mistook for permission to continue. 'When Daddy said what he said about Rosie, you see, I worked it out. Maeve wouldn't tell me the truth, but I remember now what happened that summer.' June's voice tailed away into a whisper. 'You see, when Daddy said that Rosie wasn't his, he didn't mean it that way. He didn't mean that he wasn't her father. He meant that ...' June shook her head.

Mary-Pat rolled her eyes to heaven. 'Oh, for God's sake, June, now is not the time to be coy. Spit it out, seeing as you know it all. What did Daddy mean? Put Rosie out of her misery once and for all. C'mon, you started this, so you can finish it.'

June said quietly, 'You know what he meant, Mary-Pat.'

Mary-Pat opened her mouth, then snapped it shut again, her pale blue eyes alive with rage. 'I do not.' She spat the words out, like bullets.

'I don't mean it like that. I know you didn't know about the letters. But you do know why Daddy denied Rosie. It wasn't that he didn't love her. We all know that she was his favourite, which is ironic really, given that she came from, ehm, another relationship. That's it.' June looked satisfied that she'd found the right words to describe it. 'We all know that Rosie is Daddy's. We know that. But *you* also know who Rosie's real mother is. You know you know, so don't deny it,' June said, trying to look dignified, dabbing at her nose with a folded tissue.

Mary-Pat sat back in her chair. 'You absolute bitch. You keep this from us for nearly thirty years'— she pointed to the letter — 'and you have the nerve to pin it all on me?'

Pius expected June to crumble then, to fall apart. She always did when Mary-Pat got bolshie. She wilted under the stream of her sister's sarcasm, but to his surprise, she refused to budge now, her jaw set. 'I don't think you have the right to throw stones, Mary-Pat. Face it, I'm not the only one who kept a secret now, am I?'

'I did it for the right reasons,' Mary-Pat muttered. She seemed to be scrabbling for the right words. 'I did it because I knew the woman was no good, that she was just bad news and Rosie needed to know that she had a family. That we were her family.' As she said the word 'family', she slapped her hand on the table, her face creased into a tight scowl.

'And what gives you the right to decide that?' June spluttered. 'I mean, you always were a bossy cow, but who do you think you are to play God like that, not to tell Rosie the truth about where she came from?'

'Oh, so we're talking about playing God now, are we? Well, that's rich, coming from you, Junie. You always did suck up to Mammy, so I suppose you're delighted with yourself, aren't you? June O'Connor, the Chosen One.' The pair of them were facing each other now, like fighting dogs, eyes bright, teeth bared in rage.

Pius watched himself do it in slow motion, his fist coming through the air and connecting with the pine surface of the kitchen table with a loud thud. Did I just do that? he wondered, even as his sisters jumped back in fright.

'June, I've had enough of this. I don't care what you do or don't know, and I don't know what the hell difference it makes now anyway, or who you think you're helping, but this isn't the way to do it, dragging Rosie in here when it concerns her and then talking about her as if she isn't in the room. It's not right.' And he turned to take Rosie by the arm, pulling her half out of the chair. She didn't resist but instead went limp in his arms.

June blustered, 'I thought I was doing the right thing.'

'The right fucking thing?' Pius roared, turning on his sister, Rosie hanging out of his left arm, which was killing him. 'Do you know what, June, you're thicker than I thought you were. I can't see what any one of us is going to get from this ... this mess.' He pointed to the letter. 'And you of all people, Mary-Pat, should be ashamed of yourself. I know you resented having to look after Rosie and the rest of us and it wasn't fair, and I'm sorry about it, but this is low, it really is. You had a responsibility to tell her the truth, and you shirked it.'

The anger had taken him now, a rage so vast he couldn't contain it. It felt like electricity surging through his body, but he knew he couldn't let rip any more. That would only be to dignify this charade, this travesty. Instead, he lowered his voice deliberately: 'I suppose it felt good, Junie, to be the only one Mammy could trust and I hope you enjoyed the feeling. I hope it gave you something the rest of us didn't get. Some hope, at least. Lucky you, June. I hope you think it was worth it.'

If he'd thought his sister would dissolve in tears the way she normally did, to get her own way, so that they'd all gather round and tell her how sorry they were for having upset her, he was mistaken. 'Well, Pi,' June said quietly. 'You know, it's a bit rich coming from you. You're in no position to lecture any of us on doing the right thing. You who've buried your head in the sand your whole life. Look at you. All you can do is grow those drugs of yours and mope around the place, feeling sorry for yourself that life hasn't given you what you wanted on a silver platter. Well, it doesn't work like that, Pi. You're a coward, do you know that? No wonder Daddy couldn't stand —' Her face was white with anger, her lips a thin line, eyes glittering.

'Couldn't stand what, Junie?' Pius said. 'Couldn't stand me? That's not exactly news to me, you know.' But did you have to say it, Junie, he thought. Did you have to make it real like that? That's cruel.

June's lips were pressed tightly together, as if to keep any more words from escaping. Her hands were clasped together on the table, the huge emerald in her engagement ring glittering. 'Yes, well, he didn't like me much either. He really only liked Mary-Pat because she looked after him, and even then not as much as Rosie. You were the one he really loved, Rosie,' June said, stretching her hand out to cover Rosie's, who pulled it away and said in a tight voice, 'Please stop. All of you.' She was standing beside him and he could feel her whole body trembling. He put out an arm to steady her, but she gently pushed it away. 'I've heard enough. I'm sure you all meant well, but I wish you hadn't treated me like I didn't matter. I'm not a child any more.' And then she turned and walked out the kitchen door, leaving them all staring after her.

'I'd better go find her,' Pius said after a few minutes. It took all his self-control to quietly pull on his jacket and push his chair under the kitchen table, taking his tea mug to the sink and carefully washing it out. And then he turned to his two sisters, the two women to whom he'd been closest for his whole life, and he said, 'You're right about me. I am a coward. I know it. The dogs on the street know it, but at least I can tell myself that I've never lived a lie. I haven't used someone else's pain to feel better about myself.' At this, June sat back in her chair, stunned, as if someone had physically assaulted her and Pius felt a flicker of regret, just for a second, but then he reminded himself of what she'd done. 'I don't care what she said in her letters or where she is or what she's doing. She's dead to me. Dead. Please don't ever bring up her name again.' And he turned and walked out the kitchen door.

He thought she'd be halfway to Dublin at this stage, but instead Rosie was standing quietly by the Beetle, shivering. 'I forgot the keys,' she said, teeth chattering. She must be freezing, he thought, standing outside in November in just a sweatshirt, and he hurried around to the driver's door, turning the key in the lock. 'Hop in.'

She stood there on the pavement, swaying, and he realised that she couldn't hop anywhere. She was in shock. He ran around to the passenger side and opened the door, gently easing her into the front seat and strapping the seatbelt across her. She didn't protest, just sitting back in the red vinyl seat, her head resting against the back, eyes closed. Her eyelids were blue and her lips almost grey. She looked so unwell, Pius wondered if he should call a doctor. He'd get her home first, he decided, and then he'd see how she was.

He had to stifle the urge to ram June's Jeep on the way out, although it took every ounce of his self-control not to do so.

ALL THAT I LEAVE BEHIND

They drove in silence up Main Street, which was festooned with bunting for the Monasterard Arts Festival, and over the humpback bridge over the canal. The trees had nearly lost all their leaves now, just a few scraps of rust hanging onto the branches, and a thick, silvery mist hung low over the water, which was like a long shiny mirror, not a ripple breaking its surface.

He pulled up in front of the house, turning the key in the ignition so that there was a deafening silence after the roar of the engine. The two of them sat there for a bit, and then he turned to her to say that it was time they went inside, when Rosie said, 'I knew anyway.' Her voice was tiny, like a child's, her face chalk white.

'Rosie, please don't ... she didn't mean it to come out that way ... it's all crap, it really is.'

But Rosie interrupted. 'It's OK, Pi, I know you're trying to help, but it's all right, really. I knew the minute Daddy said. At least, I knew there was *something*. I think I've always known.'

Pius was mystified. 'But how, Rosie, no one ever said anything, did they, at least, not before now. I didn't know anything —' he added hastily, 'or I would have said, honest.' And then he thought of Mammy and Daddy in the car on the way to Rosie's christening and the thought occurred to him that he had known something after all. He'd sat there in the back seat, Rosie's carrycot balanced on his knee, looking at the little red-head inside, at the way her tiny fingers curled over as she lay there fast asleep, and he'd known, somewhere inside him. It was in the set of his parents' shoulders as they sat in front of him, staring straight ahead, in complete silence, until Daddy had turned to Mammy and said, 'Thank you, Michelle.' And his mother, without looking at him, had said, 'I will never forgive you. Ever.'

He'd known. And like his sisters, he'd said nothing at all.

'I know, Pi. But they didn't have to say anything. It's funny, because I've always felt a part of the family, but there was *something*. You were all too nice to me, that's what it was.' She smiled ruefully. 'I was just your annoying baby sister, but each one of you looked after me like parents and taught me all the things I'd need to know. I wonder if you all did that because you knew I wasn't one of you, not really.'

'Jesus, we were your *family*, Rosie,' Pius said, mystified. 'That's what families do. And when Mammy left, it just seemed important. We looked after you because you were our sister and we loved you. It wasn't any more complicated than that. And nothing about that has changed, love, no matter what your sisters have said, you have to understand that.'

He'd expected her to nod, to say that, of course, she understood, but instead she just looked out the window, a faraway look in her eye. 'I went up with Mammy to Dublin ... the day she left.'

Pius shook his head. 'No, Rosie, you couldn't have. June and Mary-Pat took you to the agricultural show in Mullingar. I remember, because it was the hottest day of the year and Mary-Pat had you in a big frilly bonnet to keep the sun off. I remember,' he said again, as if trying to reassure himself. He *did* remember, he was sure of it.

Rosie shook her head, sadly. 'No ... I know I was with her because we went on the train and we came out somewhere big and noisy. It must have been Dublin. I remember lots of traffic and seagulls. We had to walk for ages and ages and my feet were sore, and then we got on a bus. I don't remember much else except that the bus was really smelly. And then I was sitting high up on someone's shoulders on a beach. I wasn't very happy about it because it wasn't Mammy.' She half-smiled. 'It must have been Maeve, that friend of Mammy's. Then later, Mammy was talking to Maeve. I remember because she was pouring coffee from a tall white coffee pot with bright yellow daisies on it and I thought it was really pretty, and Maeve said something like, "Are you going to put up with it, Michelle?" Something like that anyway, and then Mammy said, "She may not be my flesh and blood but that only makes me love her more."'

Pius didn't know what to say. Instead, he just sat there, his mouth hanging open. Say something, you big eejit, he told himself. Say bloody something.

'Ah, Rosie,' Pius managed to find his voice, 'I don't know. It was such a long time ago and, sure, you were only a baby. Mammy could have been talking about anything at all.'

But Rosie interrupted, 'You see, Pi, she looks so like me, even in those awful power suits and that big hair. But it's not just that, it's the way she stands. It took me a while to work out, but we both stand the same way.'

Pius felt bewildered now, and then the penny dropped. Of course. How had he never guessed. 'Who are we talking about here, Rosie?' he said carefully. 'Is it that woman ... Frances O'Brien?' When she nodded slowly, he shook his head. Frances O'Brien, with her shiny teeth and nut-brown skin, whom he'd lusted after as a kid. How had he been such a fool to miss that, and her living in the house with them. Jesus, they'd probably done it right under Mammy's nose.

He turned to her in the car and said carefully, 'Have you spoken to her?'

Rosie nodded. 'But I don't think she wants to know, to be honest, and it's OK, I don't mind, Pi. She's not family, I know she isn't. She's ... she might be my mother, but she's not my family. I have a family, or at least, I had.' She wiped a tear away with the back of her hand.

'Come here,' Pius said, pulling her towards him, the pair of them stretched awkwardly across the gear stick. He squeezed her tightly, feeling the sharp bones of her shoulder blades. 'You have a family. We're your family and we always will be, even if we've made a holy mess of things. Your two sisters love you, you need to know that.'

She attempted a weak smile, which Pius didn't have the heart to return. The two of them were probably sitting hunched over the kitchen table, drinking their umpteenth cup of tea, trading more secrets like currency at a market. Secrets weren't like that, though. They couldn't be revealed to win power or to score points — the two of them had got the wrong end of the stick there altogether. He'd never forgive them both. Never.

March 1981

Michelle

I see the cot out of the corner of my eye, a small white carrycot, covered in padded plastic with a pattern of pink bunnies on it. It's in a corner of the hall, and as I stand there, holding onto the door, I see it move a little, a little vibration, and a tiny mewling sound, like a kitten, comes out of it. I don't move for a long time, just stand there, until a blast of wind blows the door against the back of my legs and the pain of it shakes me into moving across the hall, slowly, towards the carrycot.

I see her hands first, or hand. A little, tightly curled fist, which pushes the pink blanket away, followed by a leg, and then the blanket is a wriggling mass of pink as she moves, her cheeks rosy above her babygro. I gasp when I see her hair, a little tuft of it, a pale golden red, sticking up from her forehead. Her tongue is sticking out of her mouth, just the tip of it, as if to show how much she's exerting herself to push the blanket off. 'It's hard work being a baby,' I find myself saying. 'Isn't it?'

At the sound of my voice, she stops dead, her little fist still in the air, and her eyes move from side to side as she listens, and then she gives a little kick and a grunt of exertion, and I find myself laughing. 'What are you trying to tell me?' She responds by giving a little gurgle.

'Are you talking to me?' I coo. 'Is that it?' Another gurgle and I think how like Junie she is. June was always on the move, wriggling and shuffling in her cot, a little blur of movement as she tried to kick her blankets off, soft 'ehs' of effort coming from her, followed by a satisfied 'ah', as she succeeded. But then I catch myself. For goodness' sake, Michelle, how can she be like Junie? You fool.

'She's a lovely wee thing, isn't she?' His voice is tender and I find myself nodding, almost as an instinct, as we both peer into the cot and, for a second, we are the child's parents, admiring our lovely newborn, looking down at her filled with love and awe at what we've produced. But so quickly, I see that it's a horrible parody, an awful sham, and I stumble backwards, and he has to shoot a hand out to grab my elbow. 'Easy. Easy, love.'

I close my eyes. 'Don't touch me,' I hiss. 'Do not put a finger on me ever again.'

He says nothing, but I can tell by the look in his eyes that he feels it, the defeat. He's given up. His grip on my arm loosens and beside me I can feel him, can sense his shoulders slumping, his head tilting forward, can almost see him bite his lip like a naughty boy.

'I'll give her a bottle,' he says. I feel like laughing out loud at the idea of John-Joe giving this little mite a bottle, he who has sung and played and bounced babies on his knee but never so much as changed a nappy in his entire life.

'I'll do it,' I say, and I lean into the cot and pick her up and she's soft and milky and warm in my arms. I hold her there for a minute. I don't expect to feel it, not for a second, that surge, that rush of love to my heart that I felt when I first held Mary-Pat and Pius and Junie in my arms. That sense that they were nobody else's but mine. Nobody's. But I do. I feel it, and it's so strong I have to steady myself, the little bundle in my arms, her tiny round shoulders, her soft little bottom, as she bumps her head off my shoulder and gives a little whine. That 'where's my food?' whine that I recognise so well.

'We'll have a little bottle, won't we?' I coo. 'Won't we?' And I carry her into the kitchen, humming a little song, and we sit down together in the old armchair by the fire.

From that day on, the baby and I are hardly ever parted. She sleeps in a cot at the end of my bed and I take her everywhere with me, pushing that huge ugly pram that Bridie gave me all those years ago up the canal and into the village, where I try to ignore the tuts and murmurs as I head up the main street, into the minimarket and around all the shelves, taking my time. I overheard Dympna O'Brien behind the meat counter say it, speak out loud the words everybody was thinking. 'I don't know how she can do that, you know. Pass that baby off as her own.' Until Paddy Deely told her to whisht, that it was none of her damn business. And I felt like saying, but I'm not passing her off. I know she's not mine. God knows, I know, but I feel it all the same, that we're two lost souls, that we need each other. She needs my love and I need hers.

And I do love her. Every day, that love grows, and if sometimes

I wonder where it will all end, I try to push the thought out of my mind. I try not to think of the damage this is all doing to Mary-Pat and Pius and June. Mary-Pat came up to me the other day when I was sitting on the bed, the baby in front of me, waving her little arms and legs in the air while I sang her a song. I was so lost in my own world that I didn't see her until she cleared her throat. 'Mammy?'

I looked up at her and it was as if I was seeing a stranger, and I felt suddenly ashamed. How long had it been since I'd been a mother to her, since we'd talked like we always used to?

'Will the baby be staying much longer, or, ehm,' she looked down at her feet, before blurting, 'will we be keeping her?' Poor love; she'd clearly been plucking up the courage to ask.

I didn't answer for a moment but took Rosie's soft little foot in my hand, feeling the tiny little toes, the wrinkles on the sole, like cracks in a riverbed. I reminded myself to rub olive oil on them later, to stop her skin drying out. 'It's just until my sister gets her strength back, that's all,' I said quietly, not daring to look at Mary-Pat, because we both knew that I wasn't speaking the truth. My 'sister' whom I had never once mentioned, who, until a few months ago, hadn't existed.

I looked up at Mary-Pat and I could see she was waiting. That she wanted me to tell her, but when I just said, 'I'm sure it won't be for much longer,' she gave me a look of bitter disappointment. I'm sorry, I thought. I truly am sorry.

'Oh, all right.' Her shoulders slumped in her school uniform, and she turned and trudged slowly down the stairs. She knows, I thought. She knows.

* * *

ALL THAT I LEAVE BEHIND

Sometimes these days, I feel so desperate that I go to the phone box in the village and I park that huge pram just outside and pick up the phone and hold it to my ear. I hear the silence, and I put a 50p coin in the slot and am rewarded with the long, low dial tone. I even dial the number, and then she answers. 'Hello?' That slight hesitation, the sense that she's wondering who can have interrupted her flower arranging or *Mastermind*. If I just press button 'A', the coin will drop in the slot and I can talk to her. I can tell her everything. I can tell her about my plan and ask if she'll help me. My hand hovers over the button, and then I hear her say, 'Who is this?' a note of alarm in her voice and I know I can't. I replace the receiver in its cradle and I want to howl out loud for my mummy, like a child. I push the pram back along the canal, the rushes hissing in the wind, the kingfisher bouncing along the edge of the canal, and I wonder how it's come to this, that this little piece of paradise can have turned into my prison.

I hope that when I get back John-Joe won't be home. I hope he'll have gone into Prendergast's or will have thought of some urgent task in Mullingar. I can't have John-Joe near me, I can't. If he walks into the room, I have to leave. Just the sense of him beside me makes me want to vomit and that bloody look on his face; as if he can't say how sorry he is, as if he can't find the words. He tried once, when he told me what he'd done to her, that girl. He said he was sorry then, but too late. 'I don't know what to do, Michelle. The nuns will probably take the baby ...' He knew, of course — he'd chosen his words carefully — that the very mention of the word 'nun' would be enough. Bridie had told me about what they did to unmarried mothers in her day, the poor young girls from the village who disappeared for the best part of a year only to reappear, grey-faced, shoulders hunched, on Main Street trying to ignore the glances, the pointed fingers, trying to bear the shame, while their babies were spirited away. I also know that nothing much has changed.

'You can leave her here,' I found myself saying.

'Thanks, Michelle,' he said, barely looking me in the eye. 'You don't know—' but I cut him off.

'Please. No gratitude, for God's sake. You'll only make things worse.'

'I thought they couldn't get any worse,' he said, a small smile flickering on his lips.

I almost wanted to smile then too, to make a little joke about just how terrible things are, but instead I say, 'Just tell me one thing.'

He looked like a guilty schoolboy.

'Why?'

He sighed. 'Because no matter what I do, Michelle, I'm not good enough for you. I just don't measure up. And so I figured, "why not". It can't make her think any more badly of me than she does already.'

'"Why not,"' I said blankly.

'That's right,' he said bluntly. 'And let's face it, it's true. You already think I'm a piece of shit, Michelle, so now you can add this to the long list of my sins, can't you?' he said bitterly. I said nothing for a moment, frozen, and I thought of that first day in Macari's all those years ago. Did I know then and just chose to ignore it? Did I fall in love with him simply to annoy my parents? Was all this hardship just the result of a teenage rebellion, because John-Joe was as far away from being Daddy as a man could possibly be? But then I remembered how much I loved him, how much I looked up to him. He was my hero.

'Do you love her?' I asked him.

He looked at me then, an expression of distaste on his face. 'For Christ's sake, Michelle.'

I see it now, that he feels contempt for me, for the woman who accepted his child, who looked at the mess he'd made of his life and agreed to tidy it up, to make it respectable, who bore the humiliation he'd dished out to her, him and that girl — who even paraded it around the town, for everyone to see. When every decent, self-respecting woman would have kicked him out, would have told him and his knacker girlfriend to take a hike. Maybe it's my revenge. I make him suffer by sticking nobly by him. But I know it's not that; it's that I just can't see any other way. The children need us, the baby needs us, I tell myself. Yes, that must be it. But I know, deep down, that I just can't think how to end it.

Part Three

Winter

13

*R*osie slipped out without Pius noticing. As she passed the kitchen door, she heard the murmur of the radio, the received pronunciation of some Radio 4 presenter. She opened the front door as quietly as she could, in case she woke Jessie, then pulled it shut, grimacing as it squeaked on its hinges. If the dog started barking, Pius would be out in a flash, asking her where she thought she was going at eleven o'clock at night.

The moon had risen, huge and yellow over the flat fields and the ribbon of water at the end of the garden. Pius's planting was taking shape, even if he'd had to stop for a bit now that it was winter. Rosie stood there for a while, looking at the familiar shapes of the henhouse and the red robin hedge at the back of the house, at the tall grasses silhouetted against the night sky, at the dark shadow of the much-hated leylandii in Sean

O'Reilly's — all the elements of her childhood home. Nothing had changed, not even one little bit, she could see that. The outline of Sean's huge chicken shed, the weathervane on top of the summer house, they were all still there, and yet they didn't look right somehow.

I wanted to know the truth, she thought. I said I had to know and now I do and all I can think is that I feel like myself and yet not like myself. I'm still me. I still breathe and eat and walk with flat feet and my hair is still red and I still have freckles. I'm sure if I ate a packet of Jelly Tots or listened to Miles Davis, I'd still like them both. I'm sure I still hate eggs and love the smell of lilies. When I look in the mirror, that woman is still me, and yet, I can't quite work out who she might be, as if the person I am inside is no one in particular. Maybe I've never known, she thought, pulling the racing bike out from behind Pius's grow-house and hopping on.

She remembered the first time she'd gone with Craig to visit his mother. Margaret was her name, a short, squat woman with a tight perm and a bright smile, who was only delighted to discover that her son was marrying 'such a nice girl. You Irish girls are so charming,' and then, slyly, 'You must be a Catholic, honey?' That had been the clincher for Margaret, a devout Catholic, and Rosie hadn't had the heart to contradict her, to tell her that her Catholicism stretched as far as her First Holy Communion and no further. Besides, she'd thought, helping herself to one of the cupcakes Margaret had made for her — iced a luminous green — what did it matter? She could be whoever Margaret wanted her to be. She'd become very good at it, even while she'd known that this life wasn't for her, that she'd felt like a cuckoo in Craig's neat little nest. She'd loved belonging to him, though, and she'd clung to that, through endless boring hikes in the mountains, full of compasses and backpacks and water bottles, through baseball games and spreadsheets and plans for the future; it wasn't fair to him, she understood, to have hijacked his life like that, it really wasn't. He'd been right all along: she wasn't the woman he'd thought she was.

Mary-Pat used to say it to her all the time, that she was like Daddy, 'a real chip off the old block', her face alive with sarcasm. Everything she'd done as a teenager, every mistake – little and big – was down to Daddy, down to his bad influence. 'The apple never falls far from the tree,' had been another of Mary-Pat's dark pronouncements. It was the one thing she'd remembered when Daddy had told all and sundry she wasn't his at her wedding. That at least Mary-Pat wouldn't be able to throw that at her any more. But now, it turned out that she was a chip off another block, a block she didn't know even one tiny bit. She thought of Frances O'Brien, of her angry eyes and helmet of hairsprayed hair, and she rolled the words around in her head: 'You are my mother.' No, they didn't sound right at all.

She was quicker on the bike now, having got used to dropping low over the handlebars of the racer and to keeping up a good speed so that she didn't wobble and fall off. She pushed hard over the bridge, past the pub and onto the main street, which was entirely deserted, the bitter November wind having driven people inside, and with no one to see her she rode along the middle of the street, her legs going faster and faster as she pushed the pedals around, her breath coming in ragged puffs, the cold making her eyes water. She needed to get there quick, she thought as she sped around the corner into a little laneway behind the church, along which was a row of cottages, each painted a different ice-cream colour. His was the eye-searing blue one; she knew that because she'd spotted him going in there one day after work. He hadn't seen her, but she'd stopped dead halfway across the little street, watching as he unloaded two catering trays out of the back of his van and carried them into the house. She'd almost called out his name, thought of asking if they could just talk, before telling herself of course not, of course they couldn't.

Now, she pulled up and parked the bike beside the ornate wrought-iron railings in front of his place. She didn't lock it, just left it there as she walked up the path and knocked on the door and waited. There was no movement inside, and her heart plummeted. He must be there, she thought. He has to be. She knocked again, and just as she was turning to leave, the door opened. Rosie blurted. 'Hi. I'm sorry to burst in on you, but I had to see you. I had to talk to you,' she began. 'You see it's—'

'Rosie,' he said sleepily. He was wearing nothing but a pair of red boxer shorts with black cats on them and his hair stood in tufts on his head. His eyes were bleary and he rubbed them for a few seconds before saying a sleepy, 'Come on in,' turning his back and shuffling along the hall, disappearing into a room at the end. Rosie hesitated for a second before following him, closing the front door quietly behind her.

The hallway was dark and narrow, and she followed the dim glow from the open door until she found herself in a small kitchen—living room. It was a little Aladdin's cave of lovely things: an armchair covered in buttercup yellow, a set of Chinese coffee tables with intricately carved legs, a comfy leather sofa with a bright orange throw slung over it. On it perched a huge grey cat, who peered at her with enormous marmalade eyes.

'Sit down.' Mark had reappeared at the door in a dressing gown, a blue-and-red striped number with a green belt. Rosie couldn't help it — she felt disappointed. He indicated the sofa, pushing the cat gently over, ignoring her mewls of protest.

'Thanks,' Rosie said, perching on the edge of the sofa, the cat having moved about six inches to the left, where it glared at her, those eyes blinking malevolently. Rosie suppressed a shiver. 'Your cat doesn't like me.'

'That's Sophie and she doesn't like anyone — don't take it personally,' Mark said. 'Anyway, you hate cats, so she probably senses it.'

'You remembered,' Rosie said.

'Yup,' he agreed, slumping onto the sofa the other side of Sophie, who blinked, tail flicking. 'But I'm sure you didn't come here to talk about your aversion to cats.'

Rosie shook her head. 'No, I didn't.'

There was a long silence, and then Mark jumped up. 'Coffee,' he said to himself, then shuffled into what must be the kitchen — Rosie could hear him clattering around, opening and closing cupboards, and after a little while, he reappeared, with a coffee pot and two mugs in his hands. Mark poured coffee into his mug and then into hers, along with a lump of sugar, giving it a stir. 'Here you go,' he said. 'Just the way you like it.'

'Thanks,' Rosie said, taking a sip. It was hot and strong and lovely, after weeks of Pius's weak cappuccinos. 'Remember our French phase?' She smiled as she put the cup down. 'When we watched *À Bout de Souffle* a hundred times on the video recorder and tried to smoke Gauloises?'

'Yeah.' He gave a small smile. 'That's where I got my liking for this stuff.' He nodded at the black coffee. 'I've never been able to shake it off ...' There was a pause while he registered that what he was saying might not exactly be tactful. 'So you didn't come here at midnight to discuss cats or French things ...'

'No, I didn't,' Rosie agreed.

'And you didn't come to tell me to shove my pity up my ass?'

'No,' Rosie said quietly. 'Sorry about that.'

'That's OK,' he said gently. 'Rosie, what is it?'

'It's ... you see ... oh, I don't know where to start,' Rosie said, her eyes filling with those stupid, useless tears again, which she dashed away with the back of her hand. For fuck's sake, can you just not cry, she said to herself. Crying achieves nothing.

He was beside her in a second, pushing Sophie off the sofa in spite of her howl of protest. Rosie wiped her tears away with a tissue that he'd pulled from a box which he kept by the sofa, shushing and soothing her, smoothing down her hair. 'C'mon, it's OK, it'll be OK,' he murmured.

'Trust you to have posh tissues,' she said, blowing her nose into a soft mass of scented hankie.

He smiled briefly. 'I prefer them to ragged toilet roll. I find it cheers me up.' And then he paused. 'What is it, Rosie? What's the matter?'

'You mean, apart from the obvious?' Rosie looked at him and sniffed, the damp tissue clutched in her hand. 'The botched wedding and the missing husband?'

'Well, yes, but that's not it either. Why did you come to see me?' His voice was soft and she found herself leaning against his firm shoulder, his arm snaking around her back, giving her a little squeeze. His hand was warm and strong, and she turned her head to tell him why she'd come and then his mouth was close to hers and then they were kissing, soft kisses, as he kissed her eyes, her nose and then her mouth, pushing it open, his tongue darting inside.

'Maybe we shouldn't,' she said, pushing him gently away.

His black eyes glittered and he laughed softly. 'No, we definitely shouldn't.' And they pulled apart reluctantly, sitting there for a few moments on the sofa, Sophie on the yellow armchair, glaring at them both.

'So,' he said.

'So,' she agreed, and then she found that she was sitting on his knee, pulling open the dressing gown, feeling the hardness of his chest, running her hands over its smooth surface while he pulled at the zip of her thick waterproof jacket. 'Still wearing the designer clothes,' he murmured, lifting the bottom of the pale lemon T-shirt she wore underneath and putting a hand on her stomach. His hand was warm and she could feel the heat of it against her cold skin: it seemed to warm her through to the inside, and she could feel the heat spreading as he moved his hand back and forth across her stomach, gently, stroking around her bellybutton, up to her ribs, his eyes fixed on hers. 'Rosie?'

'Hmm?'

'We shouldn't be doing this. You're married. We need to stop.'

'I know.' She sighed, pushing the dressing gown off his shoulders and running her hands over them. She'd always loved his shoulders — they were her favourite part of him.

'I mean it,' he insisted, pushing her gently off him, trying to rearrange his dressing gown, turning around to scrabble under the sofa for the belt.

'No, you don't,' she said, lifting her T-shirt over her head, then stepping quietly out of her tracksuit bottoms, until she was sitting beside him on the sofa in her underwear, a mismatched bra and knickers. I should have shaved my legs, she thought, remembering all the fuss she'd made about her wedding preparations, all the waxing and self-tanning. She'd been as smooth as a baby, and she was now covered with a pelt of downy orange hair, which mustn't be that attractive, she thought. And she'd lost weight in the last few months and the bra was now too loose on her, and her breasts were flapping around somewhere under the black padding. 'You know you don't.'

He groaned and pulled her towards him until she was sitting astride him, his legs bare and hard under hers, his breath soft in her ear. 'No, God help me, I don't.' He pushed her gently down onto the sofa and leaned on one elbow above her, looking at her, a smile twitching at the corners of his mouth. She hesitated, just for a second, the thought flitting across her mind, why now? Is this really a good idea? What's going to happen if we do this? But as soon as the thoughts appeared, she pushed them away, because she didn't want to question it. She just wanted to give in to the moment, no matter how passing. She wanted to lose herself in it and to forget everything that had happened. Everything.

He removed the bra with one hand, nuzzling her breasts, and then he gently removed her knickers, stroking her thighs, cupping a hand under her bottom, before easing himself down on top of her, pushing her hair off her face. 'Am I too heavy?'

She shook her head, even though he was twice the size of her and she felt that the air was being slowly pressed out of her.

'I *am* too heavy. You're so tiny,' he murmured, lifting himself up on one elbow. 'There, you can breathe again now.' He ran a finger down her shoulder and along the edge of her breast down to her hip, so that Rosie shivered involuntarily. His touch was light, as he stroked and caressed, and Rosie found herself responding, pushing against his fingers as they probed gently, letting herself be kissed and held and loved. 'Hang on,' she said after a while. 'I need to wait.'

He stopped teasing her nipple with his tongue. 'Why?'

'For you, you know.'

He didn't reply, but he let her stroke him, the smooth surface of his skin, like the surface of one of his coffee tables, kissing every little bit of him, from his mouth to his toes, learning what his body looked like. What it felt like: the hardness of his chest, the dip of his belly. He was sprawled across the sofa, the dressing gown bunched beneath him, relaxed, a smile on his face. His body was perfect, she thought, so completely his and he was so at ease in it. She couldn't help then but think of Craig and his stiff, mechanical movements, his polite 'Was that OK for you?', which made her want to strangle him.

Mark looked up at her now. 'Come here,' he said and pulled her on top of him, and they collapsed into each other, a tangle of limbs, her skin warm against his. His hands were resting on her bottom. 'Is your bottom always this cold?'

'Yes,' Rosie said. 'It always is. Enough jokes now, Mark, promise?'

'I promise. It's a very serious matter.' He made a face and she burst out laughing. 'You're an eejit.'

'But I'm your eejit,' he said softly. 'I always have been, Rosie.' He reached up and cupped a breast in each hand. 'You are just gorgeous.'

'Mary-Pat calls me Sparrowtits,' Rosie said as he stroked and kissed them, making appreciative noises as he did so.

'She's wrong, they're perfect. I can fit one in each hand,' he said. 'It's as if they were designed entirely for me.' He sighed.

Rosie giggled and then he groaned and kissed her hard and her mouth opened to his, and then he was pushing her gently back down onto the sofa, parting her legs and guiding himself inside her, and even though it was their first time, it felt right, and she knew she should have stopped him, should have reminded him about a condom, or he should have reminded her, or one of them should have been even remotely responsible, but they weren't. They were like teenagers, throwing caution to the wind, carried along with it, with the pleasure of finding each other again.

He lay on top of her afterwards, his breath slowing, and she could feel his heart beating, vibrating through the wall of his chest. She wanted to stay like that for ever, but the danger of passing out overcame the moment.

He pulled himself gently out of her and lay beside her on the couch, his arm flung across her breasts. She ran her hands through his thick, short hair, feeling the bristles against her palms, and across his face, and he grabbed her hand and kissed her fingers, one by one. 'Nice ring,' he said, when he spotted the silver and purple band.

'Thanks, it was Mammy's wedding ring.'

He looked as if he was about to say something, but then changed his mind.

'What is it?' Rosie asked.

He kissed the tip of her nose, his eyes searching hers. 'You have no idea how much I missed you.'

That wasn't what you were going to say, Rosie thought, even as she replied, 'I missed you too.'

'That's why I stayed, you know.'

'Why?'

'Because I thought if I left, you wouldn't know where to find me when you came home.'

Rosie felt stunned by the admission. She sat back on the sofa, unsure what to say for a moment.

'I suppose you think I'm pathetic.'

'No, no, I don't think that. How could you think I'd ever think that? That's just ... I never thought anyone would do that for me, that's all. It's so ...'

'Pathetic, I know,' he said ruefully. 'Abject, foolhardy, pitiable; supply your own adjective.'

'I *was* going to say romantic.' She smiled, feeling tears welling up. 'Oh, look at me,' she said, dabbing at her eyes. 'Such a fool.'

'A fool for love.' Mark reached out and took her hand and began to twist her mother's ring on her finger. 'Ever since you called around that first night, in your wedding dress, and you just stood there with it tucked into your knickers and your hair was a mess and you had a big streak of mud across your cheek, I wanted to tell you how I felt, but I was too angry and I wanted to say how sorry I was about what your father said. It was a terrible thing and I should have been there for you, but I wasn't.' He kissed her softly on the lips and her cheeks, all the way up to her ears, and she was sure then that she heard him say something. It sounded like, 'And now it's too late,' and she meant to ask him, but instead she returned his kiss, knowing that all she had to do now was to keep quiet, to say nothing, just to let things happen with Mark and be happy that she'd found him again. To be grateful for the sudden gift of it after everything that had happened. They could be happy, the two of them, she knew that. But she also knew that if she ignored what she thought she'd heard, she'd only be repeating the mistakes of the past, being whoever Mark wanted her to be instead of being herself, even if she didn't yet know who that was. And sooner or later, next week or next year or in five years, she'd find herself back where she started, alone and lost.

'Mark, what did you just say?'

He didn't look her in the eye, but instead stared fixedly into the distance.

He cleared his throat. 'Actually, I'm going to Vietnam.'

'Oh. That's nice,' she said, thinking, No, that is not nice. Not nice at all.

'I'm sorry, Rosie. I know this changes everything, but I've spent ten years planning and dreaming. I'm not sure how long I'm going for, but a while anyway. I have this idea. It sounds a bit daft, really, in this neck of the woods, but I want to come back in a bit and open a Vietnamese restaurant, a proper one.' He smiled. 'And I need to do some research, track down ingredients, that kind of thing. And I've been thinking of introducing curry sauce to the Vietnamese. What do you think?'

You told me you'd been waiting for me, Rosie thought, but she said 'They'll love it. That and battered sausages.' And they both chuckled, and he squeezed her shoulder again, and she tucked her head in the hollow between his chin and his shoulder. They were silent for a long time, and then Mark said, 'Do you think I'm doing the right thing?' He sounded like a young boy, tentative, uncertain.

She felt it then, the urge to reassure him, even though it nearly killed her, even though she knew that she could probably persuade him to stay. 'Yes, you absolutely are, Mark. It's something you need to do. It's where you come from, you know. And that's really important, to know where you come from.' I of all people should know that, she thought. 'So, when do you leave?'

'Couple of weeks. I'm going to see Mum in London first and then ...'

'Oh. Well that's good, that's great. I'm really pleased

for you.' And then Rosie decided that she'd had enough of congratulating him. She'd used up her ration of magnanimity and now she needed to go home and throw herself on the bed and howl with rage and regret that she'd left it too late.

'Oh, Mark,' she said sadly.

He gave a small smile, ruffling her hair. 'Rosie, I'm sorry. I really am, and I didn't mean to take advantage of you.'

Rosie snorted with laughter. 'It's not that.'

'What is it then?'

Rosie sighed. 'June and Mary-Pat told me something today.'

'Oh?' She felt him tense ever so slightly. Don't say it, she told herself. Don't.

'They told me that Frances O'Brien was my real mother.'

It took him a while to react, pushing Rosie slowly away from him, a look of horror on his face. 'They *what*? Tell me you're joking.'

'No.' Rosie shook her head, puzzled. Why would she joke about something like that?

His shoulders slumped and his head dropped to his chest. 'Oh, Rosie.'

Rosie felt her stomach muscles clench, that familiar tightness in her chest. 'Is that all you can say. "Oh, Rosie"?'

'No, of course not. Jesus, what a shock. I mean ...' He sat up on the sofa, arms circling his knees, the way he always did when he was thinking about something, that muscle working in his jaw.

'What is it?' Rosie said. 'Mark, talk to me.'

When he said nothing, when he didn't even look at her, the penny dropped. 'Oh my God, you knew.'

He went to reach out to her then. 'Rosie—'

But she pressed on. 'You knew and you never said a word.'

He didn't try to deny it, just shook his head, his eyes now full of tears. What the hell are you crying about? she thought. What do you bloody have to cry about?

'Who else knew? The whole town?' She sat upright on the bed. 'I mean, was there a person alive in Monasterard who wasn't up to speed on my parentage, apart from me, of course? Might there be anyone who hasn't heard the news?'

'Rosie, calm down,' he managed then, reaching out and placing two hands on her shoulders.

She shook off his hands, then pushed him violently in the chest, so that he fell back on the cushions. 'I will not calm down,' she hissed. 'I'm not some hysterical woman, so please do not patronise me.'

'I'm sorry, Rosie, listen to me. I had an idea, but I didn't know for sure. You have to believe me ...'

'Oh, fuck off,' she muttered, getting up from the sofa and gathering her clothes, yanking on her bra and bottoms, stuffing her knickers into the pocket of her jacket. She felt that she needed to do all of this quickly so that she could get out. The air seemed suddenly thick and she was struggling to breathe.

Mark got up and put a hand on hers, trying to catch her eye. 'Rosie, Rosie, c'mon, let's talk about this.'

'No. We are done talking.' She extracted herself from his embrace, stepping back, her feet colliding with Sophie as she did so, who gave a squawk of protest. 'Sorry, Sophie,' Rosie said automatically. She pushed her feet into her trainers and put her coat on, zipping it up, while he just sat there, face rigid with shock. Eventually, he managed, 'I'll drive you home.'

She turned to him then. 'You will not. You will not go near me or speak to me ever again. Do you hear me?'

His eyes widened as if to say, 'You don't mean it,' but when she didn't speak, he just nodded sadly.

I *don't* mean it, she thought as she ran out of the hall door and onto the little side street. He knows I don't mean it, so he'll come after me, I know he will. She stood and waited for a few seconds at the top of the street and, when there was no sign of him, tried to ignore the way her heart plummeted in her chest. He's not coming. I know what he was going to say earlier, but he stopped himself. That must mean he doesn't really care.

Dazed, she wandered onto Main Street, the wind buffeting her as she turned the corner, remembering then that she'd left her bike in his front garden. Crap, she thought, I'll have to go back and get it, but there's no way I can go now. No way. And then, like a ship in the night, she saw Wee Petie driving towards her in his Passat. She knew it was Wee Petie, because he drove everywhere at ten miles an hour. He drew slowly alongside and rolled down the window, the folksy country yarns of Johnny McEvoy blasting out of the opened window. 'What's a lady like you doing out on a night like this?'

Boy, am I glad to see you, she thought. She managed a weak smile. 'Oh, just going for a little walk.' As if any normal human being would be wandering around the town at midnight in November. 'Can I grab a lift?'

He turned down 'The Mountains of Mourne' and opened the passenger door. 'Hop in.'

'Thanks,' and she slid into the passenger seat, the warm blast of the heater enveloping her. He turned the music back up and drove along the street in silence, the words to 'Mursheen Durkin' reverberating around the car, his collection of holy medals and scapulars swaying from his rear-view mirror, the pyramid of fag ash in the ashtray behind the clutch. She knew that he was the same age as Pi, because they'd been to school together, but Wee Petie looked about ten years older, with his red eyes and purple, swollen nose, the legacy of too many years drinking spirits.

Rosie let herself be lulled by the heater for a few seconds, her eyes suddenly drooping. She couldn't understand it, how exhausted she felt, how weary to her very bones. The adrenalin burst she'd felt earlier at Mark's just seemed to have deserted her and she felt herself grow sleepy, the warm air blasting her face, the odour of pine air freshener filling the car. And then she was three years old, curled up on the back seat of Daddy's car under a blanket, the heater blasting her with warm air. She'd felt sleepy then, too, her eyelids drooping as she lay there, thumb in her mouth. Daddy was driving, his black hair, streaked with grey, curling over the top of his shirt as he stared into the rain, the wipers swishing back and forth across the windscreen. She could still remember the steady whump-whump as they moved, the way they cut a swathe through the silver raindrops as the car drove through the night.

He hadn't said anything when he'd collected her from Maeve's, just stood there on the doorstep, hands in the pockets of an old grey cardigan that Mammy had knitted him, shoulders stooped, his face old and tired. He'd held his arms out to her and she'd gone to him, inhaling the smell of Woodbine and woodshavings as she'd pressed her face into the rough material. 'Ah, my little Doodlebug,' he'd said gently. 'My little Rosie.'

'Mammy's gone, Daddy,' Rosie had said then. She remembered how eager she'd been to tell him, as if it was something really exciting, like a holiday or a trip to Switzers department store to see the Christmas lights. 'She told me to be a good girl and to remember her every night before I go to bed and to tell Mary-Pat and Pius and June to do their homework.' She'd looked up at him then, expecting him to exclaim that wasn't Mammy the lucky girl and they'd all miss her until she came home, but he hadn't said anything at all, just looked far into the distance, patting her idly on the head.

She didn't know if he'd spoken to Maeve — he must have done — but Rosie remembered him carrying her gently out into the car and placing her on the back seat, his breath coming in short puffs as he manoeuvred her in. He'd lit a cigarette then, she remembered that, because he'd pressed the cigarette lighter down for a bit, then lifted it out, the coils a livid orange, and put it to the cigarette, inhaling and then exhaling a great cloud of smoke before returning the lighter to its spot behind the handbrake. 'Homeward bound, Rosie,' he'd said then quietly. 'Homeward bound.' He always said that whenever they were coming back from a journey, even if only to the supermarket. And off they went, into the night, the two of them in the rain, Daddy puffing away and she almost asleep on the back seat.

And then, after a while, he'd turned the radio on and the song had come wafting out. 'A Cushla', an old song which crackled and hissed and in which the singer's voice sounded as if it were coming from very far away. 'A Cushla, a cushla, your sweet voice is calling, calling me softly again and again.' Daddy had begun to sing along then, his tenor voice filling the car, rolling around it, filling every space. He always did have a lovely voice, Daddy, sweet and strong. And as he sang, Rosie felt that he was singing it for her, that she was his Cushla, but now, as she sat in Wee Petie's car, she knew. He hadn't been singing it for her at all. He'd been singing it for Mammy. Because, in spite of everything, he loved her. And the memory made her realise that he must have loved Rosie too. She knew that, because he'd come to take her home.

'You drifted off there for a second.' Wee Petie's voice sounded loud in her ear and she jumped in fright.

'Sorry, Petie, it's late.'

'It is. How's himself?'

Rosie swallowed, groggy still. 'Oh, he's grand, Petie, thanks. He's hard at work in the garden, you know ...'

'I meant that young lad of yours.' Wee Petie's bloodshot eyes were still focused on the road ahead, but he grinned broadly, revealing an expanse of cracked yellow teeth.

'Oh, ehm.' Rosie examined the worn spot on her jeans, trying to work out what she could usefully say. 'Craig's gone, Wee Petie. He went home to America a while back.'

Wee Petie tutted, flicking the indicator as he turned slowly left onto the towpath. 'Not that fellow, I mean Mark.'

'How did you know about him?'

He grinned, revealing two rows of yellow teeth. 'Ah, you know what these places are like, Rosie, or have you forgotten? Word travels fast, even if some of it is utter shite. But you know, you've picked the right one there. A giant of a man, make no mistake about it. He's done a lot for this town and it just won't be the same without him. But, sure, we all have to leave sometime. At least those of us who have any sense.'

Rosie mumbled something in reply, willing Petie to shut up, to just stop talking, telling her how much Mark had done for the place. She didn't need to hear it, not now that it was too late. Not now that he was leaving.

'I never got out and look at me,' he said ruefully. 'I'd have loved to have gone somewhere like Vietnam — all those temples, and that food. Of course, there's the communists, but sure there's always some kind of a catch.'

Rosie listened to him ramble on. 'He deserves it, after all the hard work he's done, to take some time away. A gap year, isn't that what they call it nowadays? Still, I'd say you'll miss him, with you only just home. Are you planning to go out there yourself at all?'

'Yes, yes, of course I am,' Rosie said. She was struggling to find the right words, because she was still trying to make sense of it all. The fact that he was finally going back to Vietnam. She knew that she could have tried to make him stay, but maybe he just didn't love her enough and she didn't want to test it, to find out.

'Well, good for you, love. You don't want to end up like me, you know. I've wasted my whole life here looking for salvation in the bottom of a glass. Looking for answers and all because I was just plain scared of life. Scared of living. So I missed out on it all, kids, a wife, the lot. You don't want to be making the same mistakes, you or the young fellow.'

Rosie had no answer for him. Before she'd come home, she'd thought she was going along one path, long and straight, like the towpath, that just stretched on into the distance, and all she had to do was keep walking forward and life would just unfold ahead of her. Now she'd been thrown off it, almost violently, left to scrabble around in the bushes at the edge, trying to find her way back, with no one to guide her. No Mary-Pat or Junie to point and say, 'It's that way, Rosie,' the way they always had. No Craig ready to grimly push her back onto it if she fell off, a displeased expression on his face. No Mark waiting for her at the end, arms open, to pull her into a hug, to whisper into her hair, 'You made it. Well done.' She was on her own. She'd have to find her way by herself.

'Ah, sure, you're probably not planning on staying anyway,' Petie was saying. 'Sure who would, except for the likes of me, who has no prospect at all of leaving?' He was grimacing as he bounced over a pothole on the towpath, guiding the car very slowly in the direction of the house.

'Oh, I am staying, Petie. Sure, where else would I go, as they say?' And as she said the words, she knew that they were true. That this was the only place for her; this was where the path would begin, no matter how much she wished it otherwise.

'You're right there. Well, there's no better place than home, in the bosom of the family.' He smiled as he reached the gate up to the house. 'Families are peculiar, but they're all we've got.'

For fuck's sake, Rosie thought, I can't take any more of this, as she thanked him for the lift and waved him up the towpath, watching the tail lights of the car disappear very slowly into the darkness.

September 1981

Michelle

I only saw that girl one more time, the day of Rosie's christening. I had told John-Joe that she was never to set foot in my home again, and if I wondered why she didn't want to see her child, why John-Joe didn't take the baby down the canal to that horrible cottage where she'd been living, I didn't ask. I didn't want to know. She'd only asked for one thing: that we have Rosie christened. 'Baptised', really; as if Catholicism wasn't responsible for most of the ills in this country. Her mother would want it, was John-Joe's explanation. It seemed little enough to offer her.

It was such a beautiful day, as if nature was declaring that she couldn't care less about our silly lives, about the messes we'd made: she had other, larger things to do. The sky was that vivid blue that makes everything pinpoint sharp, the green of the leaves, the yellow of the barley in John Rogers' field. We bumped over the road to Porterstown in the Beetle, John-Joe and I in front, the kids squashed into the back seat, Rosie in her carrycot across their knees. If anyone had seen us pass, they'd have saluted us, as they all do around here, a family on its way to Mass. This normal family.

I tried not to look at John-Joe, but in the end I couldn't help it. I needed to study his face, to see if I could work out what he was thinking. What it meant to him to be driving us to his daughter's christening, whether he felt remorse or shame at what he'd done. Then I looked up for a moment into the little mirror in the sun visor above my head and I saw the three heads, Mary-Pat looking out at the fields, her soft face tired, tears gathering at the corners of those lovely blue eyes of hers, as if she was carrying the weight of the world on her shoulders. I wanted to hug her then, to hold her and to tell her it's not her fault — none of it is her fault. Pius was leaning over the carrycot, his features mobile as he made faces at the baby, rewarded by giggles and gurgles — he was in his own little world, oblivious to everything that was going on around him, and I thanked God for that. Only June was her usual self — like a sphinx, her expression unreadable. She'd dressed for the occasion as if it were the Royal Wedding — she'd been obsessed with Charles and Diana ever since we watched the whole thing in Bridie's living room, ordering a big white frilly blouse with leg-o-mutton sleeves from Dympna Moran with her pocket money.

When I looked back at John-Joe, his jaw was working and a deep groove had formed in the middle of his forehead, between his eyes, as he focused on the road. His expression was solemn, but I realised that I had no idea what he was thinking. How can

ALL THAT I LEAVE BEHIND

I have lived with this person for fourteen years and feel that I don't know him, I thought. He's as much a mystery to me now as he was the day we first met. Maybe we never really can know another person: essentially, we are all a mystery to each other.

He must have sensed me looking at him, because he turned to me, a small smile on his lips. 'Thank you,' he said quietly.

I said nothing for a moment, just pulled a battered compact out of my handbag and attempted to powder my nose, but my hand was shaking too much. And then I turned to John-Joe and the words left my mouth. 'I will never forgive you.' The words sounded like gunfire in the car, and I turned around to see if any of the children had heard, but the girls were absorbed in their staring out the window. Only Pius looked up from playing with Rosie, a look of shock on his face. Then he shook his head, as if doubting what he'd heard. I turned back to my work with my compact, dabbing powder on my nose, knowing that once the words were out, I couldn't take them back. It was over.

At the church, the girl had to stand behind John-Joe and myself at the baptismal font, watching her own child enter God's family, and if I felt sorry for her, I managed to push those feelings down; the pity I felt because she looked so worn out — all that shiny confidence gone, all that zest for life. Her face was grey and her hair was lank and her coat was two sizes too small for her. Those nut-brown eyes were dull as she cast them at the floor. And then I noticed the string of rosary beads in her hand, tightly clasped as her lips formed the words to the prayers which were so unfamiliar to me: 'Hail Mary, Mother of God ...' and I felt a certain kind of wonder that she had this faith, in spite of everything, in spite of losing her own flesh and blood to another woman. There was a part of me that admired her for it. That admired her courage as she signed the register as Rosie's godmother, her pen not wavering for a second, then picked up her handbag and tucked it over her arm and said, 'Well, goodbye then,' outside the church and walked back up the road towards God knows where, head held high.

I can still see her walking away from me as I sit in Sean's kitchen a week later, a big green ledger book in front of me. I've come over to give him a hand with his accounts; it turns out that I have a head for figures, making sense of the jumble of receipts which he keeps in an old brown envelope, being able to decipher the arcane rules behind the milk quota, the grain subsidy. It seems odd that I can focus on this kind of thing with the chaos all around me, but I find it soothing, putting the rows of figures into the ledger. Rosie is lying in the old pram, lifting her foot to her mouth, sucking her toes with a satisfied sigh. She's such an easy baby, always smiling and gurgling; she hardly ever cries. Without Rosie, I just don't know what I'd do.

'You have some expenditure that I can't account for,' I'm saying to him, my biro pointing to a row of numbers on a battered stub, almost obscured by a large tea stain. 'It says Murphy's grain and feed – was it for the hens?'

'You know, you don't have to put up with it, Michelle.'

His interruption is so sudden, I look up. He's standing beside me, too close, leaning against the range, hands in his pockets. A muscle is working in his jaw and his eyes are bright with emotion. 'I can help you, you know,' he says more softly.

I put the ledger down, and I go to the pram and I pick Rosie up. Her bottom is heavy and damp and I need to change her nappy. I coo into her ear and she giggles to herself, little feet thrust outwards with excitement.

'I don't need anything, Sean,' I say, my mouth to the top of Rosie's head.

He tuts impatiently. 'For God's sake, Michelle, how can you say that? He's left you with a child that isn't yours, humiliated you in front of the whole of Monasterard. I mean, how much longer are you going to put up with it? What kind of a woman allows her husband to do that to her?'

The kind of woman who's too proud to admit defeat, I think to myself. The kind of woman who is hanging on by her fingernails to everything she's worked so hard to achieve. The kind of woman who loves her husband, in spite of everything. Because I do love him. I love and hate him at the same time.

'Please don't judge me, Sean,' I say. 'It's complicated —' I begin, but to my horror, he comes over to where I'm sitting and he kneels down beside me, and he puts a hand on my knee. It's heavy and warm. And I look at it and I think that there might once have been a time when I'd have liked him to put his hand on my knee, to stroke my hair, to kiss me softly on the lips. But not any more. The idea of any man ever holding me again feels revolting to me.

'Why don't you kick him out, Michelle? God knows, you run the place yourself anyway. I'll help you — you can come and live here with me. I'll look after you. I'll show you that men aren't all like him.' He's squeezing my hand now and I want him to stop. 'Please, Michelle, you know how I feel about you. You've always known.' He begins to rub my knee in circles, and it's making me feel ill, and his other hand is on my shoulder and he's whispering, 'Please,' in my ear.

I jump up so suddenly I have to grab Rosie to stop her from falling off my knee. She gives a wail of surprise. 'Stop it,' I say, my voice sharp. 'Stop it now.' I lift Rosie into my arms and bundle her into the pram, then turn to manoeuvre it out the door. He tries to stop me then, his hand on my arm. 'Michelle, I'm sorry. I'm sorry. It was a mistake.'

I turn and I look at the kitchen, with its ticking grandfather clock and lovely delft, the kitchen that's been my haven so often over the years, my refuge, and I see it then, that this, too, was an illusion. I wouldn't have wanted this life, not one little bit. It would have stifled me, crushed my spirit. I could no more play the farmer's wife than fly to the moon. The only life I ever wanted, I had, the one I worked so hard for, and I was prepared to pay any price to hang onto it. Even losing the man I loved.

'You were wrong, you know,' I say.

'Wrong about what?' He looks mystified for a second.

'That all men aren't like him. They are. Goodbye, Sean.'

I feel that I've used up every ounce of energy and can barely walk out the door and trudge across the yard with the pram. I know he won't follow me. The exhaustion which now overwhelms me is so powerful, I feel I can barely walk, but instead of turning left to the house, I turn right and push the pram down the towpath a bit, my breath slowing as I walk, the whispering of the rushes and the pip-pip of the wagtail soothing me. Rosie sits high up in her perch and she looks around her, pointing at the hens, at the water, at the rushes, and then she gives a little laugh, her pudgy hands clutching her little pink blanket. It's then that I understand, that I can see clearly. It's worthless. All the years of sacrifice, pulling everyone along behind me as I marched on grimly, enduring year after year of it, of the cold, the damp, the discomfort, the sense that my life was just a huge mountain that I would never be finished climbing. For what? To stand here and to feel that the whole thing has been a waste, a sham. I know now that my life here is over.

Rosie looks at me then with those lovely eyes, which are so bright and trusting, and she breaks into a gummy grin. It's as if she's talking to me, as if she wants me to save her.

And I know now that that's what I have to do.

14

It seemed ironic, June thought, that when she'd spent her entire life trying to escape who she was, she only realised too late what it meant to her. Only when she'd wrecked what she valued most did she even see how little care she'd given it. There was nothing to do now, she knew, but to try to start again.

Gerry had moved out that night, when she'd come back from Monasterard. She hadn't asked him to leave – if anything, it should have been the other way around, but that was Gerry. He was a good man: she'd known that from the moment she'd set eyes on him, that afternoon in the Shelbourne. She'd been able to see beyond the bluster, the snobbery, the tendency to be a windbag, to the man with the good heart who would do anything for his family. Which is why it wasn't fair to blame him – the fault was all hers. There was something wrong with *her*, not with Gerry.

He wasn't looking for revenge because of what she'd done; he wasn't even angry, although he should have been. He was hurt, and that was far worse. When he'd intercepted her at the top of the stairs, he'd just held her mobile phone out to her, bottom lip trembling, like a lost little boy.

'Oh.' That was all she could think to say. 'Oh.' She had no idea she'd left the phone behind. She didn't have to look at the texts, with their silly emoticons, their misspellings. She knew what they said, and now so did Gerry.

'I won't read them out,' he'd said gently. 'They don't really bear being read out loud.'

If he'd ranted and raved, it would have been easier — if he'd yelled about the vows they'd taken and did they mean nothing to her, or banished her to the holiday home like Susie's husband Frank had done when he'd found out about Jao, the instructor, and they'd all had to go rushing down to Rosslare to drink wine and listen to her sob her heart out and feel smug that it wasn't them. Instead, he'd just looked at her sadly. 'I blame myself,' he'd said. 'If I'd been around more ... been less caught up with my job, with this stupid board meeting ...'

She'd grown angry then. 'Oh, for God's sake, Gerry, why on earth are you trying to blame yourself? I'm the one who —' She hadn't finished her sentence. The phone lay between them, all the little emoticons that Dave liked to use — the devil's horns, the endless smiley faces. She didn't even think to ask herself why she hadn't deleted them. Maybe she'd wanted Gerry to find them, or was that just too obvious?

'Is it serious?' he'd asked.

'Yes,' she'd answered.

She hadn't meant it like that, she thought now as she drove through town. She'd meant 'serious' in the sense that wrecking your whole life was serious, managing to lose your husband and family in one week was serious. She was driving him to his mother's now, a week after the family conference, the two of them wordless as they drove through the grey streets, the people huddled in the early winter wind, darting along the pavement, muffled in scarves and jackets. She pulled up in front of the smart flat on Mespil Road, with its view of the posh bit of the canal, full of barges and pristine swans, suppressing the shiver of revulsion which always gripped her whenever she slipped into her mother-in-law's orbit. She'd be only too delighted to have her only son back in her lair.

She turned to him then, wondering why he wasn't getting out of the car, to see tears streaming down his face. 'Junie, let's not do this, please. I can't manage without you, you know that.' After everything she'd done, she could hardly bear it, but she knew that they had to be strong now – that they – she – couldn't just go home and pretend that nothing had happened.

'Is it because we haven't taken Charlie out for a walk for a while?' He looked at her hopefully, as if a slight lull in the bedroom department might have set her on a course of complete self-destruction.

'Oh, God, no.' She shook her head. 'It's not that, believe it or not.'

'Look, it's the stress ... this new guy at the station – Aidan keeps going on about what a find he is and I'm fighting for my life here, Junie.' Gerry sniffed. 'They don't want old farts like me.'

'Oh, Gerry.' June leaned over and dabbed at his tears with a tissue. 'I had no idea it had got this bad. Why on earth didn't you tell me? We've always been able to tell each other things.'

'Not recently,' Gerry said dryly.

'No, you're right,' June agreed, blushing beet red. 'Gerry, I—'

He held up a hand. 'No, please, Junie. It makes it worse if you explain. I keep telling myself that it was completely meaningless. Just ... bodies and stuff. Please don't tell me otherwise.'

June shook her head and felt tears springing to her eyes. Tears that she didn't need to stem, to wipe away and pretend that they'd never happened. She cried for herself and Gerry and for the awful things she'd said to her siblings and for lying and keeping secrets and being a bad mother – everything. And when she finished, she gave her nose a good, loud blow, a honk, and herself and Gerry managed to giggle, like schoolchildren.

'I'm sorry, Gerry.'

'I know you are, love. But I'm hurt, and my ego has taken a battering.'

'And you don't trust me any more,' June said.

He didn't say anything in reply, just shook his head. He didn't need to say anything.

'I'm going now, love. Mummy will be wondering what I'm doing out here.' He nodded in the direction of his mother's place and they both looked up to her third-floor flat to see her looking out the window. Oh, Christ, June thought – what would that cow make of it? She'd be jubilant. She'd always thought June had no class.

'Gerry, before you go, can I tell you something?'

He turned around. 'Of course, Junie, anything.'

She was about to tell him then, to 'spill' as India would put it, but instead she shook her head. 'It's nothing. I'm sorry.'

'Junie, are you sure you don't want to tell me?' He was gentle. 'Don't you think not talking is what got us into this mess in the first place?'

'Among other things,' June said grimly. She took a deep

breath and let the words come out. 'I've been writing to my mother for years, and I told nobody about it.'

He'd looked puzzled for a few minutes, his forehead creased into a frown. 'Your *mother*? But she's dead, or as good as,' he'd added.

She could have taken offence, but June knew what he meant. As far as Gerry was concerned, Mammy was dead. She'd been gone for years when they'd met and her name had only been mentioned once in all the years they'd been together. Just once. The woman who'd taught her everything, and she'd mentioned her name once. June had felt a wave of shame wash over her. It didn't matter what Mammy had done. She didn't deserve that, to be wiped out like that.

June had shaken her head. 'She's not dead, Gerry.'

'Oh.' He'd shifted slightly in the seat, absorbing the information.

'That's right. She's been living ... overseas, and ... ehm, she's written to me now and again over the years.'

'And you kept it to yourself,' he said wryly. 'How well I know you, Junie.'

'I did,' she admitted.

'Why?'

'I've thought about that a lot over the past few weeks and I don't know. I thought I was protecting the rest of them, or maybe I just wanted Mammy to myself ... maybe that was it. Is that really so wrong, Gerry? I mean, it affected me too, her leaving, and no one ever gave me any credit,' she said.

He reached over and patted her gently on the hand. 'It's OK, love, it'll be OK.'

'Gerry?'

'Yes, love?'

'Why are you being so nice to me?'

Gerry shrugged. 'Look, I know that I might not have listened much in the past. I suppose that life has been pretty comfortable for me. I've just sailed on through without a single obstacle and I forget sometimes that it hasn't been like that for everyone else. Well, I suppose I'm getting my comeuppance now. I have no idea what to do with myself, do you know that?' He shook his head. 'No idea at all.' He gave a heavy sigh then and blew his nose loudly into a crumpled hankie, which he'd pulled out of his jacket pocket. His eyes were red-rimmed and his face creased with disappointment and June thought she'd never loved him more. But she didn't deserve him. She just didn't.

There was a long pause before he said, 'You know, if it's any consolation to you, I need to do some thinking too, Junie. I know, it'd be a first,' he smiled, 'but there's a first time for everything, isn't there?'

'There is,' June agreed sadly.

'And you'll triumph in the end, I know you will. You're stronger than you look, you know.'

'Thanks, Gerry. It's good of you to say it.'

'Yes, well ... if it'll bring us back to each other sooner, Junie, I'll say anything at all, you know that.' And then he'd leaned towards her and given her a gentle peck on the cheek. 'I'll be over to see the girls on Sunday, OK?'

She'd left him on the pavement outside his mother's, two suitcases beside him, waving, a lost soul. She thought her heart would break.

She texted Dave that night. 'Meet me at the Shelbourne, 6.30, Friday.' She didn't bother asking if that suited him, or if he might be at home with his family on a Friday night. He had a wife and two children — she'd seen photos of them on his desk, and he'd hastily turned them face down. And had she cared? Not really. She'd been so hell bent on getting what she wanted — whatever that was — that she didn't stop to think about anyone else. How could she have been so selfish — imagine if it were India and Georgia? And then she flushed when the next thought came.

It was the least she could do now to let him go with a bit of style, a bit of dignity.

His reply was typical, full of exclamation marks, and June had tutted as she'd deleted it. She'd need all of her strength to see this through.

She insisted they meet in the tea rooms, and as soon as she walked in, feet squishing over the heavy cream carpet, the drapes framing the windows with their lovely views of St Stephen's Green, she knew that it was a mistake. Dave was sitting in the corner, in one of those stiff wing-back chairs, in a suit and tie. She'd never once seen him out of overalls and he looked as if he were being strangled by his collar, pulling and tugging at it, eyes flicking nervously to one side. When he saw her, he jumped up, like an excitable schoolboy. June flushed a deep red. Sit down, for God's sake, she thought as she walked towards him. She'd dressed as if for a business meeting, in a dove grey wool suit. It was Chanel and she'd told Gerry not to buy it for her, that it was too expensive, but he'd insisted. Now, she was glad she had the suit of armour, could pretend that she was just another well-heeled professional chatting to a client.

As she came towards him, he grabbed her hand and attempted to kiss her full on the lips.

'Not here,' she hissed.

He flinched and sat back down again. She took up the menu and, on cue, so did he, looking at the selection of pastries and petits fours as if he'd never seen such a thing in his life. 'Any chance of a pint?' His top lip was sweating.

'They don't serve alcohol here,' June said briefly.

'Oh. Right.' He looked around the room. 'This is very you, June, very classy. You always did have your eye on this kind of lifestyle, didn't you?'

'I don't know what you mean,' June said. 'Will I order tea?'

There was a long silence before Dave put the menu down. 'You haven't invited me here for a little tea party, have you, June?'

June shook her head. 'I'm sorry, it's just … Gerry … Gerry knows.'

Dave stopped dead, his blue eyes wide with alarm. 'How?'

'He saw texts.'

'Oh, fuckin' brilliant.' Dave ran a hand through his hair. 'Why the fuck didn't you delete them? What's he going to do? Will he tell Majella or will I have to — Jesus, I'm fucked. She'll hack my balls off.' He looked around the room as if contemplating escape.

'He will do nothing,' June said quietly. 'He's been very good about it. He's forgiven me.' And she looked at Dave primly.

Dave sat back in the overstuffed seat then, an expression on his face that she'd never seen before. 'Well, aren't you the lucky one, June, to have such an understanding husband.'

'Yes, I suppose I am—' June began, but Dave interrupted, leaning forward in the chair, waving a finger.

'Do you know something, you're just a prick tease, June, thinking that you can just walk into my life after twenty-five years and get me all riled up again and then just tell me to fuck off. You know what your problem is – you're a user and you're a snob. You've always thought you were too good for people like me – but everyone knows that the O'Connors are just trash. That sister of yours who doesn't belong to anyone in particular – who the fuck knows who the daddy is there, eh? And that father of yours, prick out all over the town until he wasn't capable of it any more. Jesus Christ.' His voice had been growing louder and louder and a group of nuns, who were gathered at the next table, turned around, anxious looks on their faces underneath their navy blue veils. June wanted to kneel down and beg for absolution, beg them to ask God to forgive her.

Then the nice Russian manager was standing beside them. 'Sir? Madam? Is there a problem?'

Dave jumped up, his knees crashing off the low coffee table. The look on his face was wild. 'There's no problem … Svetlana,' he muttered, looking at her name badge. 'We won't be ordering tea after all.' Then, louder, 'June, try keeping your knickers on in future.' And with that, he was gone, head high, striding across the room.

'I'll just get my coat,' June said quietly, gathering her bags and exiting the room with as much dignity as she could muster.

When she got home, the house was empty, as it generally was these days. She went to the fridge and opened it, then closed it again. She'd find nothing there. At least, nothing that would make her feel any better. She sat down at the kitchen table, drumming her fingers on the expensive surface. Gerry had had it imported from Sweden and it was birch, a lovely blonde shade that felt cool under her touch. She laid her cheek down on it and closed her eyes. She was getting a headache, a pain right above her left eyebrow that throbbed and ached.

It's finally happened, she thought. I'm alone. The one thing I was afraid of — it happened anyway, and it was all my doing. I have no one to blame but myself.

There was only one thing left to do and it would take all of her strength to do it, but she knew that it would set them all free. And even if the others never knew she'd done it, *she'd* know. And she'd understand that, for once in her life, she'd done the right thing.

She sighed and went upstairs to the bedroom, to her dressing table and took out the lovely Smythson notepaper. She was running low and knew that the next time she'd be opting for Basildon Bond. She didn't have the nerve to ask Gerry to fork out for more. It seemed appropriate, somehow, for the next phase in her life. She sat down, put a fresh sheet in front of her and lifted her pen to write. 'Dear Mammy ...'

She was distracted then by a presence behind her. She turned to see Georgia standing at the door in a pair of grey jogging pants and a black T-shirt that said 'Queen Bee' on it. She couldn't help it, the flicker of impatience she felt when she saw her there. It wasn't fair, she knew, after everything the girls had gone through, but she wanted to get this done, without interruption, so that she could put the whole awful thing behind her.

Maybe if I just ignore her, she thought, turning back to her task, and then, after a few minutes, 'You're hovering,' over her shoulder.

'Sorry, Mum. It's just ... I need to talk to you.' Georgia's voice wasn't her usual confident boom but a little, childlike wobble.

June swivelled the chair around until she was facing her daughter. 'Look, love, I know it hasn't been easy—'

Georgia waved her away with a hand, a look of impatience on her face. 'It's not that. It's India. She's done something bad.'

India? June shook her head for a minute. 'I don't understand.' 'India' and 'bad', the two words just didn't go together. India was a good girl. She'd never given June a day's trouble. She'd studied for all her exams and never went out to social nights lathered in fake tan and wearing nothing but a bandage, like some of those girls she saw hanging around outside Wes. Georgia, on the other hand …

Georgia gave a half-smile, as if to say, 'I know. You thought it'd be me.' And then her eyes filled with tears. 'Oh, Mum,' she blurted and ran towards June, hurling herself into her arms, where she gave a little wail of distress. June put her arms around her daughter, around her solid little back, and said, 'It's all right, shush, shush,' into Georgia's hair, thinking as she did how long it had been since she'd done that, given either of her girls a real hug.

June pulled her daughter onto her knee, giving her a squeeze. 'That's my girl. See? You're not too old to sit on my knee, are you?'

'No, Mum.' Georgia's sobs had died down a little and she leaned her lovely dark curls against June's shoulders and hiccupped gently.

'Georgia, tell me what the matter is.'

Georgia took a deep breath. 'There are photos of India online.'

'Right,' June said cautiously. 'Well, she has an account. She showed me once – there were kittens on it and Leinster rugby players.'

Georgia rolled her eyes to heaven. 'For God's sake.' And she got up from June's knee and walked out of the kitchen before sticking her head back around the door. 'Wait there for a minute.' June could hear her thump up the stairs to her bedroom, and then thump back down again, her determined steps, a little terrier. She was holding her iPad, which she put on the table between them. She tapped in a password and logged on to India's profile.

'How do you know her password?' June asked.

Georgia gave her a patronising look. 'Now ...' She scrolled down through pictures of dogs leaning out car windows and American cheerleaders. 'Mum, you might need to prepare yourself. Are you ready?'

June nodded, her stomach clenched. She wasn't sure she was ready. She looked at the photo Georgia showed her on the iPad. There was silence while June tried to process the information. The photo was blurry and only showed from the bottom of India's face down, but June knew that scar on her daughter's collarbone. She'd got it when Georgia had hit her with a hockey stick in the back garden. She'd needed five stitches.

'She's not wearing any top,' June said, stating the obvious.

'No, Mum. She isn't.'

I'm not sure she's wearing any bottoms either, June thought bleakly. 'Where does this come from?'

'Probably that asshole Jamie Ferguson; he says he's her boyfriend, but he's only after one thing. Guess he's got it now.'

'He asked her to post ... naked photos of herself online?'

Georgia sounded weary now. 'No, Mum. He asked her to send them to his phone and then he posted them online for all the world to see. It's what some boys do.'

'And girls let them?' June looked at Georgia in horror.

'Well, not exactly, but it happens, Mum.' Georgia shrugged.

'My God,' June said. How the hell had she not been aware of this? What kind of world were her daughters living in … that something like this could happen? That they could be defiled like this, in front of the whole world, by a young man. June couldn't think. Her mind was a blank.

'Everyone in the school knows and Mrs Delaney says you'll be hearing from her, like, today, and she's phoned you twice and India's made me run to the phone every time it rings in case it's the Gorgon. I've had to pretend to be the Chinese takeaway twice now.' Georgia was growing agitated and June soothed her. 'Georgia, calm down. I'll ring Mrs Delaney.'

'No!' Georgia wailed. 'India will kill me. She'll know it's me. I've been trying to keep it a secret, I really have, because I know that things are so bad with you and Dad, but I just can't keep it in any more,' she said.

June held her breath, just for a second, while she tried to take it all in, patting and soothing and telling Georgia that it would all be all right. 'Daddy and I will sort it out, and you are not to worry about a thing, do you hear me? You've done the right thing,' she said, trying to sound convincing, all the while wondering how she hadn't noticed what was going on with her girls, right under her nose. How had she not seen? Maybe, she thought bitterly, because she hadn't been looking.

15

She must be pure mad, Mary-Pat thought as she tasted the sauce and decided it needed a little more salt. To think she could get her husband to love her again with a bit of nice food and underwear, but she had to start somewhere. God, these knickers were killing her, she thought, as she ran her finger around the elastic, which was digging into her flesh. Her breasts almost spilled over the top of the corset: she'd been a bit optimistic with the sizing, she realised.

She'd planned it for days, trying on the underwear and standing in front of the bedroom mirror, wondering if she'd stand any chance of seducing him in that get-up or did she look like a giant marshmallow with a little strip of purple at the top and bottom. 'Are you cracked or what?' she'd ask herself, turning around to get a view of her rear end encased in blue lace, her face flushing with embarrassment as she caught an unwelcome glimpse of her back fat. Sure why would he be interested in you? Why would he find you sexy? The thought would move her to tears. He used to find her sexy, but now, she wasn't so sure. At other times, she'd feel a rush of self-confidence as she planned the seduction menu, grinning as she thought of how much he'd love the venison steaks and steamed asparagus.

But, sure, the whole thing distracted her anyway. 'Displacement activity', Graham called it: doing one thing to avoid thinking about something else. He'd be right there. But it didn't matter what the hell he called it, Mary-Pat thought, the result was just the same. She was trying not to think about everything because it was just too much to take in, and so it was easier to focus on asparagus. Easier than to go to the phone and pick it up and dial Rosie's number, slamming the phone down before it had even rung once. She had no idea what she could say to her anyway. I'm sorry I didn't tell you about that O'Brien woman, that I kept it a secret from you because I was trying to protect you from the sordid truth about Daddy. Who the hell would want to know that her father couldn't keep his hands off any woman who happened to be passing? No one, least of all Rosie. She'd had enough to bear in her life. Mary-Pat wanted to explain to her that she'd had the best of intentions, but that somewhere along the line they'd gone wrong.

But Mary-Pat also knew that there was a part of her that hadn't rung Rosie because she couldn't forgive herself for the way she'd been with her. She wasn't sure how it worked like that, how hatred for one person could be moved onto someone else, someone entirely innocent. Her logical mind told her that Rosie was blameless, but her heart had been filled with anger and resentment. She couldn't help herself: all the years she'd given to her sister after Mammy left. She only had to catch a glimpse of Rosie's red head for it to seize hold of her, for the thought to pop into her head: if you hadn't appeared, Mammy would still be here. You're the reason she left.

Mary-Pat closed her eyes as she stirred the sauce. How could she ever make it up to Rosie? Where could she even begin?

After Pi had carried Rosie off into the night that dreadful night of the family conference, June and Mary-Pat had sat in silence in the kitchen, the only noise being the click of Duke's paws on the kitchen tiles as he shuffled back and forth, sniffing for any food that might have miraculously fallen from the sky. The two of them had blown themselves out and the silence now stretched between them.

'Well, that went well,' Mary-Pat had eventually said. She'd intended to sound sarcastic and was gratified when her sister had flinched. It was mean, she knew, but June deserved it.

June had shrugged, her eyes brimming with tears. 'Can I have one of those?' She'd nodded at Mary-Pat's cigarettes.

'You don't smoke.'

'I do now,' June had said in a shaky voice, accepting the proffered box from Mary-Pat and selecting one, inhaling deeply when Mary-Pat had lit the cigarette, then coughing and spluttering.

'Easy. You don't have to smoke it all at once.'

June had given a tight smile and there was another long silence while she had puffed away at the cigarette. Mary-Pat didn't break it. She wasn't going to throw her sister a lifeline.

Eventually, June had blurted, 'I'm sorry, MP, I didn't meant to spring it on you all like this. And I didn't mean to keep it a secret from you all these years. It was just … Mammy made me promise not to breathe a word. She didn't want the others to worry. She wanted to let sleeping dogs lie. It was an awful responsibility, MP, and I hated it, but I felt I had no choice. It was either that or lose Mammy for ever.' She'd sounded whiny and nervous, the way she always did when she knew she'd done something wrong. Mary-Pat remembered her using the same tone when they'd done something bold as children and Daddy told them he'd tan the hide of whoever was responsible. June would just look wounded and whine, 'It wasn't me, Daddy.' And, sure, who wouldn't believe her? Like butter wouldn't melt in her mouth.

Mary-Pat had thought for a long time, eyeing the little letters on the table, before saying, 'Do you think you could put them away, please? I don't want to look at them.'

'Sure.' June had tried not to look too hurt as she picked them up and pushed them into her handbag, like a bundle of used tissues, soiled and manky.

'The thing is, June, we did lose Mammy for ever. The day she left us. She was gone. And we had to come to terms with that in whatever way we could. You know what it was like, Junie.'

June had nodded silently, twirling the wedding ring round and round on her slender finger. 'It was awful.'

'It sure was. Worse than awful. It wasn't just the wondering where she was, the worrying, but also thinking over and over again about what we'd done to make her run away like that. I thought it was my fault, that I hadn't looked after Rosie well enough or something, or that I hadn't taken sides when that woman came to live with us. I should have sided with Mammy. I should have. She probably felt she had no one to turn to—'

June interrupted, 'But that wasn't our responsibility, MP. It wasn't our fault, surely you knew that. Look what Daddy was like. If it hadn't been Frances O'Brien, it'd have been someone else. She probably just couldn't take any more.'

'So she left her children,' Mary-Pat had said flatly.

'Yes, well ...'

'You and I both know that she could have taken us with her or booted him out. The law was on the woman's side in those days. No judge in the land would have argued otherwise. But she chose to leave us with him and go off and make a new life for herself.'

'And she's blamed herself ever since,' June had interjected. 'I can't tell you how many times she's said sorry—'

'Oh, for God's sake!' Mary-Pat had barked. 'Sorry, sorry. Who gives a shit about her sorries. It's far too late for that, Junie, and you should have told her that. After you'd told us, your flesh and blood, about the letters and let us all decide what to do. It was your responsibility to us, to tell us. But you chose to keep it to yourself. And I don't think I can forgive you for that, I really don't.'

'I'm sorry—' June had started to whine again.

'Oh, will you just quit, Junie?' Mary-Pat's hands had been shaking as she'd lit a cigarette and took a deep pull. She needed a moment, she'd thought. She needed to weigh the enormity of it all in her mind, to decide whether she wanted to lose another family member after everything else that had happened that afternoon. After all of those years holding it all together, through thick and thin. All those years with Daddy in this house, all the years in which what had happened in her own family had sunk deep inside of her. And Mary-Pat knew with a sureness which she'd never felt before that she'd had enough. She knew that she couldn't erase the past, but she could stop it taking a grip on her now. She could stop it poisoning her family, the family she'd created with PJ. They were what mattered now, not the others.

'Don't you want to find out where Mammy is? What she's doing? Aren't you even a little bit curious?' June's voice had sounded faintly accusatory.

Mary-Pat had shaken her head. 'I'm with Pi on that, June. Thanks all the same. And now,' she'd pushed herself up from her chair and looked around, 'this place is a mess and PJ will be back from the pub quiz any minute.' She'd taken a deep breath, her decision made. 'I'd like you to leave, Junie. I'm sorry.'

June had nodded and sniffed, picking her expensive handbag up off the floor. She hadn't looked at Mary-Pat as she put on her jacket, but when she got to the hall door, she'd turned around. 'Are you sure …?' and she'd pulled the wad of paper out of her handbag.

Mary-Pat had hesitated for a second too long. At that moment, she'd have given anything to know where Mammy was and what she was doing. But as June had come back towards her, taking the creases out of the crumpled mess of paper, Mary-Pat had found it within herself. 'No. Please, Junie. No.'

June had looked as if Mary-Pat had hit her. Then she'd nodded, stuffing the letters back in her bag and marching promptly out the front door, shutting it behind her with a loud bang. Mary-Pat had waited until her sister was long gone before breaking down. It was as if a dam had broken inside her, and it all came pouring out, the pain and resentment of it all. For the next hour, she'd held herself and howled until she could howl no more and then she'd looked at the clock on the wall and realised that she'd have to stop, because PJ and the kids were due home at any minute. By the time John-Patrick had come in, she'd been standing by the cooker, turning fried eggs over in the pan. 'Tea's ready,' she'd said.

'Thanks, Mum.' John-Patrick had pulled out a stool and sat down, pouring himself a cup of tea. 'Any news?'

'No. Quiet day,' she'd lied, putting the eggs on a plate and sliding them across to him. 'Eat up.'

She'd sat down beside him and lit a fag, before remembering that the child was eating, and she'd put it out on the ashtray on the kitchen windowsill, wincing as she noticed all the butts. He'd looked up and had given her a half-smile and she'd noticed that his eyes were their normal blue, not those scary black marbles.

'What?' She put her hands on her hips.

'Nothing.' He gave a faint smile.

'What is it, John-Patrick?'

'You normally don't stop smoking when we're eating,' he said politely, crossing his fork and knife on his plate and wiping his mouth with the cloth napkin she'd provided for him. She'd trained him to do that and she felt proud of him now.

'Yes, well, I'm trying to be a bit more considerate,' she'd muttered.

He'd nodded, as if her being considerate was the most normal thing in the world. 'Is everything all right, Mum?'

She didn't know what came over her, but she'd told him, her lovely son. It had all come out, everything, about Mammy and Daddy and Rosie, all of it, and, being John-Patrick, he hadn't interrupted or offered advice she didn't need. He'd just listened, and even though Mary-Pat had felt guilty about burdening him, she'd also felt glad, glad that it was all now out in the open and that she wasn't passing the guilt on to the next generation; the notion that you had to keep things secret. It wasn't good for anyone.

'You know, I remember the very first time I saw Auntie Rosie,' she'd said, pouring a thick brew of tea into two mugs and shoving one across the table to him. 'I'd come home from school. It was February, I remember, because there was ice on the canal and the rushes were all covered in frost. And there was a carrycot in the hall. It was like an alien had landed in the place, I can tell you. I crept over to it and just saw her, moving under her little crochet blanket, and she let out this tiny cry. She was such a scrap, all scrawny and wizened; she didn't look like I thought a baby should look. I thought they were always plump and bonny, with big rosy cheeks. Anyway, of course, your Auntie June nearly wet herself with excitement, eejit that she is. "MP, look, there's a baby!" God almighty. She always was dim.' She'd rolled her eyes to heaven then, before catching herself on. 'Sorry, that was a bit much.'

'Did you know who … it … sorry, Auntie Rosie belonged to immediately?' John-Patrick had said quietly.

Mary-Pat had nodded. 'Of course I did, because I'd met her in the minimarket when she was about six months gone and it didn't take a genius …' She'd hesitated, biting her lip. 'As far as I know, I was the only one that did know, apart from Daddy and Mammy, of course. And it made me feel anxious inside, that I had to keep it to myself, you know? And the way they made excuses for it, for her, I mean.' Mary-Pat had shaken her head. 'Mammy told us it was her sister's and they were minding the baby because she hadn't been feeling well. I never did understand that: not the excuse, but why Mammy put up with that. I can't think it was because she wanted another baby. For God's sake, they could hardly manage to feed and clothe the three of us as it was.'

John-Patrick had cleared his throat and shuffled in his chair. 'Ehm, maybe she loved him,' he'd finally said, blushing bright red at the idea.

'Maybe you're right, love. Maybe she did,' Mary-Pat had said. She'd taken a deep breath, 'Don't think badly of Grandad, love, will you?' Mary-Pat had said. 'I don't want you to think badly of him.'

'It's kinda hard not to, Mum,' John-Patrick had said, looking surprised. 'He doesn't come out of it well.'

'Maybe not, but he was weak, John-Patrick, not bad through and through. Just a weak man trying to pretend that he wasn't. Maybe try not to be hard on him, will you? Not that he'd notice if you were, but you get my drift. You'll see that when you get older, love, that it's not always easy to be strong or to do the right thing. Sometimes it takes more than we've got.'

John-Patrick didn't say anything, just put a hand over hers and gave it a squeeze. 'You did the right thing, Mum, by Rosie. She knows that.'

Does she? Mary-Pat thought. 'It's good of you to say it, love, but I doubt it. I think she blames me for everything that's gone wrong in her life, but anyway ...' She squeezed his hand back. 'You're a good listener, son. There'll be some girl out there who'll like that.'

'Thanks.' He'd shifted uneasily in his chair, not meeting her eye.

'There already is,' she said. 'Why didn't I cop on sooner? Your mother must be losing her touch.'

He'd blushed then, the poor thing. 'She's an au pair for the MacNamaras.' And then he'd coughed nervously. 'She's Swedish.'

'Oh, lovely,' she'd said nervously. 'She must be into saunas and all that.' 'All that' meaning 'taking their clothes off all the time'. The Scandinavians were awfully free like that.

He'd snorted with laughter then. 'Mum, for God's sake — talk about stereotyping. And no, she doesn't eat reindeer or listen to ABBA all the time either.'

'Sorry. Maybe I haven't changed that much, after all,' she said ruefully.

'That's good to hear,' he'd replied, carrying his plate over to the sink and carefully rinsing it, before turning his head and saying, 'Because I like you the way you are, Mum, believe it or not.'

'Cheeky bugger,' she said, accepting the brief squeeze he'd offered her, his hands damp on her shoulders, leaning her head against his chest and thinking how funny it was that only a few years before, he'd used to come to her for hugs, leaning into her tummy and resting his head there while she wrapped her arms around him.

'Love, will you promise me one thing?' she said into his jumper.

'What?'

'Don't tell your father. He's had enough of all that and he doesn't need any more of it, the burden of it, do you know what I mean?'

John-Patrick hadn't answered her directly; he'd just shrugged and muttered something about playing *Devil May Cry*. 'Later, Mum.'

Now, she dipped a finger in the hollandaise, wondering about how the roles had been reversed and if it was inevitable that the children become the parents in the end.

'Mary-Pat?'

She screamed and dropped the wooden spoon, where it clattered to the floor, sending a yellow spray of hollandaise over the floor and cupboard doors. 'Oh, shite,' she yelled, clutching her chest. 'PJ, don't sneak up on me like that. You gave me an awful fright.'

He was standing at the kitchen door, a copy of *The Sun* under his arm, looking at her warily, as if she were a wild animal he'd cornered. Compared to her, he was overdressed, in a thick sleeveless gilet and a fleece which zipped up under his chin and she suddenly realised how cold she was and how unattractive her mottled blue skin must look. She looked down at the two rolls of fat around her belly, over which she couldn't see the knickers with the ribbon detail. What had she been thinking – how on earth would he think she was sexy in this rig-out?

'Why are you in your underwear?'

'Ehm, I ... well ...' she stuttered. For a second, she couldn't think of a single word to say.

'Mary-Pat?' He was beside her in a second, but she couldn't help noticing that he didn't touch her. He just stood beside her, looking worried. Eventually, he said, 'Will I fetch your dressing gown?'

She nodded, not trusting herself to speak.

When he came back, he draped the dressing gown gently over her shoulders and tied the cord around her waist, like a little child. Then he busied himself making a cup of tea, putting one teaspoon of sugar in hers, the way she liked it. And then he handed it to her. 'Will we sit down?'

She shook her head, pulling the collar of her dressing gown tightly around her, feeling the warmth of the thick cotton surround her like a fluffy blanket. She felt glad to be covered up, not to be exposed like that, even to her husband.

He cleared his throat. 'I think we might take the sauce off the heat.'

'Oh, Christ,' she blurted and turned around to see a sticky brown mess bubbling away in the pot. She whipped it off the stove and threw it into the sink, dousing it with a jet of cold water so that it hissed and spat.

'I was making venison steak for dinner,' she eventually managed. 'I thought the sauce might be nice.'

'Steak? Are we celebrating?' He tried to joke, but when she didn't reply, just bit her lip and looked at her tea, he said, 'Mary-Pat, tell me what's wrong. Is it the others?'

She'd been about to tell him, to let it all out the way she had with John-Patrick, even though she'd asked her son to keep it quiet. The temptation was almost too much for her, but at the tone of his voice, she stopped herself. He sounded so weary, so tired of it all, and she knew that if she told him, if she fed him another morsel about her family, it would drive him even further away. He'd had enough. God, she wanted to unburden herself, but she wouldn't, because she knew that it wouldn't do any good. And she also knew that if she told PJ about Mammy, he'd only encourage her to get in touch with Mammy again, because he was a good man and because he believed in family. He just wouldn't understand why it would cause her more pain than she could deal with.

'It's not the others. It's us.'

PJ said nothing, just blew on his tea, his eyes fixed on the activity. Mary-Pat wanted to rip the mug out of his hand, and she would have done had it not contained near-boiling liquid. Instead, she said, 'I know about your one up at the minimarket. I've seen you there.' She looked directly at him as she said this, daring him to deny it, to say that she was just imagining it. When he didn't immediately reply, she opened her mouth to say something else to him, something like — 'Well? Have you nothing to say for yourself?' But she stopped herself. She didn't need always to be the first to speak. Graham and she had been working on that recently. So she just waited.

'It's nothing,' he said eventually. 'Nothing has happened. She's just a nice girl who likes a bit of a joke, that's all.' He looked at his hands around the mug of tea. He was such a bad liar, PJ, like a naughty schoolboy, all shifting from foot to foot and refusing to meet her eye.

'A bit of a joke.'

'Yes, MP, a bit of a joke, and banter and fun. The craic. We used to have plenty of it, if memory serves.'

Mary-Pat was silent for a bit. PJ never talked to her like this. She was about to open her mouth in response when he continued, 'And do you know what? I enjoy it. And I flatter myself that she fancies me, even though the dogs in the street know that she would never in a million years go anywhere near a man like me — she's got some Transylvanian body builder who waits for her after every shift — but it makes me feel better, MP. Because I know that you don't fancy me any more and you haven't for a long time. And don't tell me that's not true, because I know it is. I'm the invisible man around here.' His cheeks were a livid red with emotion and his breath was coming in short puffs as he spoke.

Mary-Pat could hardly believe it. 'I'm sorry, PJ, I know that things haven't been easy—'

He tutted impatiently. 'It's not that, love. That kind of stuff will always be there — the swings and roundabouts, ups and downs. The thing is, we've always been in it together. It's always been us against the world. Now, I feel I don't have you any more, the girl I married ... You're here physically, but in your mind you're elsewhere, somewhere I can't reach you. None of us can. And that hurts, Mary-Pat, to be shut out like that.'

Mary-Pat felt as if all the breath had been sucked out of her. She'd thought she was the one in the driving seat, the one who'd been wronged, and now ... she didn't know what to think. 'I don't know what you mean, PJ. I'm here day in day out, making your lives easy, making things comfortable, looking after you all, making sure that none of you want for anything ... If you're not happy with that, though ...' Mary-Pat folded her arms and set her mouth in a thin line.

'We are and we appreciate it, MP, we really do. But honestly, I'd trade all the ironed shirts and big dinners in Ireland for a joke and a laugh with you the way we used to. I mean, when was the last time we sat down together and talked, really talked?'

'We talk every day, in case you haven't noticed.'

'I don't mean that kind of talk — shite about what was on Pat Kenny or what that eejit Wee Petie got up to on his tractor. That's all well and good, but I mean proper talk, about what we want out of life, where we're going, that kind of thing. Remember our five-year plans?'

Mary-Pat shook her head but didn't reply. It seemed safer now to leave the talking to him, seeing as he was so much better at it.

'We used to sit down and talk about where we'd be in five years and what we'd have done. We'd have a holiday home in Wexford, or one of the kids would be studying medicine, or you'd have gone to college, that kind of thing — what we hoped for out of life. Why did we forget our dreams, MP, I mean what happened?' As he said this, he reached out and covered her hand with his, squeezing it tight.

Mary-Pat shook her head. 'I don't know. Life happened, I suppose. The kids and then the business ...' She didn't mention the elephant in the room. Daddy.

'I know. And Daddy did his best to make things stressful,' PJ said ruefully, rolling his eyes to heaven. 'But I didn't resent it, love, because I knew how much it meant to you, how much family mattered.' She knew that he was being kind, using a euphemism for the chaos that was her family. 'At least you have a family. If you don't, you quickly understand how important they are.' Mary-Pat used to find the fact that he was an only child, born to parents in their forties, now long dead, fascinating. She used to tell herself that she wouldn't actually mind being an only child – it seemed so much more peaceful – there would be none of that endless conflict, that ceaseless measuring yourself up against your siblings and finding yourself wanting. That you weren't as glamorous as your younger sister, or as pretty. That your brother was far nicer than you would ever be. That you were a complete bitch to the little girl you'd told yourself you'd given everything to. She sighed and squeezed PJ's hand back.

'You don't need to be responsible for them any more, MP. They're all grown up now. You don't have to mother them. It's not your job. It should be our time now, Mary-Pat. We've earned it.'

She bit her lip. 'I know, but I'm just afraid,' she said.

'Why?' PJ shuffled his seat a little closer to hers and reached out and folded over the collar of her dressing gown, which had been sticking up, patting it down, looking at her tenderly.

'That we won't know what to say to each other. That we'll discover that we have nothing left now that the kids are reared. That we'll just sit in silence in front of the TV for the rest of our lives.'

He smiled. 'What are the odds of that, do you think? Sure, you'd talk the hind legs of a donkey, for starters. I can hardly get a word in.'

Mary-Pat laughed. 'Well, it'll have to be different from now on. That's what's got us into this mess in the first place. You have to do some talking too.'

He nodded. 'But you have to let me, love. And you can't interrupt, or tell me what I should be thinking, or that I've got it all wrong, that I'm some class of an eejit — all that kind of thing has to go.'

'Jesus, give it to me straight, why don't you,' Mary-Pat said. 'Am I that bad?'

He kissed her softly on her cheek. 'You are, and most of the time I wouldn't have it any other way. You know me, love. I like a quiet life. But that won't work any more. We need to really talk.'

Mary-Pat nodded silently. She was itching for a fag, but she had to be firm with herself. She wouldn't give in to her cravings any more.

'You can start by telling me what the underwear is about.' He smiled.

'Oh.' Mary-Pat found herself blushing like a teenager, pulling her collar more tightly around her neck. 'I thought that it might make you fancy me again. I had no idea I looked so ridiculous.'

He reached out and stroked her cheek, his eyes tender. 'You do not look ridiculous. You look gorgeous and I wouldn't change you for the world.'

Mary-Pat thought she'd just die of embarrassment. 'Will you get up the yard, PJ, with your flattery.'

He leaned closer to her now, snaking a meaty arm around her shoulder, giving it a little squeeze. 'I mean it, Mary-Pat. I've never stopped fancying you. I just thought you didn't want *me* any more.'

Mary-Pat shook her head. 'You were wrong. But what about your one?'

He shrugged. 'I won't lie, MP, it was fun to go up there and have a bit of craic. To share a joke and a laugh. But that was it. We'd just chat a bit and I'd see myself as the man I once was. The kind of man other women might fancy. It made me feel better about myself.'

That's sad, Mary-Pat thought.

'I couldn't fancy her anyway, sure, she looks like a stick insect,' he added mischievously. 'I like my women with a bit of padding on them.'

Mary-Pat giggled.

'And now that dinner looks well and truly burned.' He pointed to the charred mess behind Mary-Pat.

'It does.'

'When are the kids back?'

'Not till late. Melissa has drama and John-Patrick's helping Pi with the garden.'

'That gives us a couple of hours.' PJ looked at his watch, then looked at her hopefully. 'Think we can go for a walk or something?'

'A *walk*? Do you think I bought this stuff to go for a bloody walk?' Mary-Pat pulled open the front of her dressing gown. 'If I'd wanted to go walking with you, PJ, I'd have bought a pair of hiking boots.'

PJ burst out laughing. 'That's more like it, Mary-Pat. That's more like the girl I used to know.'

She'd tell him in the end, she thought later, as the two of them lay in bed, PJ snoring softly beside her, her new underwear strewn on the floor on top of his jeans and boxers, where the two of them had ripped them off, they were in such a hurry. But not now. She'd only just got him back and she didn't want to spoil things before they'd even begun. It was her marriage, she now realised, hers and PJ's. And her life to do with whatever the hell she wanted. The thought was scary and exciting at the same time, and as she allowed herself a little daydream, she pushed all the other stuff into the background, all the guilt and the anger and the sadness, and the uncomfortable thought that by not telling PJ she was guilty of keeping another secret. All that didn't matter right now.

I'm free of them all, she thought. Free at last.

16

*P*ius was doing the washing up after tea, which he'd cobbled together out of the couple of rashers and sausages in the near-empty fridge, when there was a knock at the door. He tutted. He hoped Mary-Pat hadn't sent an envoy down as she had done every single day since the meeting in November. John-Patrick would appear on his bike, saying he was there to help with the garden, and then two days before Christmas, he'd turned up at the door, his breath streaming in the winter air: 'Mum wants you to come to Christmas dinner.'

Pius had shaken his head. 'Thanks, John-Patrick, but I've other plans.' The 'other plans' consisted of the Christmas edition of *The Archers* and a bumper pile of *The Sunday Times*, with a dash of self-pity that here he was, all alone at Christmas. Rosie had asked him to come to Daphne's, but he'd refused because, he realised, he probably wanted to wallow in it, in the loneliness. It felt familiar, comforting in a funny way. Anyway, Pius wished Mary-Pat would just butt out. Piss off and leave him alone. There was no way in the world he wanted to talk to anyone. He didn't trust himself. He felt as if his heart was sore, bruised and heavy in his chest.

He'd been so angry about it still when he got home, he thought now, a full six weeks later, as he put the dishes away. That Mammy had just walked out on them all, and now she was allowed to live like that, to eat and drink and laugh and have friends and all that, when she'd left them all behind. It wasn't right. His life had stopped the moment she'd walked out the door and he couldn't honestly see why hers had gone on. He just couldn't. And the other thing was that without Mary-Pat and June he felt unanchored, loose. He'd spent his entire life resenting them both, but in the weeks since he'd spoken to them, he'd felt as if there was something missing, like a limb. And that irritated him because, quite frankly, he didn't want to feel like that, not when he never wanted to talk to either of them again.

When he'd finished his supper, he'd decided to take Jessie out for a walk before he went to the greenhouse and checked on the plants. She'd be needing one. Maybe he'd ask Rosie to go with him, if he could persuade her to get out of bed. She'd been so tired lately, so quiet. A couple of times, he'd tried to broach the Frances O'Brien subject with her, suggesting that they could both go down and see her, but Rosie had shaken her head in a way that made him understand that there would be no visiting, not any time soon anyway. She'd do it in her own time — or not at all. It would have to be her choice.

He wiped his hands on a tea towel and was about to go and fetch Jessie's lead when he heard the knock, a slow thud on the brass door knocker. 'For fuck's sake,' he thought, eyeing the grandfather clock in the hall. The words were in his mouth as he opened the door. 'John-Patrick, it isn't a good time – oh.'

Dara was standing on the doorstep in his pyjamas, a pair of wellies on his feet. He was shivering, his thin little body vibrating with the cold, his cheeks a purplish blue. 'Can I feed the hens?' The request came out in a gush and, as he asked, he didn't look at Pius but around him into the hall. Pius didn't know what he was looking for, for a minute, but the penny dropped when he heard Jessie whine from behind the pantry door. She must have heard him.

Pius leaned out the door and looked left and right for any sign of the child's mother. It was nearly dark now and he knew she'd be worried.

'Well, they're in bed now, Dara. They go to sleep before dusk, so the fox doesn't get them.'

'Oh.' He looked down at his wellies, which were bright red with black spots on them, like a ladybird, and shuffled around for a bit. Pius said nothing, waiting, and when Dara looked up at him he was astonished to see the boy's lip trembling.

He wasn't sure what to do – he hadn't been faced with a crying child before. 'Come in anyway. I was going to take Jessie for a walk, but I fancy a hot chocolate first. What do you think?' he improvised.

Dara nodded silently and slunk in the door, making his way into the kitchen. Jessie's whining became more persistent now and after Pius had pulled a carton of milk out of the fridge and poured some into a pan, he opened the pantry door. Jessie bolted out and over to Dara, her tail wagging furiously, covering his hands and his knees with her slobbery doggy kisses.

Dara squealed with delight, hugging Jessie and burying his face in her neck. 'I love you, Jessie,' he muttered into her fur.

Pius smiled to himself as he opened the cupboard for the cocoa powder. You could find great comfort in animals, he thought, noticing to his relief a packet of ginger nut biscuits that Rosie must have bought.

When the cocoa was ready, he put a mug of it in front of Dara with a couple of biscuits, then sat down beside him, slinging his old grey fleece over the child's shoulders as he did so. There was silence while Dara sipped his cocoa and munched on a biscuit, showering the front of his pyjamas with crumbs. Pius reached out and gently brushed them off. 'There, we'll tidy you up a wee bit.'

'Thanks,' Dara said, then continued munching.

The boy seemed upset about something, but Pius wasn't sure if he should ask, figuring that pushing him would only upset him, so instead he said, 'I was just thinking, we might do a patrol of the perimeter out there to check the fox isn't around, and then take Jessie for a walk back to yours. What do you think? Your mammy will probably be worried.'

Dara shook his head and looked out the window, not catching Pius's eye. 'She doesn't know I've gone. I ran away.'

'Oh. Right. Something must have upset you, so.'

Dara nodded but didn't volunteer anything. I won't prod, Pius thought. I won't try to winkle it out of him. I'll just wait.

There was a long silence. 'Daddy's there, so she might not notice I'm gone.'

Pius's heart started to thump in his chest. The Waste of Space as he'd christened the man. He must be visiting, and even though Pius tried to rationalise it, to tell himself sure why wouldn't he be, the man would want to see his child, his own flesh and blood, he couldn't help the feelings of jealousy that gripped him. It was all he could do to control himself, not to show it to Dara. 'I'd say she might, Dara, if you're gone long. Tell you what, why don't we do our jobs and then I'll give her a ring just to let her know you're safe, how does that sound?'

Dara barely nodded, jumping down off the sofa and allowing Pius to put his little twig-like arms into the fleece. 'Will you get Jessie's lead for me, Dara? You know where to find it.' Jessie didn't need a lead at all because she glued herself to his ankle whenever they were outside, but it did Dara good to feel he was in control.

The garden was in darkness when they went outside, the trees black against the inky blue sky, a pale moon just skirting the edge of the water, not high enough up to create much light. Jessie whimpered and sniffed, probably scenting the fox, but Pius let Dara take her lead and walk her. She wouldn't pull too much; she was good like that, Jessie. The two of them did a circuit of the garden, along the hedge where the fox would slink every night, and around the henhouse. Dara smiled at him and gave him a thumbs-up then. 'They're OK,' he said, in an exaggerated whisper.

'That's good,' Pius whispered back. 'Let's go and check on my lettuces – we might need to pick the slugs out of them.'

Dara hopped eagerly along the path in front of him, clearly not having the same trouble that Pius was in seeing where he was going. Pius was just wishing that he'd brought his torch with him when the moon rose up above the fir tree at the edge of the garden and bathed all in a silvery light. The two of them looked up, and the night sky seemed to be alive with stars. Pius could make out the plough and, above that, Ursa Minor and Polaris, then the dusty sprinkle of the Milky Way.

'Pius, do you know what that star is?' Dara tilted his head back and looked up at the Evening Star, alone in the sky.

'That's Venus,' Pius answered. 'It's a planet.'

'I know. I have the solar system on my wall at home. And there's Jupiter.' Dara pointed to a star so far away Pius had to squint to make it out. Could the child be right? Probably. Daphne would make sure he knew important stuff like that. That's what parents did, if they were any good; they didn't just feed and clothe their children and shove them out the door: they taught them the things they'd need to know. He thought now of that night with Mary-Pat and Daddy, looking up at the stars, understanding for the first time his place in the universe, understanding, too, that it wasn't finite, that it went on for ever, a place that had existed long before him and would exist long after he'd gone. He'd understood for the first time in his young life that there was something larger than him and his own little world in Monasterard and it was Daddy who had helped him to know this. Daddy with his feet of clay, of whom he thought so little.

'Do you know that if you fell into a black hole, you'd stretch like a bit of spaghetti?' Dara was saying now. 'I know because Kevin told me. Kevin's my dad and he knows everything.'

You're right, Pius thought. He does. Until you discover that he's just a human being and that he doesn't know nearly as much as you thought. 'Cooked or raw?'

Dara dissolved into a fit of giggles. 'Cooked, of course! If you were raw, you'd just break up into little bits.'

'Ah, I can't think which is worse.' Pius smiled.

'I don't think we'd die like that, would we, Pi? In a black hole.'

'It's probably unlikely,' Pius agreed.

ALL THAT I LEAVE BEHIND

'But we will die? My friend Sinead's mother got cancer last year and she died. Does everyone die of cancer?' He was growing anxious now, hopping from foot to foot, his face creased with anxiety.

'Well, some people do die young, but most of us will live for a long, long time,' Pius said gently. 'We'll grow up and fall in love and marry and see our children grow. And we'll work and just live life and do our best with every day that comes.' And maybe, just maybe, he thought, we might discover that there is more, that there is some greater purpose to our lives, some reason for our living, or maybe we'll just slip into the cold ground knowing that all we've done is pay a few gas bills and moan about the weather. Either way, just looking at this little boy, Pius understood something for the first time, that this *was* life in all its beauty and mystery, him and Dara, here in the garden on a cold winter's night, looking up at the stars. Life was him and his sisters fighting like animals, life was him and his feelings of anger about his father, loneliness about his mother, regret at all the lost opportunities, life was the beauty of the water and the rain and the silvery rushes. It was all there, and he was living it. All these years wasted waiting for it somehow to begin, and all the time it was right there, under his nose.

'And then we'll die,' Dara said with a sigh of satisfaction.

'That's the general idea,' Pius said, 'when our work is done.'

He was about to usher the child inside when there was a sudden flurry of motion beside the gazebo and a loud voice yelled, 'Dara? Dara, are you here?' And in a blur of motion, Daphne was upon them both, catching hold of Dara and squeezing him tightly to her, murmuring, 'It's OK, it's OK,' into his hair. The little boy began to cry in earnest then, as if he'd only just realised where he was, a long wail coming from his mouth as he put his arms around his mother's neck.

The two of them remained like that, with Pius looking on. He felt a bit awkward and wondered if he should just slink away quietly, when Daphne pushed Dara away, yelling, 'Don't you ever do that again, do you hear me? I contacted Garda Kelly at the station and he has a patrol out looking for you.'

'I'm sorry, Mummy.' Dara looked down at his wellies, and his shoulders shook as the tears came. 'I just wanted to help Pius to put the hens away and you said I could,' he wailed.

'Not in the middle of the night, I didn't, you silly boy,' she said, and then pulled him towards her again in a tight hug. 'You have to ask Mummy before you go out.' She was quieter now and as she spoke she kissed the top of his head and rubbed her hands through his hair.

She seemed to have forgotten him for a few moments, and Pius wondered if he could simply make a run for it to avoid being given out to.

He stuck out a foot to begin walking, but too late. She caught him with those green eyes. 'Did it not occur to you to contact me? Do you think it's normal that a seven-year-old would wander the countryside alone at night in a pair of pyjamas?'

Pius shook his head, a naughty boy, like Dara. 'Look, Dara only turned up ten minutes ago, and I was going to ring you once he … settled a bit.' He searched for the right word. There was a silence while she digested his excuse, which he broke by saying, 'C'mon, let's go inside out of the cold. I'll ring Garda Kelly and let him know Dara's safe.'

Throwing him another glare, she said, 'No thank you. Kevin's on his way.'

'Right, then. Well, are you going to come inside and wait or stand outside in the freezing cold?' Pius barked and then turned on his heel and went into the house, leaving the door open behind him. She could come in if she wanted. He wasn't going to embarrass himself by begging.

He was banging around in the kitchen, pretending to put a pot of water on the range to boil, when there was a knock on the door.

'Come in, for God's sake,' Pius said, more rudely than he'd intended. She appeared out of the gloom, standing under the glare of the strip light. Not even the horrible yellow glow could make her look less lovely, he thought. 'What is it?'

She blinked for a few moments, and he suddenly realised how rude he'd been. 'Sorry—' he began, when she interrupted him. 'I owe you an apology.'

'What for?'

'I jumped to conclusions. I guessed pretty quickly that he'd come here, but I should have trusted you. I know you'd have called me, of course you would. I was just so *worried*.' Her lovely green eyes filled with tears and she wiped them away with the back of her hand. 'I thought I was losing my mind. I mean, you hear these things every day, about kids that go missing ...' Her voice broke.

He wanted to do nothing more than to go to her and hold her, but he stopped himself. He knew that she didn't think much of him to start with and that would only make matters worse, so he stayed put, beside the range, and said, 'I know, and it's hard, but sometimes you just have to trust that they'll be OK. And he was, wasn't he? The world isn't that bad a place, Daphne, in spite of what you hear.'

She nodded silently and sniffed.

'Dara's dad's been visiting.'

'I know. You said.'

'He's not used to kids. He doesn't see much of Dara and he expects too much of him. He thinks they should be discussing world peace and algebra, but the child is *seven*, for God's sake. And then Dara gets upset because he knows he isn't able to please his dad and oh ...' She twisted the tissue she'd dug out of her pocket into a tight knot, shaking her head, before she blurted, 'Sometimes I wish he wasn't in our life at all, does that sound terrible?'

Pius shook his head. 'It doesn't sound terrible. And if he doesn't spend time with Dara, he might not know what's ... appropriate for a seven-year-old.' He thought of the black holes and the being stretched like spaghetti. Maybe he wouldn't mention that to the Mermaid.

At this, Daphne looked up. '*You* know, and you don't have children.'

'Thanks for the reminder,' Pius said dryly. 'It's something I regret.'

She looked up at him then. 'You do? Sorry, I didn't mean it like that.' And she bit her lip and Pius wanted to reach out and kiss every bit of that lovely face. She looked as if she were thinking hard about something and then she said, 'Pi, do you know about Rosie?'

'What about Rosie?'

'You don't know then,' Daphne said. 'It's just ...' She took in a deep breath and then it came out. 'She's pregnant.'

Pius swayed from foot to foot, feeling dizzy. 'What? How? My God,' he eventually managed. Then, 'Is it the Yank's?'

Daphne gave a little giggle. 'Oh, for God's sake, no. Not *him*.' The two of them shared a conspiratorial smile, and Pius, not for the first time, wondered how on earth he'd remained completely ignorant of this new development. Rosie had managed to have a new relationship and he hadn't noticed a thing. Top marks for observation, Pi, as usual.

He looked at Daphne hopefully. 'That's good news then. Isn't it?'

'Yes. Yes it is. Except he's gone.'

'Who?'

She rolled her eyes to heaven as if he was the greatest eejit that ever lived. 'The father. You know, Mark.'

That young lad from the Chinese? Well, it fitted, he supposed. They'd been inseparable when they were kids, and he was a good lad. Not like that other creep. 'Well, she'll be needing help with it, I suppose,' he said thoughtfully, ignoring the hiss of the boiling water as it poured over the top of the pot and onto the range. Daphne would be well able for it, he was sure, and Mary-Pat, if he plucked up the courage to tell her. She'd want to know, surely.

'Time to man up, Pius,' Daphne said softly, before turning on her heel and walking out into the hall. He heard the soft thud of the front door and then she was gone.

Time to man up indeed.

Part Four

Spring-Summer 2013

17

The midwife was a bit of an old bat, but Rosie found that faintly reassuring. She wanted to be bullied and bossed around a bit. It helped her to feel more secure, because Margaret reminded her of Mary-Pat. Every time Rosie sat in front of Margaret, a stout woman from County Mayo with a big red face and size-ten feet, she'd think of her sister and she'd have to suppress the longing to have her there beside her.

She'd lost count of the number of times she'd gone to pick up the phone to her sister, since that day in November, or had started to walk with Jessie across the field to the town, turning right then in the direction of Mary-Pat's, before stopping herself. 'No,' she'd say out loud, so that Jessie would look at her, cocking her head to one side, wondering what it was she'd done. 'No, you're not going there.' It was as if she had to say it out loud to herself, to scold herself into not going. Not because she was angry with Mary-Pat, though. She wasn't. She just felt as if she didn't know her sister any more. As if the Mary-Pat she'd known all her life was not the same Mary-Pat that had sat in front of her at her kitchen table and told her that she'd always known about Rosie's mother but had chosen not to tell her. And Rosie could understand why, in a funny way. I get it, she'd thought as she'd looked at her sister's tired, too-pink face, at the broken veins on her cheeks and chin. I understand why you didn't tell me. Because it would have done me no good. But then the next step would be to assume that Mary-Pat had done it for the right reasons, out of love, but here Rosie couldn't be sure. And if she couldn't be sure, it was safer not to trust, to end up finding out that the opposite was true. She'd had enough of thinking one thing and finding out that she should, in fact, be thinking quite the opposite. Rosie supposed she was sulking, in a way, but she also knew that it was easier like this, with just herself and the baby. It was time she stood on her own two feet, even though she struggled to keep the feelings of loneliness at bay. The sense that she and the baby were the only two people in the whole world.

Once, in a fit of madness, she'd almost rung Craig. She knew that she had to ring him anyway, to discuss the annulment. In spite of everything, the letter that had arrived from the solicitor in January had given her a shock. Words like 'dishonest' and 'fraud' had jumped out at her. She wasn't dishonest, she knew that, but she was a fraud, and he deserved better than that, in spite of everything. If he preferred an annulment to a divorce, she'd agree to whatever it was he wanted, even if it was to pretend that instead of making a mistake, what they'd had had never really existed. It was as if their ten years together had simply been wiped out.

She'd gone to her mobile phone and scanned the numbers, a

little thumbnail of his strong face and bright smile popping up beside his number. She'd stared at it for a long time, running her finger across the numbers, finding it hovering over the 'call' button but then, she'd stopped herself, because how would she tell him that she was four months pregnant with someone else's baby? The thought was ridiculous. But there was something about the situation that called for his stoic presence, the completely logical way he'd have of working through the problem. He'd probably devise a spreadsheet for it, she thought to herself.

Mark, on the other hand, would not. He'd have kissed her bump and nuzzled his face into her belly, making gentle farting noises with his lips and singing to it in Vietnamese. He'd have told it jokes and cooked it spicy noodles and called it silly names. He was as light-hearted as Craig was glum, Rosie knew. And then she understood why she'd wanted to call Craig — because she so badly wanted to tell Mark but knew that she couldn't. She knew that if she told him about the baby, he'd come back for good — at least, he'd promise her that, but she couldn't ask it of him. Oh, he'd come back, she knew he would, and then one day he'd wake up and look at her in the bed beside him and he'd think, 'I missed my one chance, and all because of you.' She couldn't be responsible for that. She just couldn't.

He'd written her a letter, posting it through the letterbox early one morning before Christmas. She'd been awake, the way she was every morning since that day in November, staring up at the ceiling or peering into the grey gloom that shrouded the canal. She'd tried to run downstairs in time to catch a glimpse of him, but by the time she'd pulled on her tracksuit bottoms, shuffled downstairs and opened the door, all that she saw was an empty front path to the gate, which had been left open. She'd called out his name then, but her voice hadn't carried.

She didn't open the letter for a while. Not until she'd had a cup of tea and two digestives to give her strength. Her hands were shaking as she'd opened the light blue envelope and pulled the letter out. She'd almost smiled as she scanned the few lines written in a terrible scrawl on the paper. He never had been much of a writer.

Dear Rosie,

I'm sorrier than I can say about your mother. I can't explain why I didn't tell you, except that it just felt like the wrong thing to do. I knew that Mary-Pat loved you and Pi and June, and I didn't want to ruin that by telling you something you wouldn't have believed, not for a moment. I know it was the truth, but sometimes the truth is overrated. What good is the truth if it only causes more pain?

I hope you can forgive me. The times I've spent with you over the last couple of months have been the best of my entire life, even better than when I beat you at holding my breath underwater by at least thirty seconds when we were nine, even though you cheated. I saw you, so don't deny it.

I don't want to lose you, Rosie, not when I've only just found you again, but I also know that it's up to you. If you want me, you know where I am, or you will do, because my e-mail address is at the bottom. I hope you'll give me another chance. You only have to say the word, and I'll be back in a heartbeat.

I love you – even though we both know it's not enough, I thought I'd say it anyway. Because that is one truth worth saying out loud, many times.

Mark

I love you too, she'd thought, reading the few lines again and then again, you know I do. And I remember the competition — you took two breaths before you dipped your head into the water and then you grabbed my ankle, so I had to lift my head out of the water to scream. You cheated too, don't you remember? But maybe you were right when you said that loving each other just isn't enough. Maybe I can't love you the way you want me to because I'm not happy. Or maybe it's you — maybe you just don't love me enough to stay, no matter what. Maybe you just wanted one night with me for old times' sake. But what the hell did it matter anyway, she told herself, folding the letter up and pressing it tightly into her hand. It was too late now in any case.

The only way she could think to manage all of this was to write a list. On it were just three things: See GP. Get job. Talk to Daddy. Three things. She could manage that. She knew that she should have added a fourth, but she just wasn't ready for that yet. One thing at a time, as Mary-Pat used to say to her.

She'd tackled the doctor's appointment first, a nice clinic in Portlaoise where, if they'd wondered why she'd wandered twenty miles out of her way to see a doctor, they were good enough not to say it. She'd opted to go to Dublin for her antenatal appointments because she was less likely to meet someone she knew than if she went to Portlaoise. Pius had gone with her that first time. He'd insisted on it, driving her there and waiting outside while she saw the doctor and then taking her to the chemist afterwards, the big Boots on the roundabout. He had a list in his hand and she followed him around the aisles as he picked things out and put them in the basket.

'Pi?' she said, as he scanned the rows of maternity pads.

'Yeah?' he replied, picking out a large pack with a smiling lady on the front and putting it in the basket, then ticking the item off on his list. When he saw her looking at the pads he cleared his throat and said, 'I did some research on the Internet. They said you'd need them.'

At the birth, she thought, trying hard not to smile at the idea of her brother boning up on the essentials of pregnancy and childbirth. He'd taken to the subject with enthusiasm, ordering books from the Internet via Nancy Brady at the library and giving Rosie instructions about the best ways of avoiding heartburn. He was her rock, Pi.

Next, she went up to see Breda O'Hare. She hardly knew Breda but remembered a sunny girl with bright red cheeks and straw-coloured hair who'd sat beside her in junior infants, who was now deputy head of St Conleth's secondary school. Rosie couldn't think why the notion of teaching had occurred to her, but it seemed plausible enough and one thing she had learned from being the worst social worker in the world in that other life of hers was that she liked kids, teenagers in particular. She liked the way they thought they knew everything and the way they gave backchat all the time.

Breda had greeted her like an old friend and had led her into her office, a tiny room filled with the detritus of school life — lost gym kits, a handful of trophies and a large year planner filled with little red dots. 'I just need to do something useful,' she said. Not to mention the fact that I need the money, as my savings have almost run out and I have no idea how I'm going to support my baby. 'I'm pregnant, you see, so I won't be looking for much before the baby arrives. But I thought you might have some advice for me. She'd bitten her lip. 'Sorry, it's been a while.'

'That's no problem, but I'm afraid you couldn't teach without a HDip. You see, you're not qualified and even if you were, then you'd have to be put on a roll of sub teachers. It's difficult because of the cutbacks and all,' she explained.

'You must think I'm a complete eejit,' Rosie had said, feeling like one of the school kids who'd been hauled into the office for detention.

'Not at all,' Breda had said diplomatically. 'Sure the system here isn't like the States at all. But my sister works in a private language college in Mullingar and they're always looking for teachers.'

'And they'll take anyone?' Rosie half-smiled.

'No, you'll have to do a TEFL course, and they're very particular about vetting, but you won't need a HDip.'

Oh, I've offended her, Rosie thought. 'Sorry, I didn't mean—'

'Don't be silly. I know what you meant. And you know, I think you'll make a good teacher, Rosie. You have a great way with you. A lovely energy that people would enjoy. Good luck with it.'

In the event, Breda's sister did have a slot, providing she was prepared to spend a month, and another chunk of her savings, on a TEFL course, and to wade through the finer points of past participles and countable and uncountable nouns, before being unleashed on a class of students. The teaching gave her a boost of energy that carried her through the next three months of her pregnancy, when she began to flourish, her hair silky, her face beginning to fill out. She lost her sharp, bony edges and began to resemble a freckled marshmallow. She liked that, she thought, looking at herself in the mirror, wondering what Mark would think of her new figure.

Pius found her a little second-hand car for the drive to

Mullingar, refusing to take any money for it — 'I called in a favour or two' was all he would say about it. A vision of that weed he grew out the back flickered into her mind, but she let it drop, faced with the prospect of a comfortable drive. Anything was better than the Beetle, which was killing her. She thought the baby would be rattled out of her if she went on any longer. And as she stood up in front of a class of mystified newcomers to Ireland and pretended she was *au fait* with the present perfect tense, she felt as if she were learning with them. Except while they were learning how to communicate in this new country of theirs, she was learning to take responsibility for herself, to find her own path. It felt good.

She knew that teaching English wasn't going to be her life's work, and so, as she drove back and forth every morning and evening, she began to ask herself what might be. And then one evening, she took out her old biology textbooks and she pored over them, remembering the hours she and Pi had spent together, examining his stag beetle collection, or trawling the canal bank for evidence of otters. After so many years of sociological waffle when she was in the States, the careful facts of sixth-year biology soothed her. She felt entirely at home with genetic mutations and the chambers of the heart. There was nothing that didn't fit a pattern in biology, nothing that wasn't expected, and if it was, it was called a 'mutation'. Something that departed from the norm. Rosie wondered where this put her and if studying the subject was an antidote to her own life, where mutations were the order of the day.

Finally, she plucked up the courage to enrol in a university conversion course. The nice lady in the admissions office told her that as she was a mature student, she wouldn't need 'the requisite number of honours', which was fortunate, as she didn't have them. The course wouldn't begin for another nine months. Oh, she'd thought. I'll be a mother then.

She'd forgotten how much she liked study; how totally it could absorb her. She'd open a book to take a quick look at a diagram for an essay and, the next thing, she'd look up and see that three hours had passed. She could just dive into it and forget about everything else, balancing her bump on the huge claw-foot chair that Pius brought down from the attic, because it would 'accommodate her', as he said politely. Pius might have been her rock, but he was a faintly embarrassed one in the way that only a brother could be.

Daphne, on the other hand, continued to be typically blunt about the whole thing, discussing flatulence and other symptoms with glee. 'I could have farted for Ireland and, Jesus, my sex drive went through the roof,' she said one day over coffee. 'Kevin was exhausted by the end of it. I was forever ringing him up in Dublin to come down and service me at all hours of the day and night — what?' she said, as Pius cleared his throat. She glared at him. 'I'm only telling her the truth. That's what pregnancy is like. Your whole body is just consumed by it. You're not a woman at all, you're just a ... vessel.'

'Aha,' he said, getting up and twiddling the knobs on the coffee machine, his face tomato red, while she and Daphne snorted with laughter behind his back. Rosie wasn't quite sure what was going on between the two of them, but she knew it was something. They bickered constantly and yet there was a light in Pius's eyes when he spoke her name, and he made Daphne relax and laugh a bit. They'd be good for each other, she knew they would.

Pius had only asked her about telling the others once. 'Have you spoken to your sisters?'

Rosie had shaken her head. 'Nope. And don't ask me to.'

'Don't you think we have enough secrets in this family?' he'd tried.

'I can't, Pi,' she'd said. 'I just can't.'

He hadn't persisted, just nodded and squeezed her gently on the shoulder.

She left item number three on her list until last, until late spring, when she was beginning to show, needing to push the driver's seat a bit further back, pulling the seatbelt across her bump as she drove out the Dublin Road to the home. The girl at reception didn't recognise her, a frown knitting her brows as Rosie explained who she was. 'I don't think you've visited before,' she said grimly, a disapproving look on her narrow features.

'No, I haven't,' Rosie lied.

'Right, well, he's in the day room now,' the girl said, looking at her watch. 'The horse racing's on,' she added by way of explanation.

'Thanks.' Rosie half-smiled.

'I'll get someone to show you,' the girl said, pressing a buzzer on the desk. After a few moments, a plump, pretty nurse appeared through a set of double doors. The badge on her immaculate scrubs told Rosie that she was Imelda.

'So when's the big day?' she asked, eyeing Rosie's bump.

'Oh, in four months or so.' Rosie was distracted, hesitating as Imelda opened the double doors of the day room, a bright smile on her face, and urged her in. 'Summertime is just the best time to have a baby,' she said cheerfully, scanning the room for Daddy.

He was sitting in a large green vinyl armchair, arms folded across his chest, staring into space. He was wearing a knitted cardigan and a pair of brown trousers that looked three sizes too big for him.

'Now, John-Joe, you have a visitor,' the nurse said gently.

Rosie had been half-hiding behind the woman, afraid, but when he looked up at her and beamed, she thought she'd faint with relief. He doesn't recognise me. Thank God, he doesn't know who I am.

'You must be the new girl!' He reached out a hand and shook hers, his hand warm and smooth, his grip firm. He'd been a great believer in firm handshakes, Daddy.

'Yes, I am,' she agreed, taking a seat in the chair Imelda had gently pushed across towards her.

'I'll leave ye to it,' she said quietly.

'Thank you,' he said gaily, waving at Imelda. 'What's your name?'

'It's Imelda, John-Joe,' she said, as if it was the first time he'd asked her and not the hundredth or more.

'Imelda,' he repeated. 'And what about you, love?' He turned his bright gaze to Rosie. 'How are you settling in here? You know, my mammy and daddy are from Donegal,' he continued. 'They've been roaming the roads for as long as I can remember.' And then his face creased in a frown. 'Where have you come from?'

'Oh, just up the road,' Rosie said vaguely. 'Have you been watching the horseracing?' She nodded at the television.

He looked at her blankly. 'No.' He shook his head. 'Gambling's the work of the devil, that's what Mammy says.' At this, he seemed to grow agitated, pulling at the hair behind his left ear and shifting in the chair. 'The work of the devil.' It seemed so unfair that he couldn't remember, she thought, one of the things that had given him such pleasure, and her too, sitting up beside him, licking the pencil and marking the pink slip with the each-way bet. 'Will we be lucky today, Rosie?' he'd say. 'What do you think?'

He paused now and looked upset. 'They're all dead now. All of them.'

'All of whom?'

He looked irritated, swatting her away with his hand. 'Oh, the whole lot of them. Everyone always leaves in the end, but then you know that.'

Yes, I do know that, Rosie thought. Even you, Daddy. And all the questions I have to ask you will go unanswered. I can see that now. She reached out and squeezed his hand. 'How about a little song?'

He sat up straighter in his seat and looked pleased with himself. 'Sure why not?'

'Imelda tells me you're a great singer.'

He nodded enthusiastically. 'I like a tune.' But then he'd looked anxious. 'The thing is, sometimes, I can't remember ...'

'I know. I'll help you. Do you know "The Rose of Tralee"?'

He sat up straight then and looked thoughtful before launching into it, his fine tenor voice floating over her out into the room. He could remember every word, and as he sang, Rosie thought that it was beautiful and she wondered how such beauty could come from someone so ... 'bad' wasn't the right word. He wasn't evil, just foolish and selfish and deluded, a man who had let his impulses dictate his life. She stroked the baby in her belly and wondered why it was that the people you loved most in the world could turn out to be for ever a disappointment, no matter how much she'd wish it otherwise or how long she waited for things to be different. And she could let it crush her or learn from it, to try not to make their mistakes, to try to do a little bit better for the baby inside her.

When he finished, there was a scattering of applause from the few elderly people sitting around in the bright room. 'Good man, John-Joe,' a tall, upright man with snowy hair said. 'Good man.'

At the praise, Daddy beamed, delighted with himself, and as she looked at him, for a second, the old Daddy was there, face alive with pleasure, a twinkle in those dark eyes.

'Is it time for lunch?' He looked hopefully at the hatch from the dayroom into the kitchen, from where clattering and banging could be heard, the over-stewed smell of boiled cabbage wafting in. Rosie felt her stomach turn. 'Yes, time for lunch,' and then she squeezed his hand again. 'I'll be seeing you,' she said. 'Thanks for the song.'

'See you, love,' he said, continuing to look in the direction of the kitchen. 'Come back soon.'

I've completed my list now, Rosie thought the following week as she lay on the examining table, Margaret's broad hands feeling her bump, shaping it like a baker shapes a loaf, identifying first the head, digging around in Rosie's pelvis with surprising force.

'Your blood pressure's very low,' Margaret said. 'Been feeling dizzy?'

'I have actually,' Rosie admitted.

'Hmm. Any idea whether Mum had low blood pressure during her pregnancy?' Margaret was looking away from her, making a series of cryptic scribbles on the file and, when Rosie didn't answer, looking up. 'Oh dear,' she said when she saw the tears. 'Oh dear. Tea and sympathy.' And then she got up and left the office, leaving Rosie sniffling, looking around for a tissue. I thought I could do this, she thought to herself. I thought I was strong, that I could manage by myself, but *look* at me. She was distracted by a rustling behind the door, after which it swung slowly open and a large foot appeared, followed by Margaret clutching two mugs, which she placed gently on the table, before handing one to Rosie. 'Here.'

'Thanks,' Rosie said. The tea was hot and too sweet and tasted like nectar. And it wasn't that dreadful wee-like green stuff either, the stuff Pi kept making her drink because it was good for her.

'You're welcome.' Margaret leaned back in her seat and eyed Rosie narrowly. 'Rosie, do you want me to contact social services? They can help, you know.'

'No, God, no!' Rosie half-yelled, pulling herself into a standing position, then sitting back in the chair. 'Sorry, I mean, no. It's fine, really. I have my brother and his … friend, they're helping.'

'What about Dad?'

Rosie thought she meant Daddy for a second, but then she understood. 'Oh. He's abroad. And before you ask, no, I don't think he has the right to know. It's complicated,' she managed. She knew that she sounded defensive, and her face reddened with shame, because he did have a right to know, of course he did. And she had no real right to keep it from him, except that she felt somehow that she had to – she told herself that it was because she was angry with him, that he hadn't told her he was going until it was too late. That he'd let her fall in love with him all over again and then he'd just left her, but really it was because she just couldn't make him come back, not after all the years he'd spent waiting for her here. His life had only begun and she wasn't going to take that away from him. Not yet.

Margaret put her hands up then in surrender. 'That's fine. I'm not pushing you — I just want to help, that's all.' She looked a bit miffed.

'I know, and thanks.' Rosie cleared her throat. 'I'll ask ... my mother about the blood pressure.'

'Good,' Margaret said, making a note on the file, a cross look on her face. Then, 'And take care of yourself, will you?' Her expression softened, and Rosie thought again of Mary-Pat, longed to have her beside her, giving Margaret a piece of her mind.

She decided to phone Frances O'Brien this time. It wasn't hard to find her number because she was on the town council, beaming out from the council website in her shiny Sarah Palin suit. Rosie didn't want to arrive on her doorstep and be turned away.

Frances O'Brien answered in a kind of a trill, a telephone voice, and Rosie felt the oddest desire to laugh.

'It's Rosie O'Connor. Please don't hang up,' she said.

There was a long pause at the end of the line and Rosie had to say, 'Are you still there?'

'I'm here.' The telephone voice was gone.

'Look, I need to ask you something. Can I come and see you?'

'No!' It was nearly a shout, then more softly, 'I don't think that would be a good idea.'

Rosie tutted with impatience. 'Listen. My sisters have told me everything.'

There was another long pause before Frances said, 'I'll see you in the Moran Arms tomorrow at 12,' and then the phone went dead.

'Nice chatting to you too,' Rosie muttered, pressing the red button on her mobile. Her hands were shaking.

I need to calm down, she told herself, deciding to take a cup of tea outside to the garden, the spring sun warming her face, and she sat on one of the brightly coloured chairs Pi had bought in the garden centre to put under the pergola. His garden was really taking shape now, the bright tulip buds pushing up through the soil, the fronds of the wild grasses blowing in the breeze. It looked lovely, and Rosie closed her eyes and listened to the rushes on the canal and felt her baby move inside her, a ripple of movement across her stomach, the shape of a foot or elbow pressing against her skin. She was going to be a mother now, too, a good one, she told herself. Even if she never found out another thing about herself, she knew that: that her son or daughter would be loved.

Frances O'Brien was sitting by the fire in the hotel in an electric blue suit, her hair sprayed into oblivion, those glasses on the chain around her neck. The expression on her face was forbidding, a tight granite mask, and when Rosie walked across the lobby towards her, her expression remained hostile. And then she saw Rosie's bump and her expression changed. It softened, and she gave a smile which made her look twenty years younger, a glimpse of the girl she'd once been on those hard features.

Frances O'Brien stood up, put a hand on Rosie's arm briefly, before taking it away. 'I had no idea ... congratulations.'

'Thank you.' Rosie didn't say anything further, just sat on one of the comfy velvet armchairs, sinking into it, her bump pushing her down into the squashy centre of the chair.

'Tea?' Frances O'Brien was saying, waving the menu at Rosie, her glasses now perched on her nose. 'They have herbal tea, if you prefer it.'

Rosie wrinkled her nose. 'No thanks,' and Frances O'Brien gave a small laugh. 'I don't blame you. Awful stuff.'

'You don't like it either?' Rosie asked.

Frances shook her head. 'Builder's tea is the only one for me.' Then, as if this amounted to some kind of admission, she rearranged her glasses on her bosom and folded her hands on her knee. 'You wanted to see me.' Her tone was businesslike and Rosie felt a stab of irritation.

'I've been having antenatal appointments and the midwife wanted to know whether there was any family history of low blood pressure.'

Frances O'Brien put a hand to her throat, and when she spoke it was barely a whisper. 'Oh.'

'I'm sorry to ask, it's just ...'

'No, no, it's fine ... ehm ...' Her eyes filled with tears and she began to rummage in her handbag, producing a packet of tissues, from which she extracted one, blowing her nose. 'I do suffer from low blood pressure, that's true.'

'Right.' If Rosie had been expecting some admission, some emotional outpouring, it suddenly dawned on her that there would be neither, that she was wasting her time: whatever she'd wanted from her mother, whatever she'd been expecting, something she'd been unable to put into words, would not be forthcoming.

'I'm not sure really if I can help you any further ...' Frances O'Brien said.

Rosie shunted forward in the seat, putting a hand out on either side to push herself up to a standing position. 'No,' she said bluntly. 'You've told me what I need to know. Thank you for meeting me.'

Frances O'Brien made no move to help Rosie, and she had to turn herself sideways to lever herself up. 'Don't get up,' she said pointedly. She turned and walked towards the door.

'Wait.' Frances O'Brien's voice was suddenly loud, compelling Rosie to turn around. 'Wait,' she said more softly. She walked towards Rosie. 'I'm sorry, I can't give you what you need, Rosie,' she began.

'I don't *need* anything,' Rosie said, thinking as she said the words that they were true. She had what she needed, even if, until now, she hadn't realised it. She had a family who loved her, even if none of them was speaking to each other and she wasn't speaking to them, Pi excluded. She knew that and that everything they'd done for her had been out of love. They had a funny way of showing it, but it was still love. This woman, her mother, was just a stranger.

'I told you. I just wanted to ask you a question for the midwife. That's all. And if it's all the same to you, I need to get on,' she said briskly, about to turn on her heel.

'Your mother was a remarkable woman, Rosie, did you know that?' Frances's expression was wistful, and she twisted the chain of her glasses in her hand. 'Extraordinary. There was no way in the world I could have offered ... a baby anything like what she could give. I just didn't have it in me, that strength. And I never wanted a baby. I just wanted love. That was all.'

'Well, thank you for clearing that up,' Rosie said blankly.

'No, I didn't mean it like that. I mean, it hadn't been in my plans. I didn't mean for any of it to happen. I just saw what you had, your family and, well ... I wanted some of it for myself. I never really had it growing up,' Frances said sadly. And she gave Rosie a look as if to say, 'Is that really so bad?'

When Rosie didn't reply, Frances continued, 'And then I had no one to support me when it did happen. I was all alone. My family had disowned me and I had to go to the nuns and it was just awful, an awful place.'

And you want me to feel sorry for you, Rosie thought, remaining perfectly still. I'm not sure I really can. I don't think I have it in me.

Frances's voice was almost a whisper now. 'They wanted to take you away when you were born. That's what happened in those days: they took babies away and they sold them to rich people in America. But your mother ... she said no, that she'd take you, so you see she really saved you. If it wasn't for her, neither of us would be here.' She allowed the words to hang in the air for a while. 'I'm sorry, Rosie, I really am.' The woman was trembling now, all vestiges of Sarah Palin gone. Her mascara had smudged and there were silver tear marks in her foundation.

'You don't need to apologise,' Rosie said, trying to picture Frances O'Brien in her mind; what it must have been like to have no one to turn to, not one single person, how frightened she must have been. She wasn't sure she really wanted to understand, because then she wouldn't be able to hang onto this righteous anger she felt. And then she thought of Mark and she wondered if history was repeating itself. If she would be telling her son or daughter about him in a few years' time, trying to explain why she'd made the choices she had, expecting them to understand why she'd deprived them of a father. Would her son or daughter feel the same way she did, that she'd never really known who she was? And then she thought, but I do know who I am now. The mystery is over. And it hasn't really changed a thing.

June 1983

Michelle

I have to hold Rosie's hand really tightly because there are so many people milling about. I'm scared that I'll lose her or that she'll get taken by some stranger: you hear about that kind of thing all the time. Her hand is warm in my own, warm and damp, and when I look down at her, her little face is red beneath her bonnet and coat. It's too hot in Dublin for both of them, but it was still chilly when we set out, a damp mist on the canal, and I didn't want her to catch a cold. She has asthma and the slightest chill makes her wheeze dreadfully.

My hands are shaking as I push the 50p into the slot, but when I look down, Rosie's humming a tune to herself, happy in her own little world. I've promised her that if she's very good, I'll take her to the amusements in Bray. She hasn't a clue what they are, but she can tell by my tone that they are something to get excited about. 'The Musements', she calls them. I've asked Maeve to meet me beside the waltzers. I feel like someone in a Le Carré novel, but I can't risk John-Joe knowing where I am. God knows what he'd do.

I can see the phone ringing now in Prendergast's. I've rung there because I know that's where he'll be. If the world was about to end, he'd nip in there for a quick one. Eoin Prendergast answers, a muffled roar in the background, and when I ask for John-Joe, he mutters something unintelligible into the phone and I can hear him yelling John-Joe's name. There's a long wait, and I panic when I hear the beep-beep of the phone telling me that my money is running out. I shove a handful of coins in just as I hear his voice.

John-Joe isn't the beaten dog this time, slinking around the place, waiting for me to forgive him. His voice is loud, confident, the anger clear. 'Where the fuck have you gone, Michelle?'

'What do you care?' I hiss.

'I care because you have taken my child. I don't give a tinker's curse about you, but if you lay one finger on my child's head, I swear to God—'

'She's safe,' I say quickly. 'I'd never harm her, you know that.' There's a long silence and I blurt, 'She needs me, John-Joe. You don't want her.' And I need her too, I think. Without her, I have nothing. She's the only thing I have left.

His voice is low now, a hiss into the phone. 'For Christ's sake, have you lost your fucking mind? It's kidnapping. She's not yours and it won't be hard to prove, Michelle, I can assure you. Bring her home to me and I'll say nothing more about it. But if you attempt to keep her, I won't be responsible for my own actions.'

'But I'm her mother—' I begin, and then I stop, realising what I've said. There's a long silence and for a moment I wonder if he's there, and then he says, quietly, 'Bring her home, Michelle. This is where she belongs.'

I haven't lost my marbles completely. I know that she's not mine, but I need to protect her. I need to make sure that she doesn't suffer because of everything we've done. She is the innocent party here.

'What about the kids?' John-Joe is saying, a sly tone in his voice. 'Are you going to abandon them too?' He's playing his trump card, but I'm not going to weaken, not now.

'I have to go, John-Joe, but I'll be back for them, they're my children. They belong with me.' And before he can say anything else, I put the phone down. And then I squeeze my daughter's hand, my voice shaking, and I say, 'Are you ready for the amusements?'

'Musements,' she squeals, jumping up and down on the spot.

'That's right, Rosie-boo. Musements.'

It never occurs to me to leave her, not until the very last moment, until Maeve has the ticket booked for Holyhead, the onwards train to London Euston. I know that we'll arrive at the crack of dawn, that the station will be quiet and that the two of us will slip away, onto the Tube and under the streets of London. By this time tomorrow, I think, we'll be far away from here, somewhere where John-Joe can't find us.

We make our tea in silence, and we eat buttered bread and jam, the way we used to when we were teenagers, our feet up on the old range in her kitchen, and we listen to the six o'clock news, the two of us having used up all of our talk in the previous hours. I'd told her things I hadn't told another living soul, not even Bridie. Maeve had just listened, her round face creasing in sympathy, and not once did she ask me if I thought I was doing the right thing. She just nodded and said that, whatever I wanted, she'd try her best to help me. What would I have done without Maeve?

The weather forecast is on, the man telling us both that a front is coming in from the Atlantic, when Maeve clears her throat. 'Michelle, I need to ask you something.'

I look up at her, wary.

'Are you serious about Rosie?'

'What do you mean?' The bread feels suddenly like rubber in my mouth. I try to swallow, but it won't go down. I feel as if I'm going to choke, my eyes watering, and it's all I can do not to spit it up into my napkin. Maeve is a great believer in napkins.

'About taking her,' Maeve says quietly.

I choke the bread down, taking a slurp of hot tea while I try to think. Eventually, I say, 'Of course I am. How on earth could you think that I'd abandon my own chi—' I don't finish the word, and it hangs in the air between us. And then Maeve puts her hand on mine and gives it a squeeze and, for the first time since this whole thing happened, I allow myself to cry. And once I've started, I can't stop. I howl and I roar for what seems like hours, even though it could only be a few moments, and Maeve pats my hair and says, 'There there,' and she just lets me cry. At that moment, I don't think I could love anyone more than I do her.

Then she says, 'Michelle, I've listened to your story and I haven't said a word. I haven't judged, because it's not my place, and God knows, you don't need it.' She hesitates. 'But your children need you. Don't abandon them.'

I shake my head sadly. 'I can't be a mother to them anymore, at least, not the kind of mother they need. I'm so ... useless to them, so ... toxic. You see, I used to think that John-Joe was the problem, Maeve, but now I know it's me. I just seem to poison everything around me. Don't you see?'

'Oh, love, that's nonsense. You're not thinking straight. It's all the stress. You're their mother. They only have you, can't you see that?'

I nod silently, clutching my damp napkin. But I don't see. Not at all. I can only see how they'd be able to breathe again without me. Without me, they'll be free.

Maeve's talking again now, a low murmur, and at first, I only half-hear her. 'You need to leave Rosie here, Michelle.'

'No!' I yell, getting up so suddenly my teacup falls to the floor and rolls around, a thick puddle of hot tea steaming up from the carpet. Rosie lifts her head, her eyes wide with shock, but then her eyelids droop again and she's asleep. 'No,' I say more softly. 'That is not going to happen.'

Maeve shakes her head sadly, reaching out and dabbing at the tea with her napkin. She keeps her gaze on mine. 'If you take her, John-Joe will come after you, you know he will, and so will the authorities. It's kidnapping, Michelle, because she's not your daughter,' she says softly. 'You understand that, don't you, love?'

I think for a moment. I'm her mother. It says so on those pieces of paper, but I know that they are a lie. 'I understand that, Maeve,' I say bitterly. 'Don't you think I know? It's just ... she's all I have,' I wail. 'Without her, I have nothing left.'

'So go and find something,' she says softly. 'If that's what you want. If the only thing you can do right now is go, go. For God's sake, haven't I helped you?' she says ruefully. 'But leave the baby. It's the right thing to do, you know that. She belongs here, with her family.'

And suddenly, the final barrier between me and the world has fallen. Maeve was my only support, my only ally, and now she's gone. The only way in the world I could have done this, picked Rosie up in my arms and taken her with me, was if Maeve was behind me, supporting me. But she's not. And the reality is, I'm completely alone.

'I'm not her family,' I whisper, as if I have only just realised. 'No. No, love, you're not.'

Maeve asks Alan to drive me to the boat, with my single battered suitcase, because she says she just can't bear to watch me go. We both know that we'll never see each other again. And as she stands in the doorway, I remember the two of us on the steps of the church on Maeve's wedding day, both our lives just beginning. When I told her that I was only going to Kildare, not to Timbuktu. I might as well, for all the distance between us since I left. And I feel sorrier about that than I can say. To wish I could rewind the years to that day and start again would be to wish my life and my children away, and I don't want that. They are the only good thing to come out of this. Them and my darling Rosie. Maeve is standing there, waving, when Rosie appears behind her, her hair tousled from her nap, her eyes sleepy. For a moment, I weaken and turn to run to her, but I stop myself. No, Michelle, I tell myself firmly. No. Instead, I blow her a kiss and she catches it, the way I've taught her to, a puzzled look on her sleepy little face. Then I turn and go, and I don't look back, not even once. If I look back, I know that I'll stay. And if I stay, my life will be over.

18

June and Gerry were sitting on the end of India's bed, waiting. India was curled into a ball on her pink duvet that Mary-Pat had bought her for Christmas when she was seven. She was facing the wall, her back towards them, her shoulders heaving with sobs. She hadn't said a word when they'd both appeared at the door, just leaving it open and throwing herself onto the bed, a dramatic gesture which would have been worthy of her sister.

'India, we need to talk to you, love,' Gerry was saying and when there was no response he shot June a look over the top of his glasses. She made a face and shrugged to show that she was no wiser than he.

'India, we can't help you if you won't talk to us,' June tried.

'Go away,' India said, her back set, her voice thick with tears.

Without needing to speak, the two of them silently agreed

to wait it out, sitting at the foot of their daughter's bed just as they'd done when she was a child and they'd come back from some glamorous charity ball, and the girls would be waiting to hear every detail. Where had the years gone, June thought as she sat there, the spring sun streaming in through India's bedroom window. How had her daughter grown up like that, before her very eyes? She'd always thought there was plenty of time: plenty of time to get around to playing with them or bring them to the beach, plenty of time to sit down in front of the TV with them and watch cartoons, plenty of time to play tennis with them in the back garden. Except it turned out that there wasn't. Her time was almost up, and she'd wasted it. She wouldn't get another chance at it, she understood. It was gone.

And then India turned around, her face streaked with tears. 'OK, you win. I'm just a slut. There, does that make the two of you any happier?'

Gerry sighed heavily, taking his reading glasses off and looking tired. Tired and old. 'Love, we're not here to judge. We just want to listen to what you have to say. And whatever it is, we won't get angry, I promise.' June looked at him in wonder. Where had he learned to be that diplomatic? He was so protective of the girls and she'd fully expected him to rant and rave and that she'd end up having to calm two people down.

Mrs Delaney had told them the bare bones of it, her sharp features surprisingly gentle as she'd invited them into her pristine office at St Concepta's. She'd told them that their daughter, who had never so much as got a detention, who had never once turned up late for school or got anything lower than a 'B' in her tests, had succeeded in plastering her naked body all over the Internet. 'You may not be aware, but it happens a lot.'

'I know,' June had said, a hot flush spreading over her chest and up her neck. 'I've just read an article about it ...' She cleared her throat. 'Will we have to involve the guards?'

Mrs Delaney had twisted her necklace in her hands. 'Quite honestly, yes. Distributing child pornography is a criminal offence.'

'But she's the victim,' Gerry had protested.

Mrs Delaney had sighed heavily. 'Of course, but I'm inclined to call Sergeant O'Malley at the local garda station, to be proactive about it.' And when she saw the look of horror on June's face, she said, 'It's a safety issue here at the school. India isn't the only girl this has happened to. We need to stamp it out. And, hopefully, if we put the fear of God into them, it'll save other girls being put through the same thing. In the meantime, you need to get specialist help to delete the photo from the various, ehm, platforms.' She gave a bleak smile. 'Unfortunately, I've had to learn about all of this, so I'll give you some names. And I'd contact a solicitor, just to be on the safe side ...'

June had looked at Gerry then. His face had been chalk white, but he'd nodded briefly and managed to stay calm. 'We'll sort it, thank you, Mrs Delaney. You've been very helpful.'

Mrs Delaney smiled briefly. 'How is India?'

'Too embarrassed to come to school. She thinks everyone's looking at her and thinking about what she looks like ... undressed,' June whispered.

'I know,' Mrs Delaney said quietly. 'But my recommendation is that she come back into school and face them down. We'll be here to help her.'

June had felt a hot wave of shame wash over her. I've failed her, she'd thought. I didn't teach her right from wrong. I spoilt her and took her on outings and bought her clothes, but

I didn't teach her what really mattered. And Gerry hadn't been any better in his own way, coming down on them like a ton of bricks if they stepped out of line even a tiny bit.

'We *should* ask the boy to leave, of course,' Mrs Delaney said, 'given the circumstances ...' here, she'd blinked. 'And given how generous you've been to the school in the past ...'

Oh, I see, June thought. For services rendered.

Gerry had pulled himself upright in his chair. 'That boy needs to accept the consequences of his actions, fair and square. Do I make myself clear? And as for India, we'll talk to her, won't we, June?'

June had wanted to yell, 'No, we won't. We'll try to pretend that this never bloody happened, that's what we'll do. And we'll pray that she doesn't end up in prison.' But of course, Gerry was right. It was a lesson India would have to learn, even though she'd give everything for her daughter not to.

'India, why did you do it?' Gerry said softly now. 'Tell Dad. I won't be angry. I just want to understand.'

'Do the boys pressure you?' June said. She'd read that in the article — that the boys nagged and begged to be sent pictures until the girls gave in. Kind of like it used to be in Monasterard, except for the fact that it could all go viral now. That's what the article had said anyway, and as June had scanned it, absorbing the realities of pretty young girls like her daughter ending up on porn websites, being called THOTs or sluts, she found that she was entering a world she just didn't understand. A world that terrified her. How could she steer her girls through this when she only half-understood it? What use could she really be to them? She wondered if Mammy had felt the same thing thirty years ago, just about different issues, different worries. Maybe June was just learning how to be a parent after all this time.

India sighed and looked exasperated, as if she couldn't believe she'd inherited two such eejits for parents. 'Look, you all think I'm some kind of saint and I'm sick of it, just sick, do you both understand? You just expect me to be responsible and kind and never to put a foot wrong, never to mess up. Georgia can do whatever she likes, and you both just laugh at her because you think she's some kind of a clown, but me? Not goody-goody India,' she said bitterly. 'Well, I've had enough,' she muttered, pulling her sleeves down over her hands, a crease appearing in the middle of her pretty little forehead.

'But, darling, we've never put any pressure on you to behave a certain way,' June said, looking at Gerry doubtfully. Have we? the look said.

'You didn't need to,' India retorted. 'You just kept telling me that I was the best daughter any parent could have, that I never gave you a moment's trouble, blah, blah. It's kind of hard to step out of line. And you hover over me all the time so I can't have any privacy.'

'I can see that,' Gerry said thoughtfully.

India's face crumpled then, and she looked as if she were about five years of age and her ice-cream had just fallen on the pavement. 'Oh, Mum, Jamie told me that I was amazing. That he'd never met a girl like me. Turns out he was just like all the others — only after one thing.' And she hurled herself into June's arms. June held her and smoothed back her hair and told her it would be all right, all the time knowing that it probably wouldn't. How could this ever be all right?

She looked at Gerry, who was calmly sitting there, and willed him to say something. 'India,' he said, gently but firmly, 'we understand that you felt under pressure, and we're sorry that you felt like that. It's not right, and that … boy will be told. But do you understand what it is you've done? You've displayed your … naked body for everyone to see. And I mean everyone. Do you understand that?' His tone was quiet, but he was making his point.

India nodded, head bent, and a fat tear fell onto her knee.

'It's a precious thing, India, and you can't give it to just anyone.'

'I know.'

'You'll have to go back to school on Monday, love,' he said gently.

'No, please, Daddy,' India wailed. 'Please. Everyone's seen the photos – they've been passing them all around the school. You should see some of the comments – I can't deal with that!'

'India, I called Siobhan,' June said. 'Georgia gave me her number. She was devastated and she's coming over later. She'll stand by you, and so will Daddy and I. And Mrs Delaney. You won't be alone. And you're such a brave girl. You can do it.'

'You can, love,' Gerry added. 'You'll go in on Monday with Siobhan and you'll hold your head up high and you'll face them down.' He gave June a look. 'Come on, love, we'll leave India to have a little think.'

'Oh. Right.' June nodded, wondering if that was really a good idea, but Gerry gave her that look, the no-mollycoddle look, and she got to her feet.

'We'll talk later, love,' Gerry said softly and ushered June out the door.

'Where did you learn to be so calm?' June said once they were safely in the kitchen. 'I mean … what happened?'

Gerry gave a small smile. 'Oh, I haven't had a personality

transformation, love, if that's what you mean, but I have been doing a lot of thinking. And I know that I need to change the way I do things — take it easier, listen more.'

'We both do,' June said. Then she sighed, saying, 'I don't know. We'll need to keep an eye on her,' wishing that she could just put her in the car and take her down to Mary-Pat's for a while. A few weeks in Monasterard with John-Patrick and Melissa would knock the corners off her, set her straight. If only she could talk to Mary-Pat. She'd know what to do.

'Any coffee?' Gerry said wistfully.

'In the fridge,' June said, adding, 'it's from Lidl.' When she saw the look of horror on his face, she almost smiled. 'I'm turning over a new leaf — trying not to buy too much expensive crap.'

He made it carefully, filling the coffee maker with coffee and putting water into the reservoir, and when it had bubbled and hissed for a few moments, he filled two mugs with it and brought them over to her, placing them gently on the table. 'Any biccies? I fancy a Jammie Dodger.'

June smiled and went to the cupboard over the extractor fan. 'It's where I keep my stash,' she said, pulling down a tin out of which she took a packet of Custard Creams.

Gerry's face lit up and when he helped himself to one he closed his eyes in pleasure. 'You can't beat Custard Creams — can there be any greater pleasure in life?'

'I know, who'd have thought it — the two of us with our biccies and our cheap coffee. Maybe we're changing.'

He grunted and took a sip, looking pleasantly surprised. 'It's not bad.'

'It isn't, is it? And nor is any of their other stuff.'

'Right.' His lips quivered as he sipped.

'I know. Who'd have thought I'd shop in Lidl and enjoy it. Their frozen fish is very good, you know,' she added, and they both snorted with laughter. Then they were quiet for a few moments, sipping their coffee. June wasn't sure if Gerry was thinking what she was thinking, wondering if it was too late for change at their age. If it was too late to understand what really mattered in life and too late to teach the girls. June was still in shock about India, if she were to admit it: Mammy would have killed her stone dead if she'd so much as copied her neighbour's answers in a maths test, never mind … what India had done, but then, Mammy's standards, her principles, could sometimes be hard to live up to. June wondered now how Mammy would have coped with the world today, where things weren't black or white any more, where you couldn't just take a position and defend it because you could so easily take a completely different position and defend that, too. Maybe that's why Mammy had gone so far away, to a place which, as far as June could see, wasn't modern at all: that way, her principles would never really be challenged. June just couldn't see Mammy muddling along, trying to follow a sort-of-acceptable path through life, not doing too much harm, but probably not doing all that much good either.

'Is there any hope for us, do you think, Gerry?'

Gerry put the cup down softly on the table. 'I'd say so.'

'You would?'

He nodded and looked out the window, his pale-grey eyes filled with tears. June wanted to jump up and go to him and hold him, but she didn't, because she didn't have the right. Not after what she'd done. 'I'm sorry, Junie,' he finally said.

'What on earth do you have to be sorry about?' June said. 'I'm the one who should be sorry. The other thing … it's finished,' she began, thinking about poor Dave in the Shelbourne, but Gerry put a hand up.

'Love, if you don't mind, I'd rather not.'

'No, of course not,' she muttered.

'I'm sorry I wasn't a better husband to you, Junie. I thought it was all about providing and making a home for you all and making sure that you never wanted for anything. I know that it wasn't like that for you growing up and I just thought that if you had everything, that it might somehow make up for the years when you didn't.'

'I know,' June said, 'and I'm so grateful for that, Gerry. I have a lovely life. But, you know, I've been thinking more about how I grew up and I understand now that I might not have had a lot, but I had what mattered. I had two half-mad parents who were hardly able to dress themselves, but they cared, and they tried to bring us up in the right way. I only see that now, with India and everything. I chose not to live up to it. I just don't have Mammy's moral fibre, I suppose.'

Gerry ignored the invitation to tell her that she had. He was probably right, June thought ruefully. Instead he said quietly, 'You never talk about her.'

'No,' June said. 'For a long time, it was just too painful, because of the way she left and everything, and then because of the letters and keeping them a secret, I just felt I never could. I felt I wasn't allowed to. I wasn't allowed to give out about her or to get angry about why she'd left. And then when I did decide to tell the truth, look what happened,' she said bitterly. She'd told Gerry about the family conference and, to her surprise, he'd told her how proud he was of her. She'd been expecting a lecture.

'You did your best, love,' Gerry said diplomatically now. 'There's never a good time to deliver news like that. But it was time for the truth, even if it didn't get the reaction you'd wanted. It's a risk, Junie. You did well to take it. Anyway, the truth is all that really matters,' he said, taking a slurp of coffee, before saying wryly, 'Would you listen to Confucius here?'

June leaned back on the uncomfortable, straight-backed kitchen chair and looked out the window. There was a long silence in the kitchen, and June could make out the low hum of the radio. I just want my family back in once piece, June suddenly thought. I want to ring my sister up and bitch with her the way I used to and I want to go down and help my brother to clean that awful house up and I want my daughters not to be miserable or to be finding out about life the hard way. And I want to stand on my own two feet for once.

'Everything's broken, Gerry,' she said. 'And I just want it to be fixed. Is it too late, do you think?'

'It's never too late, June,' and then he gave her hand a little squeeze.

'I don't know where to start,' June said softly. 'There seems to be so much to do.'

'One step at a time, love.'

You're right, June thought. That's what Daddy used to say when I'd get in a sweat with my homework. 'One thing at a time, love. Rome wasn't built in a day.' How funny that Daddy, of all people, could give such sage advice. 'Listen, will you stay for dinner? I think there's some lasagne in the freezer.' And when Gerry looked hopeful, she added, 'Don't get any funny ideas. It's just leftovers.'

'Oh, so it's leftovers now?' Gerry grinned and June playfully punched him on the shoulder.

'I made it myself, actually. I spent a whole Saturday afternoon making a batch of them — can you believe it?' She laughed.

'No, I can't,' Gerry said from behind his mug.

They had a nice family supper of reheated lasagne. Gerry made India come down from her bedroom with the promise that nothing of any significance would be discussed at the dinner table, and when Orianna came to do the cleaning, Gerry invited her to sit with them and have dessert. 'Will you have a little drop of wine?'

'No thank you, Mr Gerry,' she said quietly.

'It's Gerry. Please,' he said, with exemplary politeness. It felt good, June realised, the undemanding chat. It was also good to have her family around her, Orianna included, a woman who had half-raised her girls and yet with whom she had hardly had a moment's real conversation. She couldn't remember the last time they'd all sat around like this — not dressed up to sit in the chilly dining room, to make stilted conversation about politics because Gerry insisted on it.

Gerry hadn't even commented on the lasagne, which had ended up a slight mess on his plate: he'd merely looked at it for a bit before picking up his knife and fork and tucking in. Georgia looked over at her mother and winked. She reminded June more and more of Daddy, with her funny whims and her dark hair and loud laughter. She was a blast, Georgia, but hard work with it. June instinctively knew that she'd have to spend her younger daughter's adolescence on alert: there'd be smoking and probably drinking and boys, no doubt about it. She half-smiled at the thought. It'd probably be fairly tame, though, compared to what India had got up to — it was always the quiet ones you had to watch. And she would watch India from now on – very closely – but in a way that actually mattered, she thought, looking at her older daughter, hunched over her plate in her pink dressing gown, face bleached of any colour. It was part of the job description.

And Gerry and herself? Well, they could share the same space and talk civilly, so that was a start. And he'd hated his mother's, even though she made him nice dinners and put a hot water bottle into his bed every night – June couldn't help but feel a dart of triumph.

Georgia was in the middle of a funny story about Mrs Marsh, the gym teacher, her mouth half-full of pasta because she never closed it when she ate, when the phone rang. 'I'll get it!' She was up off her seat like a hound after the scent, bolting into the hall in case she'd miss even a slight bit of action. 'It's probably Aoife wanting to Skype me,' she roared back into the kitchen.

'Good God, that child has a voice like a foghorn,' Gerry muttered, tucking into the last bit of pasta. 'When the hell did she get so loud?'

When you were living in that office at Talk FM, winding up half the population of Ireland with your nonsense, June thought. When we used to have to listen to you on the radio to know what you were up to.

Georgia bellowed 'Hello!' loudly into the phone, no doubt deafening poor old Aoife at the other end. 'Oh, hello.' The name was slightly muffled, but it must be someone they knew, June thought, because Georgia was giggling. 'Yes, I've been a good girl. No, no boys yet. Or smoking. No drugs either.' She laughed. 'Do you want Mum? Hang on.' Georgia bustled back into the kitchen. 'It's for you, Mum.' She nodded in the direction of the hall.

ALL THAT I LEAVE BEHIND

'Who is it?'

'It's Aunty Mary-Pat. She says she needs to talk to you about a baby.'

Later, June went up to her bedroom, which was chilly, and turned on the little lamp on her dressing table. She sat there under the pool of light cast by the pretty Tiffany lampshade, and she thought of what Mary-Pat had said earlier, about life being too short, and she took out her Smythson notepaper and selected a pen from the little clay holder that India had made in first class in primary school, a sweet, wobbly mess of blue and red paint. Oh, her lovely girls. They were the lights of her life. She knew that India was afraid right now that she'd let June down, and it was true, June was disappointed, but not in India, just in what she'd done. It would be so hard for her, but she'd learn, June knew. At the thought of her girls, June had to blink to keep the tears at bay. They'd have to wait. She hesitated for a few moments before beginning to write.

Dear Mammy,

How strange it is to be writing to you like this, after all the years that have passed, and all the letters that have gone between us, all the things you now know about my life and Mary-Pat's and Pius's and Rosie's. It's been a lifeline, hasn't it? Something that's pulled us both together and it's been so precious to me, it really has.

Which is why what I now have to say is so difficult. I'd like to ask you respectfully to stop contacting us. You left us a long time ago, and we've had to get on without you. To build our own lives, all the time wondering what they would have been like with you by our sides. We've managed to do this, Mammy, but some of us have been more successful at it than others. And it's been hard and so painful at times. And you weren't there for any of it. You weren't there when it mattered, Mammy. You weren't there when we needed you.

I know that this might sound like a bit of a rebuke and I don't mean it that way, but I don't think it's fair that you get to stay in touch with us on your terms. Maybe it makes you feel better about what you've done, but it's harder for us. It makes it harder to live our own lives, to love our own children and to look forward to what life has to offer.

I'm sure this letter won't be easy for you to read, no easier than it's been for me to write, but that's it, Mammy. I'm sure there are many other words I could write, but none of them would really help now. They wouldn't make a difference.

I hope you respect our wishes.

With love always,

June

19

$\mathcal{I}$t was part of his new-found decisiveness, Pius thought, as he stood on Daphne's doorstep, a bunch of spring lilies in his hand. Turning up just like that, without needing to devote a day-and-a-half to ruminating over the whole thing, debating the rights and wrongs of it, eventually talking himself out of whatever action he'd planned. He'd been getting better at that, at being decisive.

He'd taken Daphne literally when she'd told him to 'man up'. He'd gone to every one of Rosie's antenatal appointments with her, waiting outside the door while she spoke to that bossy midwife, Margaret, and if the woman thought it was a bit strange that her patient's brother should turn up every third Wednesday of the month, well, so be it. He'd tidied up the back room and painted it a nice neutral shade of yellow and had even surprised himself by tracking down instructions for a lovely handmade crib on the Internet in the library.

He was doing it for Rosie, because she needed him, but he was also doing it for himself, he knew that. To show himself what he was capable of. And now it was time to put the next part of his plan into action. Pius only hesitated when he got to the front door, holding his hand up to knock and then dropping it to his side again. His courage briefly deserted him and he was about to turn around and make for home when the door opened and she was there. The Mermaid. She was dressed in a pair of paint-spattered white overalls, her red hair jammed into that stupid bloody hat. In her hand, she was holding two slender paintbrushes. 'Oh,' she said, 'c'mon in.'

'Thanks.' Pius looked down at Jessie. 'I'll leave her outside,' he began, nodding towards the dog.

'What? No, for God's sake, she's fine. We'll get you a drink, won't we, pet?' she cooed and bent down to stroke Jessie's silky ears. 'Oh, you're a lovely girl, yes you are.' Jessie practically purred with pleasure, closing her eyes and letting out a small whimper. 'I'll put the kettle on,' she said, opening the door wide and leading him into a spacious, bright hall, in which every inch of wall space was covered with paintings.

'Wow,' he said as they walked towards the kitchen past a beautiful triptych of green-painted panels. 'These are beautiful. It looks like the canal hanging on the wall.' And then he blushed because he didn't know the first thing about art. She'd think he was a total poser. Books, he could talk about, but not art.

'Thanks. I wanted it to feel like that,' she said.

'Are they yours?'

She nodded. 'I dabble a bit,' her back turned to him as they went into a kitchen that had been painted a bright, tomato red and into which filtered a watery silver light from the pretty garden outside. Pius could see a nice agapanthus and a magnolia that needed a prune. Maybe he'd suggest it, if she had a minute, although, knowing her, she'd probably take it the wrong way.

She put a cast-iron kettle onto the hotplate of a blue-painted range. 'It'll take a few minutes.'

'I'm in no rush,' Pius said. There was a silence for a moment, the kettle bubbling away, and then he was distracted by Jessie, who was circling his legs. He reached out to pat her on the head and felt that twinge in his shoulder again, a sharp pain which made him gasp and lift a hand to squeeze the muscle which throbbed beneath his shoulder blade.

'What's wrong with you?' Daphne nodded towards his shoulder.

'Oh, I think I've pulled a muscle,' Pius said. 'It throbs a bit right here,' and he pointed to the spot.

The Mermaid said nothing, just went over to one of the kitchen cupboards and reached up onto her tiptoes, her hand almost, but not quite, reaching a brown plastic box on the middle shelf.

'Here, let me,' Pius said and went over, reaching up to the shelf easily and pulling the box down. She didn't move out of his way and he was suddenly so close to her, he could feel the warmth of her through the overalls, could smell a mixture of paint thinner and vanilla. He suddenly longed to see her red hair tumble around her shoulders. He longed to pull the hair to one side, gently, and to plant kisses from the top of her neck down to her shoulder blades, running his hand inside the collar of her overalls, tugging it back a little so that he could brush his lips along her skin ...

He swallowed, his throat dry, and then handed her the box,

awkward because she was about three inches away from him, her head level with his chest. He lowered it until she took it. 'There you are,' he said, unnecessarily.

She said nothing, but he noticed that her hands were shaking as she rummaged through the box, until she produced a small brown tub with a white lid on it. 'Calendula. Good for tired muscles,' she said. And then added, 'It's probably your age.'

'Gee, thanks,' Pius said.

'Anyway, let me know if it works,' she said awkwardly.

'I will. Thanks. Ehm, do you think you could turn off the kettle?' He nodded towards the range, where the kettle was now screaming, a high-pitched 'wheee' which was making his ears ring.

'Oh. Right.' And she walked briskly over and pulled it off the range, busying herself putting two teabags in brightly coloured mugs and adding boiling water. She went to the bin and emptied the teabags, plunk, plunk, into the bin and added milk from the carton which had been sitting on the counter — he wondered if the milk was warm. He didn't like it warm, it tasted off. She handed him the mug, taking a sip from hers and making a face. 'Sorry, milk's off.'

He took a tentative sip and winced. God, it tasted awful. 'It's lovely, thanks.'

She gave a little smile. 'Liar.'

He smiled back. 'It's horrible, actually. Sorry.' And then they both laughed. He liked it when she laughed: that frown that creased her forehead disappeared and her whole face lit up. It transformed her whole appearance. He cleared his throat. 'Ehm, I'm getting a new batch of hens next week and I wondered if Dara wanted to help me settle them in.' At least, that's part of it, he thought, putting the mug down on the counter. The lie will do for now.

'Oh.' Daphne blushed and looked at her tea. 'Yes, he'd love that. He likes doing things with you.'

'Oh, really? I thought that I was irresponsible and generally useless and it was time to "man up",' Pius said.

She put down her mug on the counter with a thump, her green eyes flashing. 'I did not say that!'

'You did. They were your words precisely. "Time to man up, Pius," and I quote.' Pius could feel the air getting thick already, the two of them taking up their battle positions, the way they always did after five minutes in the same space. How on earth could he ever have thought that they'd be good together. There was no way this would work. No way.

'Well ...' She shrugged, as if to say, 'What can you do?'

He changed his mind then. He had to say it, he just had to, or else they'd go on like this for ever. 'The thing is, I came to tell you that you were right. You've been right all along. I think that's why we keep fighting every time we meet. Because you keep telling me things that are good for me, but that I don't like.'

'We don't fight,' she said angrily, her hands on her hips.

'We do, Daphne,' he said quietly. 'That's what we're doing now.'

'Oh. Yes. So we are.' And then she looked at him, and her eyes were filled with an expression he didn't recognise. 'I don't want to fight with you, Pius.'

'I don't want to fight with you, Daphne,' he replied softly.

There was a long silence while the two of them examined their feet, the grouting on the tiles, the bit of dirt over the cooker, anything so as not to be the one to speak next.

Daphne gave in first. 'Can I ask you a favour?'

'Sure.' Pius shifted slightly on his feet, wincing in pain as he moved position. This bloody shoulder.

'Can you talk to Dara? You know, reassure him. I think he's worried because of the tension between Kevin and me, you know … It's a big ask, but he listens to you. He looks up to you.'

Pius was taken aback. He couldn't see why the child would look up to him. He was hardly a role model now, was he? And then Daphne whispered. 'We both do.'

Pius looked at her then, but she held his gaze. 'You're a good man, Pius. You make people feel safe.' And she blushed now and looked at her tea.

She reached out and took his hand in both of hers, examining first the back of it, running her hands over the veins and his bony knuckles, then turning it over and running a hand along his lifeline, sending a shiver up his spine.

'Christ,' he said then, breaking the moment.

'What's wrong?'

'I have a cramp in my leg.' And he stood up straight, hopping about on his left leg while holding his right one straight in front of him. 'It's not funny,' he said then as she snorted with laughter. 'Ow, ah!' The pain was like a knife in the sole of his foot.

'Wriggle it around a bit, that's it,' Daphne said as he hopped around.

'There, that's better.' Finally, the pain was gone and he was left standing there, hands in his pockets, wondering how he was going to get back to where they'd been.

'It was just having Kevin around again made me realise, you know? How good you are for us both. You've never asked anything of either of us, just let us be ourselves. And you've taught Dara such a lot, about nature and the garden and everything. You've been more of a father to him than Kevin ever has.' She said this last bit bitterly and, in spite of himself, Pius felt moved to defend Kevin, the imperfect father, even though it nearly killed him to do so. An imperfect father was better than no father at all, and besides, all fathers were imperfect – if only he'd known, maybe he'd have been a bit kinder to Daddy. Or maybe not. Anyway, being a father meant getting over being perfect, he'd worked that out at least.

'He's trying, Daphne. It's not easy, but he's trying to stay in Dara's life and to teach him stuff, even if you don't think much of it. That counts for something.'

She was surprised, he knew, at him leaping to the little shit's defence, but it was the truth, Pius decided. And after everything that had happened over the last few months and weeks, the truth mattered.

'It's just ... well, look, I know about Rosie.'

He stood back suddenly, feeling the heat of the range through the rear end of his trousers. 'What about Rosie?'

She gave him a look that only a woman could give, a mixture of pity and amusement. 'Pi, we talk. A lot. She's told me everything about your family. And I'm sorry.'

He could feel it all floating away from him, the little bit of happiness he'd managed to seize for himself. He could feel the black clouds gathering at the edge of things, pushing against him. He sighed heavily. 'Daphne, please. Can we not talk about this? I'm sick of it all. Just sick of it.'

'And you blame Rosie for shaking you out of your comfortable rut, Pius.' Daphne fixed him with that glare again, the one that made him really, really annoyed. Because it said that she wasn't fooled by him for a second, that she wasn't taken in by the bullshit he spun himself to make his life easier, to justify to himself why he lived the way he did. And now he had to ask himself honestly whose fault that was. Whose choice to stop living, just to exist, because of something that had happened to him when he was hardly a man at all. Lots of people lost their loved ones, every day – they died or parents split up or left and somehow they went on. But he didn't. He'd just stopped and sulked, he supposed, refusing to dress or eat properly, locking himself up in his place alone, shunning the only woman who'd ever loved him. He'd thought that if he did that, somehow Mammy would see, wherever she was, and know that she'd hurt him. And one day she'd come back and say that she was sorry. And then, the thought occurred to him. She's gone. She's gone and she's never coming back. And you have to go on.

And then he found himself reaching out and taking Daphne's hand, pulling her gently towards him until she was standing opposite him, and before he could overthink it, he tilted his head to one side and kissed her on the lips. She tasted of mint and garlic and Vaseline and her skin was so soft and pillowy. He groaned and pulled her tight to him, feeling the softness of her, the rolls of milky flesh which were so gorgeous they were almost edible. He ran his hands through that glorious hair, feeling the silky texture in his fingers. 'Thank God you aren't wearing that hat,' he blurted.

'What's wrong with my hat?'

'Nothing. It's beautiful. You're beautiful,' and he kissed her again, before saying, 'you could wear a burka, Daphne, and you'd still be the most beautiful girl in the world.'

'Oh, stop.' Daphne blushed. 'You know, you're not too bad yourself.' And she leaned back in his arms to look at him properly.

He ran a hand over the stubble on his cheeks and chin. It felt like sandpaper and he felt sorry for Daphne, having to kiss it.

'Would you mind if we took things slowly, though, Pius?' Daphne was saying now into his ear as they stood there and held each other close. 'I'm not sure I'm ready yet for, you know ...' and she blushed. 'We've been on our own for so long, it takes a bit of getting used to.'

He pulled himself back a little so that he could hold her face in his hands and look her in the eye. 'I'll do whatever you want, Daphne. But I've spent thirty years waiting for my life to begin, not realising that I was living it. That every day was an opportunity that I was wasting, sitting in this place and feeling sorry for myself. All those years, just gone and nothing to show for it. And you and Dara, well, you both made me realise that I haven't got any more time to waste.'

'That's a long speech.'

He cleared his throat. 'It is, I suppose. I probably won't speak for the next fifty years.' He smiled.

'Well then we'll have a very quiet relationship,' she said, stroking his chin, running her fingers over the stubble. She searched his eyes with hers. 'I'm glad I found you, Pius.'

'I'm glad I found you, Daphne.'

20

When Rosie went into labour, as the canal bank burst into summer life, she knew who she had to call. There was only one person who she really trusted with this, who could go through this with her, she thought as she dialled the number, closing her eyes as the phone rang, imagining her sister picking it up, wondering how she'd explain it all to her in five minutes, how she'd account for the months that had passed when her only contact had been John-Patrick and Melissa, who'd appear at the door because they were 'just passing', carefully skirting the fact that Rosie and their mother didn't seem to be talking. Melissa had been thrilled about the pregnancy, downloading an app to her mobile so that she could monitor her aunt's progress, becoming an expert on the height of fundus and stages of development, but even though Rosie loved her niece, it wasn't the same. She needed her sister.

The phone rang to some novelty voicemail and Rosie had to stifle the urge to laugh as Bart Simpson asked her to call back. 'Mary-Pat, it's me. Rosie,' she added helpfully. 'Look, can you call me?' She had to break off then as a wave of pain hit her, her mobile falling onto the floor.

She'd woken early that morning with an odd feeling of lightness in her abdomen, as if the baby wasn't there any more, and she'd had to reach out her hand and touch the mound of her belly to be sure. She sat upright as quickly as she could, a sudden panic gripping her and the sensation that something had emptied out of her. Heart thumping, she'd patted the bedsheets and then she realised that she was sitting in a puddle. The sheets were wet and clammy and she was freezing, her skin covered in goosepimples. She opened her mouth to call Pi, but all that came out was a hoarse whisper. In the end, she had to scrabble around for the mobile on the floor and ring him. His voice was a low rumble. 'Hello?'

'Pi, I think it's started.'

There was a long silence at the end of the phone, and Rosie could see the wheels turning as he tried to work out what to do. 'Will you ask Mary-Pat to meet me at the hospital?'

He cleared his throat. 'OK.' Rosie was grateful to him that he hadn't asked for an explanation. 'Can I, ehm, help you with anything?'

'No, if you could just get the car ready — not the Beetle,' she added hastily. There was a rumble then a murmur and the phone went dead, which Rosie took to mean that he was doing as he'd been asked.

She was surprisingly calm as she washed and dressed. Margaret had told her not to shower if her waters broke, in case of infection, so she dabbed at herself with a towel, then put on a comfy pair of tracksuit bottoms and a T-shirt and fleece. She'd have to ask Pi to help her to lace her trainers because she couldn't reach. The baby, who normally started every morning with a vigorous bout of kicking, was completely still in her belly, and Rosie felt a flash of panic before remembering that Margaret had also told her that that happened when you went into labour, that the baby was just 'in the departure lounge' and didn't need to move about any more.

She picked up her hospital bag and looked around the room and thought, when I come back, I'll have a baby with me. I'll be a mum. And the thought filled her with a sense of wonder. What kind of mum will I be? Will I be like Mammy or like my real mum? Will I know how to do this job as well as Mary-Pat? She'd always thought she didn't have a rule book, a road map, but now she realised that of course she had. She had one of the best.

And then she thought of Mark and wondered where he'd be right now. Somewhere out there in the world, unaware that he was to be a father. She closed her eyes and tried to picture him, but the picture was fuzzy even now, blurry around the edges. Maybe I've done the wrong thing, but please forgive me, she thought quietly to herself before closing the door behind her and shuffling gently down the stairs to where Pius was waiting, a set of towels in his hands, as instructed. 'I called Mary-Pat. She'll be along in a bit.'

Rosie nodded, not trusting herself to speak. She leaned gently against her brother, her big oak tree, and closed her eyes. 'There, there, Rosie-boo, it'll be OK,' his voice a deep rumble in his chest as he gave her a gentle squeeze. 'We'll all be there for you. Don't you worry.'

'Thanks, Pi. I'm sorry for everything.'

'Sure, for God's sake, what do you have to be sorry for? None of it was your fault,' he mumbled into her hair. 'It's us who should be sorry, love, that we made such a hash of things. We'll try to do better with the third generation.' He smiled.

Rosie tried to argue that he'd been a great brother, that she was lucky to have him, but a contraction gripped her with such ferocity she had to close her eyes and grit her teeth against the pain, the vice which gripped her abdomen and then slid downwards, a great wave of it, which made her grab hold of Pius's wrist until it passed.

'Better?' Pius's voice was soothing.

'Thanks, Pi. You're a natural.'

'Must be all the practice I've had,' he said ruefully. And then he paused. 'I'm sure Mammy would be proud of you, Rosie.'

Rosie shook her head. 'No, Pi. I'm sorry. No. She's gone. I already have a mammy, or as good as, and I don't need another.'

Pius looked down at her and then he kissed her forehead. 'You're right. Of course you are. And now, let's go before you have this baby right here. The kitchen's in a right state.'

Rosie balanced on her pile of clean towels in the passenger seat, gripping the door handle and Pius's arm as she rode the contractions all the way to Dublin. It was strange, she thought, that she could go from being speechless with pain to being able to continue chatting to Pius about the programme on the radio, a phone-in where people talked about their favourite childhood memories. He kept up a good patter to distract her. 'Do you remember the time you helped me to skin that rabbit that I shot and Mary-Pat walloped your backside because you got your good dress covered in rabbit blood? And she nearly killed me too, into the bargain. That was you, Rosie, always a tomboy, always getting stuck in.'

'Skinning a rabbit, an essential life skill,' Rosie joked, before she had to grip the dashboard as another contraction built and then ebbed away again. 'Oh, Christ, that was a bad one. Are we nearly there yet?'

'Just another ten minutes. Hang on, Rosie, we'll make it,' Pius said, shooting her a worried look.

'It's OK, Pi, I'm not going to have it in the car.' Rosie managed a short laugh before muttering, 'Oh, crap, another one.' What had she been thinking, that the pain would just be like bad period cramps? Now she knew why nobody ever talked about it — if they did, there wouldn't be a woman alive who'd go through it.

Pius put the boot down and they did the rest of the journey at about seventy miles an hour, screeching into the car park and bullying another driver out of a parking space. 'That's not like you, Pi,' Rosie joked weakly.

'Yes, well, needs must,' Pius said grimly. 'Thank God I got you here in one piece. Mary-Pat would kill me if I didn't. She said she'd break my knees if I didn't deliver you safely. Now, let's get you inside.'

Rosie couldn't walk for laughing.

Naturally, Rosie heard Mary-Pat before she saw her. Margaret was at the 'business end' as she called it, examining Rosie to see how many centimetres she'd dilated. 'Hmm, I'd say it's early days yet, but we'll see how we go. We might need to move things along if there's no progress in the next couple of hours. How are the contractions?'

'Well, they were really bad in the car, but they've eased off now,' Rosie said.

'It's because you've come into hospital. They all do that.' Margaret laughed. 'They must sense it somehow and decide that they're not ready to come out and, sure, who could blame them. It's a scary old world.'

She pulled off her gloves and threw them into the bin and went to make a note in the file when the door crashed open and Mary-Pat bustled in in a grey jogging suit and carrying a large holdall. Margaret's head shot up and her eyes darkened. 'Excuse me, no visitors in the labour rooms. Please go to the waiting area.' And she pointed to the door, in case the person hadn't quite got the message.

'I'm her sister. I'm to be the birth partner,' Mary-Pat barked and marched over to Rosie and gripped her hand. 'Howya, love. Why are you flat on your back? C'mon, get the hell up.'

Rosie thought she'd never been so glad to see anyone in her whole life. 'Mary-Pat,' she exclaimed, trying to lift herself up in the bed, knocking over a cardboard hat that Margaret had offered her to be sick into onto the ground. 'Thank God you're here. I can't do this by myself, I just can't.' She searched her sister's face for reassurance, knowing that she sounded panicky. She *was* panicky. The contractions and the pain that came with them were coming fast again now and she could feel herself getting tired and weepy and longing for something to take the pain away. Anything. She'd sworn she wasn't going to have an epidural, but now she longed for it, longed for the blessed release from the exhausting pain.

'Excuse me, I have a patient here who's in labour,' Margaret bristled. 'She needs rest.'

'She does in her nelly.' Mary-Pat gave Rosie a tight squeeze, before tugging at her gently to get her to sit up. 'C'mon, love, time to get moving or you'll never get that baby out.'

Rosie tried to shift forward in the bed, but she couldn't move. Her stomach seemed to have pinned her there — she was like an upturned crab, arms and legs waving but unable to right herself. Gently, Mary-Pat reached behind her and shifted her forward until Rosie was sitting more or less upright. As she did so, she nudged against Rosie and Rosie felt the hardness of her sister's stomach, the solidity of it. Surely —?

Mary-Pat looked down, as if seeing her stomach for the very first time, then looked back up at Rosie. 'It would seem your condition is catching.'

'You're kidding,' Rosie managed.

'Yes, well.' Mary-Pat blushed a violent shade of puce. 'It's a long story. Blame Victoria's Secret and a bottle of Chianti.'

'Oh. My. God,' Rosie spluttered, then coughed, then burst out laughing, before a wall of pain made her moan and close her eyes, gripping her sister's wrist.

When she opened her eyes again, Mary-Pat was patting her rounded tummy. 'It's no feckin' joke. I'm forty-three. And the kids are mortified, of course. Melissa says if I think she's going to push a pram around Monasterard I've got another thing coming. And John-Patrick has barely spoken to either of us since we told him — I think he's too embarrassed at the notion that these old age pensioners are still at it. Still, it was worth it, if you catch my drift.'

'TMI, Mary-Pat.'

'I know.' Mary-Pat shook her head ruefully. 'I didn't actually mean it like that. I just meant that I'm glad to have PJ back.'

I didn't know he'd gone anywhere, Rosie thought, but then, why would I? I never asked my sister about her marriage or about how happy she was. I didn't care, because I was too caught up with my own dramas. And she felt ashamed that she had no idea that her sister was pregnant. 'I'm sorry, Mary-Pat, I truly am. I had no idea. I wish to God I had, but ...'

'Sure you had your own pregnancy to be getting on with, love. And,' she put up a hand as Rosie went to object, 'I know why you didn't tell me, and that's fine — Melissa never shut up about it, to be honest — but I would have liked to be able to be there for you, to make it up to you for all the shit we've put you through. And ... well, I hope it's not too late.' Mary-Pat blushed at the uncharacteristic expression of feeling. 'I know,' she said, seeing Rosie's look of incredulity. 'I've been practising talking about my "feelings".' She used air quotes and rolled her eyes to heaven.

'Well, it suits you.' Rosie tried to get the words out but gave up as the contraction gripped her. 'Oh, for Jesus Christ's sake,' she roared. 'The pain is fucking killing me. When the hell will this baby come out?'

'That's the contractions talking, pet. Means they must be working.'

At this point, the two women looked at Margaret, who was trying to busy herself at the foetal monitor, her face a picture as she tried to absorb the story she was hearing. Mary-Pat turned to her then. 'Don't worry, we're the only two that are up the duff. The others are grand. And I'm married at least, which is more than I can say for herself here. Although that's the way nowadays, isn't it?'

Margaret nodded and said diplomatically, 'They're all mothers to us.'

'You're dead right. Now, do you think Rosie could get up and start moving around, or else this baby will never go anywhere.'

'Well, she just needs to be monitored for a few more minutes and then—' But Mary-Pat was ignoring her, ushering Rosie gently up on the bed. 'C'mon, Rosie-boo, up we get, there's work to be done.'

Margaret tutted and rolled her eyes to heaven, and Rosie shot her an apologetic look. 'Off you go,' she said reluctantly, removing the straps of the foetal monitor from Rosie's belly.

'Thanks, love,' Mary-Pat said. 'Any chance of a cup of tea? I'm parched.' And then, as the door swung shut behind the retreating Margaret, 'What's wrong with that woman? You'd swear I'd asked for cocaine.'

Rosie was shaking with laughter now as the pain gripped her, so that she was laughing and moaning at the same time. 'Oh, Mary-Pat, stop making me laugh, it's making things worse.' She gritted her teeth and grabbed her sister's wrist. 'I won't be able to do it, I won't.'

Mary-Pat held onto Rosie, matching her grip, her strong hand grasping Rosie's, giving it a tight squeeze. 'You will, love. You will, and before you know it, you'll be looking at your baby and you won't be able to believe he's yours and you'll start out on the greatest journey of them all. I know, because I've been there myself, and there's nothing like it. It's a miracle.'

A miracle. It sure didn't feel like it right now, Rosie thought. She lay back on the bed, and Mary-Pat fussed around, pulling a little facecloth out of the holdall and soaking it in cold water from the sink before folding it and placing it on Rosie's forehead. Rosie felt the damp, cool cloth soothe her, the lull between contractions a blessed relief. 'Mary-Pat, I'm glad you're here.'

'Well, I'm glad to be here too, love. And I'm sorry about everything, I really am.' Mary-Pat took Rosie's hand in hers and gave it a squeeze.

'You don't have to be sorry, MP.'

'I do, love. I was trying to protect you. It wasn't a nice story and we all felt ashamed that something like that had happened to you. You just got caught up in events that weren't of your making, pet. Sometimes people do dreadful things, even though they don't mean it. Mammy and Daddy weren't bad people, just foolish and a bit naïve, I suppose. They didn't understand that what they did affected others.'

'I know, Mary-Pat, but can we talk about it another time?' Rosie moaned, unable to respond because another contraction had gripped her. She held Mary-Pat's hand so tightly she could feel the bones in her sister's hand rubbing against each other. 'Sorry,' she managed, through gritted teeth.

'Ah, for God's sake, less of the sorries, pet. Now, before we all slit our wrists, let's take a little walk, will we?'

'Thanks, Mammy,' Rosie joked.

'Enough of the Mammy shite. Not that old,' Mary-Pat barked, but Rosie knew that she was pleased.

Later, much later, Rosie was kneeling on the bed, cursing and swearing, her face covered in a sheen of sweat. She felt as if she would split in two, so searing was the pain. The baby cannot come out that way, she told herself. He or she just can't. She won't fit. A cold sheen of sweat broke out on her forehead and a wave of exhaustion swept over her. She leaned forward and rested her head on the pillow. She was done. She'd had it. She couldn't give birth to this baby and that was it. She leaned her head against her arms and moaned softly to herself. She could hear the two women arguing somewhere behind her, but it felt as if she were underwater, unable to surface. She suddenly wanted Mark; wanted to have him hold her hand and crack jokes to distract her. He should be here, she told herself. Why didn't I tell him? I need him to be beside me. 'I need him here now,' she moaned softly to herself, then louder to Mary-Pat. 'Mary-Pat, I want Mark here now. Get him for me, please. I don't care what you have to do.'

'Let's just let Rosie calm down and gather herself for a few minutes, shall we?' Margaret was glaring at Mary-Pat.

'Look, if she gives up now, she'll just get too tired and won't be able to push,' Mary-Pat said.

'She's too tired now, Mary-Pat.' Margaret was trying a conciliatory tone.

'Ah, for feck's sake,' Mary-Pat said. 'Rosie, will you listen to me. That fellow of yours can't be here right now, because he's on the other side of the world, but we'll call him as soon as we can. Now, if you don't push, some pimply young one of a house doctor will be in here with the salad spoons to pull that baby out of you and, let me tell you, you won't like that. So when you get your next contraction, I want you to push harder than you've ever pushed before and we'll get this baby born, what do you say?'

Rosie nodded, a vision of a small doctor waving a very large pair of salad servers flashing into her mind, which alternately terrified and amused her, and she found herself laughing and crying at the same time as Margaret and Mary-Pat urged her on, whooping and cheering as if she were nearing the finishing line in a race, which she supposed she was, in a way. 'Oh, here's the head,' Mary-Pat squeaked. 'Feckin' fantastic, Rosie.'

Margaret tutted. 'Right, Rosie, one more push and we're there.'

Rosie thought the bottom half of her would just fall off. 'I have a bowling ball inside me,' she gasped. 'I can't push it out, it's too sore.'

ALL THAT I LEAVE BEHIND

'Well, you sure as hell can't keep it there,' Mary-Pat said. 'It won't like being jammed halfway up your ass, that's for sure.'

'Oh, Mary-Pat, stop,' Rosie said, bracing herself again as another contraction hit. She gritted her teeth and wondered if that burning sensation would just go on and on and whether she'd split open in the process. And then, she felt a gush of warm water leave her and the baby slid out, like a warm fish.

'Will you look at the head of hair on him,' Mary-Pat exclaimed. 'You've given birth to a mop.' She laughed as Margaret lifted a large pink thing covered in goo up.

'Congratulations, Rosie, you have a grand big boy.' She beamed and darted Mary-Pat a dagger look while she was at it.

He *was* big, Rosie thought. Big and red and angry, with his tiny fists clenched up close to his face and his eyes clamped shut, mouth wide open as he let out a loud roar.

'He has a fine set of lungs anyway.' Margaret laughed as she urged Rosie to sit down and began to tidy her up. 'You just hold him for a while, pet, and then we'll dress him to keep him warm.'

Rosie could feel herself tremble as she held her son, warm and heavy in her arms, a solid mass of gorgeous lobster pink, even now, little folds of fat at his wrists and ankles. Her teeth were chattering and her skin was covered in a riot of goosepimples, and the elation was like nothing she'd ever felt in her whole life.

'What the hell size is he anyway?' Mary-Pat marvelled. 'He looks like a sumo wrestler already, don't you, love?' At the sound of Mary-Pat's voice, he stopped roaring and listened, mewling quietly, then venturing to open his eyes, two inky black splashes underneath a heavy forehead. 'A chip off the old block, that's for sure, isn't that right, isn't it?' Mary-Pat burbled, hovering over Rosie's shoulder, a look of rapt attention on her face.

She gave Rosie a brief squeeze. 'I'm proud of you, pet. There's plenty of women who'd have the C-section booked for a grand fellow like himself, but you made it look easy. Well done.'

Rosie was speechless, looking down at her son as he gave a huge yawn, uncurling his fists so that his hands, which were wrinkly like an old man's, made a starfish shape, then curled up again as he made a little moue with his mouth. You're mine, she thought. You're mine and I can't quite believe it.

He twisted his head now and opened and closed his mouth like a goldfish. 'Oh, he wants a feed already, the greedy so-and-so.' Mary-Pat laughed. 'Will we set you up, love, and you can get started?'

Feeding? God, I have to do that, Rosie thought. I am responsible for this baby's survival. The thought made her feel panicky and elated at the same time as she let Mary-Pat lift the baby to her breast, where he latched on as if he was to die of thirst, fixing her with a beady stare as he did so.

'He's no wallflower, that's for sure,' Margaret said, laughing. 'He won't fade away, anyway.'

'He will not. He's an O'Connor through and through.' Mary-Pat beamed, lifting his bottom up and tucking him in tight against Rosie. An O'Connor; Rosie turned the name over in her head as the room fell into a contented silence, thinking that it was the first time that any of them had thought it was a name to be proud of. She felt the tears fill her eyes and spill over onto her cheeks and soon she was sobbing, clutching her soft, warm little bundle to her.

'It's the shock, love. You've just climbed a mountain and you need to sit for a while and take in the scenery,' Mary-Pat said, rubbing her shoulder.

'That's right,' Margaret agreed. 'And we'll just need a bit of quiet so you can deliver the placenta and then we can tidy you up.' She shot Mary-Pat a meaningful glare.

But Mary-Pat continued, 'And none of that shite about wanting to eat it or bury it in the garden. All that New-Age nonsense.'

Rosie knew that her sister was trying to distract her while Margaret worked away, and she was grateful. Her teeth were chattering and she wanted nothing more than a cup of tea. A cup of tea and Mark. 'He should be here, Mary-Pat. I shouldn't have done it without him. What was I thinking? I wanted him to be free of me and all of this ... stuff that I seem to bring with me. I didn't want to tie him down.'

Mary-Pat shushed her. 'For a start, that stuff, as you call it, is you, Rosie. You might not like it, but it's who you are. And I have a feeling that that fellah of yours is strong enough to cope with it. He's a good man, Rosie, better than that eejit you married anyway. You dodged a bullet there, love, when he vamoosed.'

'Mary-Pat!'

'Well, contradict me if you disagree, Rosie,' her sister said crisply. 'And do you know what's more? The timing's never right, love, God knows, I should know,' she said, rolling her eyes to heaven and stroking her own small bump. 'Nothing is ever perfect, so you just have to get on and make the most of the life you have.'

Rosie sighed. Her sister was right, of course. She was always bloody right. 'Let me take himself for a moment,' Mary-Pat said. 'We'll clean him up. Won't we, my little sausage?' she crooned, taking him in her arms. 'Yes, we will, we will ...' Her voice faded as she went out the door and it closed behind her.

Rosie leaned back on her pillow and closed her eyes for a moment. It was a lovely summer evening and through the open window of the room she could hear the clatter and hum of city life, could smell the faint metallic odour of petrol fumes, and she longed to be back on the towpath, smelling the sweet clover in the grass, hearing the rushes whispering in the wind. She could feel herself drifting now, even as the thought nudged at the edge of her mind that she wanted the baby back from wherever Mary-Pat had taken him. She wanted him in her arms. And she wanted Mark beside her. And if he couldn't be beside her, because of her own silly pride, she'd need the next best thing. She pulled herself up in the bed, reaching out to the bedside locker and pulling her bag onto the bed. God, the pain. She'd never have another baby.

She thought for a few moments. How could she say what she needed to say in a text − how could she explain it all? And then she had an idea, and she began to type, fingers clammy on the phone screen. And, before she could tell herself not to, she pressed 'send'. Then she smiled and leaned her head back on the pillow and fell asleep.

21

*M*ary-Pat had reluctantly agreed to let Margaret bathe and clean her nephew and she supposed the woman would manage, she thought now, as she sipped tea in the hospital canteen. She'd picked mint tea, even though it tasted like mouthwash, because caffeine wasn't good for the baby. Mind you, nothing was good for the baby now, was it? It seemed you could eat nothing at all nowadays; no prawns or tuna or smelly cheese. She'd lived on tuna when she'd been expecting Melissa, not knowing she'd been filling her daughter's brain with mercury. It seemed that people had become so cautious nowadays, afraid to take any risks at all. Everything was a danger, a hazard. But, sure, where would you be without taking a risk?

She sipped the warm mouthwash, wincing slightly as she did so. Funny, Rosie being a mum. Part of Mary-Pat always thought of her sister as a child, forever dancing around in a fairy costume that June had made her out of an old pair of curtains. She looked as if she were hardly old enough, but she was thirty-two, and Melissa and John-Patrick had been at school when Mary-Pat was the same age.

And now, here she was again. Mary-Pat closed her eyes at the thought of it. She'd never have the energy for it at her age, all those sleepless nights, the feeding and the colic, but she supposed she'd have to. And John-Patrick and Melissa would help, in spite of themselves. They were good kids.

PJ, once he'd got over the shock of it, had set his shoulders and said they'd just have to get on with it. 'Kids keep you young anyway,' he'd said, in a way that had made Mary-Pat guffaw with laughter. 'I know, I don't sound very convincing, but we'll be good parents, MP, I know we will. We *are* good parents.'

They said that babies couldn't save a marriage, and Mary-Pat knew that, but she also knew that this baby came after the fact, so to speak, so it didn't count. The marriage had been saved, and the baby was the result, so it was a win-win situation, she supposed. And it had all been worth it anyway, to hold PJ in her arms and feel close to him again, to feel protected, with her man by her side. You can stuff that up your gingham pinny, she'd thought as she'd lain there with PJ after, thinking of that young one and her bright smile. This man's taken.

It was funny, Mary-Pat thought as she relived the rest of that evening, looking out the hospital window, that he'd said that she was still the girl he used to know. She wasn't. She'd changed and for the better, she liked to think. She knew that she was still capable of sharp words, but at least now she could think before she opened her great big trap. At least, most of the time. The words didn't come bursting out of her before she'd had time to edit them, probably because she wasn't keeping them down all the time. Now, she was more inclined to say what was really on her mind and not just bark out smart comments.

They'd had plenty of time to chat, herself and PJ. Sure the sex had been over in about five minutes, the pair of them were in such a hurry. They'd taken their time later, but the first ... well, it made Mary-Pat blush to think of it, the way he'd grabbed the cord of the dressing gown when she was halfway up the stairs and then, oh, it had been fast and furious and just fantastic. She'd got carpet burn on her rear end and this little person to show for it, she thought, rubbing her stomach. It was like starting all over again.

She hadn't breathed a single word to PJ about the family stuff. She knew that it wasn't probably in the spirit of their new start together, but she didn't want to burden him with it. And because she knew that he really didn't want to hear it. He'd pretend he did – he'd listen attentively and ask lots of questions, but she'd know that he'd be cringing inside, waiting for the latest revelation to be over. She knew this because he'd been in no hurry to ask her why she wasn't on the phone to her sister gabbing the way she normally did. She'd rung June once, but the conversation had been stilted and she'd hung up after five minutes, not sure that they'd ever speak again. Not like they used to anyway. She didn't power walk down to Pi's either or make her daily visit to Daddy. Now, she went twice a week, on Wednesdays and Sundays, and if she felt guilty about it, she'd remind herself that she'd more than done her bit – and anyway, guilt wasn't going to be the driving force in her life. Not any more. Daddy was safe and comfortable and as happy as any man could be in his condition. Imelda had let her bring Duke with her and Daddy found comfort in that, sitting in his armchair, hand resting on Duke's head, before looking at her and asking for the hundredth time, 'Are you Jim Brogan's girl, Ailbhe?'

'That's right. That's me,' Mary-Pat would agree, the thought that, at last, he'd forgotten her name making her feel light-headed with relief. It was as if a weight had literally been taken off her shoulders. A yoke. Her family had been part of her life for far too long. It was time her marriage and her children took centre stage.

Anyway, the kids still needed her, at least a bit. They didn't want her standing over them, but they still liked to have her around, to chat to, to tell her about their plans and to ask her advice and then to tell her she didn't have a clue what she was talking about. Melissa had announced that she wanted to be in a reality TV show the other day, which Mary-Pat had just said was lovely altogether, congratulating herself that she hadn't torn a strip off the girl. And John-Patrick, well, he seemed to have found himself a bit more in the last month or two. He still liked the computer games, so that made him a bit of a nerd, she supposed, but that Swedish girl seemed to have cheered him up. God knows what they were getting up to, but she tried not to think about it too much, apart from telling John-Patrick to act responsibly. In fairness to him, he didn't state the obvious.

She took another sip of her tea and looked at her watch, wondering if PJ had got stuck in traffic. He and Pi were driving up together with the kids to see the new little man because there was no way in the world she was letting her brother rattle into the car park in that heap of junk of his.

She was glad Pi was back, mind you. And glad that he'd made the first move. It was big of him, she had to admit. He'd appeared on her doorstep one morning after Easter in a smart-looking jacket and a new pair of jeans. 'Well, will you look at himself,' she'd said, trying to conceal her delight at seeing her brother. 'Very debonair.'

He'd blushed then, and of course the penny had dropped. There could only be one reason why a man would look that happy – or dress that well. 'What's her name?'

He'd shuffled from foot to foot, muttering something about it being early days. 'Ehm, it's Daphne, you know, Rosie's friend,' and then he'd blushed to the roots of his hair, stroking Jessie's silky ears to avoid making eye contact.

Christ almighty, Mary-Pat had thought. The girl was practically half his age. She'd had to use every ounce of her new-found self-control not to say it, though. 'Come on in,' she'd told him then. 'I'll put the kettle on.'

They'd chatted about everything and nothing, the way they usually did, both of them carefully skirting the topic of the family conference. She suspected that they weren't ready for that yet. So she'd told him about the baby and he'd looked stunned, but only for a second, God bless him, and then he'd thrown his arms around her, giving her a tight squeeze. 'I'm lost for words,' he'd eventually admitted.

'You're not the only one,' she'd said wryly, and they'd both had a laugh at that.

'Actually, that's why I've come.' He'd cleared his throat, refusing her offer of a second cup of tea. 'It's Rosie. She's, ehm, in the same condition,' and he'd nodded in the direction of her bump.

Mary-Pat just couldn't believe it. The shock of it. Out of force of habit, she'd looked around for any sign of her fags, but remembered then that she was off them. She'd have to cope with this news without them. Her baby sister, pregnant, and she'd never said a word to her. And Melissa, that madam, she knew all along. That was why she was down there all the time...

Mary-Pat had felt the bitchy words forming in her throat, the hurt bursting out of her, but then she'd stopped herself. Was it any wonder Rosie had said nothing? Why on earth would she, after all that had happened? Poor little thing. 'I'll go down to her later.' She'd stood up, pushing her chair back with a scrape on the kitchen floor. 'She'll be needing help with everything. Has she got a buggy, do you know? I think I have a spare one up in the attic—'

'MP, sit down a second,' Pius had said, placing a hand on her arm.

'What?' Mary-Pat had sat down on the chair.

He'd cleared his throat. 'I think it has to come from her, MP. After everything, you know ...'

Mary-Pat had felt her heart sink like a stone. 'I suppose you're right. But how will she manage? She'll need me, I know she will.'

'Well, she has Daphne, and me — I've been to two scans so far and an antenatal class,' he'd chuckled.

'Fair dues, Pi.' Mary-Pat had managed a smile, and then she'd added, 'Do you think you might show me the scan pictures the next time you come up? I know I shouldn't without asking, but I just need to see them, do you know?' I need to feel that I'm looking out for her, she thought, that I'm there for her, even if I can't say it.

She'd paused then, toying with the sugar in the bowl, scooping it up with a teaspoon and letting it trickle back in. 'I'm sorry about everything, Pi. It's just ... I was trying to protect her. I couldn't see what good the truth would serve.'

Pi had shifted in his chair. 'I know. I know you were, MP. And we were all guilty, if that's any consolation. We all knew, in various ways, and we said nothing, so we share the blame, whatever there is of it.'

'Hmm.' Mary-Pat had been silent then. 'Do you wish you'd looked at the letters? I sometimes do,' she'd said sadly.

Pi had looked anguished. 'At one stage in my life, I'd have given my left arm to hear from Mammy. Just one word, that's all. Something to let us know that she still loved us. That she still cared.' He shook his head then. 'Ah, sure what's the point, MP, in going on about it now? What good will raking over the past do? We have to move forward. We have no choice.'

'It might help us understand, I suppose,' Mary-Pat had said thoughtfully. 'Do you know I've been seeing a therapist? I know, who'd have thought it. Me?' She'd laughed at Pi's look of incredulity. 'It really helps. I know it won't bring her back or help me to understand why she left us like that, but it helps me to make sense of how I feel about it, if you see what I mean.'

'We never will understand, will we, Mary-Pat?' Pius said quietly.

'No, that's one of the things about it. Even if we ask her, she won't tell us, I know that. At least, she won't tell us the truth. Even if we send a message through the envoy up in Dublin,' and she rolled her eyes to heaven.

'You haven't forgiven her, then,' Pi had said softly.

Mary-Pat had thought of the phone call she'd made the previous week; the conversation that just seemed to peter out after a few minutes, with June finally announcing that she had a few things to do and Mary-Pat putting the phone down, wondering if she'd have been better off not having picked it up — maybe it was too early for either of them. 'I'm probably being too hard on her, Pi, I know that. Maybe I'm just jealous that she got to talk to Mammy and I never did. I'd say that's it, to be honest. I wish it had been me that Mammy had confided in, you know? I know that if it had been me, I'd probably have done exactly the same thing as June. I'd have kept it all to myself because I'd have been so thrilled about it.'

She could see from his face that he'd been surprised at that, at the honesty of it. 'It's true, Pi. Might not make me look very good, but it's true.' Mary-Pat had shrugged. And then she'd asked, 'What about Rosie? Will she forgive us, do you think, Pi?'

He hadn't said anything for a while. He'd got up slowly and had put his jacket on, pushing the chair gently back in under the table. Then he'd said, 'Give her time, MP. Just give her time.'

He was a good man, Pi, and he'd been a rock to Rosie, that was for sure, Mary-Pat thought as she looked at her watch again. It was visiting time, so she hoped they'd get a bloody move on. She wondered then if that Frances O'Brien would turn up too. Maybe not. Mary-Pat wasn't sure if Rosie had told her anything, and maybe it was best if she waited.

Mary-Pat had taken Duke for a little walk down to the woman's place one morning after that bloody family conference, to fill her in, that her dark little secret was now out in the open. Mary-Pat knew it was cruel, but the woman hardly deserved to have her feelings minded, now, did she? But then she'd seen the look on the woman's face, the way she'd gone as white as a sheet and clung to the doorframe, and she'd understood that it had probably brought it all up again for her. She wouldn't see it as a fresh start, or a new life; she'd probably be remembering every bit of her own sad little story, and no amount of that praying she did could disguise it.

She'd almost felt sorry for the woman then, as the two of them had stood on the doorstep, Duke whining to get off the lead. 'I have just one question,' Mary-Pat had asked. 'Why? Why did you leave Rosie like that? Why did you abandon her?'

Frances O'Brien had trembled then, her body shaking in her pink fluffy dressing gown. Eventually, she'd said, 'She needed more than I could give her. She needed a family.'

Mary-Pat had waited, knowing that there was more. The woman had clutched the collar of the dressing gown tightly around her and bit her lip. 'Do you remember we met that time in the supermarket?'

Mary-Pat had nodded. How could she forget? The sight of her in that big woolly jumper, looking like the loneliest woman in the world. The outcast.

'Well, that's what decided me. I was all alone and I had nothing. No family, no friends, no money. I had nothing to offer a baby. But you ... you all had each other.' The acid in her tone was hard to ignore. 'I knew straight away that that was my only choice. To give my child what she needed.'

Mary-Pat wasn't sure whether to believe her story, that she'd made the ultimate sacrifice for her child's sake, but then, she'd never had to make that choice, had she? 'And besides,' Frances O'Brien had said then, as if anticipating Mary-Pat's next thought, 'I knew that everyone would blame me, no matter what. Nobody would blame John-Joe. I'd be the woman who ripped your family apart, not him. It's always the woman, isn't it?'

The bitterness was suddenly so strong, Mary-Pat could almost taste it. The woman was right, in a way. She'd been the Scarlet Woman, in spite of the fact that Daddy ... Mary-Pat couldn't bear to think of it any longer. And anyway, Daddy had lost everything too. He'd lost the only woman he'd ever really loved and, for him, that was everything. That was the irony: for all his messing about, Daddy only really loved Mammy.

'That's not quite right, Frances ...' she'd begun, but Frances had waved her away, her eyes glittering with tears.

'Don't tell me that I didn't make the right choice, Mary-Pat. I know that I did and nobody can tell me otherwise.'

Mary-Pat had nodded then because nothing more needed to be said.

Frances O'Brien had hesitated for a second, clutching the chain of her reading glasses, and then she'd laid a chilly hand on Mary-Pat's arm. 'Thank you for letting me know.'

Mary-Pat had shrugged. 'Yes, well, what good does all of this do if we don't learn from it? C'mon, Duke, let's go,' and she'd turned on her heel and marched back up the canal.

It was funny, Mary-Pat thought, that just a year ago she'd been in such a sweat about Rosie coming back. She'd felt as if her whole life was under threat, that with Rosie home it would all fall apart. And she'd been right. It had fallen apart, but somehow, miraculously, it had all come back together again, in a different way. And she was a different woman now, she knew that. It had sure shaken them all up. And if she thought to ask herself about June, she'd quickly remind herself that what her sister had done was unforgivable, even if somewhere, deep down, Mary-Pat would have to admit to herself that she was glad that the whole thing about Mammy was out in the open. There were no secrets any more. But still, it was easier not to fully forgive June — that way Mary-Pat didn't have to think too much about her own actions. And anyway, some things could never be fixed, not properly anyway. Oh, well, Mary-Pat shrugged.

She'd better go and see if that midwife had managed to tidy her nephew up for his visitors.

She was about to get up and leave, putting her mobile into her handbag, when she felt a presence beside her, a cloud of that expensive perfume her sister wore, the one that always made Mary-Pat feel a bit sick.

She lifted her head slowly, and June was standing there, awkwardly clutching a large blue teddy bear, an ugly-looking thing that was nearly twice the size of her. Jesus, she looked like a train wreck, all angles, her hips too narrow for her jeans, with cheekbones that jutted out and big shadows under her eyes. Her hair looked a bit weird too, as if she'd dyed it some peculiar version of her usual expensive colour. She looked as if she'd aged ten years in the last few months. For a second, Mary-Pat felt sorry for her — she looked as if she'd been diminished, somehow, made tinier and more brittle by life.

'I was just thinking about you,' Mary-Pat blurted.

'Oh, really? Was it good?' June looked hopeful for a second, running her hand through her hair in that familiar gesture, but there were no expensive bracelets on her wrists, Mary-Pat noticed.

God, you can be an awful eejit sometimes, Junie, Mary-Pat thought. 'No.'

June flinched, clutching the teddy bear to her as if for protection, her face half-hidden under a mountain of blue fur. She whispered, 'I shouldn't have come. I knew it was a bad idea.' And she turned to walk away.

Mary-Pat sighed. 'For feck's sake, Junie, you're here now. We're not going to run you out of the hospital. Besides,' she nodded at the monstrous bear, 'you'll need to put that thing somewhere.'

June blushed. 'India bought it. I would have picked something more tasteful,' she added.

'It won't go unnoticed anyway,' Mary-Pat said. 'C'mon, visiting's nearly over and I want to have a hold of him. He's a gorgeous fellow.'

June's face lit up. 'Is he? Who's he like?'

'Oh, his dad. He won't be kicking him out of the cave, that's for sure. And it's not the Yank, so you can breathe a sigh of relief, like the rest of us.'

'Oh.' June looked startled for a moment. 'Whose is it?'

'It's a very long story,' Mary-Pat said briefly. 'I wouldn't know where to start, but we'll sit down later, will we, and I'll tell you.'

June made that flapping motion with her hand, the one she always made when she was agitated. 'Oh, it's none of my business, really ...' and then she changed tack, dropping her shoulders, the tension draining from her face. 'What am I saying? I'd love to talk,' and June looked as if a weight had been lifted off her shoulders. And then she paused. 'Will Rosie be OK if I come?'

Mary-Pat shrugged. 'No idea, but what's the alternative? Are you going to lurk outside with that daft bear? Take the bull by the horns, Junie, that's what I say.'

June stood a little taller then, her grip relaxing around the teddy bear. And then she said, 'I missed you, Mary-Pat.'

'Ah, enough of that shite, Junie,' Mary-Pat began, but June waved her away. 'I need to say this, please.' And she took a deep breath. 'Mary-Pat, I'm sorry. I truly am. I never intended to keep anything from you — that wasn't the reason I never told you about Mammy's letters — I just wanted to keep the lines of communication open and ... well, I missed Mammy so much. I can't tell you what it was like just to be able to talk to her again.'

'Lucky you,' Mary-Pat said dryly.

'I know, it was selfish,' June murmured. 'If it's any help, I've broken off contact,' she began, when a large elderly woman with a full tray of roast dinner pushed by her, muttering something about people clogging the place up with expensive toys and would they ever not just move out of the way. June would normally have been all apologies, offering to help the old bat with her tray, but instead now she just turned to the woman and said, 'Do you mind? I'm trying to have a conversation here.'

Mary-Pat fought off the laugh bubbling in her chest as June gave a sigh of exasperation. 'Look, I need to talk to you properly, Mary-Pat. I think we need that at least. But I want to know something first: will you forgive me?'

Mary-Pat had to think about it, looking at her sister's anxious face peering out from around that horrible blue bear. Part of her wanted to throw her arms around her sister and say yes, of course she'd bloody forgive her. But another part of her just didn't feel ready. She felt scarred by the whole thing, somehow, unsure whether she'd be able to trust her sister again. Eventually, she managed, 'Not in a hurry, Junie, but we'll work on it. OK?'

If June looked disappointed, she tried not to show it, pulling herself up a little straighter, balancing the teddy bear on her hip and composing her face into as dignified an expression as she could manage with a fifteen-pound teddy in her arms. 'Fine.' And then another pause as she tried to formulate the question which was clearly on her mind. 'Are you *pregnant*?'

Mary-Pat tried to look nonchalant, as if it was the most natural thing in the world for a woman of her age, a woman who was closer to the big knickers and the retirement home than most, to be about to become a parent. 'It's another long story, and I'd need a few glasses of wine — not that I can drink them, but still … Now, let's go and say hello to the new O'Connor.'

'Is he an O'Connor or will he have his dad's name?'

'For feck's sake, Junie, who cares? Get a move on or the child will be one by the time we get to see him.' And Mary-Pat tucked her arm into her sister's and dragged her along the corridor to the maternity ward.

Later, when she got home, she sat down on the edge of the bed and rubbed her sore feet, and then she lay back on the bed and closed her eyes for a few moments. She was dog tired, but she knew she wouldn't sleep: the events of the day kept rolling around and around in her mind. It seemed that after years and years of being stuck, things had all come flying loose at the same time: Rosie's lovely little man, now probably roaring his lungs out at the hospital; the whole thing with June; PJ and herself and the new life that now lay in front of them. Mary-Pat felt herself grow dizzy at the thought of it all. I need to calm down, she told herself firmly, wishing to God she could take a pill and go to sleep.

And then she thought of the shell. She reached out for her handbag, pulling it onto the bed and rummaged around in it until she found it, the nubbly surface warm beneath her hand. She pulled it out of her bag and she put it up to her ear. She closed her eyes and heard the hiss of the sea and saw herself on the beach at Carnsore with Mammy that hot summer's day, all those years ago, and as she did, her breathing began to slow. She could see the waves breaking gently onto the stony little beach, could feel the hot sun on her skin. 'Every time you listen, think of me,' Mammy had said, but when Mary-Pat tried to think of Mammy, she just couldn't call a picture of her up in her mind. She seemed to have gone all blurry, and the more Mary-Pat tried, the more indistinct she became. She's fading on me, Mary-Pat thought. After all this time, she's fading away.

22

Five Months Later

*R*osie couldn't understand why Pi insisted on squashing them all into the Beetle, but for some reason he seemed to think that it was appropriate, that they all needed to make this pilgrimage in the old car. 'It'll remind us of all the times Mammy took us on day trips when we were kids.' Rosie hadn't the heart to tell him that it wouldn't remind her of anything at all, as she hadn't been part of that life with Mammy. That she had only been on one trip with her and it hadn't exactly been a day trip. But she was so pleased to hear Mammy's name spoken like that, normally, the way you would about anyone's mother, that she said she'd be happy to. Because going on a day trip with her brother and sisters meant that they were a family. A real family, not a collection of individuals, a family who did the kind of things that all families did. And besides, Josh had never seen the sea.

She didn't need to take him — there wasn't enough room in the Beetle, and Mark said he'd take him for a walk to his favourite place, the little marina at Porterstown to look at the fish. It was something they did together, every single morning, because he wanted to have his son to himself for an hour. 'Making up for lost time,' he'd put it once, and Rosie had felt the flush of shame at his words. She'd been so selfish, she knew that, and, that first time he'd held his son in his arms, she'd tried to explain: that it was too soon, that there was so much to understand, and somehow, she needed to find her own way back onto the path, but he'd shaken his head. 'No. No more explaining. I'm here now.' He'd looked at the little bundle in his arms, at the face that so resembled his. 'My son.' And then he'd looked at her as if he could hardly believe it, lifting the baby to his face and covering his head with kisses.

'Yes, your son.'

'Ehm, what did we call him?'

'Josh.'

He'd made a face then.

'What's wrong with Josh?'

'Nothing,' he'd smiled. 'But he needs a Vietnamese name, too.'

So he'd been called 'Vien', or 'complete'. And here he was, sitting between her and June. It seemed important to Rosie that he come; that he wouldn't miss out on a thing. At five months old he was hardly likely to remember, but that didn't matter. She'd be able to tell him about it later, to say, 'you were there,' and that seemed important to her.

Pius didn't protest, bless him, when she asked him to fit the car seat, spending the previous afternoon grunting with exertion as he tightened the bolt that attached to the temporary seatbelt into the single bench seat in the back of the car. 'To think we used to balance you across our knees,' he'd joked, wiping the sweat from his forehead. Rosie had tried to tell him that she could probably manage herself, but he didn't like that. He liked to take charge these days, even if she joked with him that he was turning into Mary-Pat.

Eventually, he'd managed to squash it into position, but only right in the middle of the seat, so Rosie and June had to sit either side of Josh. They let Mary-Pat have the front seat, because, as she kept telling them, she was 'about to drop', so they could hardly not. As it was, they'd had to help her in, lowering her onto the seat, with Rosie lifting her legs into the footwell. 'Jesus H. Christ, I'm too old for this lark,' she sighed. 'Too feckin' old. Could we not have taken the Jeep, Pi? Feck's sake.'

June sighed and rolled her eyes to heaven behind her sister. 'I saw that,' Mary-Pat barked.

'Yes, well, if you *will* keep moaning, MP. For goodness' sake, you're pregnant, not at death's door,' June said crisply. June had taken to saying a lot of things crisply, or briskly, that old half-smile that she used to wear now gone, along with the constant diplomacy. Her face looked better without that rictus, Rosie thought, more relaxed, and she could read her sister's emotions more easily. It was funny how she'd gone one way and Mary-Pat the other, MP becoming more laid back and her sister more direct. It suited both of them. They'd changed in the past year. But then, Rosie supposed, they'd all changed.

'Did you bring everything?' June was asking now, as Josh reached out and clutched her index finger, wrapping his little pudgy fingers around it, his eyes crossing with the effort of lifting it closer to examine it. 'Oh, lovely baba,' she cooed. 'Lovely little boy.' Josh gurgled in agreement, his black eyes dancing. His father's eyes.

'I have the map anyway,' Pius shouted over the roar of the engine as he gunned the car down the towpath, a spray of gravel shooting out behind him.

'Jesus, take it easy, Pi. You used to be such a careful driver. What's with the Fernando Alonso act?' Mary-Pat muttered, hands pressed against the dashboard.

'I just feel like living on the edge, MP,' Pius joked, teasing her by putting his foot hard on the accelerator so that the car jolted forward. Mary-Pat gave a little scream. 'Very funny,' she said. Then she rummaged in her handbag and produced a large black shell, holding it up for the others to see. 'I brought mine. What about you, girls?'

'Do I have to give away the original?' June moaned. 'It's just, I have things marked in the margins and I want to keep them. Otherwise I can't remember properly.' She looked at the tattered copy of *Gone with the Wind* on her lap. 'I need to remember,' she said sadly.

'I thought that was the whole idea,' Mary-Pat said. 'That we'd try to forget, or at least to pretend we were forgetting, even though there's no question of it, is there?' she said gaily. 'It's symbolic, that's what it is, to give us some closure, as they say on all those American talk shows. Oprah's a great fan of closure.'

Rosie couldn't imagine that you could get any closure by doing what they were doing – taking a little trip to the beach like this on a cold December afternoon. Mammy's leaving wasn't the kind of thing that you could just wrap up and leave behind you, neatly filing it under 'the past' and moving on. It had changed their lives, had changed them in all kinds of ways. Maybe they were only just beginning to discover their true selves now that they'd stopped trying to push the past away. Maybe they'd begun to accept that things were much easier if they faced up to the past, accepted that it had happened. That they couldn't change it, no matter how far or hard they ran from it. Look at her, she'd gone six thousand miles away and it had just gone right along with her, dogging her days, casting its shadow over her new life, even her relationship with Craig. Because it wasn't all his fault, she knew that now. He'd accepted her exactly as she was: how was he to know that that wasn't the real her at all?

Or maybe it was Mark that had changed her, she wasn't really sure. She was suspicious of the idea that one person could change another. It just didn't work like that. Maybe it was that he'd made her more herself. She'd put on weight since Josh was born — or rather she hadn't lost the baby weight, the kind the other mums in the village all moaned about, but which she actually liked. She liked her new softness. It felt different somehow, and she wondered if she'd developed a personality to match her new, fuller shape — more relaxed, less anxious, ready to laugh again like she used to, to enjoy being silly and having fun.

'The mother of my child,' Mark would call her, giving her a gentle squeeze around her middle, the little pads of fat that hadn't gone away since she'd had Josh. She'd push him away, laughing. 'I wish you'd stop calling me that, it's nauseating.'

'I would if you'd agree to marry me,' he'd say softly, the way he did at least a dozen times a day, putting up his hands and saying, 'All right, all right,' when she playfully punched him on the shoulder. The truth was she didn't want to get married, not again. Once had been bad enough, but she knew how much Mark wanted it, so she knew she'd probably have to do it eventually.

But she'd made him promise not to put her through another wedding. Weddings were jinxed as far as she was concerned. Besides, they already had a wedding to go to in the spring, in Italy. It had been Pi's idea and himself and Daphne and Dara had planned to spend a few months out there, 'living the good life' as he put it, courtesy of his new cash crop that had replaced the weed, which he'd manage to dispose of without setting fire to half of Monasterard in the process. Rosie had no idea that bean sprouts could be that lucrative, but there you go, what did she know? Them and the lovely potager that Pius had nursed into being and which to Rosie was a thing of wonder: the lovely beds full of leafy chard and fennel and kohlrabi, vegetables she hadn't even known existed, planted side by side with nasturtiums and peonies and cosmos. It was lovely, magnificent really, and realising Mammy's vision had given Pi a new lease of life, a new confidence and a new drive. At long last he could see a future for himself in which he was the main actor, of which he was in charge. And it had brought him Daph and Dara.

No, she wouldn't marry Mark just yet, she thought, because she wouldn't do it to please him. Pleasing someone else hadn't served her well. But they would move house, because if she had to spend another day in Mark's place she'd go completely mad. The little blue house was far too small now, particularly since Josh seemed to require enough high-tech equipment to fill a spacecraft. Mark could make all the jokes he liked about passing food out to her through the cat flap while she lived in the garden. Anyway, they'd be moving into the house while Pi was away so that she could try not to kill his garden and Mark could work on his new restaurant, a proper authentic Vietnamese. No curried chips or garlic mayonnaise in sight. It was funny how his mother used to talk about going back to Vietnam when they were kids as if it were some mythical Tír na nÓg, as if their stay in Kildare was only temporary, a staging post on their way back to where they belonged. And yet, he had gone 'home' and had come back to her and to Josh. Maybe that was where home was, Rosie thought, wherever your family was. She knew that because she'd found it too.

As she looked at the fields whizz past as they sped along the road towards Wexford, Rosie hardly dared admit it to herself, how grateful she was for the life she now had, and how, even now, the fear still lurked in the back of her mind that any minute it could all be taken away. She knew it wasn't logical, that she should just live in the moment, be mindful as the latest jargon would put it, but there was a tiny bit of her that just couldn't let go. Maybe it was because she'd seen enough of what letting go could do – living in the moment hadn't exactly served her parents well. She thought of her mother now, in her little cottage, with her miraculous medals and her relics of Padre Pio, who thought that praying a lot was a substitute for living, but Rosie could hardly blame her. She'd suffered enough.

They had a cautious friendship, Frances and herself, and Rosie wondered if they'd ever have anything more; there were too many questions that still had to be answered, too much water under the bridge. And she also knew that she could never see her as her mother. To do that would be to ignore the woman who had given up so much to raise her. And that was sad, but Rosie knew that neither of them could do much about it. And Frances adored Josh, pouring all her maternal feelings into him, forever asking to babysit, insisting that she mind him when Rosie went back to work and to finish her degree, a look on her face that suggested that she'd be devastated if Rosie refused. And of course, Rosie had had the good sense not to, to be grateful for what she was being offered.

She'd probably never get over that feeling deep inside, but she'd learn to accept it, to live with it, that tiny anxiety, as the small price she'd pay for her happiness, she thought now, holding up Mammy's ring to show the others that she'd remembered, feeling it's nubbly, bumpy surface for the last time.

'All present and correct,' Mary-Pat had said triumphantly, 'and I have the writing box in the footwell, not that I can reach down to my ankles nowadays. I haven't seen my toes in about six months.' And she beamed a smile of pure happiness, patting the huge mound of her stomach with a sigh of satisfaction. Rosie had to admire her sister: after a lifetime of grafting, of looking after everyone other than herself, here she was, about to do it all over again. She'd spent her whole life railing against something that seemed to come to her naturally. Maybe it was because she wasn't spending all of her energy on Daddy, on propping him up, guilt propelling her up to St Benildus's every single day. Now, she went twice a week: once with Duke and once with Rosie, Josh sitting on her knee examining Mary-Pat's key chain with the silver fish on it, while the two of them chatted and Daddy sat there, a faraway look in his eyes. And then, in a moment of lucidity, he'd ask to hold Josh. Daddy liked babies, he always had, and even though he gave no sign that he recognised either of them, he was happy to dandle Josh on his knee and to sing 'Báidín Fheilimí', the gentle tune they'd all learned in school, often lulling Josh to sleep. 'Haven't lost my touch,' Daddy would say, handing him back gently to Rosie.

'No, you haven't indeed, Daddy,' Mary-Pat would reply. It was their signal to leave, and they'd both walk off down the corridor with Josh, and Rosie would think about that first time she'd visited him and had first understood where life had taken him. How sad she'd been at the loss of it, how shocked at the sight of him so diminished. She would wonder if he'd ever thought to question his life and the choices he'd made, and she'd thank him, too, for having said those words at her wedding. The change had been hard and painful, but if he had never spoken, if he hadn't turned her whole life upside down, hers and everyone else's, they'd probably have spent the rest of their lives living in the past. And that was no life at all.

'Right ... it's here somewhere,' Pius was saying, slowing the engine down and turning onto a long, straight road bordered by threadbare hawthorn hedges, the grey-blue smudge of the sea just visible at the end. They were all silent as they drove on, until they got to a crossroads. 'Carnsore Strand' read a brown sign with a fishing rod on it that pointed left, but Pius turned right instead. 'If they're anything like the boyos at home, they'll have turned the signs around,' he said. 'And anyway, I seem to remember it being this way.' And he was right: a hundred yards later, a drift of sand covered the tarmac and a red-and-white bollard announced the end of the road that led to the sea.

'Hang on, MP, I'll help you out,' June was saying, opening the door, a blast of icy air shooting into the car. When she got out, her hair blew up around her face, which turned instantly blue, and she mouthed, 'It's freezing.'

'Ready, Joshie?' Rosie said, putting his arms into the padded all-in-one which she'd half-removed in the heat of the car and lifting him gently out of the seat. She held him for a second, his warm cheek next to hers, and she breathed him in, his scent of mashed banana and milk, the way his long black eyelashes fluttered against her cheek.

He sucked in a huge breath of shock when they stepped

outside into the freezing wind, his eyes round, his lips beginning to quiver. Rosie bounced him up and down to soothe him, pointing to the churning grey waves. 'Look, Joshie, the sea.'

'Right, let's get this over with before we all freeze to death,' Mary-Pat was saying. She held the writing box open. Pius was first, carefully folding the garden plan and putting it in. June hesitated for a second then put the book in, kissing her hand first and then placing it on the book. 'Oh, I can't bear it,' she muttered, her eyes filling with tears. Mary-Pat put the shell gently in then closed the box and tucked her arm into June's. 'All set, Rosie?' She looked at Rosie enquiringly, her eyes bright, her cheeks pink with the cold. For a moment, she looked like the girl Rosie remembered as a child, with her bright eyes and rosy cheeks, singing a song as she fried bacon on the pan for tea. It was as if the years had been rolled back and she was fourteen, free from the weight of all that had followed.

Rosie's hand hovered over the box in mid-air, the ring dangling in space. She tried to loosen the grip of her fingers, but they clung onto the ring as if of their own will. 'Could I ... ehm, would it be OK if I just put it in when we find the right spot? I just need another minute.'

Mary-Pat didn't reply, just reached out and squeezed Rosie's arm, then turned to June. 'C'mon, love, let's go and find a good spot, will we?' The two of them walked off towards the dunes in the early-winter light, towards the sea, the grey waves crashing on the stones. Rosie could hear the two of them talking. 'Do you remember the day we came down here with that fellow, what was his name?' Mary-Pat was saying.

'Bob,' June said. 'And you and I started fighting and Mammy slapped me. Oh, I'll never forget that slap – I can still feel the sting now.' She smiled. 'I had no idea what was going on in their lives, did you? I just knew I'd done something to make Mammy angry.'

'There was nothing we could have done, love,' Mary-Pat was saying. 'Nothing at all.'

For a moment, Rosie tried to follow what her sisters were talking about but then she relaxed. There was no point, she realised. She'd spent her whole life trying to follow conversations she didn't entirely understand, trying to feel part of the family by taking their memories as her own, by claiming that, of course, she could remember the time they'd gone to the funfair or the demonstration, when she really didn't have a clue. She hadn't been there. She had her own memories instead: of Daddy and herself walking through the fields to school, of Pius teaching her how to tie a fly or start a fire with two sticks, of Mary-Pat spending a whole rainy afternoon with her, rolling out pastry and cutting it into the shape of a shamrock because Sr Fidelma had asked them to bring something in for St Patrick's Day.

'Let me take that little fellow.' Pius was beside her now, gently pulling Josh out of her arms and tucking him onto his hip. Josh didn't protest because he loved his Uncle Pi, his gentleness and his sense of strength and the fact that he didn't fuss over him like his aunties did, making those funny, high-pitched squealing sounds that made him wince. They walked to where Mary-Pat and June were standing, June bending down to pick up the stones while Mary-Pat pointed and gave orders. 'For God's sake, MP, I'm going as fast as I can,' June was saying, her hands damp as she clawed at the sand, a grimace on her face. She didn't like dirt, June.

'I'd better give her a hand.' Pi smiled, reaching into his pocket and pulling out a small fold-up trowel in a little purple carry-case. 'I bought this just in case.' June was only too happy to let Pi dig, and in no time they were all standing over a sizeable hole, a little puddle of water gathering at the bottom of it. For a second, Rosie wondered if it was the right kind of place: it looked so dark and wet and cold, like a grave. As if they were burying her under the sand. But she wasn't dead. She was out there somewhere, living her life, moving forward while they'd all stood still. She looked at Pius for a second and he must have read her thoughts because he reached out and squeezed her arm. 'We're not burying her, Rosie love. It's not her we're laying to rest; it's the past. We have to let go of it now,' he said gently.

'You're right.' She nodded quietly, but she held onto Mammy's ring, running her fingers over the rough surface for the last time. It was the only thing she had left that tied her to Mammy, she thought. Just one ring. And then she looked down at it, at the ripple of white running through the purple stone, at the scratches on the dull silver, and she thought, it's just a ring. That's all it is. We invest objects with all of our memories and feelings, but at the end of the day, they're just things. It's the memories that remain. I don't need Mammy's ring to remind me because I know I won't ever forget her.

She found her grip loosening on the ring, and she dropped it in, hearing it clatter against the dark wood, and then she looked up and her sisters were both smiling at her. We're here, they were saying. We're always here.

They all watched as Pius put the box gently inside, covering it up again with the sand and then a thick covering of stones.

'Should we say a prayer?' June said.

Mary-Pat roared with laughter. 'Mammy would kill you stone dead if you said a prayer. How about we just put a stone each on

top and say whatever it is we have to say. To ourselves of course —
we don't need to spill it all out like we're at some kind of group
therapy session.'

Pius looked at Rosie and the two of them tried hard not to
smile. 'You first, Pi,' Mary-Pat commanded.

And that's what they did. They stood there around the little
mound on the beach, the bitter wind whipping around them,
and they each placed a stone on top, standing there for a few
moments and then nodding to say that they'd finished. Rosie
found a pure white stone with a streak of purple in it that she
thought Mammy would have approved of, and she and Josh
placed it gently on top of the large smooth grey one Pi had
selected, his little fingers clasped around hers.

When it came to her turn, she had the words ready in her
mind, but then she realised she couldn't use them. She was a
mother herself now and she knew how hard-won that word was,
how much it meant. 'Goodbye, Michelle,' she said to herself. It
was time to stop calling her Mammy now.

May 2012

Michelle

'*M*rs O'Connor?' The nurse is a lovely young woman with skin the colour of chocolate, and when she calls out my name I take a while to come back to myself, to realise that I'm sitting on a hard plastic seat outside a doctor's office in a hospital in the city, a full five hours on dusty roads from the village. I have a thick file in my hand, with my X-rays in it. The doctor first showed them to me just three weeks ago, the small shadow on my lung the size of a ten-pence piece. It looked harmless, like the radiographer had just put a thumb across my ribcage, but it's not and it had to be cut out of me. When I think of it, that area in my chest contracts in pain.

'How are we today, Mrs O'Connor?' the doctor says

cheerfully, wiping his hands with that alcohol handwash they all use nowadays. I hate the way he calls me 'we'. There is no 'we', it's just me. Maybe he assumes there is a 'we' because I call myself 'Mrs', but he doesn't know that I do it for practical reasons — it's easier in a country like this for there to be a husband hovering somewhere. It makes me appear respectable.

'Any unpleasant symptoms? Any discomfort?' he's saying, examining the small wound below my left breast. 'Nice and clean anyway.' He stands up again and goes to the sink to wash his hands. 'Well, we're ready to start chemotherapy now. It can be debilitating, but you're still a young woman and you'll respond well, I'm sure. Are you prepared for the hair loss?' He turns and flips my file open on the desk, his eyes scanning the printed blue sheets. 'It's not a given, of course, but with your medication and the treatment dose ...' he's saying softly.

I interrupt him. 'I don't want any more of it.' As I say the words, I don't quite believe I'm the one talking. The words just seemed to come out of my mouth. But as I speak, I know it's the truth. Before, I had a reason to get treatment, to get better, to keep up that relentless march forward, just as I have since the day I came to this place. Never look back, I used to say to myself, even while that was all I seemed able to do. The mantra helped me, it fooled me into thinking that my life was moving forward to a certain point, to the day that I would hold my children in my arms again. But now, it seems there's no need to pretend any longer.

He's puzzled for a few moments, before taking up his spiel again as if I haven't spoken. 'You'll probably feel quite tired, but again, that should lift towards the end of treatment and the anti-emetics will help with any vomiting—'

'I don't think you heard me. I don't want any further treatment.'

He stops in mid-sentence, the X-ray in his hand, as if only just realising I've spoken. 'Am I hearing you right, Michelle?' His beetle-black eyebrows crease into a frown.

'You are.' I sit up straight on my chair.

He clears his throat. 'Michelle, I need you to be very clear about this. Treatment will prolong your life by anything up to a year.' And then he looks at me, the madwoman who doesn't want to live for another year, an expression of horror and distaste on his face.

It's my life, I think. My life and my death. 'But I will die, isn't that what you told me?'

'Well, sooner or later. The prognosis with treatment is for extension to life by anything from months to years ...'

'Well, I'm ready to go now. I've decided.'

Dr Abdallah looks at the nurse and then back at me. When he talks, it's in the careful tones of a man dealing with a person who isn't of sound mind. 'I don't know if you realise what you're saying. Maybe you need to take it home and share it with your family.'

I close my eyes for a second and then open them again. There's a silence before I manage, 'No. No family.' I get up abruptly and my thighs squeak on the hot plastic and I say nothing more to the handsome doctor, ignoring his panic when I open the door and leave that stuffy office and walk down the endless sets of stairs to the front door and out onto the hot pavement, the sun bright on my face. I stand there for a few moments, the traffic whizzing by on the street in front of me, a blast of horns and a screech of brakes as one car veers in front of another. Joseph said he would collect me at 11.30 and, mechanically, I look down at my watch, then down the street to where the white bulk of the Land Rover is parked beside an election poster for the presidential race. 'A Better Life' is promised beneath the smiling face of the candidate, a man renowned for taking backhanders.

Joseph catches sight of me and drives towards me. '*Habari*?' he asks briefly, running around the front of the car and opening the door for me, a gesture which would once have infuriated me, but I know that Joseph is doing it out of kindness. 'Any news?'

I think to myself before responding, '*Nzuri*.' It always amuses me that the word means 'fine' and 'terrible' at the same time, which just about covers it.

'Aha.' He nods sagely and guns the car into first, the engine rumbling as we take off into the traffic without indicating or looking to see if there's anything coming, and we are rewarded by an angry honking of horns. '*Twende*,' Joseph says quietly, turning the radio on, a loud tinny blast of music filling the car.

'Yes, let's go,' I agree, and he rewards me with a flash of white teeth and I want to reach out and hug him, because I know that he won't ask me another question, not unless I speak first. And I can't speak right now. I can't say a single word. My tongue feels swollen and dry in my mouth.

Sure enough, we are silent for most of the five-hour journey home through the red dirt, watching it gradually cover the windscreen in a fine red sheen. I look out the window at the wide, flat green trees whose branches stretch out along the horizon, at the patches of dark green so carefully tended by the local women, bent over the earth, working it into submission. I smile when I see them, because it reminds me of my younger self, bent over my hoe in front of that old cottage, wondering at how I was managing to produce cabbage and potatoes and carrots out of the soil simply by looking after it. I miss that, that closeness to the soil. When I first came here, I dreamt about it. I dreamt that I was picking up great dark handfuls of it, clogging my fingers, the pinky-silver outline of a worm weaving its way through, instead of the dry red dust pouring through my hands. For me, that soil was life itself. It was a miracle, a symbol of the future that seemed to lie before me. But I've thought enough about that over the years, circled over and over the same terrain, wondering 'what if'. I suppose I can let go of that now.

The girls are waiting when I get back, and they swarm around the Land Rover like bees, laughing and waving. I flatter myself that they're here for me, but I know they're after the sweets I packed into my bag: the tropical mints and lollipops — 'my heart beats for mixed fruit drops' reads the slogan on the yellow packets of boiled sweets that the girls love. They are so beautiful, that blue-black sheen on their skin, the coils of hair tight on their heads, their long, bare legs sticking out of the end of those old-fashioned pinafores, their little cotton shirts pressed so neatly. My girls. I was wrong when I said I had no family to Dr Abdallah. I have a family. This is my family. I know I don't really deserve them, after everything I've done, but I'm blessed to have found them. Caring for them has helped me to wear away at my guilt, to rub it away so that it's now just a little hard pebble inside of me.

I climb out of the car and, even though my heart is like lead, I hug them and kiss them and let myself be carried to the dining hall by my swarm of laughing bees.

Only later do I manage to get away, to drag a plastic lawn chair out in front of my flat and sit there in the dusk, watching the sun drop low on the horizon. It happens so quickly here, you can almost see it move, then 'plop', it disappears and a blackness descends that's sudden and total. How unlike the silvery, pale sunsets of home. I sit in front of my hut and I listen to the crickets in the trees and I balance the letter on my knee. I've read it so many times that the words are burned on my brain, as if they'd been branded there. The urge to soak it all in, to examine every line, was hard to resist. At first, I didn't really register what she was saying. Oh, her meaning was plain, but I couldn't grasp it, and when I did, when I understood, I needed to process it for a while. I needed to go through the pain, the resentment, the anger at her rejection of me. I'm her mother, I thought as I scanned the lines. Does that count for nothing at all? But I suppose I lost the right to that name many years ago.

I know that June is right. I thought it was the right thing to do, to write to her, to ask her to write to me, but now I see that we've kept each other prisoner in the past. I wanted them to remain as they always were, never to grow up, and I can see now how selfish that was. June sent me a picture of Rosie's wedding, a portrait of the whole wedding party jumping high into the air, the house behind them looking a lot smarter than I remember it. I gasped in shock when I pulled it out of the envelope and it took me a while to understand: they aren't as I remember them, sitting on that little ladder in front of the house. They've lived their whole lives, have loved and worked and had children, all without me. They have got on with the business of living somehow, in spite of the pain. The thought felt almost hurtful to me. How dare they, I thought, scanning the photo to see if I could pick out my own children. How dare they live without me. But now I understand. June is right, of course, even though her words still sting. I don't have the right to contact them any more, to hold them back. The burden is really mine to carry, not theirs. They have done nothing. Nothing at all.

It's time. Time to let them go.

Oh, I need a drink, I think as I shift in my seat, chilly now that the sun has gone. I begin to get up and I jump when I hear a small, polite cough. I look up and Theo, the post boy, is standing in front of me in a pair of denim shorts and a T-shirt with 'Nerdies Sunglasses' written on it. He smiles at me and nods at the letter on my lap. 'Please, miss.'

I look at it and then up at him. 'It's from my daughter. She lives a long way away in Ireland, where it rains all the time.' Because of the missionaries, many of the local people here have been told about Ireland, but the only thing they seem to latch onto is the rain. When I tell them I come from Ireland, they mimic great clouds above their heads and say, 'Always raining.'

He smiles at me again, and I see that he's humouring me, that he wants something else but is too polite to ask. I look down again and see what he's looking at. 'Is it the stamp? Is that what you want?'

He shakes his head, as if nothing could be further from his mind, which I take to mean 'yes'. 'Here.' I hand him the letter. 'I won't be needing it any more.'

If he's wondering why I'm giving him the whole letter instead of tearing the stamp off the envelope, he doesn't say. Instead he grins and says, '*Asante*,' and puts the letter carefully into the red satchel he has over his shoulder, the faint outline of Royal Mail still visible on the plastic. And then he walks away.

I lean back against the warm wall of the house and I close my eyes. I think of what John-Joe told me that time, about the last words his mother said when she lay on her bed in the upstairs room in Donegal, her family gathered around her. 'My work is done,' that's what she said at the end of her long and busy life, surrounded by everyone who was dear to her. And I know that when I die I'll be alone and that it's my choice. It has all been my choice, all along. I have to accept that now, that and the fact that I'll never see my children again. It's finished now. I'm tired. My work is done.

AUTHOR Q&A

The title of the book is quite emotive, and it could refer to Michelle or to her children, all of whom are leaving something behind in their own way. How did you come to decide on the title?

I came to the title, *All That I Leave Behind*, quite late, and really, because I only belatedly realised how much of the novel belonged to Michelle. In an earlier draft, she wasn't actually as present, because I wanted to explore how a mother's leaving might affect her children, rather than herself. I think I was possibly a bit angry with Michelle myself, for having left them! But then I came to understand that it was as much her story as theirs — the impact of leaving was as profound on her as it was on them. She was heartbroken, but felt that she had no other choice. And so it became 'All That I Leave Behind' — meaning the whole of her life, really. And the children, too, end up leaving things behind

— the past, in particular. They really all live in the past in so many ways — none of them has moved on, at least, not inside themselves, since Michelle left. Mary-Pat has made a life for herself with PJ and her children, but inside, she's still in a rage with her mother for having left, and for having burdened her with the responsibility of the others; Pi is literally stuck, refusing to move outside the narrow world he's created for himself; June is stuck with the image she has of herself as a perfect, middle-class mum, and yet, she's bent on self-destruction; and Rosie hasn't really begun to find herself yet, to understand who she really is.

The 'children' are understandably very angry at their mother throughout the book and in the end start to come to terms with the fact that she's never coming back. Yet, Michelle remains a sympathetic character throughout — did you find this difficult to balance?

Yes, I did. It was a tricky balance, because how do you make someone who abandons her children sympathetic? It goes against nature, doesn't it, to leave your children, and yet I wanted to explore how that might actually happen and what might drive a woman to making that choice. I remember reading a newspaper article while I was thinking about the story early on, profiling women who left their children and why. I found the piece revelatory, not least because some of the reasons weren't that profound. One lady, I remember, simply felt that she should have been a writer, but that her children prevented her from doing so, which I found particularly interesting, because for me, it was the opposite, but I could understand how that might be — how some women might find having children could somehow squash their true nature. Motherhood is such a complex state, and raises difficult emotions, I think.

ALL THAT I LEAVE BEHIND

Would you say that motherhood is something of a theme for you in your writing?

Yes, most definitely. I'm interested in motherhood as a subject — it never really grows old! I'm interested in how women who choose motherhood become mothers, good and bad, what emotions come to the surface, what 'tapes' from childhood still play, and what patterns are repeated through generations. I tackled the subject in non-fiction terms in *In My Mother's Shoes*, and now I'm looking at it in novel form — which allows me more freedom to get to the heart of it, I think. I believe fiction can touch on truths that are universal, and if I want to understand a subject, I find novels are more helpful than non-fiction.

Michelle's chapters are set in the early 1970s and 80s. Was this period important to you and how did it shape her character?

Michelle was very much a child of the 60s. She'd grown up in a rigid, old-fashioned household, the only child of two doting, but overpowering, parents, and she wanted to rebel against that. I think many people in that generation did — they wanted to push against the old order and create something new. I think they were the first generation to feel that they really could change the world. And then, of course, it all fell apart, politically and personally, for many people. For Michelle, John-Joe was the perfect vehicle for that rebellion — the kind of man her parents would just hate! Unfortunately, that spark that Michelle saw in her partner wasn't anything more than being a bit of a chancer, which is why she felt so let down by him and alone in pursuing her ideals. I was also interested in how children can unwittingly pay for their parents' choices, as these four children did, both materially and emotionally. So much of growing up involves

the death of idealism, and yet, for Michelle, she never really
did grow up.

*It's interesting the way each of the children sees Michelle and John-Joe differently.
Pi hated his father, but Rosie adored him. Do you think this is true to life?*

I've always been interested in the notion of 'favourites' in a
family. Parents insist they don't have any such thing, but I think
it's part of family life — and children can see it. I think most
parents love their children equally (although some don't, it has
to be said), but they may have an easier relationship with one
child than with another. It's complicated — some parents might
struggle with one child because they see so much of themselves
in them, or might bond with another because their personalities
gel. Family dynamics are always interesting. Pius loathed John-
Joe and yet in so many ways, he was like him and was certainly
pursuing the same, aimless life. Mary-Pat was essential to
Michelle as a helper and support and yet, she felt the burden
of that role, and June, as she said herself, was the 'overlooked'
one, who didn't have a strong relationship with either parent,
which left her at sea. I think it's also interesting that children
can carry that childhood self on into their adult relationships
with their parents, so Mary-Pat still brought Daddy his *Racing
Post* and his chocolate — because that was her role.

*There was a parallel drawn between Michelle and Rosie throughout — both of
them left home, both of them 'married' a man unsuited for them and the life they
wanted to lead, both of them tried to change/hide their true selves to fit into a
different kind of life. Did you think about their similarities as you wrote the book?*

Not consciously, but I'm very interested in how children repeat the patterns of their parents in many ways. As a parent myself, I see that! Often, I think we're not aware that we are doing the same things as our parents did — creating the same marriage, family patterns, etc. I don't want to be overly deterministic about it, because I think people can create something new for themselves — Rosie could have repeated Michelle's mistakes, but she was aware of that and steered a new path for herself. She became aware, when she was pregnant, that she was about to repeat the past, in not inviting Mark to be a father, and that awareness helped her to change.

What gave you the idea for the book?

A few things came together at a particular time. First, Michelle's voice came out one day, when I was on holiday, and I wrote the prologue to the book, but it seemed to be detached for a while from any kind of story. I couldn't work out who she was or how she'd connect to something greater. And then I read Mary Lawson's *Crow Lake*, which is a wonderful novel about family life, and felt a frisson of excitement — here was the story I was trying to tell, albeit differently. And then, I happened to take a walk with my husband along the canal in Co. Kildare, because he likes to fish it, and something about that still, silent landscape really appealed to me. It took me a little while longer to locate Mary-Pat, Pius, Rosie and June, but eventually, it all came together. Writing a novel is a bit like unravelling a knot of twine or solving a puzzle — it's about pulling clarity out of what initially seems to be a muddle, distilling it until eventually, clarity emerges.

Alison Walsh

How do you make time for writing?

Well, I do read about other writers who spend entire days writing, but that's actually never been part of my life, because I have a 'day job' as an editor and a family. Writing, for me, was and still is an oasis carved out of a busy day, two hours of peace and quiet, bedroom door shut, earplugs in, trying to ignore the punch-up in the boys' bedroom. My children feel the urge to communicate with me once the door is shut! I've always written like that — it's my time and I try to make the most of it. I also find that as long as I commit to that regularly — six days a week in general, that it works for me. Although I did read about a successful author who spends twenty minutes a day writing and felt a slight twinge of envy ...

When did you start writing?

Writing is in the family, so to speak. My great-grandfather, Maurice Walsh, was a writer, and very popular in his day, and when I was a child, I'd often be asked if I was going to be a writer like him! An impossible question to answer when you're nine. However, it's true that I always did love reading and writing. I'd always written bits and pieces: stories about gymnastics when I was in primary school, adventure yarns, an essay on the Crusades (about which I knew nothing) in secondary school, but I never thought writing was for me — I think it was a confidence thing, really. I'd read huge amounts, particularly in college, but never thought I could actually write. Instead, I went into publishing and worked as an editor. And then I found myself at a loose end during my first pregnancy and went to a creative writing class in London, where I then lived. And I wrote something which just seemed to emerge onto the page from some part of me I didn't know existed — and that's where I realised that I might have a voice somewhere. It took me another ten years or so, and three children, to fully tune into that, but it's all part of the process.

Acknowledgements

Thanks to my family: to Colm, for everything, not least for listening to me moan for two years, and to Eoin, Niamh and Cian for constant interruptions/entertainment. I thank my agent, Marianne Gunn O'Connor, for her persistence and support and many hours of chat, Pat Lynch and also Vicki Satlow for her reading and feedback; to my editor, Ciara Doorley at Hachette Books Ireland, sincere thanks for her enthusiasm and guidance, and to Joanna Smyth, Breda Purdue, Jim Binchy, Ciara Considine, Ruth Shern, Siobhan Tierney and Bernard Hoban. A note of thanks also goes to Emma Dunne for her helpful suggestions, particularly with the timeline and to Aonghus Meaney for his excellent proofreading. Finally, I thank Mary Behan for her help when most needed.